Publisher's Note

This book is a collection of stories from writers all over the world. For authenticity and voice, we have kept the style of English native to each author's location, so some stories will be in UK English, and others in US English.

Also From Cohesion Press

SNAFU
An Anthology of Military Horror

Edited by
Geoff Brown
and
Amanda J Spedding

Cohesion Press
2019 (Print)

SNAFU:
An Anthology of Military Horror
Geoff Brown and Amanda J Spedding (eds)
REISSUE 2018 (ebook) 2019 (print)

Anthology © Cohesion Press 2014
Stories © Individual Authors 2014
Frontispiece © Greg Chapman 2014
Interior Art © Montgomery Borror 2014
The Battle Of Spotsylvania by Henry Alexander Ogden p22
Source Pixabay
Cover Art © Mel Gannon 2014
Internal Layout by Cohesion Editing and Proofreading
Set in Palatino Linotype

COHESION PRESS

Cohesion Press
Mayday Hills Lunatic Asylum
Beechworth, Victoria
www.cohesionpress.com

Contents

FOREWORD

War is hell.

Nothing puts people closer to their base state than a threat to their life. Nothing reveals their animal nature more than the desire for survival at any cost. People trained for war have to deal with these extremes time after time, surviving for a greater purpose. Or, at least, one hopes so. Because survival in a personal fight can be selfish, but survival in war might mean the fate of nations, or even species. And pretty much every permutation of that kind of fight for survival is explored in the stories you're about to read.

Don't be fooled into thinking an anthology of military horror is just a book full of Platoon or Aliens knock-offs. In these pages, the variety of story you'll find is staggering.

Historical and imagined, science-fictional and contemporary. Mythos, the Wild West and Special Forces. Great wars, small wars and the American Civil War. Shapeshifters and ghosts and extraterrestrial parasites. Japanese demons and supernatural special agents. Monsters large and small. Battles fought with raging gunfire and earth-shattering explosions and battles fought cold, with paper trails and subterfuge. Battles won and lost in moments and battles that stretch across aeons.

There's great variety in story style and length too. From very short stories to novella length yarns with lots of meat ready to be stripped off their bones. This book is a fine achievement and a great example of a theme superbly explored.

You'll enjoy all the approaches here, and the great writing from both established names and emerging talents. But no matter the variety, one thing that doesn't change from tale to tale is the underlying truth evident in every one. Lives are at risk, great stakes are being played but throughout every page we're never allowed to forget that regardless of the nature of the enemy, the real horror is war itself.

Alan Baxter, NSW Australia, 2014

BLACKWATER

Neal F. Litherland

Fisher's Cove was drowning in the fog. It pressed against the dead eyes of dark windows, laced its fingers through rotting fences, and poured itself down alley mouths. The white ghost of the Pacific possessed the seaside town until even the monotonous heartbeat of the reef's warning buoys could barely be heard. In places, a gabled roof or weather vane broke the surface, clawing at the sky.

"And thus I came to a place where dreams and death lay down to sleep," Frost whispered.

"Jesus Christ, you got to do that now?" Carmichael muttered.

"Might not have a chance later." Frost readjusted his rifle sight and took another long, slow scan across what they could see of the little town.

"Giving me the fucking heebeegeebees," Carmichael said, running one hand back over his dark, shaved scalp.

"I can't give you anything for that," Hernandez said. "Now if Frost gave you the clap, then I could maybe do something."

"Cut the static," Leo said, voice cracking like a teamster's whip. They went silent, even CB who hadn't said anything. "Frost, movements?"

"Impossible to say for certain," Frost answered, fiddling with his sight again. "Fog isn't staying steady; we've got a west wind pushing at it. All the buildings are dark, no movement. Visibility's maybe ten yards once you get into the bank."

"CB, report."

"No chatter," the rangy redhead said, lifting his face from his scanner's shadowed blackout screen. "No cell or sat signals going in or out. Last confirmed contact was a big rig on the interstate testing the air waves two hours ago. No one in the town replied, no indication they knew he was there, or vice versa."

Leo nodded. His men watched the darkness, hands on their weapons and minds on the job. Each one of them knew his role, and they knew they were not part of a democracy. If Leo said they waited, they waited. If he said they went in, they went in. If any one of them had a problem then he should have mentioned it before lacing up and gearing out. Leo unslung his weapon, and popped the long clip out of the cut-down M4. The others did the same, flicking safeties and racking slides, offering up one last prayer to the assault-rifle gods that their sights were straight and the brass didn't jam.

"Frost, take point," Leo said. "Carmichael, Hernandez, myself, then CB. Previous intel says the gathering's going to be at the church, so we get in and get out quick, clean, and quiet. This place is full of sectarian nut jobs, and they may not take kindly to us stealing one of their flock. They give her to us, we walk away. They put up a fight, show them the error of their ways with strict prejudice. You get me?"

"We get you," they said. No one called Leo sir. Those days were behind them, and they didn't pretend otherwise. Leo slid an indigo balaclava over his head. The others did the same.

It was like a child's game. Leo pointed, and tapped Frost on the shoulder. Frost ran bent over, his low profile a caricature of some inbred beast loping through the shadows. He slid behind cover, swept the area, and signaled the all clear. Then the next man went, and the next, and the next. Rear covered fore, then fore covered rear, all of it in total silence. Leo chose the next spot, and the whole cycle began again.

They ducked behind rusted-out cars sitting on busted rims, and slipped silently past hedges grown long and wild in the sea air. They crouched near rotting doorways with peeling paint, breathing through their mouths and squinting into the swirling night. Pot holes and cracked curbs tried to trip them up. Busted doors creaked in the night breeze, wailing and whining on rusted hinges. The place reeked of swollen, rotting wood, and when they breathed too deep a slimy, fishy scent coated their tongues. The ocean rumbled as the surf rolled in, and shushed when it went out; the snoring of some invisible giant whose dreams the shadow men had no interest in.

The town felt wrong. None of them said anything, but they all felt it. Frost stroked his finger along the outside of the trigger guard like his personal worry stone. Hernandez crossed himself every time a loud noise turned out to be the wind in the eaves rather than an alarm bell. CB blinked away thick droplets of sweat from the bridge of his nose – uncharacteristic for a cold, autumn night. Carmichael hummed show tunes under his breath.

"Mute your chute, Jukebox," Leo hissed, glaring over his shoulder at Carmichael. The big man went silent and shifted his grip on the street sweeper he'd insisted on toting. Leo shifted his gaze to the others. "Put it on ice, all of you. You can puke your guts and shit yourselves on your own time."

They made the last dash for the church as a whole, every man watching and running with his weapon socked to his shoulder; a hair-trigger phalanx with no safety just begging for a target. Nothing shambled out of the fog, slick and wet from the sea floor. No one shot at them either. They pounded up the stone steps, Leo taking up position to the right of the iron-bound double doors and Carmichael taking the left. Hernandez and CB took a knee at the base of the stairs and watched back the way they'd come. Frost stood calm and easy, halfway up with his suppressed barrel pointing at the sky.

Leo crouched, and put his ear against the place where the doors met. He stayed there for a three count, then jumped and slid back out of the doorway. CB and Hernandez swiveled, and Frost crouched down low just as the latch lifted and the door swung inward. A silhouette stepped out of a watery rectangle of light, and Carmichael swung a hard, looping right into the figure's belly. There was a harsh gasp, and the target stumbled forward. It reached beneath its coat, and Leo kicked it behind the knees. The man went down, and a knife spun out of its fingers. Carmichael put a boot on the man's back, and the wide mouth of his trench gun against his head.

"You make so much as one little bo peep, and I'll smash your pumpkin all over, you get me sucker?" Carmichael growled, putting more of his weight onto the prone body. The captive didn't speak, or even so much as twitch.

At Leo's signal, Hernandez and CB hit the door, criss-crossing as they went through. There was silence for a long moment, broken only by the sounds of doors opening. A small eternity later each man whispered, "clear" back into the night. Frost picked up the dropped knife, and ducked inside. Carmichael looped an arm around their prisoner's throat, and hauled him inside. Leo followed, closing the door quietly behind them.

The sanctuary was old. The boards gleamed with varnish, and the rafters were dusty with a hundred years or more of votive smoke. The walls held candle brackets, the flickering flames hiding just as much as they revealed. There were no trappings of any faith the men had ever seen before, though. In the bare places once graced by the portraits of saints sat stone shelves holding sunken, graven images of creatures whose forms were nearly unrecognizable. An altar of smooth, black stone sat on the dais, flanked by gilded statues of tumescent creatures with dozens of blank, empty eyes. A heavy, leather-bound book rested on the sea-green altar cloth, and on the wall above and behind, burnished letters spelled out the legend *The Esoteric Order of Dagon*. The place was otherwise empty.

Once inside, the team took a good look at who they'd sandbagged. The captive was a portly man with a shiny, bald head and a sunken chin. His long, black robe was frayed at the cuffs, and though a little too big, it marked him as a priest clearly enough. He scrabbled at Carmichael's arm, digging pale, fish-belly fingers into the choke hold. Frost held up the knife, a wavy-bladed tool more useful in ritual than in combat, and the bald man went still. Frost patted the man down, turning out his pockets and checking all the logical places for hold outs and surprises. He didn't find any. Frost tucked the decorative dagger behind his web belt, and stepped back out of the line of fire.

"I'm only going to say this once, padre," Leo told the man. "If you do what I tell you then you'll live through the night. If you try to scream, or attempt to fight me or my men, I will have that knife in your gullet before you've taken a deep breath. Do you understand? Blink once for yes, and twice for no."

The prisoner stared at Leo with watery, wide-set eyes. He blinked once.

"If I have my man release you, are you going to co-operate?" Leo asked. Again the single blink. Leo nodded. "Let him go, Jukebox."

Carmichael released his hold. He stepped back and to the side, bringing up the shotgun as he did. The man in the black robe coughed, and kneaded at his wattle. He sucked air, and gagged slightly before he managed to get himself under control. When he spoke his voice was breathy, like he was trying to talk with a hole in his lungs.

"Who are you?" the priest rasped. "What do you want?"

"Sarah Prendergast," Leo said, ignoring the first question in favor of the second. "Turn her over, and we can all pretend this night didn't happen."

The priest shrugged his shoulders, hands clasped at his waist. "I do not know anyone by that name."

"Five foot five, blond hair, blue eyes, pale," Leo said, pointing his muzzle right between the holy man's eyes. "Eighteen years old; runaway. Birthmark on the right cheek, and a jagged scar below her left knee. She came here seven months ago."

"Ah," the priest said, nodding. If he noticed the gun, or its proximity to his head, it didn't seem to bother him any. "And what do you want the girl for?"

"Doesn't matter," Leo said.

The priest looked at each of them. He nodded again, agreeing with some unasked question. "I suppose not. If I refuse to assist you?"

"Then you might meet whatever gods you pray to sooner than you think," Hernandez said.

The priest smiled, and his wide, thick-lipped mouth curved at the corners without showing any teeth. He held his hands up slowly, palms out in surrender. "As you wish. The girl you seek is down below, along with the rest of the congregation. I can lead you to her if you wish?"

"I do," Leo said, toggling the selector switch on his rifle. "Frost, if he tries any party tricks drop him. Jukebox, you're on crowd control. CB, Band-Aid, cover our tails and make sure no one sneaks up on us."

The priest led them to the rear door of the sanctuary, moving with the lurching, awkward gait of someone more used to sea than land. Beyond the door was a short, dark hall lit only by spillover from a cramped, spartan office. Aside from the light the office's only unique feature was a huge map of the western seaboard. Hundreds of red push-pins were jabbed along the coast, marking the locations of offshore reefs. The man in black pushed open another door, and they stepped into the night.

The church yard may have been well-cared for once-upon-a-time. A wrought-iron fence enclosed the small space, but the iron was warped and pitted from the salt air. The barrier leaned drunkenly too, as if contemplating a leap over the edge of the bluff. Crumbling headstones and canted crosses were half-buried by the overgrown verge. In one corner rotting vegetables gave mute, fecund testimony to a garden gone to seed. The priest followed a trampled path through the foliage, witch grass and burrs snatching at his hem and sleeves. He paid the plants no more mind than he did the men following him.

"I don't like this, boss," Hernandez whispered. "It's too easy."

"Seconded," CB said, wiping his nose on his sleeve. "I can't see shit in this black."

"Just BOLO, boys," Leo said. "Fingers on triggers, and we're done before dawn."

The priest paused, and fiddled with a rusty gate at the end

of the path. The men fanned out into the grass, crouching low and trying to look everywhere at once. The priest grunted, and the gate squealed as it swung inward. He stepped into the void without a backward glance.

Frost sucked in a sharp breath, and Carmichael swore. The priest stood in midair a moment longer, his robe flapping in the wind from the ocean. Then he turned, and slipped out of sight.

"Do not lose contact," Leo said.

Frost slid gun-first toward the yawning hole. "Stairs," he said, jerking his chin to give the all-clear. A moment later he was gone, and the others followed.

A stairway was carved into the living rock. Barely wide enough for a broad man, the steps had been worn smooth by more than a century of wind, rain, and regular travel. The steps would have been dangerous in full daylight. In the dark and the fog they were suicide. They moved as quickly as good sense allowed, aware of the empty gulf on the left. Each man felt along with his boots, and kept his gun leveled at nothing. All they heard was the sound of the wind, along with the rhythmic pounding of the ocean. There was no sign of the priest.

After one hundred steps and a single switchback, the fog began to clear. Twenty yards below was a stubby shelf of black rock, worn smooth and decorated with the detritus of the retreating tide. The shelf extended out into the water; the natural rock becoming a carved bridge to nowhere wide enough for a convoy to ride two abreast. Heavy stone pylons ranked every fifteen yards or so, but there were no railings between them. Silhouettes moved in the distance, back lit by flickering orange flames and casting dark, monstrous shadows in the remaining mists. The wind blew stronger, carrying slurred consonants chanted by a congregation of ghosts. Carmichael started humming the theme to *The A-Team*.

"I take back what I said about this being too easy," Hernandez said.

"Noted," Leo said. "Assume the padre is sending company. Anything that comes our way in a black robe that doesn't have blond hair, shoot first and ask questions when we're out of this fucking freak show. Conserve ammo, keep it quiet if you can. Keep your poppers handy, but don't pull the pins unless I give the word. We don't know how strong that bridge is, and I don't want to swim back."

No one appeared out of the mist by the time the squad reached the shelf. A quick sweep turned up seaweed, some smooth pieces of bottle glass, and what was left of the priest. The left side of his head was bloody, and he'd had the misfortune of slamming chest-first onto a log. The driftwood had splintered, punctured his lungs, and pulped his ribs. The body stank, the trademark scents of freshly voided bowels mixing with the digestive juices in a ruptured stomach. Hernandez did a cursory check, and shook his head when he didn't find a pulse. Leo swore.

"This change anything boss?" Frost asked, keeping his muzzle trained on the bridge.

"No," Leo said. "We get in, get the girl, get out."

Up close the bridge was more than stable. A solid, stone structure, it looked as if it had been carved by hand and smoothed by a millennium of ocean currents. The support pylons stretched a full ten yards above the bridge proper. Roughly six feet in diameter, the shafts were inscribed with faded pictograms of sea creatures, men, and things which were a little of both. At the pinnacle of each pillar perched statues of bulbous, black creatures; things with glassy eyes and distended mouths atop rounded bodies with flabby bellies and lithe, powerful limbs.

Leo gestured, and they formed a staggered line. There was no cover except the thin mist, the darkness, and the sounds of whatever the Dagonites were conducting. If anyone glanced back across the bridge their cover would be blown. The men advanced, stepping carefully across the slick rock with their shoulders hunched low and their weapons trained on the flickering shadows that grew more distinct all the while. The bridge ended a hundred yards into the ocean, terminating in a huge cul-de-sac. Pylons ranked like standing stones, and beneath each one stood a young woman with her arms chained above her head. Dozens of robed people stood in a crescent facing the ocean. Flames leaped from a central pit, painting the scene like a fresco on the wall of a chapel in hell. The chanting rose higher, then higher still; a single cry from a hundred throats shrieking up at the clouded stars like a signal beacon.

Suddenly the chanting ceased. The wind died. Even the waves, which had pounded toward the shore, calmed to a gentle lapping. The squad split to either side, crouching and blending their bodies with the outlines of the pylons. They listened. For several moments there was nothing but the sound of the ocean and their own nervous breathing. Beyond the fire, something splashed out of the ocean, and hauled itself onto the platform with the meaty slap of flesh on stone. The stink of fish oil, and the heavy, acrid smell of brine wafted on the breeze. The water parted again and again as others broke the surface and clambered onto the temporary shore. In moments the newcomers outnumbered the congregation, standing in the spaces between the pillars at the very edges of the firelight. The chorus moaned, and there were no words in it; just a raw, animal sound of elation and anticipation burbling into the darkness. Someone screamed; a high-pitched shriek only a young woman in abject terror could manage.

"Shit" Leo snarled, surging around the pylon. "Go, go, go!

They rushed the platform, and the last of the mist parted like rotting silk. The congregation whirled, robes open shamelessly as they stared at the interlopers. Flesh drooped from their bones, hanging in pallid folds the color and texture of pale cheese. Their long-fingered hands bore delicate webs, and thin, watery drool ran from the corners of mouths grown too wide to close completely. Stooped and hairless, they were a world apart from the women hanging from the pillars all around.

"Nobody move," Leo said, raising his voice along with his rifle. "Just stay where you are and – "

Something moved. Darkness parted, and firelight danced over something out of a scuba diver's nightmare. The thing

13

had a jaw set with the thick, curving teeth of a barracuda, the pebbled, monotone skin of a shark, and the black, empty eyes of a predator. It stared at the invaders, flickers of too-human curiosity in its dark gaze. It sucked a heavy breath through the thick, fleshy flaps along its ribs. It opened its mouth, and the back of its head erupted in a spurt of gore, punctuated by the muted crack of a single rifle shot.

Time slowed. The first creature flopped to the deck, and its fellows rushed to its aid; a phantasmagoric wave of upended evolution that was all claws and teeth, suckers and tentacles. The beak of a mollusk snapped beneath the deflated, slitted remnants of what might once have been a nose. Hands gone boneless and rubbery reached out from the ends of arms that bore bony fins and spiny spurs. Voices that could once have spoken the words of men howled animal defiance, and were answered in kind.

Leo fired a burst into the over-developed chest of a thing with a squid's head and scapula like a manta ray's wings. Carmichael blasted buckshot into something that looked like the love child of a flounder and a puffer fish whose guts stank like rotting kelp. CB and Hernandez stepped into the gap, firing short bursts one after the other until the rapid-fire chatter blended into a single, continuous snarl. Frost squeezed his trigger, and every round carved a .30 caliber trench through a target's brain pan.

It was over in seconds. Shell casings littered the ancient stone, and cordite clouds hung thick and blue as cigar smoke. The creatures, whatever they were, didn't need silver bullets or mumbo jumbo to make them stay dead. Blood ran in not-quite-red pools, and two dozen bodies lay in twitching, leaking heaps. The worshipers lay alongside the fish men, caught in between men and monsters even in death.

"Reload," Leo called. His voice was calm, but his hand shook. It took him two tries before he popped his empty clip.

"What... what the *fuck*?" Carmichael demanded. His eyes were very wide, and his nostrils were flaring as he took shallow, rapid breaths. "Leo, what the *fuck*?"

Leo took two fast steps and slapped Carmichael hard

across the face. The big man stumbled, and wheeled around. Carmichael brought his weapon up, but when he squeezed the trigger the hammer made an empty, hollow click. Leo held his gaze, and Carmichael looked away. He took a shaky breath, and swiped a thumb beneath his balaclava.

"Shit," Carmichael said. "I'm bleeding."

"Bleed on your own time," Leo said. The words were barely out of his mouth when the ocean around them erupted. Water spumed up, and something in the darkness howled. The howl was taken up, until the very sea keened. "Find the goddamn girl! We lose her, this whole thing goes tits up!"

They ran, adrenaline and purpose kept them moving. Some of the girls were dead, their nude torsos punched through with bloody holes. A few others had been slashed by the creatures, their glazed gazes contemplating the carnage with vacant curiosity. Three of them were still alive, and one of them was Sarah Prendergast. She stood on the balls of her feet, every muscle trembling with the effort of holding completely still.

"Get them down, and let's get the fuck out of here," Leo said.

Frost drew his sidearm and fired. It took seven shots, but in seconds the survivors were free. A dark-haired girl sobbed and ran past them, slipping through blood and bodies as she headed for the shore. The second girl stumbled forward, lips trembling. Her skin shone like obsidian, slick from the ocean and tight with goose flesh.

"Who are you?" Sarah asked. Her voice was airy, and her tone politely curious.

"Your father sent us," Leo said.

Before he could say anything else Sarah launched herself at him, scrabbling for his sidearm. Her eyes blazed, and she bared her teeth in a horrible rictus that wiped away any beauty she had left. It was a look that said she belonged here, in spirit if not in body. Frost holstered his pistol, and in the same motion drew a small stun gun. The girl was wet, and she went down like a sandbag.

"Christ almighty," Leo grunted, re-adjusting his pistol.

15

"Frost, carry the girl. Carmichael, take point. CB, back him up. Band Aid, you're rear guard."

"What about me?" the other girl asked. Her accent was hard to place, but it probably had roots south of the equator in Africa.

"Run," Frost said, snugging a pair of restraints around Sarah's wrists and ankles.

They ran. The sea boiled and writhed as the keening creatures gave chase. White caps pounded like breakers, and the putrid denizens of the deep rode those waves like war horses. Bipedal eels slithered up the pylons, lashing at the runners' legs and snapping at their faces. Men with the faces and fingers of toads leaped onto the bridge, only to be torn to pieces by steel-jacketed hornets. More came, and more after them, with hoary skin and hard shells, with eyes on stalks and with earless, wall-eyed heads.

Carmichael howled and stumbled, his shotgun rending a swimming shadow into chum. He kept firing, but he stopped running. There was a long, spiral spine jammed straight through his left thigh. CB ran past, clearing the way with short, three-round bursts. Frost followed, nostrils flaring as he carried Sarah and emptied his pistol into anything that got too close. Hernandez knelt, and Leo covered them.

"We've got to get a tourniquet on this," Hernandez said.

"Just go!" Carmichael snarled, reloading. His fingers shook, and his lips were going a light shade of blue. "We won't make it if you slow down any more. Go!"

Leo clapped Hernandez on the shoulder, and sent him on. When the medic was running, Leo hung an extra grenade on Carmichael's belt. "Don't let them take you."

"Wasn't planning on it."

Leo nodded, and ran. The steady thunder of Carmichael's pump gun rolled almost until they rest of the squad reached the beach head. Four seconds after the heavy gun stopped firing, a fireball went up behind them. The bright light in the darkness tore stone from the bridge and splintered shrapnel from the nearest support pillars. The school parted around the blast, darting away from the explosion with instinctive fear. That hesitation bought the pursued enough time to make the stairs.

They climbed into the sky, and in less than a minute were again lost in the fog. The thick cloud blotted out the sight of the horde, but it also distorted the things' howls and wails. They sounded closer, then farther away, eventually reduced to noise on the wind. The squad slowed, climbing by feel as they focused before and behind. Nothing came at them from below, and nothing descended on them from above. An adrenaline-fueled eternity later CB pushed the iron gate wide and the others ran back onto solid ground. As soon as everyone had cleared the threshold Leo slammed the gate closed and rammed the stock of his weapon against the latch until he'd deformed it into a meaningless hunk of immobile slag.

"Status?" Leo snapped, turning to the others.

"The girl's out cold, but breathing steady," Hernandez said, crouching over Sarah. He withdrew a pre-loaded injector and pressed it against her bare shoulder. "Basic sedative ought to keep her out. If it doesn't I doubt she'll be able to do more than drool."

"She's your responsibility now," Leo said. "CB, Frost, sweep the church. We're going out the way we came in, and I want to be sure one of those fucking things didn't sneak up here ahead of us."

Frost reloaded his pistol, and vanished through the door right after CB. Leo turned to the other girl who was hugging herself and shivering in the damp. Leo shrugged off his jacket and handed it to her.

"You got a name?" He asked.

"Dikeledi," she said, slipping into the jacket and buttoning it quickly.

"Dikeledi, you've got two choices," he said. "You walk off now and go your own way, or you come with us. You come with us, I'll do my best to get you out of here, but you do what you're told when you're told to do it until we're clear, you get me?"

"I understand," she said. She kissed the palm of her hand, and pressed her fingers to Leo's forehead. "Thank you."

A low, sharp whistle sounded from the doorway, and Frost was gesturing them into the church. Hernandez lifted Sarah in a fireman's carry, grunting as he headed toward the church. Leo followed, Dikeledi on his heels. Leo jerked his sidearm and offered it to the girl.

"You know how to use one of these?" he asked.

"Well enough," she said, taking the weapon.

"Safety's off, and there's one in the pipe," he told her. "You see one of those things, kill it."

The church was just how they'd left it. Leo slammed the door, shot the bolt, and kept moving. Hernandez was handing Sarah over to Frost, and the girl's head was lolling. There was blood on her lips, but not very much. CB had his scanner out, and at Leo's look shook his head.

"Dead air," he said.

"Don't jinx yourself," Hernandez said, taking a deep breath and reloading.

"CB, take point," Leo said. "Frost, you and Dikeledi are with me. Hernandez, keep an eye on the back trail, but don't get lost."

"We leap-frogging again boss?" Frost asked.

Leo shook his head then cracked his neck. "We hit the door and don't stop moving until we're pedal to the metal. Due east, fire at will but do not stop to engage."

They nodded, and took their places. CB set his feet, and took several, deep breaths. He gripped the knob for a long moment, and listened. Without a word CB rushed the darkness, and the others charged into the blackness.

The town was alive. Shadows swarmed out of the ocean below, slithering through gutters and darting across buckled roads. The nightmare mass rolled in like a flood tide, suggestions of shapes and bodies of two separate worlds mingled into a hideous whole. The creatures raised their heads like hounds sniffing the air, or dragged themselves along the ground to taste the man scent. They called out in garbled, incomprehensible voices, and made ear-piercing shrieks as they swept closer. The pursuers moved slowly, but there were a lot of them and they were gaining.

All at once, everything went silent. The shambling foot beats ceased, and the dread chorus stopped. No doors slammed, no shutters creaked, and even the endless drone of the ocean seemed to fade away. The squad stopped, chests heaving as they tried to look everywhere at once. Their ears strained at nothing, and their eyes scrabbled at the fog, desperate to see what they couldn't hear.

"Boss?" Frost panted.

"Quiet," Leo said.

Frost sucked in a breath, but before he could say anything CB started shooting. He ran into the fog, howling loud enough to be heard over the quick, staccato bursts of his weapon. Bullets smashed glass, and thudded into brick and steel. The others ducked, eyes darting back and forth. Nothing came at them. CB kept firing, moving further and further into the fog until first his footsteps, and then his shots vanished.

"Go," Leo said, and they ran for the trees.

Their retreat was a graceless, disorganized run through the underbrush. Roots snatched at their feet. Low-hanging branches rasped at their sleeves and across their faces, but the forest was just a forest. Beneath the wet, low-hanging limbs the shadows were nothing but patches of darkness. The fog stayed silent, and they didn't look back.

The van was right where they'd left it, stashed beneath a mottled, indigo tarp and out of easy sight. Leo snatched the tarp, and Hernandez got the back open. Frost got Sarah onto the medical bench, and cut the restraints. When he realized he'd used the padre's kris knife he threw it out into the trees. Hernandez strapped the girl in, crouching down and checking her vitals. Leo climbed behind the wheel, and Frost got into the passenger seat. Dikeledi slid into one of the rear-facing jump seats, fastened her belt and watched out the window. She never let go of the pistol. Doors slammed, the engine rumbled, and minutes later they were on the highway.

The silence stretched thick as midnight. Leo drove with both hands on the wheel, eyes flicking from the road to the mirrors and back again. Frost took long, slow breaths. His fingers moved almost of their own volition, as if he was playing a piano only he could see. Hernandez coughed and shuffled, clicking a pen flash into Sarah's eyes and checking her pulse. He coughed again. Then a third time.

"What's your malfunction, Hernandez?" Leo said, jerking the wheel into the fast lane and stepping down on the gas.

"Nothing," Hernandez said. "It's just the girl."

"What about her?"

"Her vitals are off," Hernandez said. "No immediate problems, but I can't put my finger—"

"She is pregnant," Dikeledi said.

Leo swerved. Frost swore. Hernandez lost his grip, and banged his shoulder against the wall before falling onto the floor. The van coasted. Frost turned around slowly, looking at Dikeledi.

"Pregnant?" he repeated. "Pregnant with what?"

The girl wasn't looking at him. She was looking at Sarah, and her face may as well have been carved from the same, dark stone as the bridge. Then without a word Dikeledi raised Leo's pistol and fired two rounds into Sarah's belly. The gun roared, deafening in the tight confines, and blood fountained as the hollow points ripped through the girl's innards. Before Dikeledi could fire a third shot, Frost put a bullet in her head. The gun fell from her hand, and she lurched against her safety harness.

Leo drove, and his leather gloves creaked as he gripped the wheel. Hernandez tried to staunch Sarah's bleeding, alternating between praying and cursing. Frost slid his sidearm back into its holster, and stared through the windscreen.

"Dammit, Frost, get back there and help him," Leo said.

"No."

Leo went still. He slowly turned, and looked at Frost. "What do you mean, no?"

For a moment Frost gave no indication he'd even heard. He kept staring out into the night, his fingers keeping time with the broken, white lines. When he spoke his voice was very soft.

"Where do you think all those things came from?"

"What does it fucking matter where they came from?" Leo said. "There's no time for this—"

Frost looked at him. His eyes were bright, and glacially cold. "She's pregnant Leo. Pregnant with what?"

Behind them, Hernandez started screaming.

LITTLE JOHNNY JUMP-UP

Christine Morgan

Mullins was first to admit to having seen the boy. He did so in a way that said he expected to be ridiculed for it, laughed out of camp, made fun of… or be accused of sneaking the drink, wild tale-telling, or worse.

As it happened, we'd all seen him.

We'd all seen him, and the accounts, they lined up too well to be anything other than the truth.

That we could each describe him to a fare-thee-well, that was nothing surprising. We'd all gotten a plain enough look, plain and sorrowful, when Sergeant Lewis picked him up from the Virginia mud.

How the rain had come down that day. Washed the smoke from the air but raised steam from the ground in its place. It raised steam from the bodies of the fallen as well, even as it washed the blood from their ashen faces. The smell of wet wool hung heavy in the air, mingling with the sharp stink of spent powder, and the lower stink of death.

There was scant dignity in it, death. Same as for war. Might start off proud, with talk of God and glory, flags waving, the fifes and drums, cavalry sabers flashing in the sun, muskets gleaming… but what was there by battle's end?

Death.

Stiffened limbs and cooling flesh. Mouths agape. Eyes staring. Whether your uniform was of the blue or the gray, there in the mud and blood it no longer mattered.

Some men, the lucky ones, went easy. Went quick. Never saw it coming, or it was over before they barely knew. A shot, a jerk like being horse-kicked, and over they'd go, dead before more than a look of surprise even began to form on their faces, before the red stains blossomed and spread on their shirts.

Others, not so much. Others fell with their legs blown off or their guts blown open, bones shattered; men who were just sacks of shredded meat held together by ropes of gristle; men with their brains bulging through snarls of hair-clots and chunks of broken skull… screaming their agony… howling for mercy and for mother… scrabbling to hold parts of themselves together or pick up parts no longer attached…

No, there was precious little dignity to be found among the dead. Or the dying. Or the living, for that matter. We'd seen brave men cowering, begging, pissing themselves in their terror, and that wasn't always even in the thick of the battle. We'd seen men who'd been just chock-full of boasting faint like church biddies with the vapors at the first boom of the cannons.

It tried the soul as much as it tried the body, war did. They liked to say how it'd bring out the best in a man. Often as not, it'd do the opposite. We knew of men who'd slunk away and run, deserters, yellow-bellied dogs, despicable, but could anyone blame them? When you'd seen your friends and brothers dying all around you, when you had to crawl over corpses – of those selfsame friends and brothers, like as not – or ignore the pleading clutch of desperate hands so you could save your own wretched life… oh yes, it tried the soul.

Death was bad but survival wasn't always pretty either. Sometimes, what went on in the surgeon's tent was more horrible by far. Bonesaws and amputations; the cautery iron heated until it glowed red-hot and sizzled the wound with the smell of roasting pork or frying bacon; the gangrene, and the maggots poured into the sores to gnaw away the infection…

Then, about when you'd thought you had gotten numb-minded to it, inured to the horrors, something would come along to prove you wrong.

Something such as the boy.

He shouldn't have been there. He had no earthly business being there. On a battlefield, on such a dark and rainy day.

What had possessed him? All we could reckon was that he'd been out looking to have himself an adventure, or maybe hoped to steal himself some food – not that he would've had much luck, supplies being what they were. Or could be he was looking for someone, his daddy gone marching off to war or the like.

We'd never know. All we did know was that he shouldn't have been there. He shouldn't have been there; none of us had seen him until it was too late… and it was the mules. The damned mules.

If we'd still had the horses it might not have happened. The horses were better about it, not as prone to panic. We'd had six, but two had been shot, one took sick, and that bastard Hollister 'requisitioned' the others out from under us – his detachment had more need, he said, more import. A 12-pounder Napoleon was more use than our old bronze 6-pounder, the one we'd dubbed Little Johnny Jump-Up because of the way it leaped when fired.

Lewis had argued, but that bastard Hollister was on better backside-kissing terms with the commander. So, he got our horses and we had to make do with the damned mules.

The mules, they'd killed the boy.

Not themselves, no. He'd thrown himself flat in a ditch, dodging their hooves.

But they'd still been harnessed, the team of six strong and stubborn beasts. Harnessed to the limber that towed Little Johnny. Instead of balking and rolling the way they did when the enemy artillery shells went shrieking overhead, the mules bolted. Downhill and gaining speed, and Little Johnny's two wheels – hickory and iron – thunked right into that muddy ditch.

If the boy had time to scream, we couldn't hear him. Nor could we hear what must have been the terrible, mortal crunching sound of ribs and spine.

Another barrage passed by then and that time the mules did buck and squeal and roll, and got so entangled they could go no further. We reached them and as we tried to calm them back under control, Sergeant Lewis gathered up the boy in his arms.

So small, he was. Six years old, seven at the most. Towheaded, in homespun trousers and a sack-shirt, and just… just broken; broken like a jointed twig-doll someone had trodden on. The way his arms and legs dangled… the way his neck lolled… we'd all seen enough death by then to know he never would've had a chance.

It had been quick, though. There was that.

We tried to find out his name, where he'd come from, or who he belonged to. There were women who accompanied the army – laundresses, seamstresses, officers' wives, cooks and nurses, among others – and a few of them had children. There were farms and towns around the area. Some family was missing their boy, some mother her child, some father his son, but nobody ever came forth to claim him.

In the end, we saw to his burying ourselves. Each of us put in toward his coffin out of our own wages. Sergeant Lewis had the detachment's chaplain say a few words. We called him Johnny, for lack of anything else.

Not six weeks later was when Mullins spoke up, there by the tent as we ate our supper of salt pork, beans and cornbread.

He'd seen the boy, he said.

We'd moved on by then, left that sad spot far behind. Yet not one of us doubted Mullins for an instant, because we'd all seen him too.

The same boy, the same towheaded boy… but not a broken twig-doll. The boy, up and lively, chipper as a chipmunk… capering around the gun limber, happy and clapping, laughing fit to split. Not that we heard him, not that we could hear him, but we'd seen him, sure as Christmas, and there was no mistaking that delighted gap-toothed grin for anything but joy.

So, we'd all seen him, but what of it? No one else seemed to, but what of that, either? Wasn't doing any harm. Wasn't like he scared us. If anything, it was the opposite; when Dobbs and I went to talk to him one night, he vanished like a dream upon waking soon as we said a word.

It got so we were accustomed to it. He'd just be there, sitting on the ammunition box or astride the gun's bronze barrel like it was a rocking horse or broomstick pony. Came to be like he was our mascot of sorts.

And why not? There was another detachment with a dog, a scruffy and spotted mongrel that followed them around, even wore a unit kerchief around its neck. A man with the 16th had a tame barn owl he'd raised from a fledgeling. I'd seen an artillery unit in Louisiana who lugged around an old ship's figurehead mermaid as their Lady Luck touchwood.

Was it so strange, then, that we had our boy?

Some of us – again, we didn't know who'd gone and done it first – took to leaving the odd biscuit or piece of jelly fold-over out by Little Johnny. They'd be gone by morning but that was hardly surprising, what with the birds, mice, and other scavengers about.

Dobbs, hardly more than a boy himself at fifteen, started leaving some of the trinkets he collected: snail shells and buckeyes, interesting stones and the like. These, too, would be gone by morning.

Same with the candy. One of the Brubaker brothers, Tad, had a powerful sweet tooth and a weakness for the sanded hard candies sold by the camp sutlers. Lemon and butterscotch if he could get them, sassafras or horehound if not. He guarded them the way some men might guard lockets with snips of their sweetheart's hair or letters from home, but now he'd spare at least one from each bag.

Then there was the matter of the socks.

Carey's maiden aunt had been in the practice of regularly sending him care packages – soap, tinned oysters, sewing packets of needles and buttons and thread, tooth powder, scripture pamphlets, gloves, rum-cake, decks of cards, cookies – which he shared out generously among the rest of us. Some weeks after his father had written to inform him that influenza had carried the elderly lady off, a parcel arrived by mail-wagon. It had undergone months of misdirections and delays before finally reaching Carey. The wrappings were tattered, the ink smudged and worn, but it was intact with the contents undamaged.

There were canned peaches and a drawstring bag of coffee beans, some peppermint sticks, and several pairs of thick wool socks, with a note to the effect that her church knitting circle had made them and she hoped they'd included enough for "you, my dearest nephew, and your gunnery friends. Love always, Aunt Agnes."

Few comforts in all this world are so simple and so welcome as the putting on of a new pair of warm, dry socks. When you're a soldier, feet pruned white and rubbed raw inside your boots after miles of marching in the wet and cold, it's a blessing beyond compare. Only a meal of hearty home cooking comes close.

We praised Carey's aunt. We doffed our caps and held them to our chests, heads bowed, in a moment of silent prayer for her God-rested soul. Each of us made haste to peel off the worn and ragged old socks he wore and replace them with the new. They felt like cradling mothers' arms, the woolen embrace of angels.

There were indeed enough for us all. And then, as he was gathering and smoothing the crumpled newspapers with which his aunt had stuffed the parcel – we'd read them, eagerly, however mundane and months-out-of-date they might be – Carey paused.

He'd found another pair of socks tucked into the very bottom of the box, as if they'd gotten in there by mistake somehow. He held them up without a word. We all saw that, unlike the ones we now wore on our feet, this last pair was… small.

No one spoke.

I had a chill; I doubt I was alone in it.

We looked at those socks. Those small socks. The size a child might wear.

Still without a word, Carey got up from his seat by the campfire. He walked over to Little Johnny, where the 6-pounder sat under a canvas shelter between our tents and the mule-pen, and placed the socks under the bronze smoothbore barrel.

Then we went to our bedrolls. In the morning, the socks were gone.

It went on for some weeks. Mullins won a shiny new tin cup playing dice, but left it out and kept using his dented one. Thomas, who whittled, made some spinning wooden tops which he painted with bold striped colors. I traded my old jacknife to a twelve-year-old drummer lad for a pouch of clay marbles. We didn't discuss it. We just… did it.

And the things were always gone the next morning.

I wondered, suspected even, that Sergeant Lewis was behind it. That he crept out there in the night to retrieve whatever the rest of us might have left. Not meanly, no … kindly, in his way, thinking it better not to dishearten us, to give us something to believe in and cling to, foolish superstition though it may be.

Ghosts, after all…

Who believed in such things?

We did.

So, I soon learned, did Sergeant Lewis. He didn't collect what we left. He had no more explanation for it than the rest of us.

One evening, he wrote a letter, but instead of taking it to the company post-master, I saw him set it atop the ammunition box and weigh it down with a rock so it wouldn't blow away.

The sergeant caught me watching. He flushed some, and told me it was a letter to his brother but he would just as soon talk no more about it.

I did not press the matter. After all, I knew Sergeant Lewis had just one brother, who'd died at Fort Sumter, back at the very start of the war. Died fighting for the other side, as it happened. Lewis said how they'd had harsh words the last time they spoke, and there'd never been a chance to square things between them.

Next morning, that letter was gone just like everything else, but the rock was exactly where it had been, atop the ammunition box.

There was not, to our mingled disappointment and relief, a reply.

Bit by bit we began to notice other little peculiarities.

The mules, for instance. The damned, confounded, stubborn

mules. They grew so well-behaved, so placid and docile and compliant, that it made us almost uneasy. They stood as calm under fire as the best-trained cavalry horses any of us had ever seen.

Our powder never seemed to come up damp, no matter how bad the weather got. We'd hear that bastard Hollister swearing from halfway across the field how the blue hell he was supposed to fire his Napoleon with damp powder, but ours was always just fine. Bone dry, dry as salt. Our slow match never went out at an inopportune moment, leaving us unready at the fuse.

And we hadn't had a misfire in… we couldn't hardly remember. Since the boy. No misfires, no injuries to our detachment, not even with the way Little Johnny Jump-Up had earned his name. We had no powder burns, no poorly-placed toes crushed by the recoil, not so much as a cinder or speck of ash landing in anybody's eye. Our 6-pounder, sneered at by the likes of Hollister, was proving one of the most reliable artillery pieces in the unit.

Reliable, and accurate.

Uncannily, even eerily so.

The sound had changed, too. Or so it seemed to us. The bark and boom of Little Johnny's bronze throat now sounded like a shout of laughter, a child's excited whoop.

Then came the day.

The dark day. The terrible day.

They were as surprised as us, there was that much at least. We hadn't marched straight into an ambush. Nor had they. Both our armies must have simply been going along, trudging, heads down as the rain dumped in sheets and buckets from black clouds so low in the sky you felt you could reach up and scoop away a sodden handful. The lightning-flash and thunder-rumble all around in the hills made it impossible to hear much of anything else.

Until the bugles rang their brassy cries, that was.

Generals in their right minds, you'd think, might have held off until the worst of the storm passed. Maybe each reckoned the other side would be caught unprepared and unaware enough to offer up an easy victory. Maybe tempers and moods were just as foul as the weather that day.

Regardless, the battle was on before we half knew it. Slick grass and slicker mud... horses and mules stamping with their breath steaming in hot plumes... orders being yelled... men running... muskets and cannons being loaded...

Hollister's 12-pounder took a direct hit and exploded into twisted shards of smoking metal. The blast shook the earth. Bodies tumbled. A string of rattling, thudding coughs followed – the powder packets from their ammunition box. I saw a man's severed arm whirl clumsily through the air, a pinwheel of fingers and blood. Another man stumbled from the spot, hands clamped to his char-burned face.

We returned fire. Fast as we could, swabbing and ramming, loading, aiming. Little Johnny jumped with recoil. The wheels dug deep in the soggy earth.

A canister shot burst nearby, spewing deadly iron shrapnel. Mullins and one of the Brubakers went down. Carey's cap was torn from his head, and a ribbon of scalp torn off with it. I felt a tug at my side, a jabbing needle-stitch from an impatient seamstress.

Our mules got the brunt of it, two killed outright, a third that should have been but was too ornery to die. The rest of the team suffered wounds of varying severity and their earlier uncanny calm was no more.

Sergeant Lewis opened his mouth to give orders but a musket ball smashed his jaw before he got more than a word out. He sat down hard, cupping his chin, blood and teeth spilling through his fingers. Carey started for him and fell, shot in the thigh.

The other Brubaker threw himself on his wounded brother. Dobbs, Thomas and I got the panicking mules unhitched from the limber before they could tip Little Johnny over. Trickling wetness soaked into my shirt.

Our unit was a shambles, disorganized. Some tried to rally a defensive line as the enemy infantry advanced.

Little Johnny Jump-Up fired again. Round shot plowed into the oncoming soldiers.

None of us were anywhere near the 6-pounder. Had we even reloaded?

I wrenched myself around, squinting through rain and pain.

Again, our smoothbore barked that sound so like a child's whoop of glee. Fire belched from Little Johnny's bronze muzzle. More round-shot flew, and more men were mown down.

And again.

The boy… our same small towheaded boy…

I saw him there, clear as day, capering and clapping his hands. I heard his bright, joyful laughter.

Then the boom of cannonfire and the crack of muskets shifted as the battle lessened near us and intensified further downfield.

Sergeant Lewis stepped up beside the boy, patting him on the shoulder as if to say that enough was enough. The boy smiled up at him. Lewis smiled back, his chin not smashed after all.

I looked again, looked to where the sergeant still sat, slumped over, a dark gory bib of blood covering him from his ruined jawbone clear down to his belt.

Yet there he stood, by the boy, whole and unharmed.

There also stood Mullins, cheerful while at the same time his own body sprawled dead and face-down in the mud.

Not Carey, and not Jed Brubaker, both of whom were badly hurt… Tad missed it, frantic as he was trying to save his brother's life… Thomas, Dobbs and I all saw them and agreed.

We saw the three of them walk off together, until they vanished into the haze of smoke and mist rising from the battlefield.

The six others of us survived. The war went on.

But Little Johnny Jump-Up never fired again.

COVERT GENESIS
Brian W. Taylor

Staff Sergeant Solomon Watkins understood something strange was happening when the pilot, Captain Ruiz, said, "What's that?" A heartbeat later a bright flash of bluish light – it reminded him of lightning – flooded through the cockpit and into the cargo hold. The metal frame of the C-17 vibrated and hummed all around him, like someone tapped a tuning fork. He pushed himself up in his chair and saw lights on the instrument panel flickering and flashing before going dark.

Watkins pulled his seat belt tighter when the co-pilot, Lieutenant Bigsby, yelled, "We're hit!" It was all he could think to do to keep his mind off the fact that they were in real trouble.

The roar of the engine turbines subsided until clacking to a stop. All of them. At the same time.

"What's going on up there?" one of the Delta Force guys shouted from the rear of the aircraft.

Watkins ignored him and listened as the pilots flipped switches, mashed buttons, and anything else they were trained to do during engine failure.

"Whatever hit us took out the electrical systems," Captain Ruiz said to the co-pilot, his voice even, calm. "We've got to try and jump-start her."

The C-17 went quiet. The aircraft swayed on the edge of a great and terrible fall. It was like sitting at the apex of the tallest hill on the tallest roller coaster Watkins had ever been on. He willed the pilot to find some kind of solution and get the engines running. Gravity, however, would not be denied. It wrapped invisible hands around the nose of the aircraft and pulled. Watkins' stomach felt like it pressed against his throat.

"Mayday, mayday... radio's fried too," Lieutenant Bigsby said, unable to conceal his concern. "We're dead in the air."

Through the small window Watkins saw how the dying embers of the sun shone red on the clusters of Sugar Maples, White Cedars, and Eastern Pines of the Adirondacks below. It reminded him of a bloody and jagged smile coaxing them lower into its waiting maw. His mouth went dry.

"Strap in, we're going down!" Captain Ruiz shouted over his shoulder.

Watkins clutched the armrests and was thankful he hadn't wandered from his seat. A short distance away his friend and electrician, Sergeant Treadway, caught off guard by the sudden power outage, flailed before slamming into a Humvee as the aircraft lurched downward. His death was heralded by the sickening crunch of skull on metal. Blood sprayed as Treadway's corpse rag-dolled backward, flailing end over end – a human tumbleweed.

Clouds parted as the aircraft was spit from the sky, hurtling downward faster and faster.

Anything that wasn't strapped down took to the air. A helmet ricocheted off the windshield of the Humvee leaving a spider-web crack. The jet engine mechanic, Lopez, was praying. Her lips moved as she crossed herself. Treadway's corpse thudded onto a supply crate then floated sideways into Lopez who shoved it away. Watkins watched as gravity guided it, blood and all, straight at him. Unable to move, he waited.

"Level up!" Ruiz yelled, no longer calm. "Pull damnit, pull!"

Treadway's mouth seemingly parted in a death-defying smile as the body slammed into Watkins. He kicked at the corpse but it rolled up over his leg and along his chest, pinning Watkins to his seat. He tried to grab it – to push it down, securing it under his feet – but slipped. This wasn't the way Watkins wanted to die – strapped to a chair, pinned under a corpse, and possibly crushed by cargo or blown to bits. Their mission seemed pretty straight forward: recover and repair a downed C-17. He should have known something was amiss when the Delta Force squad boarded. Routine R and Rs almost never included heavy firepower. At least not Stateside.

The plane groaned like an injured beast as their descent hastened. Watkins could actually hear air rushing over the frame of the plane. Treadway shifted, jerking up. The force of their two skulls connecting sent stars washing over Watkins' field of vision. Everything became one giant blur. He felt something warm rolling down his scalp. His eyes rolled up as the familiar coppery scent of blood filled his nostrils, his dead friend still grinning as if pleased with his actions.

The last thing Sergeant Watkins heard before unconsciousness settled over him was, "Brace for impact!"

* * *

Something hurt. Pain was a good thing. It meant Watkins was still alive. He took in a breath and winced as fiery pain stabbed at his mid-section. His ribs, he realized, were likely broken. He sat there a moment clearing the cobwebs from his mind. From somewhere nearby came the crackling noise of what Watkins assumed was fire, followed closely by the pungent smell of cooked meat. *Please, God, don't let it be me.* He remembered Treadway's corpse and opened his eyes.

Much of Treadway's flesh had been charred black and crispy. The chairs to Watkins right were still smoldering. Thankfully, it looked like Treadway had shielded him from the blaze. Watkins grimaced, pushing what was left of his friend away. The corpse slid down the walkway until coming to rest on some kind of metal case. Where once Treadway's face had been was an unrecognizable mess of melted flesh. Smoke wafted from his empty eye sockets, lending a hellish vibe to the already chaotic scene. Treadway's dog tags had been fused to his flesh. There was no way Watkins was going to try and dig those out.

Where had everyone gone? The better question was why had they left him strapped to a chair in a burning wreck?

Watkins disengaged his seatbelt and stood, careful not to shift his broken bones too much. He had to steady himself on the nearest seat as the floor seemed to be on an incline. It wasn't just the floor he realized, but the entire aircraft was askew, like it was lying on its side. One look at the windows and the earth poking through the broken glass confirmed his suspicions. He struggled his way over a row of seats toward the cockpit. The first thing Watkins noticed was a trail of blood.

The cockpit had collapsed under an ancient White Pine where the aircraft had scraped to a stop. Captain Ruiz had been folded in half as the instrument panel pressed his legs up. Watkins felt for a pulse. There wasn't one. The other side of the cockpit was relatively clear of damage or debris. No Lieutenant Bigsby. The trail of blood looked like it originated from the co-pilot's chair and trailed off toward the rear of the wreckage.

Watkins turned and noticed a giant crack toward the aft section of the aircraft. A sizeable gap had opened up where the tail tried to pull away at some point during the crash. The metal creaked as Watkins stepped past the blocked front entrance. No way to get through the rolled over door.

Further along the belly of the aircraft Watkins noticed two bodies pinned under a Humvee. They were Delta Force judging by their attire. It looked like the vehicle broke from the cargo straps and crushed them against the wall. He thought about trying to retrieve dog tags when the C-17 shifted. It whined in protest as it rolled toward the right. Watkins scrambled away from the wayward vehicle. He looked from the Humvee to the corpses and couldn't help but feel thankful that wasn't him. The poor bastards probably never saw it coming. The aircraft eased to a stop, the floor leveling out some. A HK416 assault rifle – he knew because he made it a point to ask one of the Delta Force guys, Haley from California – slid from under the Humvee and came to a stop after hitting Watkins' boot. He wasn't sure why he grabbed the weapon. All he knew was that it didn't feel right leaving it behind. Other than a scuff on the butt, the weapon seemed ready for action.

After the aircraft settled, Watkins knew he had to get the hell out of there before it rolled back to its normal position. If that happened, he'd be a stain under the Humvee too.

A bang came from outside the wrecked aircraft. It droned through the silence like a ghost through a graveyard. Another bang. Watkins followed the sound in the direction of the right wing.

The banging continued in regular intervals. Someone was out there.

Watkins double-timed it through the cracked fuselage. He emerged to find several rows of sugar maples cut in two by the crashed aircraft. The trail of chaos was at least a mile long. It was easy to see where the C-17 first hit by the giant divot in the ground. Skid marks were clearly visible at regular intervals until the aircraft clipped the outer edge of the Adirondacks. Watkins could see the matte grey-blue paint of the left wing some distance away in the vegetation where it had broken free.

He turned his attention to the source of the noise. There were two people, one on top of the wing and another below the inboard engine. It looked like they were trying to knock it down.

Something didn't seem right. Why wouldn't they be helping the injured or salvaging supplies from the wreckage? They definitely should have moved the bodies to a more stable location until contacting Command for rescue.

Watkins crouched and inched along the outer fuselage, watching. One of the Delta Force guys was lying on his stomach hitting the engine with a long chunk of metal. The engine swayed, spewing fuel on the ground below. If the fire reached it, well, Watkins didn't want to think about what would happen.

"Hey, dumb ass, what are you trying to do, kill us?"

The person on the ground turned at the sound. There was no mistaking Sergeant Lopez as she faced Watkins. Her long black hair had fallen from what was left of her bun, blood sticking long black strands to her face. Her arm hung loosely at her side like it was broken. She definitely needed medical attention. Why hadn't Watkins thought to look for a first aid kit?

Watkins took a step closer. "You okay, Lorena?"

Lopez tensed, her eyes darting from Watkins to the engine with a frantic energy – looking at him with what he'd thought was longing. No, it was something more. She had the look of an addict, of need, just like his cousin back home in Trenton. She inclined her head and narrowed her eyes. It was almost like she was unsure what to do. Her eyes moved around and Watkins could almost see her brain working with thought.

"It's me, Solomon. What happened to you?"

Lopez's lip curled up in a snarl. A low growl rumbled from her chest and up to her throat just like a dog.

Watkins stopped, tensed. As Lopez's eyes moved, he thought he noticed that her sclera weren't white. He stared. The next time her eyes moved toward the engine he was positive. Each sclera was blue – the color of electricity – instead of white. Weird.

Think as he may, Watkins couldn't come up with anything that would turn a person's eyes that color. No disease, condition, or sickness… nothing. This whole scene seemed a little too surreal. Maybe he was still strapped to the chair in the C-17 in a coma. Maybe he was dead. That would make more sense than what he was seeing.

Lopez took a step toward him, spewing a guttural challenge; her eyes no longer unsure but wild and threatening, soulless.

"Don't move, Lorena." Watkins raised his weapon.

Without warning Lopez raged toward him, screaming at the top of her lungs. Watkins watched dumbfounded as her head ballooned outward with each step. His legs seemed to know what to do before his brain. He slowly backed up until a large stump stopped his retreat. Lopez kept coming. She was about twenty yards away and closing fast.

Watkins could see her scalp rippling. It looked like two shapes were moving, almost scrabbling around between her skull and scalp. Faster and faster the lumps moved around the circumference of Lopez's head until she abruptly dropped to her knees, clutching her skull. She was less than ten yards away and her screams of agony echoed off the mountainside.

Watkins instinctively pointed the gun at her.

Lopez reached a hand toward him, the snarl replaced by a look of confusion, pleading. Under her skin the two lumps sped faster and faster. Watkins actually heard her skull crack. Lopez screamed one last time, clawing at the ground, pulling herself closer to Watkins. Then, incredibly, her head burst apart like a piñata at a kid's birthday party. Instead of candy, bone, brains, blood and… something else rained down.

Watkins jumped back, pain knifing through his ribs. His mind raced, trying to comprehend what he'd just witnessed. This wasn't supposed to happen. People's heads didn't just explode. He was only a mechanic sent to fix an aircraft. Nobody was supposed to die.

He looked down at the body and saw a quick flitter of movement. Watkins leaned forward for a closer look. It was difficult to pinpoint through the remnants of Lopez's head, but eventually the thing slithered onto her back.

It looked like some kind of black worm, about two inches long with barbed pincers. Its polished body reflected what was left of the light and reminded Watkins of obsidian. He took a few tentative steps forward. The thing – because he had never seen a worm like that before – stopped moving and almost seemed to be waiting. Another emerged from the carnage that used to be Lopez's head, moving through the grass toward Watkins. Nasty little buggers.

"Back away. Slowly," a voice whispered from behind. "They don't live long without a host."

Watkins wanted to turn and see who the voice belonged to but didn't. It was nice to hear a real, human voice. He moved back with steady, even steps while watching the black worms. They were moving faster now slithering around in circles, probably looking for a new brain to explode. Why weren't they going for the idiot banging away at the engine?

As if on cue, the Delta Force guy smashed the engine one more time. A moment later it crashed onto the ground below, jet fuel pissing from the broken manifolds.

Lopez's worms had slowed. They raised their tiny heads to the sky and opened their pincers, screeching. With a buzz and an arc of what looked like electricity they exploded.

"What the hell were those things?" Watkins turned and saw a soldier dressed in head to toe black crouched near the crack in the fuselage. The soldier motioned him back.

"The worms? I wish I knew." He pointed to what was left of Lopez, "That your friend?"

Watkins crouched and nodded.

"The same thing happened to a couple of guys from my squad. We call them screamers. Next time put a bullet through the host's head before they get too close. The worms will still bust out but at least they won't get inside you. I've seen one slither up a guy's nose. It isn't pretty."

"Got a name for him too?" Watkins asked pointing to the Delta Force soldier who was pressing a shard of metal the size of a small book into his stomach. There were already pieces of metal covering his arms. His eyes shone with the same electric-blue light as Lopez's.

"Those would be ironhides. They stick metal all over themselves like homemade armor. Even seen one pick up a gun and shoot another man down." The soldier took two silent steps forward and fired. The bullet struck the infected soldier in the eye. As the fresh corpse fell, three worms broke free from the confines of his head. "RIP brother."

"Who are you?"

The soldier smiled. "I'm Chen. We were sent to investigate a... discovery." Chen looked up at the darkening sky. "C'mon, let's get away from here before more freaks show up. The worms seem to be able to communicate. That screeching you heard was a call for help." He looked inside the wreckage. "That Humvee operational?"

"Beats me," Watkins said with a shrug. "I didn't have time to find out as I was falling out of the sky and crashing, not to mention all the weird shit going down after I woke."

Chen looked from the Humvee to Watkins. "We've got to

find out. That's probably our best chance at getting the hell out of here in one piece. There's a naval base not too far south of here. Edgerton Springs."

Chen crept through the tear in the fuselage, Watkins staying close.

Chen glanced through the passenger-side window. "Steering lock. If we can find the loadmaster, we should find the keys."

"He's not here."

"Duh," Chen said. "I just want to make sure the Humvee isn't fried."

Chen tried the Humvee's door. It opened. He looked around a minute before releasing the hood. "Take a look and tell me what you see."

Watkins walked around to the front of the vehicle. To his surprise everything looked in order. The battery didn't have any char marks like he thought it would. "Looks good," he whispered back.

Careful to make as little noise as possible, Watkins eased the hood down.

"I want you to stay here while I get the others," Chen said, inspecting his weapon. "I'll be back in five."

"But you just said we should get out of here. What do you want me to do?"

Chen pointed to the open Humvee. "I want you to get in and be quiet."

A feeling of dread settled in the pit of Watkins' stomach. He eyed the corpses suspiciously before looking back at Chen. "I'm just a mechanic."

"C'mon, there's nothing to be scared of. Those guys won't be getting up anytime soon."

"You don't know that," Watkins snapped.

The smile faded from Chen's face. "Look, I move faster alone. You'll only slow me down. And, besides, someone has to stay with the Humvee."

Maybe Chen had a point. If the Humvee was their only means of escape, someone should guard it. Even though he didn't like it, Watkins nodded.

"The challenge word is 'egg roll.' The response will be 'pizza.' If you challenge and don't get the right response, shoot. Got it?"

"'Egg roll,' seriously?"

Chen's smile returned. With a shrug he said, "What, I'm hungry."

Watkins got into the vehicle and slouched down as far as his long frame would allow. He watched Chen disappear through the crack. This was going to be the longest five minutes of his life.

After a few minutes of watching the fuselage, Watkins thought he heard something. It was a rustling noise, like someone running through tall grass. He dismissed it as the wind only for the sound to persist. As the sound approached, he thought he heard heavy breathing – a person out of breath. He cocked his head and held his breath, concentrating.

A shape blurred past the crack. It was too fast to see.

Watkins heart sped as adrenaline surged through his body. His fight or flight instinct kicked in. Chen gave him a code word for a reason. But what if some of the Delta Force squad had survived?

Something stopped in front of the crack. The falling sun didn't provide enough light to see. It could be an infected freak or one of the other passengers from his flight. The only thing Watkins knew was it wasn't Chen.

He watched as Lieutenant Bigsby took a tentative step through the crack. As the Lieutenant turned, Watkins saw he didn't have any eyes. In their place was what looked like miniature television screens displaying static; a myriad of different-colored wires pressed into his temples. His flight suit was shredded in places, wounds visible beneath. The weird thing was they weren't bloody anymore, but a deep blue. Watkins had never seen anything like this before. He clutched his weapon tighter as Bigsby opened his mouth. Instead of a voice, the sound of a radio tuner searching for a signal blipped static over and over.

Two ironhides came through the crack. They fanned out and started rummaging through the debris toward the rear of the wreck focusing on scraps of metal and little else. Watkins noticed the loadmaster and cursed his good fortune. Dispatching one worm-infested freak would be difficult, but three, by himself, would be a tall order. Maybe too tall.

Bigsby crouched, looking from side to side. An image of the cockpit flashed on the miniature screens that were his eyes. He walked on stiff joints, almost like a baby who had recently taken its first steps. After a few steps he turned and more blipping static shot out of his mouth toward his two comrades.

The two ironhides dropped their metal haul and moved to Bigsby.

They were communicating.

Watkins palms started sweating. He took slow, measured breaths to help quiet his thundering heart. Somehow he couldn't shake the feeling this wouldn't end well. Yet he wasn't about to sit there and wait to die. Even though he hadn't fired a weapon in over six months, he eased it up, resting the barrel on the dash. In his mind he had two choices: start shooting now and hope he hit Bigsby, or wait for the group of freaks to get closer and pray they didn't notice him, blasting all three of them.

Sweat dripped from Watkins brow.

He waited.

Bigsby led his fellow freaks at a cautious pace. It was almost like they could sense Watkins lying in wait. They circumvented some supply crates only a few feet away, slowly but steadily getting closer.

Just as Watkins prepared to burst from the Humvee, he heard Chen say, "Pizza."

Bigsby spun with purpose and screeched, an ear piercing sonic noise. Watkins covered his ears. The two ironhides ran with urgency toward the cracked fuselage, long metal shards in their hands like swords.

"Pizza," Chen said a little louder, closer.

Watkins took aim, careful to target Bigsby's head. He sucked in a breath, held it, and squeezed the trigger. Bullets forced their way through glass. Bigsby, turning at the sound, was struck in the cheek and neck. He wobbled before falling, a gurgling hiss escaping his mouth. Deep-blue blood flowed from the fresh wounds.

A hail of gunfire erupted from just outside. Watkins could hear Chen and another man shouting out enemy positions.

Through the searing pain in his ribs, Watkins exited the Humvee. He hurried over to where Bigsby was trying to crawl away, a snail trail of blue liquid marking his meager progress. When he was reasonably close, Watkins fired another burst. This time he didn't miss.

Worms slithered from Bigsby's ears, nose, and the hole in his head. There were at least a dozen of them. Watkins scrambled toward the crack in the fuselage, not wanting the electric exploding worms to damage their ride. He yelled, "Pizza," over and over so he wouldn't be accidentally shot.

The loadmaster's head exploded as Watkins emerged from the aircraft, bloody chunks and black worms hitting him in the face. Watkins immediately dove sideways hoping to avoid any more worms and bullets. He felt at least one slithering up the front of his neck. More shots echoed around the crash site.

"Ironhide down," Chen said.

The worm worked its way up to Watkins' lips, scrabbling and nipping with its pincers. When it was halfway through, Watkins bit down. His teeth caught the soft spot between armored sections splitting it in two. The pincers continued squeezing his tongue for a moment. Before he could spit it out, a buzzing electric current arced through the space between the roof of his mouth and tongue. Watkins twitched, the zap momentarily stunning him. Following a tiny pop, the worm exploded, coating his tongue in bitter-tasting worm guts.

There was no stopping the second coming of the ham and cheese omelet.

"Cease fire," Chen said, holding up an arm. "Watkins, get out of there."

Watkins rolled over and saw half a dozen worms slithering after him. He hopped up, his broken ribs hampering him little but hurting him plenty. After hearing several pops, he turned back.

"You okay?" Chen asked.

Watkins held an arm out, palms facing Chen and two others. "Stay back. I may be infected."

The second Spec Ops soldier raised his weapon. A woman who didn't look very soldierly yet, for some reason, was dressed in the same black uniform, pushed past him, pressing his gun down. "Ease up, Lawson. If the worm didn't make it to his brain, he's clear." She walked over the loadmaster's corpse to get a closer look at Watkins. He opened his mouth when she asked. She pulled his eyelid down and made him move his eyes around too. "See?" she said. "His eyes are normal."

She patted Watkins on the shoulder. "I'm Doctor Emily Staniszak, parasitologist extraordinaire and all around lover of cheese." Her smile warmed the fullness of her face. "Why were you yelling pizza like some kind of whacko?"

"That was the challenge word. Didn't want to be confused with one of those wormy freaks."

Staniszak laughed. "Let me guess, Chen picked the challenge word."

"What?" Chen said, patting his stomach. "I told you I was hungry."

Watkins walked over to the loadmaster and rifled through his pockets. "Thank God." He pulled a set of keys from the corpse's jumpsuit and held them up. "We can get out of here now."

"You're not going anywhere," Lawson said with a sneer. "We don't know enough about those worms. We don't even know if they're actually parasites. What we do know is one of them exploded in his mouth. It's too risky to take him with us."

Lawson seemed like the typical grunt – square jaw, fresh buzz cut, in peak physical condition, and apparently no sense of humor. He stood, poised to shoot. Watkins didn't dare move.

"Cut it out, Lawson," Chen said, moving between the two men. "We go together, or not at all. Doc says he's good to go. You smarter than her?"

Lawson looked from Watson to Staniszak before looking at the ground. "No," he mumbled.

"I didn't think so. Our mission hasn't changed. We need to get the Doc to safety so we can figure out what in the hell is going on."

Doc Staniszak peeked in the wrecked C-17. "Holy shit." She turned toward Watkins. "You do that?"

Watkins leaned against the wheel well and nodded. He grabbed his weapon and eyed Lawson. While he understood his intentions were noble, or at least he was giving him the benefit of the doubt, it didn't change the fact that that son of a bitch had just tried to shoot him.

"Whatcha got?" Chen asked.

"He killed a technophile all by himself."

Chen turned toward Lawson and said, "And you wanted to shoot him. Dumb ass."

Lawson stormed off toward the tree line grumbling. He turned like he wanted to say something but didn't.

"What's with him?" Watkins asked.

"Oh, I don't know, it might have something to do with the fact that he had to shoot his friend in the face a few days ago. Lawson's never been the most sociable guy to begin with. Throw some freaky alien worms who take over people's brains and you can respect his crankiness."

Watkins grabbed his ribs. "We've all seen some freaky shit. Doesn't give anyone the right to fly off the handle like that. I thought he was supposed to be trained for high-stress situations?"

"He is," Chen said, his tone darkening. "Most of us Spec Ops guys don't get many days off. We get orders and we go. No questions asked. We literally live for this."

"Sorry," Watkins offered. He understood the life of a soldier. He'd watched a friend forced to serve six months longer than his enlistment due to 9/11. The brass called it stop loss. Watkins called it bullshit.

A gunshot rang out from the direction Lawson had taken.

"Stay here with the Doc and get ready to go. I'll be back in two minutes." Chen didn't wait for an answer and took off for the tree line.

Watkins tossed Staniszak the keys. "Fire the Humvee up. I'm going to make sure their way back stays clear."

Staniszak caught the keys. "Don't do anything stupid."

Watkins cracked a smile as she walked through the cracked fuselage. He focused on the tree line, finger on the trigger. From inside he heard the Humvee's engine turn over and chug to life. Staniszak eased the vehicle out through the already open cargo door of the crashed airplane and waited.

True to his word, Chen came tearing through the tree line after two minutes, Lawson and an injured Delta Force soldier a short distance behind.

"Get in the Humvee," Chen shouted, hopping over a downed tree. He was moving fast. "We've got company."

As the three soldiers neared the wreck, a static hiss cut through the mountain dusk. A chorus of screeches seemed to answer the call.

Chen skidded to a stop after reaching Watkins. He raised his weapon and fired into the tree line. Watkins jaw dropped when he saw three screamers come tearing into the clearing. Right behind them were half a dozen ironhides carrying assault rifles, followed by two technophiles.

Lawson pulled up. He turned and shot, providing covering fire for the injured Delta Force soldier who was running with a limp, blood leaking from a bullet hole in his thigh.

One of the technophiles spit static and as one, all six ironhides fired. Lawson took a bullet in the shoulder but held his ground. The Delta Force soldier wasn't as lucky. The first bullet ripped through his midsection while the second went clean through his good thigh, sending him sprawling. Chen fired on the screamers. He put a bullet through the fastest one's brain and just as quickly took out another. The third plowed into Lawson sending him tumbling over a stump.

Watkins fired at the line of ironhides. Bullets hit metal and ricocheted away. He got lucky and struck one in the chest and it fell. Without a fresh clip, he tossed his useless weapon aside and ran for the injured Delta Force guy.

One of the technophiles opened its mouth. An electric blue glow, faint at first, shone from its throat. A rumbling noise came from its chest. It reminded Watkins of a jet engine powering up.

"Take that glowing bastard out," Chen shouted. "He's trying to fry the Humvee."

Watkins remembered the blue flash that hit the C-17 right before they lost power. He could hardly believe what used to be a man could be capable of such things. He could hardly believe anything anymore.

The blue glow intensified as the sound raced faster from within the technophile.

Chen was yelling but Watkins didn't hear what he said. The Delta Force guy was on his back firing into the thick of the worm-controlled freaks. A bullet tore through the glowing technophile's calf and it fell to a knee. The blue glow abruptly stopped.

The ironhides fired back.

Watkins danced around as chunks of ground erupted from the hail of gunfire. Someone yelled that they were reloading. An ironhide fell, blood squirting from its neck. Lawson was running toward the Humvee. Watkins slid down next to the injured Delta Force soldier. "Time to go."

The guy didn't answer.

Watkins checked for a pulse, couldn't find one.

Lawson, limping now, hobbled closer, his weapon gone. Watkins hurried to him, placed an arm around his waist and aided his retreat. Chen continued firing. "Last mag," he yelled, slamming the cartridge into place.

The ironhides had tossed their weapons aside. Instead of running, they walked briskly toward the survivors, jagged metal tearing into their flesh. Maybe all the metal prevented them from running.

"Move your asses," Chen shouted. One of his bullets struck an exposed head. Worms wriggled around under the freak's scalp until bursting through his skull. Chen moved with ease over a downed tree, doing his best to cover them.

Staniszak leaned on the horn.

Through gritted teeth Watkins pulled Lawson along, ignoring the pain burning like lava under his skin. He'd be damned if he'd die in the middle of nowhere, his brain food for the worms.

Chen was at his side then and together the two of them pulled Lawson into the Humvee. The uninjured technophile spoke statically to the ironhides who immediately retreated. They ran to the aid of the injured technophile, two of them carrying it toward the downed aircraft.

As Staniszak weaved through the trees, night fell over the Adirondacks like a lid on a coffin. Watkins leaned back and closed his eyes for a moment.

Lawson tapped him. "Thanks for the assist."

"Together, or not at all, remember?"

Lawson nodded, cracked a smile. Maybe he wasn't so bad after all.

Staniszak slammed on the brakes, swerving around two screamers in fluorescent-orange hunting vests. She threw the Humvee in reverse.

"Hit those sons of bitches," Chen said.

"Hold on." Staniszak slammed the Humvee in drive and plowed into the freaks. One flipped over the hood and landed with a crunch on the already cracked windshield, the glass giving way. The Humvee rose and fell as it passed over the second screamer.

Chen grabbed the screamer and struggled to force it back out. Staniszak slammed on the brakes and it flew forward as the vehicle stopped. Chen pushed, sending it onto the hood. Staniszak pressed down on the accelerator, swerving before the screamer could recover. It slid over the side of the Humvee and into the night.

"Wait!" A helmetless soldier in standard camouflage came running like a bat out of hell from the woods. He looked over his shoulder as he ran. "More crazies behind me."

Watkins opened the door and the Delta Force soldier hopped in. It was Haley. Staniszak hit the accelerator and the Humvee shot forward as about a dozen sets of electric-blue glowing eyes raced into view.

"Glad to see you made it." Watkins said.

Haley nodded. "Me too. Thanks for stopping." He panted a moment, leaning his weapon against the seat between his legs, the barrel pointing up. "I owe you one."

They drove on, the screams and screeches of the infected fading. Watkins noticed long faces all around the Humvee. He wondered if anyone else had noticed the civilian freaks. The parasites had already spread to the civilian population.

Eventually they followed signs until reaching the naval base. The front gate looked abandoned, a headless soldier their only welcome. A large explosion rumbled in the distance. Watkins sank back feeling deflated, worn.

"Out of the frying pan and into the fire," Chen complained. Haley passed him a clip. They both readied their weapons.

Lawson clutched his wounded shoulder. "We should keep moving. The base is a lost cause."

Staniszak tapped the fuel gauge. "We're not going anywhere without fuelling up first."

Lawson punched the door.

"We've got work to do," Chen said, opening his door. He hurried past the dead guard and opened the gate.

The Humvee sputtered to a stop just inside the base. "Looks like we're walking," Staniszak said, her face paling. It was the first time she looked genuinely afraid.

Watkins exited the Humvee to the sound of distant screams. "What do we do now?" he asked.

"We survive," Chen said with grin.

BUG HUNT
A Joe Ledger Adventure

Jonathan Maberry

-1-

The last words I heard were, "Something hit us. We're going down."

Yelled real damn loud.

Then a big black nothing closed around us like a fist.

We were gone.

If that meant we were going down then I had to wonder, in those last fleeting seconds before the chopper hit the canopy of trees, how far down was the ride? Was it just to the trees, or to the forest floor below? Or would the world open its mouth and swallow us whole, gulping men, weapons, equipment and everything those tools of war signified? Would we slide all the way down into the pit?

Yeah, maybe.

We probably deserved it, too.

I'll leave that for philosophers.

I was too busy dying. I was by the open door, hunkered down over the minigun. When the Black Hawk tilted I felt myself begin that long, bad fall.

-2-

I have expected to die more times than I can count. Nature of the job.

I'm a first-team shooter for an organization that pits special operators against terrorists who have bioweapons based on absolute bleeding-edge technology. In those kinds of fights a lot of people on both sides take long dirt naps. A lot of my friends have preceded me into the big black. Most of them were better people than I'll ever be, but being a good person doesn't make your Kevlar work any better. It doesn't armor plate you, or make you immune to poisons, venoms, and biological agents.

Each time I expected to die and didn't, I felt like I was cruising more and more on borrowed time. When it comes to counting the grace of God – or whoever else is on call for this little blue marble – I'm overdrawn at the bank. One of these days they're going to foreclose on me, and I won't have any luck or grace left to pay the bill.

I thought today was that day.

Today should have been.

Just as being a good person doesn't give you any added protection, being a right bastard doesn't necessarily guarantee that you'll meet the fate you deserve.

The helicopter went down.

I didn't.

Not entirely.

I woke upside down.

In a tree.

A long goddamn way from the ground.

Not the first time *this* has happened to me, either.

My life blows.

-3-

The first rule of survival is: Don't panic.

Panic makes you stupid and stupid makes you dead.

Panic also denies you the opportunity to learn from the moment. You take a breath and judge the immediacy of your experience. You need to assess everything. Mind, body, equipment, environment... all of it.

The bright blue of the sunny sky had faded to a washed-out and uniform gray, so I had no way of telling the time. No way to judge how long I'd been out. Five minutes? Hours? I wasn't hungry or thirsty enough for it to be longer than that. Our Black Hawk had been hit by something – probably a rocket-propelled grenade – at around ten in the morning.

My mind was fuzzy. That was the easy part to figure out. There was a big lumpy hot spot on the back of my skull where I'd hit something during the crash. My helmet was gone.

Most of the rest of my body felt sore and stretched, but hanging upside down will do that. Plus there would have to be some minor dents and dings from when I bailed out of the Black Hawk.

I paused, frowning.

Had I bailed out? I couldn't remember doing that, though I must have because I wasn't crumpled up inside the fallen bird.

Moving very, very carefully, I leaned back and looked down. The floor of the forest was about forty feet below me. Long damn drop.

Then I took a breath and tightened my stomach muscles to do a gut-buster of a sit-up. On good days I can bang out a whole bunch of these. Flat, on inclines, and clutching weights to my chest. Today was not a good day, so it took a whole lot of whatever energy I had left to lift my upper body high enough to see what was holding my feet in place.

I expected to see a tangle of branches. Or something from the chopper – rope, a cable, some of the net strapping used to secure cargo. I stared at my feet, at what held me to the tree.

No rope.

No cables.

Nothing that had been on the Black Hawk.

Nothing that belonged in this forest, either.

Nothing that belonged anywhere.

I was lashed to the branch by turn-upon-turn-upon-turn of glistening silk.

The strands were as thick as copper wire. And far stronger.

I turned and looked around at the rest of the tree. That's when I saw it. It wasn't that the day had become hazy and gray with clouds. No, there was more of the silk stretched in wild, haphazard patterns between the trunks and leaves.

All silk.

I wasn't hanging from a tree.

I was caught in a web.

Yeah.

A fucking web.

-4-

It's moments like this that make you want to seriously freak out.

I mean go total bug-eyed, slavering ape-shit nuts.

A spider web big enough to cover half a mile of treetops and hold a two-hundred-pound man – complete with combat gear – suspended? Yeah. Panic time. That is *not* normal, even for me. That is not something you start the day either psychologically- or tactically-prepared for.

Which changed the process.

Instead of letting calm passivity inform you and help you plan, you go bugfuck nuts and get the hell out of there.

Maybe you scream a little.

I did. Sue me.

I snaked out a hand and caught the thickest part of the branch I could, careful not to grab more of the webbing. Once I steadied myself, I reached into my right front pants pocket for my Wilson rapid-release knife. I wear it clipped to the lip of the pocket and it was still there. I pulled it free and flicked my wrist to snap the three-point-eight inch blade into place. That blade is short, but it's also ultra-light and moves at the speed of my hand, which means it can move real damn fast.

I slashed at the web, terrified that the blade might stick or not be tough enough to slice through the fibers.

"Come on, God, cut me one frigging break here."

The blade bit deep and the fibers parted.

I chopped and slashed and even stabbed at it, nicking my boots, slicing my trouser legs.

Suddenly I was free, and gravity jerked my feet straight down. My steadying grip on the branch immediately became the only thing preventing me from plunging down to a bone breaker of a landing.

I couldn't close the blade one handed so I had to risk putting it into my pocket still open. Somewhere up in Valhalla I could see the gods of war raise their eyebrows and blow out their cheeks as if to say, "Boy's tough but he's a bit of an idiot."

Whatever. I needed my other hand and I didn't want to throw away the only weapon I had left. My rifle was probably in the chopper, and my holster was empty; the Beretta had probably fallen out while I hung upside down.

With a growl of effort and a lot of fear-injected adrenaline I swung sideways and up and caught the branch with my other hand. The bark was rough, but the wood was solid.

I hung there.

Boots swaying above the ground.

Streamers of spider web hanging around me.

What on earth had spun those webs? What on earth could have spun anything that big? The thought of some lumbering monster as big as a Range Rover scuttling toward me on eight massive legs was unbearable.

Was that what this was, or was my imagination taking the facts and spinning them out of control? Distorting them into science fiction implausibility. After all, there were spider colonies that made webs as massive as this. There were wasps and moths that covered trees with their nests.

That's what this could be.

Not one big monster, but many small ordinary-sized ones.

It sounded good. It sounded great. It was doable. I could bear that.

Except that the strands hanging down around me were too thick. Too damn thick. No tiny insect body had spun them.

My mouth went totally dry.

Then I saw something that made it all much, much worse. Up there, tucked into the folds of the webbing, half-hidden by boughs of pine, were bones. I hung there and stared at them. I could see the distinctive knobbed end of a femur. In my trade you get to know the difference between animal and human bones.

The thing I was looking at was a human thighbone. Above it, obscured by shadows, were a half dozen curled and cracked ribs still anchored by tendon to the sternum.

Get out of here, I told myself.

I lingered a moment, though.

I listened to the trees, tried to hear past the soft rustle of branches stirred by leaves. Needing to hear any sounds that didn't belong.

There was nothing.

Nothing.

And then…

Something.

Not close, but still too close. A scratching sound.

Like something climbing.

Then a brief, high-pitched cry. Not an animal cry, though. This was a chittery sound. Like a locust or a cicada.

Get the hell out of here right now.

My heart was hammering like mad, and sweat poured down my body. I had to get out of here right damn now.

I began climbing sideways, sliding one hand and then another to move along the branch. It was strong, but I was a solid two hundred pounds. The green wood creaked. And then there was a single gunshot-loud crack and suddenly I was moving downward. Not falling. Swinging. The branch broken but didn't snap completely off. It swung me down like a lever and I thudded hard into the trunk and started to slide down. I instantly lunged for a second branch. It was smaller and broke right away, but it slowed my rate of fall. Not much, just enough for me to snake out a hand and catch another branch.

Which broke.

And another.

Which broke.

And that's how I went down the tree. Each branch cracked and folded inward, slapping me over and over again into the trunk. Each time I cried out in pain, and each time I slid down the rough bark. I couldn't hear the scratching sounds of whatever had made that nest, but no doubt it was coming. It was an awkward, painful, lumpy, uncertain process of fleeing by falling.

When I reached the lowest branch it held and I clung to it with desperate force, panting, praying, locking my fingers around it and holding on for dear life. When I built up the nerve, I looked down.

My boots were maybe six or seven inches from the green grass. I almost laughed, but instead I let go and thumped down onto the grass. My knees buckled and I dropped to them, then toppled sideways, my body feeling raw and beaten, my arms aching.

Above me the trees swayed and shadows seemed to curl and roil under the gray webbing.

I got back to my knees and carefully reached into my pocket for my folding knife. It was there, but as I drew it out I saw that it was the wrong color. Instead of bright silvery steel, I saw dark red smears.

That's when I felt the warm lines running down the outside of my thigh. Very little pain, though. Or maybe so much pain elsewhere that I didn't really feel it; but I knew that somewhere on my thigh was a cut. Couldn't be too deep. I hoped. I had no first aid kit.

The trees above me rustled.

Get out of here, I told myself. *You're not bleeding to death, so get your ass in gear. Go anywhere but don't stay here.*

But that was as much bad advice as good. Fleeing was not really an option.

I tapped the earbud I wore, but there was only static. I figured that much. I quickly checked, and the little battery signal booster I wore was no longer in my pocket; until I could find it, I wasn't going to be making any long distance calls. At best I might pick up chatter from anyone within a mile and on the same frequency.

I was in the Pacific Northwest, in the vast and seemingly endless forests of the Washington State timber country. All around me were millions of trees. Douglas fir, hemlock, ponderosa pine, white pine, spruce, larch, and cedar. The whole world was the green of pine needles and the dark brown of tree bark.

There had been four other people in that Black Hawk. There had been a briefcase filled with biological samples that I needed to get to my boss, Mr. Church, because he needed to get them into a goddamn vault where they would never see the light of day again. I was on my way back from a quick and dirty piece of business on the Canadian border where I'd helped dismantle a small but effective bioweapons lab. The bad guys were Serbians who had shanghaied a couple of biochemists and forced them to make designer bioweapons. Nasty stuff. Not doomsday plagues, but pathogens lethal enough to kill sixty percent of the crowd in Times Square on New Years Eve. That's six hundred thousand potential victims.

I went in with two of my guys, Top and Bunny. My right and left hand. Top was First Sergeant Bradley Sims, a former Ranger who'd come out of retirement to fight in the Middle East war that had killed his only son and crippled his niece. He'd been recruited into the Department of Military Sciences because he was very probably the best special ops team leader in the business. Bunny was Staff Sergeant Harvey Rabbit, a six-and-a-half foot kid from Orange County. Looked like a surfer boy, fought like one of the Titans from Greek legend. Stronger than just about anyone you're ever going to meet.

Top and Bunny.

They were out here. Somewhere.

Alive, I prayed.

Or dead, I feared.

The other three were the crew of the Black Hawk. I didn't know them. They'd been sent to extract us when the Serbians went ass-wild on us and put forty guys in the woods with RPGs and LAW rockets. Our chopper had made maybe six of the eighty-two mile journey to the nearest populated town before it was brought down.

I needed to find my men. I needed to find that metal case filled with weaponized pathogens. A working radio would be pretty damn nice, too. So would a gun.

I froze. Above me I could hear the scratching sound.

Louder.

Closer.

I got to my feet and ran.

-5-

No, I don't know what I was running from.

Maybe another guy – an ordinary chap or even a regular soldier – would have been stalled on that one thing. The giant web. And, sure, I was pretty freaked out about it. However I'm not an ordinary chap. I work for the Department of Military Sciences. We see the truly weird stuff that's out there. Sure, most of the time that's either a designer pathogen, a doomsday plague, transgenic manipulation, biotechnology like exoskeletons and cybernetic implants, nanites, or a dozen different madhouse attempts to cook up a super soldier. Frankenstein stuff. Jekyll and Hyde, if Jekyll worked for the government and Hyde was a field op. In the five years I've been rolling out with Echo Team and the DMS, I've seen horrors that stretch beyond anything I'd imagined was even potentially real before I'd joined. A prion-based plague that turned people into something too damn close to flesh-eating zombies. Genetically-engineered vampire assassins. Ethnic-specific diseases cooked up by modern day Nazi eugenicists.

Like that.

Giant spiders? Scary as shit, but if I could get me a good handgun or, better yet, a machine gun, I was going to ameliorate my terror by proving that armor-piercing rounds are an adequate answer to just about all of life's little challenges.

The downside to that kind of bravado?

Yeah, I didn't actually have a gun.

So, like any sane person who thinks there might be giant spiders in the trees, I ran away.

As fast as I could.

Then I skidded to a stop.

Far away and far downhill I heard the chatter of automatic gunfire. Heavy caliber rifles. AK47s, without a doubt. You go into combat on a regular basis you get to know the sounds of different kinds of guns.

Serbians.

Then I heard another sound. A long, ripping, soul-searing shriek of total pain. A human voice raised to the point of red inhumanity. It rose and rose and then was suddenly gone. Shut off. Torn away.

The sounds – gunfire and screams – had come rolling up the slope at me. Somewhere downland, bad things were happening. That was a direction I absolutely did not want to go.

But it was where I had to go.

God damn it.

I bent low, faded behind any available shrubs I could find, and ran toward the sound of battle and death.

-6-

There was a steep gully cut into the landscape and it provided shelter and an easier path downhill, so I slid down the side and jogged along the bottom. The ground here was moist and marshy and it was a good ten degrees colder. It was also much darker than I expected and soon I had to slow down and feel my way through sections that were black as night.

I fumbled my way around a bend in the gully when I smelled something burning.

Correction. Something *burned.* A past-tense smell.

Oil and copper wires and plastic. Meat, too.

I rounded the bend and there it was. Sprawled across the gully, its back broken, its skin black and blistered.

The helicopter.

The vanes were all gone. So was the tail section. The Black Hawk's hull was crumpled from the impact with the ground, but I couldn't see the kind of blast signature a rocket-propelled grenade should have made. And yet something had hit us hard enough to knock us out of the sky.

As I crept toward it I could see shapes inside. Twisted and withered from the heat.

Two of them. Both buckled into their pilot's chairs.

Gone. Neither of them had ever had a chance. They'd stuck with it, fighting the controls of the dying chopper, and it had killed them down here in the moist darkness. Crushed them and cooked them.

Two men whose names I didn't know. Part of an extraction team. Men I would probably have gotten to know once we were back in the world. We would've had beers, swapped lies. Become real people to one another.

Now they didn't even look like people.

It took me three minutes to find the third man. What was left of him, anyway.

He lay against the steep slope of the gully forty yards beyond the smashed nose of the Black Hawk. His legs and face were burned, but it wasn't fire that had killed him. When we'd boarded the chopper he'd taken possession of the metal suitcase in which the bioweapons were stored. Per our protocol, he'd sealed the case and then cuffed it to his own wrist.

The wrist and the cuff were still there.

The man's hand lay on the ground between his feet. The case was gone.

The soldier's body was riddled with so many bullets he was in shreds. Hundreds of shell casings lay in the damp earth. The Serbians had slaughtered him, a needlessly brutal demonstration of force to recover their bioweapon.

In the distance there was more gunfire.

They were still fighting. Their team had not been extracted and I had to wonder why. If they had the case, then why linger? Even if Top and Bunny were both out there, what use would it be for the Serbians to hunt them down? They'd won. All they had to do was leave and my guys would spend a couple of long, hard days walking out of these deep woods. By the time Top and Bunny reached a working phone, the Serbs would be back home, or they'd have vanished into a safe house.

Why were they still fighting?

Questions, questions.

I moved back from the dead soldier. Another man whose name I didn't know. But I nodded to him, brother to brother. Acknowledging his life, respecting his death, making promises to his ghost I hoped I could keep.

I looked for any weapons. Nothing. I ran.

The gully split open and flattened into a streambed. One side of the stream was thick with trees, the other side a natural clearing. A Chinook helicopter lay in the field. Not stood. Lay.

It was over on its side, its propellers twisted like broken legs, the gray hull smashed in. Thin gray streamers of smoke curled from the engines. The grass and dirt was torn up and littered with more spent brass. And the exterior of the Chinook was splashed with blood and pocked with bullet holes.

I came up on the blind side and slunk along the bottom of the dead bird, but when I glanced inside I saw nothing but debris. No bodies at all.

And again, damn it, no weapons.

All I found was a torn open backpack, its contents spilled out like entrails. Among the junk I found two power bars and a full canteen of water. My stomach clenched like a fist at the sight of the food, and I tore open one of the wrappers with my teeth. I crammed the nearly tasteless bar into my mouth and chewed faster than I could breathe, then washed it down with half the water. It took an effort of will not to scarf down the other bar and to conserve the rest of the water.

In the distance the sound of gunfire had slowed to a few random shots. No more screams that I could hear. My best guess said that the shots were two to three miles away, and I still had no gun. There's a lot of logic to the old saying that you should never bring a knife to a gunfight.

And yet…

I moved off in the direction of the last few shots I'd heard.

Now that I was in the open I was able to get a look at the sun. It was later than I thought. I must have been out for hours. I figured it for about two o'clock, give or take. That meant I had four hours of daylight left. After that…

It was going to be a moonless night, so despite some starlight, the woods in Washington State were going to get very dark, very soon.

I began walking again, keeping my pace steady so that I stayed cautious but still covered distance. It was almost fifteen minutes before I saw the first sign that I was going in the right direction.

It stood upright in the grass, almost perfectly vertical, like a post erected for a new fence. Slender and gray. A vane from the Black Hawk's rotor. Snapped off near the base, driven inches deep into the wormy soil. The angle was right. The dying chopper must have hit the tops of the trees and then hurtled past this point to where it crashed and died in the gully.

As I drew near it I saw a couple of things that made me slow down and approach with greater caution.

The first thing I saw was that there was a slot of disturbed dirt at the base of the vane. From the angle of the resulting mound of pushed-up soil it was clear that the vane had struck at an angle. Then someone had come along and lifted the thing so that it stood improbably straight.

The second thing was writing. Someone had written a note in very crude fashion. The crudest. A fingertip and what looked like fresh blood.

COWBOYS AND INDIANS
SOMETHING IN THE TREES
~~FOOTBALL~~
PETER PARKER – FRIEND?

I grinned. Cowboy was my combat call sign. The reference to 'Indians' was a reference to 'Indian country' – a shorthand soldiers use for an area filled with hostiles. He was telling me about the Serbs. The second line was easy, too. No need to translate what the 'something in the trees' was. The word 'football' referred to the steel biohazard case, and the strikethrough was Top's way of telling me that it was gone. Balls. If the Serbs had recovered it, then we were back in deep shit.

I squatted there on my heels and considered the last line from the note.

PETER PARKER – FRIEND?

What did that mean?

Then I got it, but it still didn't make sense. Peter Parker is the name of the secret identity of Spider-man. I got that much; Top was telling me about the spiders. But why 'Friend?' Was he trying to tell me that the spiders were our friends? That made no sense at all. Spiders, natural or unnatural, were ugly, scary sonsabitches. I am not a fan.

And they were insects. How can an insect be a friend or not?

Did he mean that they weren't carnivorous? Something like that? It made no sense to me.

The note had been coded because there were hostiles on the ground. Fair enough. I pushed the vane down flat on the ground and smeared out the message with the sole of my shoe. Feeling enormously insecure about the way this was all playing out, I set off to find my men.

Top was alive. Maybe that meant Bunny was, too. And if my luck was starting to turn, maybe all three of the chopper's crew. Doesn't hurt to ask the universe to throw you a bone every once in a while.

I located the footprints that headed away from the spot and followed, moving as quickly as caution and observation would allow.

And that's when a strange day began getting stranger.

I found a dead Serbian.

Maybe 'dead' isn't the right word. I found a big red splotch of wetness on the ground and, all around it to a distance of thirty-five feet, were parts. Arms, legs, chunks of meat. The man looked like he'd been hit by a grenade, but there was no sign of shrapnel, no signature of detonated explosives. Just a body destroyed in a way I couldn't explain.

A dozen yards away was a second kill point, except the thing that had died there could not have been human, and this time there was clear evidence of the impact of a rocket-propelled grenade. Used at close range, too. The thing it had hit had been nearly vaporized. All that was left were glistening chunks of what looked like crab shell. Chitinous and rough, with faint yellow and blue spots. There wasn't enough of it to make sense of its shape, though I still had that bad feeling in my head ever since I woke up with my foot in a web.

Some kind of mutant insect?

Maybe.

The shell casings on the ground told an interesting story. There had been a firefight, with the Serbians capping off a lot of rounds. The creature had apparently tried to take cover behind a pain of twin pines, but the RPG had blown the trees and it apart. The kicker was that there were 9mm shell casings in the woods on the far side of the combat scene. From the angle the brass had dropped, it was clear they were firing at the Serbians. The Serbian rounds had been fired mostly at the dead thing, with only a few shots returning fire from the guys with the small arms.

Did that make it a three-way fight? If so, the evidence suggested that the Serbians were more concerned with the creature then they were with Top and Bunny.

Not sure how to read that. Top and Bunny are generally scary enough to command full attention from any hostiles we meet. What could have unnerved the Serbs enough to more or less ignore them in a fight? The answer to that opened up new and very disturbing lines of speculation. I didn't think I wanted to go down that path right now.

I kept moving.

I found a footprint punched deep into a spot of moist earth. Big shoe, military tread. Size fifteen-extra-wide.

Bunny.

The print was angled toward what looked like a game trail and as I bent low to follow it, I saw that there were more prints. Same shoe. No second set with the same tread. I had to think about the message back at the vane. It was definitely Top's kind of thing, so why wasn't I seeing his footprints?

And why were Bunny's so heavy?

The answer came to me a split second before I saw the first drops of blood.

All along the game trail, scattered around the big man's footprints, were random droplets of blood. Closer when the tread suggested Bunny was walking; farther apart when he was running.

The depth of the prints made sense now. Top was hurt and Bunny was carrying him.

Christ, has Top written me a note in his *own* blood? It seemed likely.

I moved on, and six hundred yards down the game trail I found another body. It was a Serbian. I think. There wasn't a whole lot of him left.

His head was gone. Not just cut off. It was gone. Someone had taken it away.

One hand was gone, too. The lower leg was nearly off. The body lay in a pool of drying blood. All around the corpse were shell casings that matched the AK-47 still clutched in the man's remaining hand. The barrel of the rifle was twisted almost at a right angle; the metal pinched shut as if it had been caught in a vise.

Sound carries, even in a dense forest. I should have heard these shots, unless they'd been fired while I was still unconscious. The blood was moderately fresh, though. So what did that mean in terms of timing? This fight had to have taken place no less than half an hour ago and probably no more than two hours before I woke up.

All around the scene were dozens of small, round indentations in the ground. I placed my right index finger into one and it was nearly a perfect fit.

No idea what the hell they were, though.

I looked around. The forest was still. Above me the trees were thick with dark green needles through which I could see patches of blue sky.

I moved on, keeping my knife in my hand, though it felt like a useless little toothpick.

The second body was a quarter mile farther on.

There was even less of this one. Just lumps of ragged red meat scattered around. If a guy swallowed a lump of C4 and exploded, the spread would be about this, though I didn't think that's what happened. Something had torn this guy apart. Torn him to ribbons.

I found no head, no hands.

There was another damaged AK47 and the boots on the dead feet were Timberland knockoffs. This wasn't anyone from my crew.

Thank God.

But it was clear whoever was hunting these Serbians was also hunting my team. And it had killed two men who had been armed with machine guns. I had a knife. My confidence in the little pig-sticker was waning, let me tell you.

Still kept going, though. What choice did I have?

A half mile deeper into the woods I heard a sound. A voice. A fragment of something.

"...see that thing... Christ... Bunny..."

Then nothing.

I froze and tapped my earbud. "Cowboy to Echo Team, Cowboy to Echo Team."

Nothing.

I repeated it.

Still nothing.

"Cowboy to Green Giant," I said, using Bunny's combat callsign. When that didn't work I tried Top. "Cowboy to Sergeant Rock. Do you copy?"

"... boy...?"

A fragment of a reply whispered in my ear.

And was gone.

Top's voice, though. I was sure of it.

Without the signal booster the radio had less than a mile's range. In these woods, with this density of trees, maybe half that. They had to be close.

I faded to the left of the game trail and instead ran through the tall grass. The trail wound through the trees, over hummocks, down through a gully, and deep into a shadowy grove of fir trees. I made no sound at all as I moved. I'm good at that. Last thing I wanted to do was draw fire if there were more Serbians. Or, I have to admit it, attract the attention of whatever was killing them.

I heard three things at almost exactly the same time.

The first was a rattle of automatic gunfire interspersed with the hollow *pok*s of small-arms. Overlaid with that was a strange clicking sound. Almost metallic, but not quite.

Dominating both sounds, though, was the rising, ear-splitting, agonized shriek of a human voice calling out for God and his mother. In Serbian.

-7-

I began to run.

That turned out to be a stupid choice.

I was so intent on following Bunny's footprints that I spent too much time looking down and not enough time looking around. Rookie mistake. Unforgivable, even if I was in shock.

The path followed rain runoff paths. Sometimes the ground was soft enough to take a clear print and sometimes exposed rock left me nothing to find. I reached a spot where a fallen tree blocked the path and I stopped and tried to imagine how Bunny carried an injured Top past the obstacle. There was no obvious route right or left, so I did the dumb thing and climbed atop the trunk to take a look. Sounds like a sensible plan if you're out hiking with your friends. Not so much when the woods were filled with hostiles.

As soon as I stood up on the trunk there was a *crack* and something hot burned past my right eyebrow. The bullet couldn't have missed me by more than a quarter inch.

Shit.

I threw myself forward, hit the ground and rolled, and as I came out of the roll there were two more shots. I heard them hit the tree. I spindle-rolled against the trunk, listened as a fourth and fifth shot chipped splinters off the wood, and then got to fingers and toes and ran like a scared dog north along the trunk. The shots were coming from the far side. There was a pause and someone said, "Dimitrije, go around, go around."

The man spoke in Serbian. Not my best language, but I can understand the basics.

The speaker sounded like he was close to the torn-up roots of the fallen tree, which meant he was close to me. Dimitrije was probably going to circle the tree from the top end. Fair enough. Nice pincer movement.

I moved away from the roots and squatted down behind a copse of young spruces. In special ops they teach you how to become completely still. It's not simply a matter of not moving, but a way of thinking. You become part of the natural landscape. You breathe slow and shallow, you blink slow, and if you have to move, you do it in time with the wind moving through the surrounding foliage. People who are bad at it move when they feel the breeze, which means they're moving slightly behind the wind. Out of tune with it. The smart fighters listen to the approach of the breeze and they let it *push* them. They move at the same speed as the wind. They don't make sounds that a forest wouldn't make. Everything is about harmony.

I already had my stupid moment. Now it was time to be smart.

The Serbs had guns. There's a tendency in people who have superior numbers and superior firepower to act as if they don't require stealth. This is not so.

I saw him come around the tangle of torn-up roots. A big man. Taller and broader than me, with a crooked nose and black hair pulled back into a ponytail. Not Serbian regulars. These were probably ex-military mercenaries. Fine.

He held his AK47 well, making sure his eyes and the barrel moved in concert. But he was walking upright, ready to kill. Not ready to defend.

I made him pay for that.

As he passed the line of spruces I noted the cadence of his footfalls. Everyone has a gait, a walking pattern. He came within five feet of me and when he turned my way he saw trees and shadows and nothing else. His face turned and the barrel turned with it as he passed.

I rose up and as he took a step, so did I, matching pressure and sound.

Until I was directly behind him.

Then I reached out with both hands. My left was empty and I snatched his ponytail and jerked it back and down as hard as I could. The leverage in something like that is devastating. His head snapped backward, his back arched, the gun flew up and his finger jerked the trigger and fired a single shot into the sky. I wanted him to do that.

The second I jerked his head backward my right hand moved. The little Wilson rapid-release knife was blade down in my fist and I drove the blade into his eye socket, gave it a wicked half-turn and tore it free. His scream was high and shattering, but I was gone before his body thudded to the ground. He landed hard, twisting and thrashing and screaming. I hadn't stabbed him deeply enough to kill him. Not yet.

I spun away and ran around to the far side of the tree, listening as Dimitrije came pounding up, yelling, firing randomly into the woods. He stopped over his friend and stood there, emptying his magazine as he turned in a half circle, killing a lot of leaves and chipping bark off of trees. None of his rounds came anywhere near me. By the time he'd emptied half a magazine I was on the other side of the tree and scrambling up atop the trunk. I peered over. Dimitrije blasted the spruce trees and clicked empty. His friend was still screaming and thrashing.

The killer inside my head smiled.

Then I was in the air, leaping at Dimitrije, hitting him between the shoulder blades as he slapped his fresh magazine into place. He star-fished in the air and his gun went flying. I bore him to the ground and let his body take all the impact, then scrambled up, drove my knee into the small of his back, grabbed his short blond hair with my left, jerked his head back and cut his throat from ear to ear.

I pivoted and leapt onto his friend. He had both hands clamped to his bleeding eye, so I corkscrewed the knife between his forearms and buried it to the knuckles in the hollow of his throat.

Silence dropped over the forest.

I tore my knife free and wiped it on his jacket, but my hand and wrist were soaked with blood. The knife went back into its holster in my pocket and I snatched up one of the AK47s. They are not my favorite weapon, but they're sturdy, reliable and I had two of them. Between the two corpses there were six magazines. Fun. No grenades, though. And no satellite phone. Would have been nice to call my boss and arrange for the entire United States military to come rescue my ass. Not an option.

I slung one rifle, held the other, ran sixty yards into the woods, stopped, knelt with the gun raised as I listened to the forest.

No shouts in Serbian. No gunshots.

But I heard that strange high-pitched chittering sound again.

Close, too. On the far side of the tree, near to where I'd left the bodies. I heard it but didn't see it. I waited a long time. The chittering sound faded and then vanished, leaving the forest sounding like a forest again.

After a long time of waiting, watching, and listening, I trusted the landscape enough to begin moving again. It took me twenty minutes to find another of Bunny's footprints.

Armed now, I began hunting in earnest.

-8-

I raced the edge of a clearing and looked upon a scene from hell itself.

It was a war zone.

Three-sided and totally bizarre.

On the far left side of the clearing, squatting down behind a tumble of boulders, were eleven Serbians. Eleven. All of them heavily armed. All of them yelling and firing.

On the opposite side of the clearing were two of my guys. Bunny knelt beside the trunk of a massive tree, his Benelli combat shotgun smoking and roaring in his big hands. A few feet away from him, Top had a rough splint on his left leg made from tree branches and canvas strapping from the helicopter. His pants leg was dark with blood and his brown face was pale and grainy, but he held his Sig Sauer in rock-steady hands.

In many ways that was what I was expecting to see. Two groups of combatants engaged in some kind of a stand-up fight, with me as the X-factor that hopefully gave my side the winning edge.

Hope springs eternal.

Life, on the other hand, sucks.

Between the two sides, standing in the center of a hail of bullets, was something so very wrong.

It was a metal ball.

A big, broken metal ball.

Well, it *looked* like a ball. It was round, at least. Forty feet across, dull silver, with a double row of colored lights, most of which were smashed and dark. The remaining lights flickered with a sluggish green glow. A hundred feet behind it was the total ruin of a second one. That one had split open and burned; the shell was coated with black ash. Both balls lay at the end of long trenches and there were mounds of dirt pushed up in front of them. From the angle and the depth of the trenches, it looks like they'd come in fast and hot from a long way up.

Between the two balls were several humped forms. Maybe

they had been spiders, or something spiderlike, but the force of that double impact had torn them apart and flung burning pieces across the ground.

Then I caught movement beyond the first of the balls. A form moved from the lee of the big craft and scuttled toward a small boulder.

The Serbians immediate shifted their barrage from trying to kill my men to trying to destroy this thing. The shape darted back to cover and a loud, high-pitched chittering sound trailed behind it.

Speech? Or the fearful cry of a creature in peril. Absolutely impossible to say.

All of this happened in a second, but my mind replayed it in slow motion because a lot had happened in that second. I ducked down into shadows to process it.

The thing that had come lumbering out was a spider. Okay. That just happened. It was maybe eighty pounds, gray-green with bright blue and yellow spots.

I recognized those spots.

A giant spider.

I had to give that a moment. Even though I'd been *expecting* something like a giant spider, let's face it --you never really expect to *see* a giant spider. It's like checking in your closet or under your bed and seeing a real boogeyman. You've been afraid of it all this time but you don't actually think you'll ever see it. Then bang!

So, yeah, okay. Giant spider.

Giant fucking spider.

By a big silver ball that might be some kind of landing craft.

Or, if the world was even more insane than I thought it was, a spacecraft.

I had to ask myself if I was ready to accept the reality of a giant fucking spider from outer space. Not the easiest question to ask.

And it's a real bitch to answer.

Every molecule of your body, every neuron in your mind

wants to say, "No, bitch. Get real." But my eyes had just seen it. My team and a bunch of Serbians shooters were clearly seeing it, too. Reacting to it. As much as I might have wanted to, I couldn't dismiss that as being a product of my own warped mind. This was happening to all of us. It was happening.

Giant alien spiders.

This entire chain of logic and acceptance took maybe a full second.

Then my mind shifted gears to analyze the scene the way a professional soldier should. The way a cop should. I'm both, so it was my job to make sense of this based on evidence and assessment.

There were two ships. One was clearly destroyed, the crew dead. The second was damaged, though I couldn't tell how badly. Some of the lights were still on, the hull looked intact.

Survivors?

At least one.

I thought about the extent of the web network up in the trees, and the bodies I'd found along the game trail. Could one of these creatures do all that?

My gut said no.

That's when I took a closer look at the boulder the spider had been trying to reach.

It was covered with soot and partly hidden by the shadows of a small pine tree.

As I studied it, the boulder moved.

Slowly, weakly.

It wasn't a boulder, of course. As it shifted I could see yellow and blue dots. And blood. Dark red and as thick as tree sap.

A spider. Wounded, maybe dying. Trapped in the no man's land between the two shooting positions.

I hunkered down behind a thick tree trunk. So far no one had spotted me, which was good. The Serbs were closer to me than my own guys, but that could be a good thing.

I tapped my earbud and very quietly said, "Cowboy to Sergeant Rock."

There was static.

There was a burst of noise that sounded like a marbles bouncing around in a steel drum.

And then…

"…Rock to Cowboy. Repeat Sergeant Rock to Cowboy."

"This is Cowboy. I'm on your eight o'clock, fifty yards back." I could see Top turn his head to stare past the Serbs. I moved my head two inches out from behind the tree and back again. Just enough for him to spot me. Not fast enough to spook the Serbs.

"Damn glad to hear your voice, Cap'n," said Top.

"Damn glad to be heard. Status report?"

"Doing moderately poor. Got a busted leg. Farm Boy stood a little too close to some shrapnel. We got the bleeding stopped, but we ain't going to be running marathons."

"Hoped for better news," I told him.

"Yeah, well life's all blowjobs and puppies, ain't it?" said Top. "You got a plan?"

"Working on it," I said. "Want to tell me what in the wide blue fuck is going on?"

"Don't know much," said Top. "Pretty sure one of those round ships clipped our bird. Took us both down. Farm Boy got me out, but the crew…"

He didn't need to say. Didn't want to say it, and he knew I didn't need to hear it.

"Hostiles converged and we lost the package. We've been looking for you and playing tag with them. Trying to recover the package. And then our friends joined in. Been a moderately interesting picnic in the woods."

"Copy that."

"What have you got on our 'friends'?"

"Big and ugly, but they don't like the Serbs."

"Why not?"

"Call it a failure to bond," said Top. "Soon as the hostiles saw them they opened fire. Cut a couple of 'em down. And Bunny thinks that it was a Serbian RPG that took *both* of their birds down. Rocket hit them while trying to hit us, and that was like cracking pool balls. Serbs hit them, they hit each other, and one of them hit us. Now the Spiders from Mars are pissed off and looking for some payback."

I almost laughed. Top wasn't one for pop culture references, but he was old enough to remember *Ziggy Stardust and the Spiders from Mars.* Bowie's best album.

"Copy that," I said. "So…basically these Serbians dickheads pissed off our visitors from the great beyond."

"Works out to something like that. We saw a couple of those critters ambush the Serbs. They do not play nice."

"I saw the leavings. Does all this make them friendlies?"

"Enemy of my enemy is my friend," he suggested.

"All well and good if we're talking bipedal mammals, Top, but how's that going to apply here?"

"I'll be *god*-damned if I know, Cap'n," he said, and that's when I caught it. Soldiers tend to use trash talk or banter a lot. Sometimes we forget why. It's not because we actually make light of the dangers and horrors of combat, it's not that we feel we're invincible killers, or that we're the life-takers and heart breakers of legend. No, the jokes, the bullshit, the light-hearted chatter is all about pushing back the fear. The genuine fear that any rational person feels when they're about to go into battle, or when they've survived one fight and they wonder how much of their supply of luck they've already squandered as the next fight approaches. I know Top is tough. None tougher, and I've met the best of the best. He's an experienced soldier who has been in more firefights than most people have had hot dinners. He's walked with me through the valley of the shadow of death so often his footprints are indelibly cut into the ground. He's helped save the world. The actual world.

Right now, though, hearing his voice over the radio as killers and monsters, he was right there at the edge of it. Of his courage, of his ability to process terror, at the limits of his potential for handling stress. He was on that ragged edge where control is by no means a 'given', and circumstance and overwhelming odds make failure a rather likely option.

It hurt me to hear it. To know it.

It hurt just as much to feel it in myself. To know that even the pattern of my thoughts – the almost blasé way in which I've been accepting and processing the impossible data from today's events – are the product of my mind trying to make light of it. To do otherwise would mean dealing with the reality of it.

Now, crouched down here at the end of the hunt, the bravado – inside and out – was burning off. Two of the three members of my team were injured. We had guns and ammunition, but we were badly outnumbered.

And there were the spiders.

I joked about alien spiders before, not I had to face that. Not just giant spiders. I've dealt with too many mutation and genetically-altered freaks in this job to really be brain-fried about that part.

Alien, though.

Alien.

A couple of years ago my team skated on the edge of a case involving a kind of Cold War that had grown up around technology that may – or may not – have been scavenged from crashed UFOs. I'd met two people who claimed to have some alien DNA mixed with their own. I'd seen a craft that I'm pretty sure did not come from around here – and by *here* I mean our planet and maybe our solar system.

So, even with all that you'd think I'd be prepared for what we had here.

You'd think that, but you'd be wrong.

Seriously, say the phrase 'alien space spiders' aloud and tell me if that's ever going to fit comfortably in your head. Ever.

I could feel the change in my body as the absolute truth of it burned off the last of my 'this can't be real so I'll just cruise with it' self-deception. It started in my fingertips. They went cold right around the time they started to shake.

You know why?

Because in every single fight I've ever been in, it's been good guys versus bad guys. Human good guys – me and my crew –

versus human bad guys. Those bad guys, no matter how many or how bad, were still human. They were a known quantity. I could look at them and know how much force was needed to crack the hyoid bone, how many pounds per square inch it would take to shatter an elbow or knee, how exactly to rupture a kidney or spleen with a certain punch. All of that was knowledge already in my head. Even when outnumbered I was on safe ground.

But... aliens?

Spiders notwithstanding.

Aliens?

In my earbud Top said, "Cap'n—?"

"Still here," I said. "Working it through."

"Work fast," he advised, "'Cause something is happening."

He was right.

Something *was* happening.

And it all happened real damn fast.

There was a flash.

A series of them.

Suddenly the whole forest went from a collection of shadows in purple and gray to a uniform white that hit the eyes like a punch. I cried out and reeled back, the rifle falling from my hands. The light was so bright that closing my eyes, squeezing the lids shut didn't do it. I jammed my fists into the sockets.

I think there was a sound, too. Not an explosion. Something else. It was impossible to describe. I felt the noise as much as heard it. There was a sensation like a heavy vibration. Low and powerful, but it was like something inside my head was vibrating rather than something outside that I was hearing. There's nothing in my experience that will make sense of it. The feeling – sound, sensation – was like how I imagine a microwave oven would sound. That kind of invisible, relentless, and powerful wave of force. My ears rang the way they would if I was standing next to a giant bell, but there was no real noise.

The sound and the vibration were terrible. Thank God they only lasted for a few seconds.

When it passed, whenever it was shut off, I collapsed onto the ground as completely as if I'd been dropped from a five-story roof. I felt breathless, smashed flat.

Then I heard something else. A familiar chittering sound.

Right behind me.

I rolled over. *Tried* to roll over. Reached clumsily for the AK47, and as I turned I saw something bulky come rushing at me.

Two somethings.

They were big and gray and spotted with yellow and blue dots. But they weren't the same as the spiders I'd already seen. These had some kind of mechanic implants on their bulbous heads. Like a kind of hood, or maybe goggles. Hard to tell. It covered most of the creature's many eyes. And they came at me really damn fast. The first one slammed into me and knocked me flat again. It leapt onto my chest and bent low toward my throat, snapping at me with jaws that snapped like pincers. Clear drool hung from the gaping mouth and splashed like acid on my skin.

I cried out in horror and disgust and punched the thing in the side with an overhand right. The spider staggered off of me, but then it immediately recovered and jumped back. This time its front legs jabbed at me, striking pressure points in both shoulders and leaning into them. My arms went dead. Just like that. The creature glared down at me, chittering in that high-pitched voice of theirs. The real eyes were dark and intense; the machine eyes burned with red fire.

I tried to twist my hips to buck it off; tried to kick. Tried hoist my dead arms to bash it off, but it countered every move by striking another pressure point with another of its powerful, articulated legs. It had more legs than I did, and somehow it knew enough about human anatomy to shut me down.

Then the second spider came scuttling over. It was smaller and its carapace was crisscrossed with scars that gave it a look of great age. And, somehow, of great power. Like it had earned those scars. Like they told its story. It had the same metal helmet covering half of its monstrous face, but even this was dented and dinged as if from hard use. As the creature advanced to climb atop me, the younger spider retreated in clear deference. The spider studied me for long seconds, but what it saw and what it thought were beyond me. I had no way to interpret the dark lights that burned in its eyes.

And yet...

The scars, the aggression, the combat skills. The cold confidence the creature seemed to exude – collectively, perhaps they did tell me something. They suggested something.

These were different from the other spiders. These were clearly warriors of some kind. Perhaps these were the special operators who did for their race what guys like Top, Bunny and I did for ours. Maybe I was letting my imagination run amok, or maybe I was seeing what was in front of me. Seeing what was actually there, rather than the horror-show image suggested by their alien appearance. Or, maybe it was the warrior in my head, the killer in my soul, who saw and recognized some kind of kindred spirit.

The spider turned and leaned toward my dead right hand. It bent low toward the bloodstains on my skin and on the cuff of my right sleeve. It sniffed at the blood; then bent closer and tasted it.

The chittering sound rose higher and higher for a moment, then faded away.

It turned quickly and looked at me again. The dark eyes fixed mine and for a moment we looked at each other with a kind of shared understanding that I've only ever had with fellow warriors on a battlefield. The kind of shared awareness that cannot be spoken, but which speaks volumes in that private language of the true warrior. Alexander the Great could have looked into the eyes of General Patton, and they despite a million differences they would have nodded to one another, understand something that cannot be expressed in actual words. I've even had that exchange with enemies, when catching the eye of the man you have come to kill, but fate opens a window in the smoke and fire and for just a moment you both realize something that no one else could ever grasp. Maybe not even most of your own troops. It's reserved for those people who are defined by war, who are born to it, and who know that they will walk forever on the blood-soaked ground while a black and featureless flag ripples in the wind above them.

The spider studied me, and then slowly, slowly, it backed away, crawling off my body until it stood in the trampled grass. The younger spider looked from his older companion, to me, and back again. Confused. Not sharing in that moment of insight.

Forty yards away the Serbians had recovered from the explosion of light and sound and were firing at the metal ball. My guys were returning fire, but it was a fight they couldn't win. The Serbs were spreading out, sending squads out in a flanking maneuver that was very quickly going to catch my guys and the remaining spiders down by the ball in a shooting box.

"Do something," I snarled to the older spider. Sure, I know it's stupid. I don't speak spider and he clearly didn't speak English. But he turned to watch the Serbs.

He did two things.

First he snapped out at me with one of his legs and the round tip of it struck me on the shoulder. In a nerve cluster. He hit me really hard and the pain was ex-fucking-quisite. I screamed and flopped around like a beach mackerel.

Then he twisted a leg so that he touched a fitting on his helmet. Immediately he and the other spider dropped down flat and curled their arms around their heads.

I had a half second to do the same, and as I did I realized that my arms were no longer dead weight. I wrapped them around my head and squeezed my eyes shut and screamed.

Another big fucking white light.

Another wave of the vibration that shook me all the way down to the bones.

Maybe their version of a flash-bang grenade.

Alien shock and awe.

I could hear, somewhere beyond the wall of blistering light and sound, the Serbians screaming. Maybe my own guys were, too. Probably.

Then the spiders were up and moving, the two of them flashing down the slope at incredible speeds. They raced toward the dazed Serbians and then they were among them.

I fought to get to my knees, to grab the AK47 and fire it. To join the fight.

All I managed to do was fall face-forward onto the ground.

A big black well seemed to open up beneath me and I fell and fell and fell.

-10-

I woke up to see that the sun was a dying red ball behind the treetops.

A voice said, "Welcome back to the world, boss."

I turned my head. Just a simple thing like that took a lot of goddamn effort. Bunny sat with his back to a tree. His face was bruised and bloody. His shirt was torn to rags and there were crude bandages wrapped around his huge arms and chest. Beside him, Top Sims lay asleep. He looked fevered and weak.

"Is he...?"

"He's bad," said Bunny. "Shock. And his leg's a mess. They're going to have to be creative on it. I set it the best I could, but it's going to need more than that."

I looked around.

"I was able to salvage a sat phone from one of the Serbians. I made a call. Mr. Church is sending an extraction team. Should be here in a couple of hours."

"Thank god."

"Yeah."

We were on the highest point of a clear slope. There was a campfire burning, the smoke spiraling up into the darkening sky. Farther down the slope was a dark, lumpy tangle of things that might have been human beings. Might have been. Bunny followed the line of my gaze.

"The Serbians."

"Oh."

"They did that."

"*They?*"

He nodded up at the sky. "They."

"Shit."

"Yeah."

I looked around. "What about the briefcase?"

Bunny snorted. "They melted it."

"Melted it?"

"Yup. One of them opened it and suddenly made that weird high-pitched noise they make. And then they pointed some kind of thing at it. Maybe it was a ray gun, the fuck do I know? Next thing the whole case and about ten feet of ground around it is a puddle of boiling mud and liquid metal." He shrugged. "Guess they're not big on bioweapons."

"Points for that," I said.

We sat in silence for a long time. Real long.

"Not sure how to talk about this," Bunny finally admitted.

"Me neither."

"At the end there, before everything went to shit... I saw two more of them spider things. Like the others, but...different."

"I know."

He cut me a sharp look.

"I saw them, too," I said.

"You saw that they were different, right?"

"Oh yes."

Bunny started to say something several times and stopped each time. Finally he gave it up shook his head.

"Yeah," I agreed.

After maybe five minutes of silence during which the forest grew darker and the fire grew brighter, he tried it again. "This is going to sound stupid but..."

"Say it."

"I think they were like us."

"I know."

"I mean, I think they were soldiers."

"Yeah," I said. "I know."

"Like us."

I nodded.

He nodded back. After a while. Above us the first stars ignited. Somehow it made the sky look bigger. Farther away. Stranger.

"Those things," he said. "The ones that were getting killed, not the ones that came after. They weren't fighters."

"No," I agreed. "They weren't fighters."

"So the others. The two that came in later? What were they? Some kind of extraction team?"

I thought about it. Nodded.

He nodded again, too. The answer seemed to offer him some measure of relief. It was a theory and it made a kind of sense. Enough sense that you could tie a rope around it and use it to keep your sanity from flying off into the air.

"Boss—?" he asked much later.

"Yeah, Bunny?"

"Think we'll ever find out who they were? Or... where they came from?"

I shook my head. Not because I didn't think so, but because I simply did not know.

Above us more and more of the stars were kindled to brightness as the day burned away and night took possession of the world. We lay there, confused, scared, hurt, and watched the stars and planets and galaxies appear in their numberless brilliance. Which one of those was the home of our visitors? Would we ever know?

I sat and watched the wheel of night turn.

When I looked at Bunny I saw a single tear on his cheek. It glistened, reflecting starlight. I reached over and gave his shoulder a single squeeze. Didn't say anything. Nor did he.

Somewhere far off to the south we could hear the faint beating of helicopter rotors.

SPECIAL OPERATIONS INTERVIEW PTO-14

Wayland Smith

This is a transcript of an interview between an OSS operative and a United States Marine, regarding the Marine's experiences on the island of [NAME REDACTED]. This file is rated for the BLACK FILE section, clearance level ULTRA SECRET. The names of the participants have been redacted. They will be referred to simply as MARINE and OSS. Unauthorized perusal, removal, duplication, or distribution of this file will be considered an act of espionage and treason, and will be punished accordingly.

– – – – –

MARINE: So that's one of those recorder machines? I just talk and it can play the whole thing back later?

OSS: Yes, that's right. You're here to talk about what happened on [NAME REDACTED] Island.

MARINE: I never hear that name again, I'll be okay with it. That's the strangest damn thing I ever saw. Oh, hey, is it okay if I swear with that thing on? I don't want to get in trouble or something.

OSS: Tell me however you need to.

MARINE: OK, then. I was assigned to the [NAME REDACTED], and we were out doing recon, to see if we could find any Jap ships to call the bombers in for, or maybe a sub.

Some damn thing went wrong with the engine, I don't know what it was, I never was a mechanic. So we had to put in somewhere and fix it, and the navigator, he looks at the chart and says we're close to [NAME REDACTED] Island. We find a little lagoon and anchor there, so the mechanic can fix the damn boat. Me and some of the guys, we get told to grab our rifles and our canteens and go scout the island, look for fresh water and any stray Japs, right? So, I go. I'm a fightin' man, I'm here to fight, that's jake by me.

We all split up, mostly looking for water. This is just a small damn island near nothing, so why would we think we'd actually find a Jap? But I did. I'm going over this hill, figuring there might be water at the bottom on the other side, right? But halfway down, there's this clearing, see, and that's where I found the Jap. I was so startled I just sorta stood there a sec. The place felt wrong. Like, when I was a kid, my granddaddy took me to these old Indian ruins? The place was abandoned and everyone said it was haunted, and it felt like that, cold and dark and just wrong. So I'm trying to get my hands to work so I can get my rifle up, and the Jap starts yelling. I thought he'd seen me at first, and was calling his buddies, and I thought, "Oh, God, that's it, I'm dead."

But he didn't even look at me. He had this strong tone, like I've heard the preacher use sometimes, when he was preachin' about something he really thought was important and special.

OSS: What did he say?

MARINE: Hell, I don't speak Jap. I got no idea. But he says this stuff, and the rocks scattered in the clearing start glowing, I swear, like the sun was coming up and hitting them square on, but the sun was on the other side of the hill by then, see? And then this smoke comes out of the rocks. I sound like I was on a bender or been raidin' Doc's pills, but I swear, I was stone cold sober. This smoke, it twists, like a snake or something, and it swells, and then gets thicker. All of a sudden, there's this huge I don't know what the hell it was standing there.

OSS: What did it look like?

MARINE: I'm gettin' there. It was eight feet tall, easy, and was huge, muscles like the biggest circus strongman you ever saw. And I swear to you, I saw it just like I'm seein' you now, it was blue. It's skin was this blue like a real clear sky back in Texas. It had this huge club in one hand, looked like it was metal. And it had two horns comin' out of its head, and this thick tuft of white hair around the back of its head, like a guy goin' bald? And it had on, I don't know, this little bathing suit looking thing, but it was made out of tiger skin, or looked like it.

OSS: I see. What happened?

MARINE: They kinda yelled at each other, but it wasn't just yellin'. There was something else going on. I don't know, it started feeling like... You ever been too close to a lightning strike? That tingly feel all over and your hair standing up? Like that, but worse. I'll tell you... This is all secret, right?

OSS: Right, no one hears this but a very few people, and they won't know your name.

MARINE: Yeah, OK. It was scaring the hell out of me. That feeling? It was like I was waiting for it to just cook me or turn me inside out, or something. I knew the Japs weren't Christians, but I never knew they were sorcerers.

OSS: He was working with it?

MARINE: Well, that's what I thought at first. I mean, it looked like he called it up, like you read about in the Bible, see? But when they were screaming at each other, that was a fight, sure as the ones I've been in with bullets flyin'. I don't know how I know, but you could just tell. And the Jap, I mean, he's a Jap, he's the enemy, I get that. But this demon thing, it was just wrong. It wasn't human. You could feel cold and evil coming off it. I know I sound like I'm ready for a long rest in a white coat somewhere, but I swear, it's true. All of it.

OSS: I believe you. What happened next?

MARINE: Well, yeah, that's the thing, ain't it? They finish screaming, and the demon roars, like some kind of lion, but louder. I've seen lions, the zoo, the circus, see? I know what they sound like. This was louder, and stronger, and it made me scared. I won't say that much. I been shot at, stood up to the enemy, seen buddies of mine blown to hell, but that thing? It was just different, and wrong. So, they finish screaming, and the Jap, he had one of those damn swords they have, see? The big ones? You seen those?

OSS: Yes, I've seen them. They call them katanas.

MARINE: They can call them Ish Kabibble for all I care. But he pulled the damn thing out, and there was like, fire on the blade. But it wasn't fire. I don't know how to say it. It was like fire that burned blue, but the damn sword was metal, and metal doesn't burn. And fire isn't blue. I don't know. But that's what I saw, blue fire on a metal sword, running up and down the blade, and kind of pulsing, like a heartbeat. That's what I thought when I saw it, it was a heartbeat, and it was alive.

OSS: Did the man seem surprised by that?

MARINE: Naw, he didn't look twice at it. The demon, it was surprised. It roared, but it wasn't strong and commanding like it was before. It almost sounded afraid, if you can imagine something that big being afraid. I mean, it was huge, and it was moving that big metal club around like it was nothing, I'm not sure I could have lifted it at all. But it sounded afraid and mad.

OSS: What happened next?

MARINE: Yeah, sorry. I was thinking about that, and just... Is it cold in here? I'm gettin' all goose bumps. Anyway. Yeah. It roars, and then it throws its head forward like a guy whose gonna puke or something. But it belches, like, and this fire comes out of it. The sword had a blue fire, so maybe that's why I wasn't so surprised that this was a green fire, light green. It belched out this fire, and the Jap, he moves like damn Fred Astaire or something. Not like he was dancing, exactly, just, that kinda easy way Astaire moves? Do you know what I'm trying to get at?

OSS: He was graceful?

MARINE: That's a funny word for it, especially in the middle of a fight. But yeah, that's it. He, the Jap, moved gracefully, like he wasn't barely trying, but somehow he wasn't where he'd been, and the fire just made this char mark on the ground. And I felt it. It was a wave of heat, even from back where I was hidi – watching. It was this wave of heat, like if you open an oven, a big one. My uncle worked in a bakery, and it was like that. But the bakery always makes you hungry, even if you just ate, and this? The heat, the fire, it smelled like hell. Like something died and was rotting. It made my eyes water just smelling it, but the Jap, he was closer than me, and he didn't care, or didn't notice. He just moved again, and it burned like a flamethrower, and missed him. The Jap just wasn't there again. He was moving like he was out for a Sunday stroll, but he just wasn't where the fire went. Yeah, maybe it was like dancing a little.

OSS: [NAME REDACTED]? Are you all right?

MARINE: Yeah, yeah, sorry. I was just seeing it again, in my head. It was kind of like a dance, I guess. And the fire was burning that weird green, and it was giving everything this hellish glow, if Hell is green. I guess it could be. I never thought about that, what color Hell was. I'm sorry, I know, I'm off wool-gatherin', that's what my Pa always called it. My head hasn't been quite right since that day. I guess that's why I got the vacation here with all you guys, huh? All I ever wanted was to fight for my country and I'm Section Eight like someone from the loony bin.

OSS: You're going to be OK. The doctors are helping you, aren't they?

MARINE: Yeah, some. I can even sleep sometimes now. And I know you don't care about any of that. The story, you just want to hear what happened. It's all anyone wants to talk about. Only, the docs, see, they want me to say it wasn't real so I can get better, "Make progress," they all say. But you, you know its' real, don't you? You've seen things. Hell, I might not even be telling you the craziest thing you heard, right?

OSS: We're here to talk about you, not me.

93

MARINE: Yeah, you guys never want to talk about you. Ok, so the demon thing... Hey, you know what the sword was called, do those things have a name? The demon thing with the blue skin?

OSS: They are called Oni.

MARINE: Oni. I don't know what that means, but it's nice to have something to call it. Are they all blue? Yeah, yeah, I see you lookin' at your watch, you don't want to answer my questions, just have me tell this damn story. Again. Where was I? Oh yeah, it's spittin' fire, like those English planes? They call those Spitfires, but this was the real thing. It belches fire at him again, and the Jap, he catches it on his sword. I don't know how, the blast, the flame, whatever, it should have been bigger than the blade was, but it worked. The green fire from the Oni *audible chuckle* and the blue fire on the blade, they met, and the sword held up, somehow. The Jap, he's saying something, maybe a prayer? I'd have been praying if that thing was trying to cook me, I'll tell you that for nothing.

The Jap, he's doing this dancing, moving, whatever, and just barely not getting singed, and the Oni, it's getting powerful mad, you can tell. And the Jap, he gets too close, and it lunges at him, swiping with that big club, but the Jap knew what he was doing. He just folded himself up, like a damn circus acrobat, and the club missed him, but he cut the thing on its arm. It howled, and that sound was the worst one yet. My hair was standing up, my knees were knockin', the whole bit, like when Lou Costello sees a monster in the movies? We don't get many movies in here.

Yeah, the monster. I know. Oni. That. The Jap has the sword there, and it's pushing the flame away. I guess the prayer worked, maybe? The fire goes out, and it roars, and swings that club at him, and he just dances off to the side. Gracefully, like. And the club hits the ground and it was like a bomb going off, and brother, believe me when I tell you I know what *that* sounds like now. I'm thinking, how are the boys not hearing this? The roars and the fire and the club hitting like a bomb, how is no one hearing this and yelling, or comin' running, or something?

They go at it that way a while. The Oni is snarling, and the Jap never says a word after that prayer or whatever it was. The Oni, it's stronger than he is, stronger than any man. But the Jap, he just keeps moving. Now, you gotta remember, those islands, in the summer? It's hotter than Hell there. Well, maybe not. Maybe that's why the Oni didn't care, if it's a demon, Hell is home, so it's used to being hot, right? But the Jap, Hell, I was damn near melting just standing there watching, and he was jumping all over like a frog or something, and I'm not even sure he was sweating. I sure was. It was beautiful and terrible and, I don't know, fierce, all at once. And the Jap, he's gettin' close more than it thinks, and he's cut it, a dozen times now. The Oni, it's bleeding and it's a real dark green, it's not right for blood, or anything else. It shouldn't be green. It's just wrong, that green.

OSS: Are you OKAY? Do you need a cigarette?

MARINE: *sound of chair scraping on floor* NO! No, thanks. No cigarette. I don't like fire much anymore. I just can't stand it. I don't want it near me, see?

OSS: OKAY, no cigarette, and I won't smoke either, OKAY? See, I'm putting it away.

MARINE: Yeah, thanks, buddy. I just... No fire, OKAY? So, the Jap cuts this thing over and over, and it's roaring and bleeding this green that isn't right green blood, and that's when [NAME REDACTED] shows up. I guess he'd finished doing his scout, and he was looking for me or something. This kid, he's green, like we just got him before we shipped out for this cruise. And he sees this blue Oni, demon, and the Jap, and he screams, but it's not a scared scream. It's like a challenge. And he yanks his rifle off his shoulder and he shoots the Oni. The Oni and the Jap, they both just stopped when he showed up, like two teenagers caught necking. But [NAME REDACTED] just shoots once, twice, three times, and he's hitting it, I can tell. I can see it grunting a little, but the bullets, they're not going in. They're not getting through its skin. It's like those guys shooting Superman in the funny books. But this ain't so funny.

The kid, he's game, and he blasts it again, and it does that thing with his head, and I want to warn him, but my mouth is so dry, and I can't get a sound out. Not a word. And [NAME REDACTED], he dies because I can't even talk. The thing spits at him, like, but it's that green fire again, and the kid goes up like a torch. He's burning and screaming, and thrashing around, and the green flame is covering him, and the screams are getting weaker...

OSS: Do you need some water?

MARINE: What I need, they don't let me have in here, brother. But yeah, water will do. *sounds of movement, liquid, gulping* Thanks. You're OKAY, even if you just want to hear this damn story, like everyone else.

OSS: Have you told many people?

MARINE: *choking laughter* Enough to land here. But who am I going to tell who doesn't think I'm totally crazy? *sound of drinking* Yeah. The kid, he dies. All burned up. The Jap, he knows what to do, like he was waiting for it. The Oni is burning the kid like kindling, and the Jap jumps at the thing, and it's a high jump, and he swings that damn katana? Is that what you called it? Yeah, OKAY, katana, and it takes the damn thing's head clean off. The head flies through the air like a basketball, and the fire on the sword, it burns brighter, like it's celebrating. Maybe it was. The Jap, he yells something, like a war cry, sounding all triumphant, you know?

OSS: And what did you do?

MARINE: Well, there's a war going on, right? And he's a Jap, even if he did just kill a demon, or an Oni, or whatever it was. And if he'd been faster, [NAME REDACTED] might have lived through it all. But he wasn't, and [NAME REDACTED] was dead, and the Oni, it turned back into that smoke and drifted apart, like when my granddaddy used his pipe to make smoke rings. You ever see that? A big smoke ring, and something hits it, and it just breaks apart?

OSS: What happened next?

MARINE: Right, yeah. So, he killed a demon. But we're at war, see? And the kid just died. So the Jap is turning, and facing the sun, and talking or praying or whatever the hell he was doing. And I pulled my rifle off my shoulder and I shot the son of a bitch like I shoulda oughta done when I first saw him. And all that grace? It was gone. He fell like a sack of potatoes. Just fell on the ground like.

OSS: And what did you do?

MARINE: Hell, what could I do? I took his pistol and his sword for trophies, like. And I found his pack nearby, and his damn little tent, and wrapped up [NAME REDACTED] in it and I sorta carried him, sorta dragged him back to the boat. I'm not sure they believed me about what happened. No, not the Oni, I wasn't that dumb. I told him we surprised a Jap who had a flamethrower, and [NAME REDACTED] got too close.

OSS: Did you tell anyone?

MARINE: *bitter laughter* Yeah, I had to. The boys, they saw I was acting screwy when we left. They thought I was shell-shocked or something, so they made me talk to the shrink. And he, he just kept asking me what happened over and over, and he knew when I was lying, I swear. So, finally, I broke down, and I told him what really happened. And now I'm here in the bug house. Preacher always said, "The truth will set you free." Not this time, huh?

OSS: Thank you, you've been very helpful.

MARINE: Yeah, that and a nickle would get me a cup of coffee, if they let me drink coffee in here. Am I ever getting out of here? Really?

OSS: I don't know.

MARINE: Well, thanks for not shining me on, anyway. *sound of chair scraping* I don't know what else I could've done. We're at war. He was a Jap. He could do things a normal guy couldn't. I had to shoot him. Didn't I?

OSS: That's not for me to say. But thank you again for telling me this.

INTERVIEW ENDS

– – – – –

Recommendations: The Marine can't be allowed to share this story. Someone might believe him at some point. He needs to be silenced. The sword has already been recovered from his effects, and our experts have it now. They disagree as to whether or not it's a normal sword. It's better if it's kept out of the wrong hands. This file needs to be sealed and categorised TOP SECRET at least.

MAKING WAVES

Curtis C. Chen

You check those corners, sailor?" the Chief of the Boat barked. "Those lines are off by half a degree and our visitor doesn't materialize!"

"Re-measuring now, Master Chief!"

The COB was exaggerating, but I'd learned early in my naval career not to argue with a superior. If it wasn't likely to kill me, I just did it.

I placed my protractor on the dowstone panel we had strapped to the deck and re-checked all the angles in the chalked pentagram, then inspected every stroke of every rune around the circle. Then I climbed the ladder and verified the matching dowstone on the ceiling. Satisfied both stones would activate correctly, I stepped back and reported my progress.

"Very well," the COB grumbled. "Rosebud!"

The seaman's real name was Roseler, but after that Orson Welles flick, everyone called him 'Rosebud' as a tease. He jumped forward, holding his clipboard. I did my best to get out of the way. The COB's quarters weren't exactly spacious. Roseler and I didn't both need to be here, but we were apparently the only two sailors on the *Bowfin* rated for magic, and the Master Chief wanted us to double-check each other.

"You got the incantations there?" the COB asked Roseler.

"Aye, Master Chief!" Roseler said, his voice cracking. And people said *I* sounded like a girl.

"Corrected for position and depth?"

"Aye, Master Chief! I've got the math right here—"

"I can't read your damn chicken scratches." The COB waved the clipboard away and checked his wristwatch. "Rendezvous in twenty seconds. Make sure you're doing it right."

Roseler looked like he might cry. "M-maybe you'd like to do it yourself, Master Chief?"

"Do I *look* like a motherfucking magician?" the COB roared into Roseler's face. Their noses couldn't have been more than half an inch apart. "Now incant that fucking spell so we can receive our goddamn visitor!"

"Aye, Master Chief!" Roseler buried his face in the clipboard. I made a fist, ready to give him a kidney-punch if I heard the slightest mispronunciation. I didn't want to be within a hundred yards of the *Bowfin* if anything went wrong on the receiving end of this teleport.

"Five seconds, sailor!" the COB shouted.

"Aye, Master Chief!" Roseler began making unnatural noises. "*Hagitaa, moro-ven-schaa, inlum'taa...*"

Both pentagrams pulsed blue and white. Roseler finished the incantation, only going a little flat on the last syllable, and a pillar of light flashed into being between the two circles. A moment later, the light faded, and an officer stood inside the pentagram, carrying a large suitcase and wearing a... skirt?

"Permission to come aboard, Master Chief," the woman said.

She looked to be about my mother's age. Unlike my mother, she wore lieutenant's bars and the most perfect makeup I'd ever seen. But the expression on her face and the fact that she'd just teleported nearly seven thousand miles onto a submerged attack boat in the South Pacific told me she wasn't here to entertain anyone. Her nametag read: MARKEY.

"Permission granted, ma'am," the COB said without missing a beat. I guess you don't get to be a Master Chief by balking at the unexpected. "Sorry the captain couldn't be here to greet you himself. We're playing hide and seek with the Japs."

As if on cue, the entire boat groaned and rolled to starboard.

I was impressed that the lieutenant kept her balance in those heels.

The COB shoved Roseler and me back. "If you'll follow me, ma'am?"

Markey looked at the pentagrams. "You're not going to clean this up?"

"These two can handle—"

"You secure those surfaces, Master Chief," Markey snapped. She looked straight at me. "You. What's your name?"

I blinked, surprised that she would address me directly. "Uh, Hatcher, ma'am."

Markey nodded. "Seaman Hatcher can escort me to see the captain."

* * *

"A kraken?" Captain Channing glared at Lieutenant Markey. "Is this a joke?"

Everyone else in the control room, myself included, was doing their best to listen in without looking like they were eavesdropping. Markey had handed over an official envelope from COMSUBPAC, and the captain and XO had verified the code sigils with their authorization amulets before unsealing the *Bowfin*'s new orders.

"No joke, Captain," Markey said.

"We're at war, and some egghead in OP-20-G wants us to go hunting for a sea monster?" The captain turned over the paper in his hand as if looking for something more on the back. "What makes you think this creature even exists?"

"The Japanese are very chatty," Markey said. "They don't know we've broken their codes, and they talk about all kinds of things over the wireless. Lately they've been diverting their ships away from the western side of Kyushu Island, to avoid disturbing something they call *nemuru kaiju* – a 'sleeping beast.' Surely you've noticed the changes in your patrol routes."

"Yeah, we noticed," the captain said. "But maybe they *do* know you've cracked their codes and this is a trap. We've been doing a lot of damage to their merchant fleet. They must be looking for ways to kill more of our subs."

"I'm not here for a conference, Captain," Markey said. "You have your orders."

"I've got a question," the XO said.

Markey looked up at him. "Yes?"

"Let's suppose this kraken is real," the XO drawled, "and as powerful as you say it is. How come the Japs haven't already woken it up and sicced it on us?"

"The people of Japan live on a collection of small islands surrounded by the entire Pacific Ocean," Markey said. "Most of their mythology tells of how dangerous the sea and its inhabitants can be. They live with that danger every day. The Japanese aren't going to risk waking the monsters under their bed." She turned back to the captain. "But *we* can."

"Okay, fine," the captain said. "If the Japs are busy fighting off this kraken, they're not making war on us. Good plan. But we have to find the damn thing first."

Markey smiled. "That's why I'm here, Captain."

* * *

Lieutenant Markey insisted on using the head right after leaving the control room. I didn't understand why she would need to piss when it had been only minutes since she'd left the comfort of Main Navy. There was no privacy door for the toilet, so I stood in front of Markey with my back turned while she squatted. My body also blocked the sound of her voice when she spoke.

"So how long have you been using that glamour, *Miss* Hatcher?"

My stomach leapt into my throat and my heart rate must have tripled. I was glad she couldn't see my face. "I'm sorry, ma'am, I'm not sure what you mean."

"Please. I know a conjured disguise when I see one. Can I give you some advice?"

My fear soured to irritation. "Can I stop you, ma'am?"

"You need better scent concealment," Markey said. "I'm guessing that's a fake bandage on your hand, to explain the smell of blood, right? But that trick won't work every month. And you don't want to get a reputation for being clumsy."

My hands were both behind my back, at parade rest, and I fidgeted with my bandaged left palm. "Do you have a suggestion, ma'am? Other than dousing myself with cheap cologne?"

"Yes." Markey stood and flushed. "But we should talk in private."

* * *

The COB wasn't happy about giving up his quarters for our visitor, but the captain refused to have a woman sharing rack space with a bunch of sailors. I wondered what he would do if he ever found out the truth about me.

Markey interrupted the COB as he and I were preparing to carry his personal effects to a temporary bunk. "Excuse me, Master Chief. I'd like to speak to Seaman Hatcher alone."

I winced. The COB looked from Markey to me and back again, his eyes wide. I had no doubt I'd get a good yelling-at later. "Of course, ma'am." He glared at me. "You know where to find me, Seaman."

"Aye, COB," I said. He shut the door behind him.

I turned back to Markey, who was already making herself comfortable on the COB's bed. She kicked off her shoes and rubbed the soles of her feet.

"With all due respect, ma'am," I said, "I'm trying to *not* call attention to myself here—"

"Relax," Markey said. "I'm just a crazy dame from Washington. They won't suspect anything. Now."

She reached into her wavy hair and pulled out a bobby pin. Then she twisted the metal – it looked like copper – until it became an impossible shape, and even I could see the energy rippling off its surface like a heat mirage.

"You're using a visual glamour," she said. "This will extend the illusion to mask odors. Just keep it in contact with your skin at all times."

She held out the object and I took it with a trembling hand. If Lieutenant Markey could turn a bobby pin into a charged talisman, and if the Navy had sent her, alone, to locate a kraken, she would be one hell of a powerful friend to have.

She also scared the shit out of me. People who seem too competent always make me nervous.

"Thank you, ma'am," I said. "This is – I mean, I don't know how I can repay you." What I really meant was: *I don't know why you're helping me.*

"Well," Markey said, "you can start by finding me some trousers and boots. I don't plan to spend the next two weeks showing off my legs."

"Yes, ma'am." I tucked the hairpin under the bandage wrapped around my left hand. "If there's nothing else?"

Markey looked at me with dark, unfathomable eyes. "Tell me how you ended up here."

"In the Navy?" That was easy: I wanted to kill Japs. I tried to think of a nicer way to say it.

"On the *Bowfin*," she said.

I frowned. "I didn't exactly get to choose my posting."

Markey shook her head. "Why disguise yourself as a man?"

I should have figured she'd ask that. "I knew Uncle Sam wouldn't let a girl do any real fighting. And that's bullshit. Pardon my French."

"Why do you want to fight?"

"You're kidding, right?" I gaped at her. "They attacked us! Stabbed their damn aluminum planes through the Pacific defense screens and into Pearl Harbor. I was born in Honolulu. When I saw the photos – all that black smoke filling our sky – I *hated* them. I wanted revenge, I'm not afraid to say it."

I felt my hands shaking, and I folded my arms to hide them. "Not to mention their Nazi pals are killing or enslaving their way through all of Europe. If we don't stop the Axis, ma'am, they're going to take over the world, and I don't want to live in that world."

Markey nodded and seemed to relax. "Sorry to interrogate you like that, Hatcher, but I'm never sure whether to trust people in disguise."

"Yeah, well, we can't all look like movie stars."

"Don't imagine for a second that makes things any easier

for me," she snapped. "And I will thank you to address me as 'Lieutenant' or 'ma'am', Seaman Hatcher."

I looked down at the floor, my face warm. "Yes, ma'am. Sorry, ma'am."

"This is not a costume I'm wearing." Markey touched her uniform. "I earned my rank. I had to fight to get this job, and I fight every day to keep it.

"Yes, there are advantages to men finding you beautiful, but that perception also limits you. They think all you are is a pretty face and a nice body. They only care about what they can see." She shrugged. "But I don't have to tell you how appearances can be deceiving."

"No, ma'am."

Markey sighed. "What you're doing now is very brave, Hatcher. But when this war is over, you'll have to go back home – back to being a woman. Have you thought about how you're going to handle that?"

"Well, ma'am, since most of my time in the Navy's been spent cleaning one thing or another, I expect I'll be well trained to be a housewife." My words came out sounding more bitter than I intended.

"You have the talent, Hatcher," Markey said. "More than that, you clearly have the will. These two things are powerful in combination."

This conversation was becoming very uncomfortable. "With all due respect, ma'am, why the hell do you care? You don't even know me."

Markey stood and walked over to me. "I won't be pretty forever. I'll get old, and men won't want me anymore. But this?" She held up a hand, then snapped her fingers to create an illusory flame bobbing in midair. "The talent will be with me until the day I die. And to know that, to have that and not use it for something good – that would be such a waste."

I couldn't decipher the expression on her face. Was she feeling some misplaced maternal pity for me? Or did she have another agenda?

After a moment, I decided I really didn't care.

"Thanks for the advice, ma'am," I said, "but we both have to survive the fucking war first."

The floating fire winked out. "Dismissed."

I couldn't get out of there fast enough.

* * *

I did my best to avoid Lieutenant Markey for the next several days. It wasn't easy, since we were both stuck on the same three-hundred-foot, sixty-person submarine. And it wasn't that I didn't respect her. She clearly had major pull in OP-20-G to rate a teleport halfway around the planet. But she was calling as much attention to me as she was to herself, and I didn't need that kind of exposure.

Fortunately, she spent most of her time in the control room or the conning tower, doing whatever she did to track down the mythical kraken, and I was assigned to the aft torpedo compartment. The captain had decided we would fire the fish from there once we were ready to wake the beast – we'd be facing away and ready to run like hell.

Markey had brought aboard divining bolts to replace the magnetic detonators in our Mark 14s. The magnets were supposed to explode a torpedo right underneath a ship's hull, causing more damage than a broadside impact, but the damn things had never worked right. Markey's instructions were to replace the magnets with D-bolts, which would make our fish detect monsters instead of metal.

The plan was to find the kraken, poke it with a couple of torpedoes, then skedaddle before it was fully aware of its surroundings. The kraken's reported location was close enough to populated areas that it should – *should* – hear the noise from those cities and move toward Japan instead of anywhere else.

Working on the torpedoes occupied me for most of the time, but Markey's questions kept bugging me. What *was* I going to do after the war ended?

Maybe I wouldn't survive. Maybe that would be the best outcome for everyone: if I died in the line of duty, and my family didn't find out until later what had happened to their daughter – that she'd given her life for her country.

Maybe they'd be proud of me. And maybe the good ol' U-S-of-A would stop questioning our loyalty then.

I hadn't thought about my future in a while – not since I first enlisted. It had always angered me to know how limited my options were, and now I was angry at Markey for reminding me, for making me worry about things I couldn't change. That's what I was thinking about that day, when the COB pulled Roseler and me out of the torpedo bay for another special assignment.

* * *

"We're submerged in hostile waters, less than a hundred miles from enemy shore," the captain said as I climbed into the conning tower. "We can't surface, and we can't outrun anything that swims. Anything goes wrong here and we are *fucked*."

He was talking to Lieutenant Markey. Roseler was already crowded into the tight space around the periscope. I handed him the *Bowfin*'s codex, which I had retrieved from the control room. He gave me a clipboard and a frantic look as I wedged myself into a corner next to the captain and the COB. It didn't seem like all five of us needed to be here, but I wasn't going to debate that.

"This will be a one-way tunnel," Markey said. She might actually have looked better in trousers than a skirt. I tried my best not to feel jealous and failed. "There's no danger of us being detected."

"But why does Rosebud have to do the spell?" the COB asked. "Aren't you the professional, Lieutenant?"

"Seaman Roseler is doing the easy part," Markey said. "We don't have a focus object, so I'll need to guide the far end of the tunnel."

The COB did a double take. "*You're* going to be his crystal ball?"

Markey sighed and looked at the captain. "We can spend all day discussing the finer points of scrying procedure, Captain, or we can get this done."

"Carry on, Lieutenant," the captain said.

I made as little eye contact with Markey as possible while she read off map coordinates for me to inscribe. I joined our target location and *Bowfin*'s mantic signature into the spell, combining sonants and inflects from the codex reference tables and triple-checking each finished sequence. In principle, writing up the scry tunnel was simpler than describing a teleport path, but I did not want to be on the hook if this thing went sideways.

A few minutes later, Roseler and Markey were holding hands, their eyes closed as Roseler recited the full incantation.

Next to me, the captain muttered, "I'll be glad when we're done with all this black magic bullshit."

"Yes, sir," I said.

He glanced over as if noticing me for the first time. "Your family have talent, Seaman?"

I thought of my grandmother. She had introduced me to the occult, sneaking some mystical instruction into my language lessons every week. We never told my parents. They would have disapproved, to say the least.

I said, "Not that I'm aware of, sir."

"Thank fucking God," the COB said, on my other side. "Give me science and engineering any day of the week. I don't trust anything I can't take apart and see how it works—"

Roseler started screaming. It came suddenly, without even an intake of breath, and the sound was inhuman. He shrieked like an animal caught in a trap. I dropped the clipboard and covered my ears with both hands.

"Get the doc!" Markey shouted. "We need a tranquilizer!" Roseler's body began convulsing. She wrestled him to the deck. "Hatcher! Help me hold him down!"

The captain leaned down the ladder and yelled for the corpsman. I jumped over him and grabbed Roseler's shoulders. His eyes had rolled back into his head. He was still screaming, and his legs kicked around despite Markey's iron grip.

"What the hell's wrong with him?" the COB asked.

"He made contact!" Markey said. "Dammit, COB, you didn't tell me he was a sensitive!"

"How the fuck were we supposed to know?" the COB said.

My stomach knotted. Not because I was concerned for Roseler, but because I was afraid if he died, Markey would order *me* to incant her spells.

"As you were, both of you!" the captain said over the screaming. I could swear Roseler hadn't taken a breath in more than a minute. "Doc's on his way. Now how do we—"

Roseler stopped screaming. His mouth closed, then opened again, and he said a word which was not a word.

My head exploded with pain. No, pain's not the right thing to call it. It wasn't just that I hurt. When that not-word entered my brain, suddenly nothing in the world seemed *right*. What I saw, what I heard, what I felt – from the dinner I was still digesting to gravity itself – everything was wrong, and my body wanted it to stop.

I saw the captain fall to his knees, clutching for a handhold. A dark stain spread across the front of his trousers. Behind him, the COB vomited all over one wall of the compartment. Markey doubled over, blood dripping from her nose.

Roseler's lips parted again. I slapped both hands over the bottom half of his face before he could make another sound. He kept shaking, and the only thing I could think was: *I'll kill him if I have to. How do I kill him? What's the fastest way to kill him?*

"Good," Markey grunted, pressing her hands over mine. She turned her head and spat out a mouthful of thick, dark blood. "Keep him quiet until we can sedate him."

"What the fuck just happened?" I asked.

"Our intel was wrong," Markey said. "They're not kraken."

Some small part of me was happy that she'd screwed up. Most of me wanted to shit my pants. Then my brain finished processing Markey's words.

"Wait, 'they'?" The urge to empty my bowels increased. "There's *more than one?*"

* * *

By the time the corpsman had chloroformed Roseler and tied him down to the bunk in Markey's quarters – she ordered him gagged and isolated; nobody argued – I had finished collecting all our gear out of the conning tower and cleaning it off. The captain and the COB had changed into fresh uniforms and regrouped in the control room. They argued with the XO in low tones as I stowed the codex above the weapons station, locked the safebox, and returned the key to the captain.

I was just about to leave the control room when Lieutenant Markey came in, blocking my exit. Her face and uniform were still smeared with blood. Most of the officers and crew looked away. I backed myself into a corner and did my best to seem small.

"Two knots, Captain," the helmsman whispered. We had been running silent since we made contact with the monsters.

"Very well," the captain said. He turned to Markey. "Lieutenant, what are these torpedoes going to do to the kraken?"

"I'm aborting the mission, Captain," Markey said.

The captain frowned. "Come again?"

"We cannot disturb those things," Markey said, lowering her voice. "We need to get the hell out of here."

"Oh, we're moving," the captain said. "But we did not come all the way into the goddamn lion's den just to have a look-see. We are going to do some fucking damage before we leave."

"Aft tubes loaded, Captain," the weapons officer said behind me.

"The intel was bad," Markey said. "Those are *not* kraken out there. They are Elder Things. Two of them."

"Older than what?" the XO asked.

"Elder," Markey repeated. "Not 'older'. *Elder Things.*"

I didn't recognize the name, but 'elder' usually refers to something supernatural that's had centuries to develop its powers. And that's always bad news.

"That's not real descriptive," the XO said.

"They are unlike any other life form in creation," Markey said. "We don't know *what* to call them, except... Things."

"I don't care what fucking kind of sea monsters they are," the captain said. "I just want to know what's going to happen when we wake them up. The Mark 14s have a nine-thousand-yard range—"

Markey stepped closer and glared at the captain. "*I don't know* what will happen if we disturb those Things, Captain. But it's going to be at least a thousand times worse than what happened to Seaman Roseler."

"I don't care," the captain said, "as long as it happens to the Japs and not us. Now how far away do we need to be when we shoot off these fish?"

"No," Markey said, her voice tight. "Elder Things are not just monsters. They are the worst monsters ever. They are beyond imagination. You saw – you *felt* what a single word in their language did to us."

I shivered at the thought of what might have happened if we hadn't silenced Roseler. The sounds and symbols we use for magic aren't human – they're ancient, prehistoric – and we don't even understand how most of them work.

"Cults have worshipped Elder Things as deities – *Old Gods*," Markey continued. "Do you understand? The mere sight of one can cause madness. If these two Things wake up, it could mean the end of the world."

The XO grunted. "You just said you didn't know what would happen. Now you're saying it's Arma-fucking-geddon. Which is it, Lieutenant?"

Markey replied without breaking off her staring contest with the captain. "We don't know exactly *how* bad it would get. But I am not authorized to take that chance. And neither are you, Captain."

"Then you *get* authorization," the captain said. "Use a comm spell to contact your superiors."

"I can't," Markey said. "We're too deep. Too much water, too much iron." She touched a pipe above her head. Both of those substances restricted the range of any enchantment. It was tough enough for me to maintain my glamour in this steel tube; there was no way she could send a message through several hundred feet of seawater.

"Eighty-five hundred yards, Captain," the helmsman said.

"Eighty-five hundred, aye," the captain repeated. "Weapons, flood aft torpedo tubes."

"Aye, sir, flooding aft tubes," the weapons officer said.

My stomach fluttered, but it wasn't fear. It took me a moment to understand that I was actually excited. I *wanted* the captain to go through with this.

"Captain," Markey said. She clenched both her hands into fists. Was she actually thinking about throwing a punch? "Listen to me, please."

"Master Chief, get our latest orders and bring them in here," the captain said.

"Aye, sir." The COB turned and maneuvered his way forward.

"Lieutenant, in seven minutes we're out of range and we don't get another shot at this." The captain spoke softly but firmly. "So we're both going to look at those orders and see precisely what the fuck we're *authorized* to do."

"Listen to me, Captain," Markey said with an unnatural calm. "You cannot do this. You cannot unleash those Things upon the world."

Why not? I thought. *The Japs brought the war to us. The least we can do is return the favor.*

"Aft tubes flooded, sir," the weapons officer reported.

"Open outer doors," the captain said.

"Opening outer doors, aye."

Yes. Hell yes. I *wanted* us to shoot off those fish. I wanted those monsters to wake up and destroy our enemies. So what if we got caught in the crossfire? This was war. One little submarine for untold devastation on their shores was more than a fair trade.

And if I died out here, I would never have to worry about going home. I would never again need to worry about fitting in, either with or without a disguise.

The sea would take me, and the sea didn't care about my race, sex, or skin color.

The COB shoved his way back into the control room. "Our orders, Captain."

The captain took the folded paper. "Thank you, Master Chief."

"Eighty-eight hundred yards, Captain," the helmsman said.

"Very well." The captain unfolded the orders. His eyes scanned across the page once, twice, three times. How many times was he going to read it?

I looked at the clock above the weapons station. Less than two minutes until we were out of torpedo range. And what if the captain decided to abort?

No. *I* had decided. If Captain Channing was just going to stand there with his thumb up his ass, if Markey didn't have the balls to follow through on her own goddamn orders, I would fucking do it myself.

The weapons officer on duty was Lieutenant Goldman. I didn't know him well, but I had played a trick on him in the mess hall once, making him think he was taking the last piece of cake. In fact, he had grabbed a bowl of coleslaw, and I got that delicious cake.

I had glamoured him once, and I could do it again.

I moved toward the weapons station, wriggling between other sailors and around their control stations. I had to be close for this to work. I closed my left hand into a fist to help focus my energies. My disguise might falter for a second when I bore the new glamour, but nobody here was watching me anyway.

The captain looked up from his orders.

"Captain?" Markey said quietly.

The captain handed her the paper. "Weps, close outer doors and stand down."

That's what he actually said. What Goldman heard, loud and clear, was: *"Fire torpedoes."*

* * *

I don't know how long it took for the commotion in the control room to settle down. As soon as our fish flew out the back door, the captain ordered Goldman placed under arrest, and the COB and the XO seized him. I followed them out of the control room, hoping to slip away in the chaos, but Markey grabbed me and dragged me back to her quarters. I hadn't expected her to be so strong.

"Why?" she asked after locking us inside. "Why did you do it, Hatcher?"

I stared her down and spoke slowly. "Do what, ma'am?"

She shook her head. "It's my own fault. I should have been paying more attention to you instead of the captain."

There was something about the way she said that— "Jesus fuck. You! You put a glamour on the captain."

"Nice to meet you, too, kettle," Markey said.

"You disobeyed your own orders!"

Markey's eyes flashed. "You don't know *what* my orders are, Seaman. I couldn't gamble on the captain making the right decision on his own."

"Yeah, neither could I."

Markey glared at me. "You know why I wanted to stop those torpedoes. Why did you want to fire them so badly?"

I took a breath. "Like the captain said, ma'am. We came here to put some hurt on the Japs. Didn't seem right for us to leave without doing something."

"No. It's more than just that." Markey studied me for a moment. "What's your real name?"

"Carl Hatcher."

"No," Markey said. "Your *real* name. The one you were born with. The one that's on the books at whichever Japanese-American internment camp you escaped from."

I felt suddenly deflated. "You – you knew?"

"I saw past your glamour when you took my bobby pin. That's why I asked you all those questions. You can disguise your looks, but you can't disguise your emotions." Markey sat. "I had to make sure you weren't a spy."

I clenched my teeth. She had never really wanted to help me after all. She had only kept me close in case I turned out to be an enemy.

"My family name is Hachiya," I said. "I am a native-born American citizen, and I am loyal to my country."

"I'm not questioning your loyalty! I'm concerned about your judgment," Markey said. "Would you really rather die here, under a false identity, instead of facing life as your true self?"

An unearthly roar saved me from having to answer. The entire boat shuddered, and I imagined the ocean itself trembling.

"Guess they're awake," I said.

"You don't know what you've done," Markey said. "No matter how much you might hate them, the Japanese don't deserve what's going to happen when those Things reach shore."

"War is hell, ma'am."

She grimaced. "You know nothing about Hell, little girl."

* * *

Captain Channing surfaced the *Bowfin* as soon as we were back in international waters. Official information about what was happening in Japan remained spotty, but Markey, or rather, Roseler, had a direct line to a primary source. She was still able to connect to the now-catatonic seaman – just like she had during the scry – and report what she saw through the monsters' eyes. That lady never stopped scaring me.

The Things were faster on land than anybody had expected. Both surfaced on the western shore of Kyushu Island and crawled into the nearest population centers, causing massive damage by their sheer bulk – news reports varied, making them anywhere from fifty to two hundred feet tall, with claws, wings, tentacles, or some combination of all three.

But the worst of it radiated outward from them, as people apparently driven mad by the Things' mere presence set upon each other. Simple killing was the least of the atrocities Markey reported seeing, and which she ordered me to transcribe in gruesome detail.

She was right. Nobody deserved this, not even the Japs. I wouldn't have wished this fate on Hitler himself.

But I refused to let myself feel guilty about it.

I hadn't created those monsters. They were older than

humanity. Someone or something would have roused them sooner or later. And no matter what Markey said about their cultural inhibitions, I knew the Japs would have eventually unleashed every weapon in their arsenal and every kind of magic they could muster against the Allies. Just like we were doing all we could to defeat them.

It was inevitable. This was war, all-out war, *world* war. It was them or us, and I would always choose *us*. My country; right or wrong.

Every nation in this conflict was doing terrible things. Every single person was doing things that would have been unthinkable before the war. Me breaking out of Manzanar, disguising myself as a man, enlisting in the fucking Navy? That was three hundred percent insane. But I had done all of it in the name of victory. I had to do it. I couldn't have stayed in that internment camp for one more hour. I refused to continue being a victim. I needed to fight back. I had to do it.

It didn't stop the nightmares or bring my appetite back any sooner, but that dense nugget of conviction gave me something to hold onto. And I needed it as Markey spent hours on end dictating the relentless details of every hideous, profane, revolting scene she witnessed through Roseler's link. I did my best to write down her words without thinking about their meaning, repeating slogans in my head to block out comprehension.

This is war. Kill or be killed. Better them than us. I had to do it. I had to do it. I had to do it.

In the end, OP-20-G was right. The Elder Things didn't seem interested in moving out of Japan any time soon. Mission accomplished.

Markey code-named the monsters Alpha and Bravo. The Japanese evacuated their coastal cities and mobilized heavy artillery. They bombarded both creatures for days. Bravo didn't budge, but the ground forces managed to drive Alpha back into the ocean. Less than twenty-four hours later, Alpha resurfaced at the southwestern tip of Honshu Island and headed inland. The Japs finally surrounded Alpha at Second Army headquarters and kept it from going anywhere else.

But stopping the Things was one matter; killing them seemed to be impossible. Machine guns, Howitzers, and even high explosives only irritated them. According to OP-20-G's researchers, Alpha and Bravo were immortal, had existed for millions of years before mankind evolved, and we might have to invent completely new weapons if we actually wanted to destroy them.

For the foreseeable future, the cities of Nagasaki and Hiroshima would remain sealed quarantine zones.

* * *

Markey summoned me to her quarters the day she left *Bowfin*. She had changed back into a standard woman's uniform, presumably to avoid ruffling any brass feathers when she arrived in DC. Her eyes were as dark and unreadable as ever.

"I teleport out in a few minutes," she said, gesturing at the dowstone circle she'd inscribed herself. A fat bundle of files sat inside the pentagram on the floor. "I need you to wipe the inscriptions after I'm gone."

"Yes, ma'am," I said.

She stepped around me and closed the door. "I also want you to know that I'm not going to expose you."

I blinked. "Uh, thank you, ma'am."

"Lieutenant Goldman will go before a court-martial. There's no way around that," she said. "But I'll testify on his behalf, tell the jury his mind was touched – a side effect of *Bowfin*'s proximity to Alpha and Bravo. Nothing anybody can disprove. He'll be fine."

"That's good," I said, not knowing what else to say.

"But you, Hatcher," Markey said, "you will have to live with what you've done. Disguise yourself all you want, run away from home, hide under the sea, but you can never escape who you are on the inside, Miss Hachiya. Remember that."

"I'm not a coward," I said. I wasn't sure if I believed it.

"No, you're not." Markey stared at me. "That's why I like you so much."

I had no response to that. After a moment, Markey's wristwatch made a noise. She stepped into the pentagram, picked up her files, and said, "Do you enjoy serving on this boat, Seaman?"

I raised an eyebrow. "Is that a rhetorical question, ma'am? I'm trapped inside a metal tube with sixty men who don't wash for weeks at a time and smoke like chimneys every second they're awake."

"Well, then," Markey said, "can I give you some advice?"

I was sure I wouldn't like what came next. "I can't stop you from talking, ma'am."

"Maybe it's time you considered a less forward position in the Navy," she said. "This war isn't just about combat. The President has ordered the formation of a new, covert intelligence agency: the Office of Strategic Services. And OSS could use people like you."

I felt blood rushing to my cheeks and ears. "Are you offering me a job, ma'am? Or just blackmailing me?"

Markey's wristwatch chirped again. I stepped back as she incanted her end of the teleport spell. Then she looked at me, grinned, and vanished in a flash of light. A second later, I realized her final words had been in English:

"I'll be seeing you, Seaman Hatcher."

THE FOSSIL

Greig Beck

There is life on other worlds.
But it is not alien.
Instead it is us, looking back from the future.

~1~
Neanders Valley, Germany
48,000 BC

Drun staggered, the skin on his upper body raw and weeping where it had been burned away. The pain was like nothing he had ever felt before in his long and arduous thirty years of life.

He needed to rest – he needed to hide – and he needed to find the Drawing Cave. For days, he and his tribe had been aware of the strange newcomers in their territory. He had urged his people to ignore them and simply wait until they passed on, as they had done many times before. But Orlak, Orlak the angry one, had managed to convince the young warriors to attack them, steal their goods and let all the peoples of other tribes know that this land belonged to the Urdan.

Drun had argued, but no one listened to the old chief anymore. Orlak carried the spear of leadership now. Only his voice would be heard.

They had crept closer to the strangers, like any other hunt.

There had only been two of them, and they were weak and small. It should have been easy – two quick kills for Orlak to crow about.

Orlak was first, as always, leading the tribe in a whooping charge that had surprised the pair of visitors. Spears were thrust into the shimmering body of one, making him collapse at their feet. But the other was faster and had not fled as they expected, instead turning to point at them, some small object flaring in its hand. Immediately most of the tribe had been covered with fire and light.

Drun whimpered as he remembered the pain of the burning rays – it was like staring into the sky at the great ball of heat and fire. His eyes still ached. Once again, Orlak had been first. He simply vanished in the beams of light that had flown from the stranger's hand. Many of the Urdan had burned along with their new leader, their screams of fear cut off as they were turned to ash. Drun had been close, partly shielded by the body of one of the young . Even so, the heat had been unbearable, and it had seared his flesh deeply.

The old warrior staggered on, finally spotting the refuge he sought. It was the deep cave they used to capture the spirits of animals they would hunt by painting their images. Drun himself had drawn bison, musk ox, and the greatest prize of all, the giant mammoth.

He crawled deep inside, the precious thing still held tight in his hand, and dropped down against the cave wall. He grimaced as another wave of pain wracked his body. He breathed deeply for a few moments, trying to ease himself into a more comfortable position, and rested his head against the cool damp stone. He listened for the sound of pursuit, or some other beast that might have taken up residence deeper in the cave. Nothing save the continual drip of milky water.

Drun opened his hand to examine the mysterious object. When he had fallen, he had found himself on the ground near the speared visitor… and beside him had lain the beautiful shiny thing – hard as a piece of stone, but so polished and smooth it defied belief. And now when he looked closely, he could see there was something bright inside it. Something like fire.

He held it in one open hand, pressing and stroking it with a blunt finger. Immediately a beam of lightning shot from its narrow end, striking the ceiling of the cave. Rocks fells, dust rose, and the small vestiges of light from outside were shut out.

Drun cried out, and his hand locked tight again over the object. Before the dust had even settled, he knew he was trapped. He cried out again but the echo of his voice was absolute. He was sealed in. He wept; sorry for himself, sorry for his lost brother warriors, and sorry for not being strong enough to stop Orlak from making war on the strange visitors.

He lay back, not caring that the drip of the water fell upon his matted hair. Drun closed his eyes and let his mind wander, taking him away from the darkness and the pain. He dreamed of his youth, of his mate, of hunting in warm spring sunshine. He exhaled, the long breath leaving him slowly for the last time.

The water continued to drip down upon him.

~2~
Neanders Valley, Germany
Today

"There's something in there."

Klaus Hoffman shone his flashlight onto the wall of the new cave, moving it slowly back and forth, letting the beam penetrate from different angles. He felt rather than heard Doris creep closer. She did little more than sniff in the cold darkness, letting him know her disinterest was peaking.

"Look, look." He turned and grabbed her sleeve as he crouched down, pulling her toward him.

"Ow." Doris pulled her arm away from his grasp. He'd thought his girlfriend had been slightly interested in entering the cave. He couldn't count the times she had seemed to sit spellbound as he had recounted his many spelunking adventures over the past few months. Perhaps her interest had been feigned, or perhaps her interest only extended to hearing about caves – entering them was a whole different ballgame.

"I don't see anything." She looked away and down into the interior of the cave. "It's too dark."

Klaus muttered in annoyance and tugged her sleeve again. "Here… don't look at the rock, look into it. It's called a limestone flow, and it's rather like solidified dishwater… cloudy but you can still see through it."

She had folded her arms, leaned forward and craned her neck. But after a few seconds she slowly shook her head. "Nope, nothing."

Klaus started to groan in frustration and then had a thought. He held up a finger and then fumbled under his jacket for his water bottle, uncapped it, and splashed the liquid onto the cave wall. The smooth limestone revealed looked like glistening wax. He smiled and sat back on his haunches. "It's the result of tens of thousands of years of water dripping down to coat everything in micro-mineral particles that hardens to a semi clear covering. It's the geological equivalent of capturing flies in amber." Klaus changed the angle of his light beam once again.

"Oh yeah, I can see inside – yuck – that thing looks weird." Doris wrinkled her nose, but crouched beside him.

"Looks beautiful to me." Klaus tipped some more water over it.

"Is it a man? He looks deformed or something." Doris got to her feet, but also kept her flashlight trained on the wet stone.

"You mean, was. And no, I don't think he was deformed. Judging by the depth of mineral coverage, I'd say he's been trapped in there for about at least forty thousand years, maybe even sixty thousand." Klaus leaned in, his nose almost touching the slick stone. "Not deformed, more like proto-human… probably Neanderthal."

He shone his torch at the cave wall and ceiling, before letting it rest on her face. "The sink hole we entered only opened the cave a few days back, and so far the emergency services have kept everyone well away. We're probably the first people to set foot here for tens of thousands of years." He raised his eyebrows theatrically, but she just nodded without enthusiasm.

Klaus shrugged, still feeling the tingle of excitement ripple through him. He leaned in close again, inhaling the smell of the ancient stone. From behind there came the sound of a metallic flicking, followed by a spark of light.

He spun. "Doris… are you shitting me… you're smoking?"

She pointed the cigarette at him like the barrel of a small glowing gun. "I'm nervous. You know I smoke when I'm nervous. I'm nervous, cold, hungry… and horny." She tilted her nose in the air, but looked back at him out of the corner of her eye.

Klaus snorted. He knew when she threw in the horny angle she wanted him to do something. Normally she got her way, but this time, his focus remained firmly above his waistline.

"You smoke when you're nervous, drunk, happy, sad… face it Doris, you smoke all the time. Show some respect; this cave probably hasn't seen people for about fifty thousand years… and do you mind not dropping ash everywhere?"

She wobbled her head. "I've seen you smoke too, Mr. High-n-mighty. Besides, who's going to complain … him?" She jerked her thumb at the lump in the wall, jammed the cigarette between her pursed lips, and flashed a quick glance at the blue Seiko dive watch on her slim wrist.

Klaus ignored her, and looked back at the encased body. "Maybe… and for the record, it might be a her. We need to dig it out – looks really old and if it's a good quality fossil, which I think it is, it could be worth thousands." He half turned. "And the smoke could damage it."

"Thousands." Klaus heard her softly repeat the word, and then came the sound of a foot grinding something into the cave floor.

He nodded sagely. "Sure, collectors pay a fortune for this stuff. They'll even pay for pieces of it. We need to get some tools, and cut it out before anyone else finds this cave."

Doris crowded in beside him squinting. "Good idea." She pointed. "Hey, I think there's a light in there."

He followed her finger. "Hmm, might be a reflection – or an opal. Could make it even more valuable."

~3~
New Berlin, Euronesia
50,000 AD

Let's go, let's go, let's go." Jax slapped each soldier on the back as they jogged past – twenty of the best – combat professionals and genetically bred to be big, tough and fearless. Zone-Cleaners, ass-kickers, terminators; call them whatever you wanted, but they got the job done, the harder and dirtier the better. He had his war party, and they were ready to kick ass.

The portal flared as they all lined up to one side, awaiting his final inspection. Nano-body armor over iron-hard muscles, fusion bombs, magnetic kill-darts, and burners with enough power to fry a city block. He walked along the line, nodding to each, their eyes straight ahead. He balled his fists and faced them.

"We are the hammer, and they are the nail. When we strike, they fall. We will not fail… we *can*not fail." He raised a fist, his jaw jutting. "Anything gets in our way, it's dead." Jax began to turn away, but paused, his head tilting. He spun back and roared. "I can't… fucking… hear you."

As one, the squad yelled in return: "Anything in our way is dead."

The squad leader grinned without humor. "Damned right." He turned to the glowing portal. "Let's go and burn some Gimps."

He turned his back on them and waited for the portal to open fully and settle itself. The zone they were about to enter was dangerous. The Gimps had evolved, changed, become clever and far more deadly.

Jax was the senior officer in charge of the top cleanup crew, and he was fearless. He knew his men would follow him to hell if need be… and that was good, because where they were going, there were devils. The Gimps, prehistoric monsters that defied belief.

He breathed deeply and cast his mind back to how they had got to this point. His lips moved in a silent curse; damn science officers and their weak-willed approach to everything. He was sick of hearing their advice to command: we don't need to take Cleaners on jumps; the Gimps fear us more than we fear them; we must hold out the hand of peace. *Ha*, he thought with a little vindication, *hold out the hand of peace and you'd fucking lose it*. As the science team had just found out… yet again.

He snorted as he checked his burner's power cells. Gilbred, that worm, and his know-it-all colleague Hindoy… now deceased. He remembered when the puny excuse for a man had returned from his expedition, shaking like a leaf.

He glanced at the chronometer. The portal's synchronizers had identified their destination and started the countdown.

Thirty… twenty-nine… twenty-eight… twenty-seven…

There'd been too many trips now. They had burned, interrogated and tortured their way across a lot of the primordial hellhole to get to this point. Now, it all came down to this last zone jump.

As he waited for the portal to stabilize, he let his mind wander over the events of the past few days. Back to Gilbred and when he had first returned.

* * *

Jax lunged forward and yelled into the seated science officer's face. "You fucking lost it? You get attacked by dumb Gimps, let them creep right up on you and spear your companion. Then you let them take his damn burner?" Jax paced, his jaw clenched. He spun back. "You'd upbraid my soldiers for stepping on a single bug, but in a blind panic you fry ten Gimps." Jax rushed back, getting in close to the cowering scientist. "Do you have any idea what sort of problems this will cause?" He brought his face so close their foreheads almost touched. "Well?"

Gilbred squeaked something incomprehensible. Jax stepped around the science officer, his lips tight in barely suppressed fury. He stopped behind the man and leaned in close to his head. "If you had left his body behind, I'd damn well make sure you spend a week in a pain chamber… of my choosing." Jax straightened, his hands clasped behind his back, chin lifter. "Why do you science guys always think you know what's best?"

Gilbred shook his head. "We knew the Gimps were in the area, but they had been so docile before. We didn't think they'd…" His voice, already high and strained from fear, trailed off as Jax turned, a scowl pulling his face into deep fissures.

Gilbred hung his head. Jax smiled and patted the man's shoulder. "You didn't think. Don't worry. That's what we do… and that's why we told you we needed to accompany you on your jumps." He snorted. "But you knew better." Jax growled. "Yes, you brainy types always knew better."

Gilbred lifted his head. "I can show you where…"

Jax's voice was so loud Gilbred nearly fell out of his chair. "Shut the fuck up; you've done enough." He exhaled loudly. "The burners do not corrode, erode, or malfunction – we designed them that way. This thing will be in operation for a quarter of a million years."

He sighed and placed both hands on Gilbred's narrow shoulders, leaning in close to one ear. "Do you know what will happen if those Gimps get that technology? Next time we drop in on them they'll fry us." Jax pushed back off the man and walked around in front of him.

"We need to find it." He stopped and stared down at the cowering man. "You need to find it. We can't go back to the same zone twice, so you need to locate the lost burner's xenon radiation trace and then follow it back up the event slope. Give me a place and a date, and we'll go get it ourselves."

Jax's voice became soft. "A warning, though. Make sure you're accurate. It costs a small fortune to open those portals, so we better find it before the general finds out… or it'll be all on your head."

* * *

The chronometer indicated the unique radiation traces had appeared again, many millennia after Gilbred had lost his weapon, and in a time they were loath to visit. As a further complication there were many traces showing. Somehow, the burner had infused objects around it with the xenon particles, and now they were spread over a large area. Jax and his team had to check every damn one of them.

His Cleanup crew was a good one – tough and brutal, and all professional zone-jump soldiers. Jax knew they'd need to be. Coming to this type of zone was not recommended. It was too dangerous. The Gimps had evolved a base intelligence, a hunter's smarts to add to their monstrous muscle power.

Jax was first though the portal. He stepped into the dark space, only just remembering in time to snap down his faceplate. The air was foul, and the gasses would quickly sear his lungs. Only the giant Gimps, with their enormous bellow-like breathers, could absorb the mix of primordial gases.

He looked around. *So fucking big*, he thought. Even though he was a veteran of the class and gender wars, and as battle-hardened as they come, these creatures scared the shit out of him. Each stood three times as tall as his biggest man, and most Gimps could literally tear him or his men to pieces.

Jax circled his finger in the air, and his team started their search. There were familiar radiation vestiges, but they were faint – the burner had been here. His team examined, probed and searched their way across the dark expanse where the initial trace was detected.

It only took them a few minutes to return. Nothing on scanners, nothing on visual. Arcad, his lead Cleaner shrugged. "Not here. Might have been once, but not now. What do you want to do?"

Jax thought for a moment. "Broaden the search area. If it's not here, I want to know what happened to it. Let's do a quick check in the outer areas."

"Outer areas?" Arcad's head snapped up. "There are indications of current habitation."

"That's right soldier… and that's why they pay us the big bucks." Jax moved to the entrance of the large space and froze, holding up one hand as he heard a sound from outside. He and the team froze.

Arcad eased up next to him. "Go or no go?" He looked over his shoulder to the portal gateway shimmering in the darkness behind them.

Jax held up a hand and waited, listening. He placed his ear to the entrance, and then shook his head. "Nothing." He half turned to his second in command. "I don't like it either, but we're here to do a job. So... we do it." He pulled the huge barrier back towards him. It opened easily, with only a faint whine of protest.

He was first through, his team stacking in behind him. Jax was the most skilled Cleaner in Euronesia and as soon as he orientated himself he knew there was danger. He sensed rather than saw the Gimp as it loomed over them. The sound that smashed out of the darkness made them all want to cover their ears and flee. The greats beast's maw was open, a near perfect circle, and huge teeth framed the ear-shattering screech that smashed at them like a physical force.

The Gimp raised one colossal arm. Jax didn't wait to see if it held something dangerous, he lifted his burner, set to wide beam, and fired. The beast shimmered for a moment or two as the beam struck it, the sound of its terrifying call shutting off as it disintegrated.

"Shit, shit, shit." He had no choice. They were loath to remove Gimps from this zone as they had strong social bonding. *Too late now*, he thought. "We need to move quickly. Give me a thorough search, and then let's get the hell out of here." He bristled. Those assholes back home better find him the right zone next time, or he'd personally feed them to the Gimps.

It took them only a few more minutes to confirm there was no sign of their missing burner. Jax herded his team back to the portal, taking one last look around. He had sealed the entrance, and was sure he had left no evidence from his team. The other creatures would find the remains of the giant beast soon enough, but as long as the crew wasn't there, the Gimps would be as clueless. *Primitives*, he thought. *And no burner, either. Waste of fucking time.* He stepped back through the glowing portal and it immediately snapped shut behind him. The surroundings rapidly cooled, and silence settled once more.

~4~
Berlin, Germany
Today

Monroe drank his beer and watched Raptor, his second in command, bring the man down over his knee, the man's backbone making a noise like a snapping tree branch. He let the jerking body slide to the floor. Monroe knew Raptor didn't care whether his opponent walked again, or died right there at his feet. Neither did Monroe.

Raptor's opponent had been big, beefy, and knew how to throw a punch. Probably won plenty of fights in his time. From the minute Monroe and Raptor had walked in through the doors, the asshole glared, sized them up, and then to the delight of his drinking buddies, decided to get in their face. Monroe told him to walk away. The redneck chose not to. Raptor had gotten to his feet and on his way up, had collected an almighty uppercut under his chin. That was Beefy's last mistake.

Monroe grinned and shook his head, watching Raptor stand like a bloody colossus looking around the bar – blond crew cut, pale blue eyes were so light they almost looked alien. Both men stood six foot three, and were as solid as iron from their special forces training. But Monroe was athletically long-limbed, and Raptor was a human bulldozer.

Monroe pivoted his head, taking in the other bar room patrons; some of them had been drinking with the man Raptor had just brutalized. No-one looked at either of the two men. Raptor's brutal and efficient violence had made them invisible.

Monroe's pocket buzzed. He frowned. It was extremely rare to get called on down time. He and his team belonged to an internal military body simply called Defense. They operated on orders issued from a few generals, and the president himself – they didn't exist until they needed to. He pulled the disc-reader. *Something big must be going down*, he thought. He read the message: POSSIBLE NT INCURSION. He grunted.

NT.

Non Terrestrial.

Monroe clicked his fingers and headed to the exit. Raptor followed, but at the door he paused to look back. Not a single person looked up, their drinks now the most interesting thing in the world.

* * *

"Victim's name is Doris Sömmer – at least we think it's her." Sergeant Artur Amos led Detective Ed Heisen of the *Kripo* – the *Kriminalpolizei* – the through the stinking, dark apartment.

"Based on an imprint of the driver's license at the check-in desk, we got a twenty six year-old female, approximately five-eight tall. But… fingerprints gone, weight unknown, hair and eye color also unknown."

"Unknown? I thought you said you had a body." Heisen followed the older policeman, squinting to try and improve his vision in the semi gloom.

Amos half turned and shrugged. "Meh." He handed Heisen a sheet of paper with some basic background information and a copy of the girl's driver's license. A small photo showed a healthy young woman beaming at the camera.

"What about other prints?" Heisen asked while reading the page.

"Millions of 'em." Replied the short cop.

Heisen looked up as Amos slowed at the doorway to a room floodlit by halogen lamps and bustling with several shapes in white biohazard suits. Amos flipped a page from his notebook, and read some more.

"Evidence of a metallic band on the fourth ring finger indicating a possible engagement, but the diamond is gone, and there's evidence she was with someone. So we're still looking for trace." He snorted and stood aside. "And yeah, we thought we had a body too." Amos pointed with his pen.

Heisen stepped past the smaller man and looked down at the carpet. There was an ash outline, almost too perfect in detail. He didn't know whether to laugh or stagger from the room screaming his head off.

"Jesus Christ! What'd they use, a freakin' blowtorch?"

The body, or what had once been a body, was just a thin layer of grey-brown ash in the shape of a figure holding an arm up, either warding off a blow or trying to shield her vision from something.

Amos pointed again with the pen. "No idea what caused it. But whatever it was, it was fucking hot. We think the ring…" he leaned forward and indicated a darker area on the end of the ash-arm pile on the carpet, "once had a diamond. Well, we think that's what it was, as the lab boys tell me that there's a small trace of mineralized carbon ash denser than that rest."

Amos looked up at Heisen. "Do you know how hot a fire needs to be before a diamond burns?"

Heisen shook his head. "I didn't even know they could burn."

"Me neither, but I looked it up. It usually takes about fifteen hundred degrees. But this must have been even hotter and faster, cause if you heat girl's-best-friend up slowly, it explodes. We reckon this was a burn of about two thousand degrees, and it occurred over a few seconds."

"That's incredible." Heisen squatted beside Amos.

The cop waved his pen around. "That's nuthin; look around, detective." Amos swiveled his head theatrically, and then faced Heisen, his eyebrows raised. "Nothing else is burned. The heat happened right here, right on her, just on her, for a few seconds, and then just as miraculously, turned itself off."

Heisen grunted and looked up – the ceiling was also unharmed. He nodded. "Well, wasn't a flamethrower, that'd fry the plaster overhead, or at least leave a helluva stain."

He sniffed. There was a strange smell, but not the greasy odor he expected when a body was cooked. He'd seen people burned up before and the fact was, Joe or Jane Doe contained a good percentage of fat, women more so. Even a healthy woman carried about ten percent body fat – burning it should have filled the room with greasy smoke and the smell of fried pork. Instead, there was nothing but a sharp metallic odor.

Heisen pulled on his lower lip as he thought for a moment, and then clicked his fingers. "Microwaves."

"Huh?" Amos looked at him as if he had just started to speak in another language.

"Microwaves. You know, like what you get in a microwave oven. I hear that the military is working on some sort of device to project the waves that'll cook you from the inside out – leaves all the buildings intact."

Amos's expression didn't soften, but his head tilted by about half a degree and one of his eyebrows went up by just as much. "Rays? Army fucking mi-cro-waves? Is that your deduction, detective?"

Heisen half shrugged. "Well, what've you got?" He didn't really think that. He'd also read that the devices were as large as a good sized refrigerator – not exactly something you'd cart up to the first floor of some back-alley flea-pit, use it to fry a young woman, and then slip out the back door with it hidden under your coat.

As Amos turned to speak to a couple of uniformed police-men, Heisen stepped back to look down at the outline again, trying to imagine how the girl had been standing before she had fallen back or been pushed to the ground. One arm was up, appearing as if she had the arm across her face at the moment of death, perhaps trying to protect herself from whatever killed her.

Heisen tried to twist himself into the right shape. With his legs splayed, one arm out and the other over his face. He let his eyes move to a doorway on the other side of the apartment. She would have been facing that room. Whatever had killed her had come from there. The door was closed.

The shove to his back nearly threw him to the floor. He spun to see six enormous human beings, all dressed in plain black coveralls, push into the room – five men, one woman, all with faces hard enough to dent a steel door.

One calmly started giving orders, and immediately the group began to spread out, some waving strange devices, the rest joining the guys in hazmat sits and taking their reports from them. Heisen noticed all had powerful looking sidearms strapped to their thighs.

"Hey, who the fuck are you guys?" Amos charged over waving his arms, flanked by two young policemen. The senior policeman went to grab one of the men by the arm. The effect was immediate and alarming – like lightning, Amos' hand was grabbed and twisted. The senior cop screamed, and the two policemen went for the guns. Before they could even get close to drawing them, five weapons were all aimed at the policemen. The young cops swallowed; behind them the technicians froze. The policemen's eyes slide to Amos.

Heisen recognized the guns – all Heckler & Koch USP Tacticals. What caught his attention was the modified o-ring barrel with polygonal bore profile and taller sights for using sound suppressors. It also had a slide rail for laser sights – these were not your standard kit, even for the *Kommando Spezialkräfte*.

"Let him go," the leader said softly.

Amos was released, and he rubbed his hand, looking like he couldn't decide whether he wanted to walk away or go for his own gun. The leader, and the only one who hadn't bothered pulling a weapon, touched something at his ear and spoke a few words. The cop's phone began to ring.

"Answer it," he said to Amos.

Heisen watched as Amos kept his eyes on the big man and pulled out his phone. He lifted it to his ear. "Amos." He listened, his brow folding.

He disconnected and turned to his officers. "At ease; that was the boss." He shrugged "Actually, further up the chain of command." He turned away, rubbing his arm. "Let these… agents… look around… and give them any assistance they need." Amos turned back to the man he assumed was in charge. "What's your name?" The older cop tilted his chin, waiting.

He was pushed aside and the agents went about their tasks. Heisen sidled up next to Amos. "Who the hell are these guys?"

Amos shrugged. "From Defense." He began to walk away.

"Huh? Defense what – army, navy, *Spezialkräfte*, homeland, who?" Heisen got in front of Amos.

Amos motioned with his hand to the huge agents. "Be my guest."

There was a woman amongst them, and Heisen switched on his most disarming smile, and approached. "Hi there, I'm…"

"Fuck off." She kept walking.

"Thank you." Heisen waved. He decided to watch and backed up to the wall. It seemed the Defense were going to give them nothing. He could try again, maybe beg them for information, or he could do his job. He moved away from the wall, knowing he only had a few minutes before these guys, whoever they were, shut them all down. If he wanted answers, he'd have to get them himself… and quick.

He stepped around the forensics guys down on their knees sifting and lifting minute bits of evidence from the carpet. As he went by he reached down to lift a rubber glove from one of their cases and held it loosely in his hand. He crossed to the closed door the disintegrated woman had been facing, and gripped the handle. He turned it –locked.

From behind him, Amos confirmed what was now obvious. "Locked or jammed tight, and so is the other side door – we haven't got in there yet and the landlord doesn't have a key. We're waiting on a locksmith. And before you ask, we've already stuck a peep-pipe in, and found nothing. So… we sit tight."

Heisen backed up looking around the old door, and then reached up to feel around the frame. From behind, Amos must have been watching.

"Done that – jammed up and no hidden keys. Be too easy wouldn't it, Heisen?"

"Locked from the inside maybe?" Heisen rolled his eyes and half turned to speak over his shoulder. "Thanks Amos; I'll take a poke around."

He didn't wait for a reply, instead sliding past the cop and then making a sharp turn down a narrow side hallway, continuing on until he came to a door he guessed was a rear exit to the room he had just tried to enter. Using the glove again, he jiggled the handle – loose but also jammed. He looked at the frame – this one was more promising – the wood looked old and damp-softened.

Heisen reached inside his jacket, slid free his handgun, and put his ear to the door. Though Amos had said they'd stuck a peep-pipe, a cord camera, into the room, he knew from experience if someone wanted to hide, they could fold themselves into a freakin' suitcase.

Heisen let the large gun hang by his side and put his shoulder against the door. He braced one of his legs against the opposite wall in the narrow hallway, and pushed. He gently applied more and more pressure until he felt the wood crunch softly as the lock was torn from its bed in the rotten cavity. He eased the door open and stepped inside. That weird smell again, but stronger – like an electrical short. The word ozone immediately leapt into his mind.

He quickly stepped out of the doorframe's halo of light – nothing like a little backlighting to make you an easy target. He waited for his eyes to adjust to the gloom, and gradually the piles of dirty clothing, food wrappers and assorted rubbish on a bench-top took on greater definition. The only sound came from the forensics team on the other side of the far door.

Heisen remained motionless and just let his eyes slide around the room. Against the wall there was a new pair of jogging shoes, with clean socks tucked into them – incongruously neat amongst the general disarray. On the bench top, a gold chain with small heart locket, an Yves Saint Laurent wallet open and with several cards in place, a wristwatch – blue Seiko dive model – expensive. Not theft then, he thought. Unless what was taken was something completely different.

Heisen looked around, and grunted. It didn't fit. The entire apartment block was nothing but floor upon floor of piss-smelling flophouses. The picture of the girl, nice, wholesome, the expensive shoes and personal items – just didn't fit.

Heisen finally walked towards the centre of the room, and

holstered his gun. What's wrong with this picture? He tugged on his lip and he slowly turned in a circle. He hadn't been in the apartment long, but as far as he could tell the place hadn't been tossed. So, whoever had killed the Sömmer girl had found what they were looking for, or the objective was the girl herself – a hit.

Heisen sighed and put his hands on his hips. Or theory three, it was some sort of freak natural phenomenon – ball lightning, maybe? He snorted softly and finally pulled the single glove over his hand. He used a couple of fingers to lift the wallet, carefully sorting through the contents. No receipts, no paperwork, or even a bus ticket… but plenty of cash. *A runner's wallet*, he thought.

He lifted open one of the sleeves and dragged out a picture of the girl – standing with a smiling young man holding an old brown skull. She wore a slightly bored expression, and was holding what looked like a weird brushed-metal fountain pen. He turned the photograph over. In small script there were three words: *Klaus and me*. He turned it back, now having a name to the young face.

"Klaus, huh? What did you two kids find?" He studied it for a few more seconds before slipping it into his pocket and checking the wallet's other compartments – all empty.

Heisen sniffed again – ozone. Ozone, and piss, and stale cigarettes, and booze and sex. No Club Med, and definitely not a place you'd expect to find a pretty young girl in new running shoes wearing a Seiko dive watch. From the little information Amos had given him, she'd come here a month ago and paid her rent cash-in-advance. In places like this, residents came here for hookers, to do drugs deals, or to hide out. You didn't stay for the atmosphere or the local restaurant's cuisine.

He briefly pulled the picture from his pocket and looked again at the smiling face – no way do young girls from good families come here to be incinerated in a two thousand degree microburst. Instead, they come here to meet lovers their conservative parents didn't approve of… or to hide out. He tapped his chin with a knuckle. *A runners wallet*, he thought again. But running from what?

He flicked the light switch but no glow came from the bulb - it was blackened inside. Looking to the door where Amos and his team worked, he saw no key sticking from the lock. On closer inspection, he could see that the locking mechanism was fused – welded shut. He frowned. Whoever came out of this room to freak Doris out and then burn her up, had then come back in here afterwards, and then made sure the door stayed closed.

Heisen looked around; whoever it was, had come out of here, come back in here … and had stayed in here. He turned slowly, the Glock hanging loosely at his side.

Where the fuck are you? he thought.

Only one place left to look. He stepped towards the old closet against the wall, and brought the gun up. He laid his hand on the doorknob. An image of the ash outline on the floor flickered in his mind, and he worked to calm his breathing.

One-two-three; he whipped open the door, and immediately something leapt at him. He smashed the Glock into it as he turned side-on, his heart galloping in his chest as he rolled away. He was back on his feet in an instant, gun pointed in a two-handed grip. His vision tunneled as he focused laser-like on the mound lying before him.

"Fuck you too." He exhaled and laughed softly. "A fucking raincoat." He holstered the gun; relieved he hadn't let off a round. He could imagine the look on Amos' face when the cop busted in to find he had just shot the shit out of a plastic coat.

Heisen lifted his eyes back to the empty closet to continue his investigation. First thing he noticed was that wooden backboard was blackened. Clothing framed the cupboard rear as if it had already been pushed aside. Heisen reached in and touched the back of the big piece of furniture – it was solid, scorched, but solid. He pushed it – no false wall, or sliding panels.

He lifted one of the jackets free and noticed that one side of it was missing. "What the hell?" He brought it closer to his face – it was singed, like the sleeve had been cut away by a red-hot knife. He turned it over in his hands – the other side was untouched. He hung it back up, and pulled a shirt from the other side of the cupboard – same thing, but the opposite sleeve – subjected to heat, but no flame – cauterized.

He leant in and looked down at the cupboard floor – no ash. The sleeves and material just… gone. He replaced the shirt and stood back, hands on his hips again. The scorch mark was oval, about three feet high, and he could see now that where the oval and the clothing had overlapped, the sleeves, and other material had simply vanished.

"Fucked if I know," he said softly to the dark interior. He pulled off the glove and stuck it in his pocket. He'd run a trace on the girl, and try and find out who the mystery man was. At least now he had a name and a face, and somewhere to start.

Heisen paused at the door, looking back at the room. From this angle, the dark oval in the cupboard looked longer… almost like a tunnel. He shrugged. *A trick of the eye,* he thought. He closed the door behind him, just in time.

* * *

Monroe watched his team move through the rooms like a school of sharks parting the smaller baitfish as they went. His Defense team didn't work with the police, or any other law enforcement body. What they usually fought didn't obey the rules, so neither did they.

Monroe looked around the room, taking everything and everyone in. His agents, Harper and Felzig squatted by the outline of the body, taking digital pictures, samples, and readings, and in a few moments, Agent Carter appeared at his side, leaning in close, small box in hand.

"What've you got, Carter?" Monroe said.

Carter held up the tiny illuminated screen. "Weird; I've got extremely high gamma radiation traces, bordering on dangerous. Also, some other form of background trace I can't identify here." He nodded towards the locked door. "And that's the focal point."

Monroe turned to the door. "Let's have a look then." Monroe crossed the room.

"Locksmith's on his way." Amos called from behind him.

At the door, Monroe didn't stop, and simply lifted one huge boot and kicked out. The old door exploded inwards. He stood in the centre of the doorframe, just letting his eyes move over the empty space. Beside him his agents had already formed up, weapons pointed onto the room.

"Clear." He walked in, followed by Benson, Carter holding out his reader, and Raptor with gun probing the dark. They went around the room quickly and professionally. The first sweep was looking for anyone or anything trying to conceal itself. Then they performed a more focused search – looking for trace and clues.

Monroe stood before the cupboard, looking in at the oval scorch mark. Carter held the reader towards it, and half turned.

"Off the scale, right here." He tapped the burn mark with his knuckle. "Solid."

Raptor had appeared beside him. For a big man he moved silently. "Want me to tell you what I think that looks like?"

Monroe exhaled. "You don't need to." He turned to Carter. "Get those readings back to base. I want to know what that unknown radiation signature is. And I want it locked in for tracking."

"Move out." Monroe turned away. "We've already missed this party. Let's try and get in front of the next one."

At the door he stopped and gave Amos a small salute. "Thank you for your cooperation, officer."

"Like I had any choice." The old cop snorted as Monroe left the room.

~5~

The General's voice boomed inside the large room. Senior science officers and Cleanup team leaders sat looking down at hands clasped on the desk.

"Every zone trip costs us close to a trillion euroyuan." He looked from Gilbred to Jax. "And both of you are now into me for about ten times that much." The General walked slowly along behind the rows of seats, and sighed. "This is turning out to be a real shit day." He continued for another few feet and stopped behind Gilbred, who obviously sensed the big man, and visibly gulped. The General leaned around in front of the science officer.

"Gilbred, isn't it?" The General grinned like a shark and didn't wait for the man to respond. "You and your entire science division better start pinpointing better zones for us right now. Because, if we keep stepping in and out of that sort of zone, sooner or later something bad is going to happen." The General's jaws worked. "Because in that zone, they're getting smarter, and I for one, don't want one of those big ugly mothers working out how to follow us back here." He straightened, but kept one large hand on the back of the man's neck. "So, just to be clear. I couldn't give a fuck about you, your division, or anyone else in this goddamn room."

The general pushed off from Gilbred and turned to face Jax. "Take a proximity bomb – if you can't get your hands on the burner, then get as close as you can and take every-fucking-thing out nearby. I authorize you to use all force necessary to retrieve or destroy the device."

"Sir, yes sir." Jax sat straighter. "Permission to take language converters and conduct Gimp interrogation, sir."

The general turned. "Authorized, Master Cleaner." He folded his arms, and glared at Gilbred. "Get it done, and get it done quick. Retrieval or destruction – no other options."

Jax stood and half bowed. "Retrieval or destruction, Yes sir."
And Gimp interrogation authorized.

That's more like it, he thought.

~6~

Klaus Hoffman scribbled the note as quickly as he could, folded it once and dropped it into the box on top of the fossil. Picking up the tape gun, he set about sealing it, then writing a name and address on the top. He finished by plastering it with way too many stamps. He held it up and looked at the name he'd written. The only teacher he had ever listened to – Professor Matt Kearns. When it came to all things old, Kearns seemed to know everything about everything.

"And no charge for this one." He giggled with just a hint of panicked insanity. "My last good deed."

Hoffman looked at his watch. Half past four – he had to get back to Doris and check in before it got dark. She'd panic if she didn't hear from him by nightfall. It was his idea that they split up, as he bet they were looking for a couple – at least this way, he could move quickly if he needed to.

He jumped to his feet and walked to the door, placed his ear against it to listen for a second and then quickly unlocked the multiple bolts. He opened it an inch, and looked through the crack. He planned to run to the mail chute, throw in the package, and be back inside in fifteen seconds.

A door at the end of the corridor opened and old Mrs. Silberman starting easing herself out – all tent-like, stained cotton dress and wiry gray hair, also in need of a wash. He slammed his door and leaned back against it, surprised at how his heart rate had jumped for nothing.

"Calm down, calm down. Next thing you'll be the one seeing goblins," he whispered to himself.

He laughed again as he let his eyes slide around the small decrepit room. The place was a mess, but it didn't matter, he and Doris would move again by the end of the week. It only took Doris a few days before she said she felt like she was being watched. It was always the same – there was whispering going on in the walls and she was sure her place was bugged. Klaus sighed; he loved her, but she was driving him crazy, becoming more paranoid by the day – making *him* more paranoid by the day. The final straw was when she told him she thought she saw a goblin… a freaking *goblin* for chrissakes.

He looked at his room again – all the windows were taped over with newspaper, the phone had been pulled from the wall, the power sockets taped over, and even the door keyholes blocked up. *She's paranoid, but I'm fine*, he thought, giggling again.

His one luxury was the ancient television that remained on day and night. He looked across to the old black and white box as the robotic newsreader reeled off the names of the latest drive-by shooting victims, domestic violence punching bags, and other assorted attacks on the human sheep of life. But the next story about a bizarre murder was like an ice pick to the back of the neck – Professor Julius Cohen, the head of paleontology at the University of Tübingen, was believed the victim of a bizarre execution. His remains were as yet formally unidentified, and it was expected that confirmation might not be possible given the state of the body.

Klaus walked towards the television, the package still under his arm, and stood trance-like before the flickering screen. The final part of the story nearly made him double over. Cohen's apparent murder brought the number of bizarre killings to three, as Julius Cohen now joined Professors Carl Ingram and Rudi Hokstetor as victims in what police were dubbing the Incinerator Murders.

Klaus' mouth hung open. He knew those men, knew all of them. He had sent each and every one of them a piece of the fossil skeleton. He flopped back into a ratty armchair and grabbed his head. Did he do that? Was it his fault they were dead? Was someone killing anyone who touched the bones? He knew that the complete skeleton was valuable but he didn't think it was worth killing people for. He put the box down, and backed away from it.

"Think, think." He paced quickly around the small room. "Gotta get out." He started filling his pockets with his wallet, phone, and keys when a knock on the door made him cry out. He quickly put a hand over his mouth and listened.

The knock came again. "Klaus? Hello Klaus, are you there? Timmy Boy has got out of his cage again and I need your help. Klaus?"

Oh for fuck's sake. He exhaled. Old Mrs. Silberman and that parakeet would be the death of him. Do one good deed and suddenly you're an adopted son… and one required to do everything from change light bulbs to recapturing bad tempered parrots that had more escape tricks than Houdini and a beak sharp enough to slice bacon.

Klaus stayed where he was, thinking through his options. Should he scream at her to fuck off? That'd send a clear message. He grimaced; nah, much as he'd love for her to leave him alone, he wasn't quite ready to be a total asshole. He eased himself down in the chair. He'd wait her out. The knocking continued. He looked at his watch again and rubbed his head, glaring at the door.

C'mon, Mrs. Silberman, go home, willya? He needed to get the fuck outta here and find Doris. He suddenly had a bad feeling about this place.

~7~

Heisen read through his notes. In the following days, more bodies had turned up – or better said, more bodies had burned up. The coroner had hinted at spontaneous combustion. Alcohol abuse, ball lightning, faulty wiring; all were listed as possible causes. But none of the suggestions actually explained the heat generated, the peculiar explicit targeting of individuals, nor the ability of the heat source to simply switch on and off.

Funny thing was, Heisen was beginning to see a pattern. The closer he came to finding this Klaus guy, the more the ash trails began to pile up. Coincidence, or was there a link? Heisen bounded up the stairs, knocking once on the open door, holding up his badge and heading straight over to where Amos talked with some other uniforms.

"Officer Amos; another nice day for a cookout?" Heisen raised an eyebrow and winked, but the older cop half turned, gave him a look like he'd just noticed dog shit on his shoe, and immediately went back to talking softly with his younger colleagues. Heisen waited, awkwardly.

Finally, Amos issued instructions to his men and turned to him. "You would be the brains of the *Kripo*, huh?" Amos said as he sauntered away.

Heisen followed. "Hey, lighten up will ya? I just…"

Amos spun at him, stepping in closer. "You just what? Listen, Heisen, why don't you shut the hell up, unless you've got some answers for us? You know; from all your de-tect-ing work."

Ed Heisen frowned, taken back by the animosity in the normally laconic police sergeant. The guy must have been getting his ass kicked by his boss. He held up his hands. "Okay, sorry." Heisen motioned to the forensics guys moving about in the next room. "What have you got: another carbonized corpse?"

Amos lips compressed, but he led the detective into the kitchen. Heisen smelled the odor that was becoming too familiar to him – ozone. Amos pointed to the corner.

Heisen winced. "Christ."

The body, or partial body was laid out on the floor – the arms and legs were nothing but ash outlines, to the shoulders and hips, where the body was intact again. The head was still attached, but gruesomely, one eye, the ears and the nose were gone – seared away, but black and cauterized. As usual, there was no sign of blood, as if something had snap-burnt the limbs and facial features away.

"Well?" Amos went down on one knee, and swept his hand over the body. "C'mon, tell me what you think?"

Heisen crouched beside Amos to study the woman, or what was left of her. Mid-seventies, cheap cotton dress in need of a clean, nothing of value on her. Her hair was wiry and gray, and looked like it needed a wash. But it was her face that drew his attention – even though one eye, the nose and ears had been removed, he could see the mix of pain and fear still imprinted there.

"Torture."

"Jesus Christ!" Amos jumped as the word floated in from behind them. Heisen spun to see the tall black-clad agent standing behind him, towering over them. His eyes moved over the old woman's remains. He squatted beside Amos, not apologizing for startling the old cop. Amos swallowed, and shook his head, turned back to the crime scene.

"Who are you?" asked Heisen.

"Call me Monroe," said the big man. He clasped his hands together on his knees. "In Iraq, we lost a man on a mission. When we finally found him... recovered his body, his bones had been broken, starting at the fingers and toes, the impact trauma moving slowly up to his hips and shoulders. Would have taken hours... been agony."

Heisen grunted. "I've seen that before as well – on the poor saps the Columbian drug gangs had their fun with. Pretty vicious stuff... especially to an old lady." Heisen looked across at him and nodded. "Detective Heisen."

The big man looked at him for a moment, then nodded. He

got to his feet, and yelled over his shoulder. "Carter, got a body in here."

"Wait a minute." Amos frowned and turned. "Tortured?" He pointed at the partial corpse. "Agnes Silberman, seventy-seven, with arthritis in both hips and chronic diabetes. She's on the freakin' pension and lives by herself. Why the fuck would someone want to torture her? What the hell has this old lady got that someone would do that to her for?"

Heisen, still crouching, looked at the dry scabbing on the wounds. "What has she got? Maybe not money, maybe nothing... or maybe she had information."

Another agent, Heisen assumed it was Carter, entered with a box case and immediately set to work sampling the air, examining the body, and even slicing away some of her skin at her arm's cauterization line. He pulled out a probe, and lifted an edge of her dress. He let it drop, and then examined the ground beside her, leaning in close to a small outline pressed into one of the ash pipes that used to be a leg. He turned to Monroe. "Got something." He reached into his bag, pulled out a small can, shook it, and then sprayed something that foamed up onto the small indentation. After a second it changed color and settled flat. He carefully lifted it out, and dusted off the excess ash. Carter stood and showed it to Monroe. Amos and Heisen tried to see around him. Monroe looked at it, his eyes narrowing. He waved it away. "Bag it."

Amos squinted at the object as Carter placed it into a small clear envelope. "Is that a footprint?"

Heisen nodded. "Looks like one... if you're about three feet tall."

"Kid maybe?" Amos responded, eyes following the bag as Carter took it back to the case he's brought in with him.

Heisen shrugged. "Sure it is, and why not. Some kid with a laser. You can get all kinda shit on eBay these days."

Monroe glared at them both.

"Boss."

Monroe's head whipped around at the sound of the voice.

"Yo." He turned back briefly to Carter. "Finish up." Monroe left the room.

Carter was down low, waving a small box around. He pointed it at Mrs. Silberman's ruined corpse. Heisen knelt beside him.

"Weird shit, huh?" Heisen said.

Carter grunted, keeping his eyes on the small box. Heisen looked over his shoulder, and decided to try his luck. He nodded towards the small box. "Pretty unusual readings."

Carter grunted again, staying focused on the small illuminated screen. "Got that right. At least we identified it – xenon."

"Xenon? That's the weird stuff used in flash lamps isn't it?" Heisen looked back at Mrs. Silberman.

Carter shook his head. "Not this type. This is 135. Normally Xenon is a gas that occurs in the Earth's atmosphere. Consists of about eight stable isotopes, and five times that many unstable ones – pretty normal stuff. But 135 is different; it's not naturally occurring. Used as the propellant for ion thrusters in spacecraft, it's a neutron absorber in nuclear reactors, and is usually the result of nuclear fission. Nope, Xenon-135 should not be here at all."

Heisen stood. "Like I said; weird shit."

Heisen turned to Amos, grabbed him by the arm and led him out of the room. "Hey, have you looked in the other apartments yet?"

Amos shook his head. "Next thing on the list."

"Good." Heisen let him go. "One more thing; anything else weird in here?"

Amos frowned.

"Burn marks in odd places maybe?" Heisen asked.

Amos' frown unlocked. "Oh yeah, in the bathroom. Looks like the old bat set fire to something – big black oval on the wall."

* * *

Monroe stood with Felzig in the bathroom. There was a three-foot black scorch mark on the wall under the sink. Felzig turned and raised her eyebrows, holding out the small reader in her hands. Monroe exhaled. "Let me guess, gamma off the scale, and more traces of Xenon 135." She nodded. Carter and Benson joined them, and Monroe turned to Carter. "What could have done that?"

Carter shook his head. "We've got HEL tech mounted on our destroyers. Those High Energy Lasers work at around a hundred kilowatts – that'd do it. Also some industrial lasers, but they're not portable." He shrugged. "Bottom line; nothing we've got."

Monroe stared back out into the hallway. "Well, someone or something is coming in and out, with some pretty high tech… and given what they did to the old woman, seems they're here to play hardball." Monroe turned away. "We can do that too."

* * *

In the apartment down the hall, Heisen went quickly from room to room, stopping at one littered with packing tape and brown paper. On the debris strewn table sat an unsent package. He spun it around and read the label – Professor Matt Kearns. He ripped it open.

"Alas poor Yorick." He lifted out the skull, holding the brown relic up in his hands. He smiled. "Nice to finally meet you the elusive, Mr. Klaus."

Heisen put the skull down and dug deeper into the package, finding an envelope addressed to the professor. He tore it open and quickly scanned it. There was a brief introduction from Klaus, and then description of his find – a complete Neanderthal skeleton, plus one other item. Heisen frowned remembering the picture of Doris Sömmer holding the small metallic device. "One other item, hmm?"

He turned slowly in the small room. There was a dark scar on the far wall. The curtains hanging beside it had been seared away in a perfect facsimile of the oval burn. Heisen looked back at the letter in his hands. It was signed 'K' and had a single mobile phone number at the bottom.

He pulled out his phone and dialed. It answered after the first ring.

"Hello Klaus."

~8~

It took Heisen most of the day and a dozen calls to convince the young man he was who he said he was. But eventually Klaus relented, and… spoke. The kid sounded at near mad panic stage, and after hearing about his girlfriend, he was close to disappearing for good.

Heisen wanted to meet with Klaus. He sat on a park bench, waiting for his phone to ring. He looked up at the sky, watching the clouds lengthen and fragment, and he turned his focus inward, sorting through what he knew in his mind. Klaus and Doris had found something in Germany – a Neanderthal skeleton and something else, as yet undetermined. The kid wouldn't give him any details over the phone, but confirmed they found something strange entombed with the fossil – something that didn't belong there.

Now, the girl was dead, many of the scientists that Klaus had sent bits of the skeleton to were dead, and his landlady was dead… and added to that, she died horribly. It was a trail a mile wide, and leading straight to Mr. Klaus Hoffman.

If the group had just been hit over the head, or stabbed or shot, Heisen might conclude they were only after the skeleton. A find that one museum expert suggested could be worth half a million. Big money, especially considering you could get someone whacked for a measly fifty bucks these days.

But the way the murders were executed defied belief. Forensic analysis and the subsequent Coroner's report said that the incineration reached temperatures in excess of two thousand three hundred degrees. And the concentration meant that it was consistent with some sort of high intensity laser. But one that left no burn residue, just a nice neat cauterization.

Nobody had any idea what type of device or weapon was used – even one from the military's research and development arsenals. And the kicker was the throwaway comment by the Coroner – out of this world, she said, as she closed the book on the Sömmer girl's inquest.

"Out of this world." Heisen repeated softly.

He jumped when the phone rang in his hand. "Shit." He quickly jammed it against his ear.

"Detective Edward Heisen." There was a pause.

"It's me."

Heisen breathed a sigh of relief at hearing the young man's fear filled voice. "Hi Klaus. How you doing?"

Several seconds of silence greeted his question, and Heisen thought he would ring off. But there came an intake of breath, a clearing of the throat and then Klaus came back on.

"Not good."

"We can help you," Heisen responded automatically.

"Bullshit. No one can. There's fucking little people after me… and they can walk right through the walls."

Heisen squeezed the phone as he concentrated. "What do you mean by little people?"

"I'm not mad." Klaus said softly.

"I know you're not. In fact I believe you. Tell me where you are, son." Heisen felt he was holding his breath.

The silence stretched again. "Wilson Street… number seventeen. Third floor, apartment 3B. It's an old brownstone."

Heisen knew the area, and told him so. "It'll take me twenty minutes to get to you. Stay inside and keep the doors locked."

"Are you shitting me? I'm never going outside again." Klaus rung off.

* * *

Heisen pulled in to the curb and sat for a moment as he examined the dark brown building on Wilson Street.

"Little people," he said to the windscreen as he searched for anything out of the ordinary in the building's third floor windows. "Fucking little people."

If he'd had the conversation in an Irish bar he would have got the joke. But the weird oval burn holes, the even weirder way people were being killed, and the tiny footprints left behind in Mrs. Silberman's ash outline – those tiny, perfect footprints – he

154

didn't think it was a kid for a second. The foot was too narrow – like an adult's, but much smaller. Something was seriously weird and it was no joke.

"Little people," he said again softly and then snorted. "Little fucking people with laser guns, executing our citizens." He laughed out loud. "Haven't had a drop to drink, Chief… honest."

He pushed out of the car, checked his gun and then sprang lightly up the several flights of stairs to 3B on the third floor. Heisen knocked once and immediately stood to the side – old habits die hard, especially after you've seen half a dozen hollow nose slugs tear through a door dead centre in response to the old *open up, it's the police* request.

Heisen waited. There was movement inside.

"Who is it?" whispered from behind the door.

Heisen stayed with his back against the wall. "Detective Heisen, Klaus. Lemme in."

"How do I know it's you?" Klaus' voice was high and tight with fear.

Heisen groaned and resisted the urge to swear, deciding instead to cut the kid some slack given he still sounded scared shitless. "Klaus, we just spoke twenty minutes ago…" He lowered his voice. "… about the little people."

A bolt slid back, and then what sounded like packing tape being ripped from around the frame. The door opened a crack, the security chain still hanging in place. The eye ran him up and down, and the door closed for a second, to be immediately pulled back open.

Heisen guessed he looked enough like a cop to pass the test. He stepped inside. A pale youth stood in the muted darkness wearing a stained t-shirt, jeans and bare feet. His eyes looked sunken – the kid needed some hot food and about a week's sleep.

Heisen quickly looked him over for weapons – old habits again. He sniffed; the place stunk of body odour, cigarettes and mildew.

Klaus half smiled. "It's not much, but it's home."

Heisen smiled and nodded, letting the kid unwind.

Klaus motioned to a formica table and chairs. "I'd offer you a drink, but there's nothing left. I ran out of food a few days back and have been too scared to go out. Uh… do you have anything? Food I mean." Klaus asked.

Heisen shook his head. "Just some gum."

Klaus seemed to think about it for a few seconds, and then shrugged. "Okay." He held out his hand.

Heisen gave him the pack and Klaus jammed a few sticks into his mouth, chewed for a few seconds, and then swallowed the entire mass. He quickly stuffed the rest in and did the same.

Heisen sat down. "So, tell me about the little people?"

Klaus swallowed again, breathing heavily and savouring his first meal in days. He sat down heavily, and looked up with exhausted eyes.

"They're after me."

"You said that." Heisen said. "What do you think they want?"

"They want what I found." Klaus responded lethargically.

Heisen shrugged. "The skeleton – the Neanderthal – that?"

"No, no, I don't think so. I mean I did at first, but not anymore. It was what the fucking cave man had in his hand." He rummaged around in his pocket. "This… they want me because of this." He placed his fist on the table. He opened his hand.

Heisen leaned forward. It looked like a fountain pen, brushed chrome and about four inches long with a slight bulge at one end. He squinted. There seemed to be a glow coming from inside.

"It's still working." Heisen sat back.

Klaus licked his lips. "I know, and that's impossible. The matrix we dug this from was at least fifty thousand years old. Whoever, or whatever, dropped this thing was around at the time these Neanderthals were spearing mammoths on the German steppes." His mouth worked for a second or two before finally finding the words. "I don't think it came from our world."

Heisen frowned as he stared at the object. "And now they want it back."

"I've got to get rid of it. You take it." Klaus slid it across the table.

Heisen didn't move to touch it. "What does it do?"

Klaus' eyes went wide. "I don't know, and I don't fucking care. I just want to get rid of the damned thing." He lunged at Heisen. "I know… I know what it is… it's a goddamn homing device or something like that. That's why they keep finding me."

He stood so quickly his chair flipped back onto the floor. "I just need to give it back and get on with my life." He paced, wringing his hands. "But these little things came out of the wall – just walked right out of it. I held it out to them, but they freaked. I bolted, and ran into Mrs. Silberman's apartment. I… I jumped out her window and ran, and kept running." He snatched the thing up in his hand and shook his head, his eyes crushed shut. "Is… is she okay? Mrs. Silberman, I mean. I tried calling her, but a cop answered."

Heisen continued to watch the young man, not feeling any urge to tell him he got the old lady tortured and killed.

"Klaus, we'll get you to a safe house. Get someone to have a look at that device and find out exactly what it is. Maybe work out why they want it so bad."

Klaus scoffed. "A safe house? There's no such thing with these guys. Have you not been listening to me? These freaks walk through walls. I'd last about…"

"We'll have you guarded twenty-four-seven. I give you my word." Heisen shrugged. "Besides, once it's out of your possession, they'll probably lose interest, right?"

Heisen waited a few seconds. He could see the young man's mind was ticking over. He looked again at his emaciated frame. "One thing's for sure, you can't keep going like this; you'll be dead from starvation in a week."

Klaus dropped his head into his hands and rubbed the fingers hard through his shockwave of greasy hair. "Maybe I'd be better off dead." He sighed and sat back, his eyes and cheeks sunken like a shipwreck survivor.

Heisen noticed Klaus' lips were so dry they were flaking.

157

He got to his feet. "Stay here kid. I'll get you some water. Then I'll call in some back up and we can get out of here." He smiled down at the cowering youth. "First thing though, I want a doc to look at you, okay?"

Klaus nodded, resting his head back in his hands. The device remained on the table, glowing softly. Klaus stared at it as though in a trance.

Heisen pushed through the small swing door, and blew air through compressed lips at the sight of the pile of dirty dishes. The congealed food smelt like a blocked drain. He'd seen worse; one guy had drowned his cat in the sink, and then hung himself. After a week, they found him… and the cat. By then, the animal had turned into feline porridge and they needed HazMat suits to even get near it.

Heisen guessed there were no clean cups, so grabbed one with the least amount of crap buildup and rinsed it out – he doubted a bit of extra bacteria was gonna kill the kid now. He turned the water off and froze. The rim of the swing door glowed, and the smell of ozone filled the air. He stared at it, confused for a second or two, half cup of water still in his hand.

It took him a few more seconds to guess what might be happening. He gently lowered the cup to the bench-top, crossed to the door and eased it open a crack. Klaus stood, arms up, as if surrendering to someone. He gibbered for a second or two, shaking his head until a tiny shaft of light struck him. The kid glowed for a moment, before falling backwards. Before he even hit the ground, his body was collapsing into dust.

"Fuck!" Heisen felt a shock run through him from his toes to his scalp. He pulled his Glock, sucked in a breath and kicked the door open, immediately diving and rolling. He came up fast, shooting at multiple targets. He missed.

A golden beam came out of nowhere, slicing through his shoulder and taking his arm. Then it all went to shit.

Monroe held up a fist. Behind him Raptor, Harper, Benson, Carter and Felzig froze and waited, focused just on him. They had cut the power to the building, throwing the old brownstone into darkness. Now each had L-3 Warrior night vision goggles pulled down over their eyes.

Monroe turned, his four red eyes taking in his team. He nodded, and then turned back to the door. Its outline was clean and green-lit by the NVGs. They were the latest tech, with two lenses pointed forward like traditional goggles, giving him his hunter's depth perception, while two more tubes pointed slightly outward from the center to increase his peripheral view, allowing Monroe and his team to more quickly move through the OODA loop – Observe, Orient, Decide, Act – in a few seconds.

Monroe pointed two fingers at his team – Raptor moved fast, attaching a shaped charge to the door in a large 'X' pattern. Then he attached a silver sheet from the top that unfurled covering the door – they wanted the entire wooden frame to be obliterated, out of their way, and most of the percussive blast to enter the room for maximum disorientation. Felzig had the EMP disc in her hand, rotated it, lights on its outside counting down as she slid it under the door.

Both agents got behind the wall to take cover. Monroe held up a hand, fingers splayed, and counted down, one finger at a time. He reached one and signaled the assault.

Raptor triggered the breaching charge. The door exploded inwards. Monroe and his five-strong team charged in, their laser sights quickly finding the small goblin-like creatures scattering in the darkness. There would be no attempt to communicate, no compromise, no hostages. These things had come here to kill – brutally – Monroe's agents, the Defense, would return the favor.

Monroe counted at least fifteen moving bodies when they came through, in seconds they had halved that amount, even though the creatures seemed to be wearing body armor and moved agilely and quickly, like a cross between wolverines and deformed children.

Raptor took the centre of the room, gun up and spitting rounds into the smoke-filled darkness, his laser sight picking out bodies, and his unerring aim just as quickly putting them down.

Then it all changed. There came a high pitched squeal from out of the dark, and then a yellow beam shot out to touch Raptor. The big man froze as a hole the size of a dinner plate opened in the front of his body. There was no wet-matter dispersal, and no projectile follow-through, just an enormous hole burned clean through that didn't even bleed. The big man fell backwards like a tree.

Carter targeted the shooter, following its nimble movements as it scurried from position to position. But from his three o'clock another beam shot out. This time there was no clean hole. Monroe watched as Carter's entire body shimmered where the golden beam touched and stayed on him. The man simply collapsed into a mound of powder before Monroe's eyes.

Monroe had to dive and roll as more of the deadly beams criss-crossed the room. He stopped with his back to an upturned table.

"Go to full auto," he roared and dived again, flicking the selector switch on his rifle and firing back at the source of the beams. Around him, his remaining agents changed up their delivery, moving out of the OODA loop, and into a lethal spray mode – the intermittent coughs of the silenced weapons became a staccato beat as high velocity rounds punched through anything they touched.

The Defense backed up, keeping each other out of the crossfire, targeting anything below waist level. Beams and bullets crossed in the small room. Monroe felt like they were fighting a pack of high tech furies, so ferocious were the small beings in their resistance.

He saw Felzig go down on one knee to reload. Like magic, one of the small creatures appeared beside her in the smoke and pointed a small device up at her. She spun, but before she could react further, her face took the small beam front-on. Her entire head simply vanished, leaving a stump of neck seared dry. She stayed upright for a second or two, the arms dropping and then her body toppling sideways.

Monroe's teeth clenched, feeling the fury ball in his chest. He liked Felzig. He'd *fucked* Felzig. She was a tough woman, an insatiable alley cat in the bedroom, and a tigress in the field. Now, she had simply ceased to exist – no scream of pain, no bleeding bullet wound or loud explosion, just a golden rod of light, and then... gone.

From his position, Monroe saw a small figure disappear into the shimmering doorway at the end of the room. The three foot glowing oval was fixed to an external wall, and inside looked to be a long horizontal tunnel. Given there was a three-story drop on the other side of the wall, this doorway had to lead to somewhere other than a Berlin street. Monroe remembered his initial code call – Non Terrestrial Incursion.

"And you guys sure ain't going home." He lifted his gun, sighted on the shimmering doorway and fired into it, emptying his magazine. Horns blared from somewhere deep inside it, and the portal snapped shut with a rush of charged air. "Fuck you. The rest of you are mine." He ejected the empty magazine and snapped in another, yelling over his shoulder as he scanned the carnage in the room.

"Agents, count off."

From out of the dark, Benson and Harper yelled in return. Monroe waited, the smoke was settling, a broken window creating a small draft of clear air. There was a tinkle of falling glass, the soft sound of dripping water or blood, and soft moans of pain from the downed beings. He held his breath. Silence settled around him.

He slowly pulled off his night vision goggles and blinked once, his eyes quickly adjusting to the semi-gloom. In his peripheral vision he detected a tiny movement, and snapped around to fire a single round at the small figure, as it tried to improve its position in relation to him.

His bullet blew it off its feet, spinning it doll-like across the floor to land face down on the debris-strewn carpet.

161

"Cover."

Harper and Benson came up behind Monroe, facing away from him, scanning the room for movement. Monroe knelt to examine the creature. He kicked its weapon away, placed one huge boot on its back and pressed down. It groaned. They were small, the same size as a three year old, but slim and perfectly formed. A helmet was pulled down over its face, and even though it looked to be wearing some sort of body armor, he saw that it was no match for the slug that had obliterated its shoulder.

He used the barrel of his gun to turn it over – it groaned again. He reached out and lifted the visor off its head. There was a rush of weird smelling air, and then a face from a nightmare. Monroe grimaced – it looked like a hairless, deformed child, with no nose, large eyes and small shovel-like teeth. The skin looked transparent with pumping veins pushing dark blood into a large pulsating brain inside its potato-shaped head. It glared at him with a boiling hatred and revulsion that Monroe had never experienced before in his life.

One handed, he lifted the small being and stared into its face. His own features twisted in disgust. "What the fuck are you?"

There came a disgusted noise from the back of its throat and it bared its teeth. The eyes still burned into his own.

"Yeah, feelings mutual, buddy." Monroe pointed the big gun at its face. "Got something for you from Felzig – open wide."

The small being began to smirk and reached up with its remaining good arm to punch a button on its belt.

"I'm Jax. Die, Gimp. It's clean up time," it hissed at him.

Monroe's eyebrows shot up. "So, you can talk."

A blinding light engulfed the small smashed body, then Monroe, then Benson and Harper, the room, and then the entire building. In another moment there was just a crater where the brownstone had stood for fifty years.

* * *

A month later, Detective Heisen sat in a taxi across the road from the empty lot where the brownstone used to be. His eyes were glazed.

"What do you want to do, buddy."

"Huh?" Heisen blinked at the sound of the driver's voice. "Give me a minute." He got out and crossed the road to stand at a line of police tape still strung across the sidewalk – he didn't know what it was there for – there were no clues, there never was to begin with. There was nothing to see, and nothing to steal – nada, zero, zip – case closed.

He flipped up the tape and ducked under, groaning as the back-brace cut into his waist. He was out of work, pensioned off at thirty-eight – a one armed detective, with several separated discs in his back from the blast that had thrown him out the window that night. The injuries, along with the potential therapy for the rest of his life, wasn't exactly Officer of the Year material. His former squad hadn't been real supportive. *That's the guy who saw hobbits, elves, leprechauns*, they'd sniggered. Well, fuck 'em all. His curse turned into a groan; his salad days had turned to boiled cabbage nights in the blink of an eye.

Heisen walked in to stand in the centre of the vacant lot. Beneath his feet, pumic-like material crunched. The boffins had told him the bricks, the steel, everything, had been super-heated to a point of molecular transformation. He looked up, trying to judge where he had fallen from, trying to remember what happened; what was real and what was the result of impacting with a sidewalk after a thirty-foot fall. He lifted his stump, staring for a moment. A gas explosion had been the official explanation. A gas explosion that had been as hot as a sun had neatly cut away his arm and cauterized the wound so cleanly that an industrial laser could not have been so efficient.

Heisen blew air through compressed lips. Nothing left but ghosts and memories. The agents, the Defense they had called themselves, had all vanished in the blast, as well as the tiny creatures he knew existed. For all his digging, no reference to the special agents, to the tiny beings, to Klaus, or to the case was on file anywhere. Even Sergeant Amos had been reassigned, and wouldn't take his calls. Someone way above even his superintendent's pay grade had shut this down and zipped it up so tight that even thinking about it was a dismissible offence.

This case had been buried and him along with it. No loose ends, nothing to see here, move along folks, and enjoy your new life as a crippled ex-detective, Mr. Heisen.

The cab honked and he turned to wave. But there was something they all forgot. He used to be a detective, and a damned good one. Agent Carter had said there was a strange radiation present. Xenon-135 he had called it. He had an in-law that worked for the university in the physics lab. If anyone could trace Xenon-135, it would be her, and if that material turned up again, then he was going to be there, waiting.

After all, everyone knows that if you capture a leprechaun it's good luck. He'd be waiting all right.

A Tide of Flesh

Jeff Hewitt

I was torn from the ethereal green fields of England and slammed back into the heathen sweat of India by the sound of musket fire and screaming. I thrashed against the mosquito nets as I sat up.

"Lieutenant Crawford!" One of the ensigns – I had yet to learn his name – stood outside my tent. I peered at him through the mask of nets. His features seemed distorted in the growing light of morning. "What in bloody... What is going on?" I demanded.

"I... uh... Captain Dartmouth. We request your presence—"

"You bloody moron! Fetch me Sergeant Stuart and get the hell out!"

"Y-Yes, sir!" The ensign fled with due haste and I took the opportunity to dress. The sound of combat made my fingers clumsy. As I tied my stock, Stuart appeared.

"Yes, *sor!*"

"What the hell is everyone firing at?"

"Enemies at the walls, *sor.*"

"Have they brought up guns or attempted to scale the walls?"

"No, *sor.*

"Who are they? Whose men?"

"We haven't been able to determine that, *sor.* It's still dark out."

I pulled on my leather boots and slung my sword. Last, I checked my pistol and pulled the hammer to half cock.

"Join me on the wall, Sergeant." I walked through the parade ground of our wooden frontier-fort and climbed a ladder to the fire steps.

"Hold fire," I ordered.

"Hold your bloody fire!" yelled Sergeant Stuart. He whacked a few privates with his halberd, yelling until there was relative quiet on the walls. The light of the torches flickered, pushing against the dark. When the powder-smoke cleared, I spotted a handful of corpses in the ditch surrounding the fort. A few men still shambled around the glacis of piled dirt abutting the ditch. They didn't move like normal soldiers. They didn't come in waves; they didn't run for cover; and they didn't scream or yell challenges. They just... walked about, as if on a stroll.

"Sergeant, has their disposition been like this the whole time?"

"Aye, *sor*. They spooked the boys, but they ain't been at the walls like they mean it," he said.

I scanned my surroundings. "Sergeant, where's Captain Griffin?"

Stuart made a show of checking the muskets of some of the men on the walls.

"Sergeant, where is he?"

Stuart looked supremely uncomfortable. One of the privates finally spoke up; a tall man with a wicked scar that ran the length of the right side of his face from forehead to jaw line. "Buggered off 'e 'as. No good for anythin', that git."

The sergeant whirled to give the private a hide tearing, but I stopped Stuart short. "It's okay for him to speak freely in this case, Sergeant." I turned to the private. "When did he leave?"

"Soon as they was spotted, sir. Took a look over the wall and was off on the first 'orse 'e came to," the private said.

I shook my head.

"Bloody yellow bastard," muttered a nearby private..

I gave the man a sharp look then pulled Sergeant Stuart aside. "Is this true? He deserted?"

"Aye, *sor*."

"Is there anyone else? Any senior officers?"

"Just Captain McKee, with the dragoons, *sor*."

"Christ," I said. Stuart nodded. I looked over the wall again; the men stumbled into the ditch and piled up, shuffling about and wandering aimlessly. "What the hell are they doing?"

Just as I spoke, there was a rush of small bodies that moved with eerie rapidity. I drew my sword and pistol as the first wave rushed over the top of the wall.

The creatures were monkeys of all shapes and description, and rotten to a one. Their bodies were disgusting bags of dripping fluids, clotted blood, and matted hair. Their eyes, when they were present, either bulged grotesquely or were a creamy, blind white. Their dirty-yellow teeth were bared in a hateful grimace. They swarmed up and over and attacked the men, leaping onto backs and chests. They pulled hair, bit at throats and exposed skin, tried to gouge out eyes, and tore at the men with jagged nails.

One of the stinking beasts leapt onto my back. I tried to cut at the bastard with my saber but couldn't get a good angle on him. Crazy scenes of carnage whirled past my vision as I tried to get the shrieking monster off. Men grabbed monkeys from their friends and crushed those heinous heads beneath hobnailed boots.

Sergeant Stuart whirled his halberd in a cyclone of steel and crushed bodies. Monkeys stuffed my men's eyeballs, nerves and all, into their gaping mouths and leaped about like madness manifest. Men unlucky enough to lose eyes and limbs rolled on the ground, screaming in puddles of blood as the beasts feasted on their flesh.

I dropped my saber and reached over my shoulder and grabbed the monkey. Small bones snapped beneath my fingers, and the flesh came away in a stinking patch, releasing a horrible stench that burned down my throat. I dragged the monkey free. The rotten simian shrieked in my face and raked my cheeks with its nails. Pistol now in hand, I shoved the barrel into its midsection and pulled the trigger. The hammer snapped forward and a fountain of gore blasted out the back of the devil. I threw the corpse over the wall, grabbed my saber from the floor, and laid about myself. I slashed at the beasts attacking my men, chopping off little heads and furry limbs in a pattering rainfall of ripe organs and decayed bones.

After what seemed an eternity, the monkeys were beaten back – little backs snapped and heads burst under musket butts. Men who had lost their weapons during the melee literally tore the monsters apart with their bare hands. When the last beast was thrown back over the wall, the men cheered their victory.

I was soaked in black, clotted blood and bits of offal. Sergeant Stuart was the vision of Death himself. The only bit of him that didn't drip with blood or gore was his eyes, which were wide, red, and angry. At that moment I think he could have killed a man or tiger with a mere look. He raised his bloody halberd above his head and roared:

"Take more than monkeys to put our lads in the ground!"

A cheer rose around him.

I wiped my saber clean and sheathed it at my side. When the cheering died down, I motioned to Stuart. "Good fighting, Sergeant. Get the men ready for another assault. Muskets primed, bayonets set."

Stuart nodded and yelled orders.

The sound of the bayonets snapping into their locks as one thrilled me. I had never before been in a battle such as this – a desperate fight in close quarters. I found I rather liked it, but I had my doubts about command. Captain Griffin was a veteran, had regaled us many nights in the officers' mess with tales of his combat prowess. To make such a man flee… I shook my head.

I walked the parapets to take stock of the wounded and killed. We'd lost several men to blindness – their eyes punctured or even torn out. Many more had severe bites that left bloody crescents oozing languid blood. The dead were taken to the fort chapel until we could give them a proper ceremony.

As I walked the wall, the enemy shambled into view. *My God, there's thousands.* We were completely surrounded. A cold chill stabbed through me. How would we ever defend against such a numerous enemy?

I schooled my face, showed no outward sign of my fear as that would only serve to panic the men – they were worried enough by the attack and the desertion of our captain. I made light talk with the ensigns, to let everyone know I was in command. I inspected muskets and personal weapons; made sure each bayonet was sharp and well-attached. These men were ready for a fight. I came to the last little stretch of wall and found the big Scottish captain of the dragoons.

Captain McKee was a huge, handsome man. He wore a full, black beard, despite the tradition and regulations that dragoons be clean-shaven. His eyes sparkled with deadly mirth, and the carbine he was aiming over the wall as I approached looked like a toy in his hands. The carbine roared, spat fire, and one of the enemies in the ditch fell, pierced right through the head. A small mound of bodies testified to his accuracy.

"Ha! I haven't had this much fun since Assaye!" The big man laughed as he reloaded his carbine.

"Captain McKee, sir!"

He turned to me. "You can call me Robert. I think the circumstances rather allow it."

"Yes sir… er, Robert. I want to formally offer you command of the infantry, being the most senior commander, and in light of your—"

McKee held up a hand to cut me off. "Nay, Nick. Keep your infantry. I'm a cavalryman and would nay know what to do with your men. Not properly."

"Thank you, Robert." I stepped close. "May I come to you for advice? I've never… that is, never had the command, to…"

"Never led men in combat. Aye, I know. Yes, of course you can ask for my help. Given the situation," he said, with a wave of his hand towards the walls, "I think you may end up relying on yourself more than you think anyway." He turned back to the wall and fired off another shot. A body fell into the ditch. He grinned. "If we've got enough shot and they decide to keep up the ducks in a pond act, I think we'll do rather well."

"I estimate they number in the thousands. We have plenty of shot and powder, but not enough to kill every man in an army."

McKee turned a critical eye to the men piling into the ditch. "Every side about the same?"

"Yes, sir. Robert."

He nodded. "Aye, I agree, then. Probably a few thousand so far." He looked thoughtful. "I'll take me lads out and have a look. Get the full scope of the enemy's disposition."

"We'll make sure the gate is clear. Which do you want to use?"

"The south gate. I gather the enemy is mostly coming from the north?"

I nodded.

"Good, then the south it is. They'll be lightest there." McKee hurried down the ladder and into the parade ground. "Dragoons! Form up, lads! We're ridin'!"

I pulled more men towards the southern side of the redoubt – two hundred in all. Sergeant Stuart joined me.

"Infantry, form line!"

They ordered themselves into two rigid lines.

"Shoulder arms!"

Two hundred muskets came up.

"Fire!"

Two hundred muskets spoke, roaring with voices of fire. A line of men outside the walls shook and fell apart. Musket balls blasted off limbs, gore showered into the air, and as the powder-smoke cleared, only a few crawled along the ground or clawed at the air. Two hundred men reloaded and prepared another volley.

"Ho! Dragoons, out!" The dragoons swung into their saddles and rode out of the fort and into the darkness of the Indian night. The guards fired a few shots as the enemy approached the gate and then pulled it shut.

I paced the wall, trying to see through the gloaming. A distant popping of musket fire; the clash of steel; screams of men. The enemy shuffled towards the sounds in the gathering night, seemingly attracted to the noise. When the outriders grew quiet – I assumed on reconnaissance – the enemy near the walls returned their attention to us.

A quick patrol of the walls and the enemy was still pouring in on three sides: north, east, and west. They were wandering into the south ditch but not at near the same rate as the other sides. They were packed in tight, some trampled by their comrades.

A pounding of many hooves racing for the fort got my attention. The patrol was coming back!

"Open the gate!" I yelled down. The guards obeyed and the dragoons thundered through. Captain McKee was at the back, following one of his men who dragged an enemy soldier behind him on a rope.

I ran down to the parade ground. McKee stepped down from the saddle and unbuckled his helmet.

"What did you see?"

His face was grim. "Bloody thousands. It's hard to get an accurate count, of course. It's dark, but my God… must be over a hundred thousand. You've got a great bleeding horde around the fort, thick as flies, and more coming in from the north in droves. They're not in formations; they're just coming on. We couldn't reach the head of their column. It's just too far, and they're too scattered. And there's something else…" he nodded towards the prisoner.

The men were formed in a circle around the enemy. They jeered and baited him, throwing rocks and punches. McKee shoved some men aside and we took in the captive.

On the surface, he was indistinguishable from the thousands of the sultanate's troops. Dark skinned, light-colored robes, and boots of fine leather. His manner, however, was nothing less than demonic. He growled and tugged at the rope, trying to reach any man he could. His skin and uniform were dirty, almost as though he had clawed his way out of a grave.

"Look, Nick! His chest!" McKee pointed.

I felt the blood drain from my face. "Those look like musket wounds," I said.

McKee drew his cavalry saber, heavier than my own, and stepped forward. The man lunged at McKee, but was brought up short by the rope. McKee swung downward – a brutal stroke – audibly shattering the prisoner's knee. When the monster went down, McKee chopped again, breaking its back. Yet, it gave no yell of pain, no scream at having its bones broken. It lay on the ground, clawing at the air, and slobbered with eager mouth at the big Scottish captain.

McKee put his boot on the creature's throat, for it was no man. Now that it was on the ground and relatively still, the wounds that should have killed it long ago were obvious. Two big musket-ball holes pierced its chest, and gray bones were exposed from where it had been dragged along the ground. The eyes held no spark – soulless.

"It's a demon," I said.

McKee nodded, gripped his saber with both hands then drove it with brutal strength through the creature's skull. It shuddered as thick black blood welled up around the shining steel. The blade was wrenched out with a scream of steel on bone. The creature finally lay still.

McKee wiped his sword on the dead man's robe. "Aye, 'tis a demon. But demons die, same as men," he said.

Those men who had born witness to the kill muttered prayers, to God or any divine being that might listen. They would take help from wherever it came.

I pulled McKee aside. "How do we fight such an army? Is it the dead of India in its entirety?"

"I don't know, lad. With the men, with our guns and swords, with our lives, if need be."

"But... how many men have we killed?" I thought of the monkeys. "And beasts?"

"The butcher's bill may be more than we can pay, lad," said McKee. "But we'll send him home with bulging pockets all the same."

A sudden volley of musketry from the eastern wall seized our attention. Sergeant Stuart was already running along the wall towards the men who were frantically re-loading. "What the hell do you—"

A guttural roar shattered the night.

Two huge, dark shapes clawed over the wall and leapt at the line of soldiers. The men scattered, screamed, as the beasts growled, bit, and slashed with long, wicked claws.

Soldiers leapt from the wall, risking broken limbs as the monsters cleared the fire steps.

"Tigers," said McKee in a voice filled with both awe and dread.

My own throat turned dry and hot as we watched the tigers chase the last of the men off the fire step. Sergeant Stuart, madman that he was, stood at the south-east corner screaming a challenge to the beasts. One of the tigers, terrifying in its speed and ferocity, rushed the man and his whirling halberd.

The other tiger preferred the prospect of a chase, and left the string of dead and dying men on the wall to pursue those in the parade ground. It took a graceful leap and landed on a man, snapping his back and tearing out his throat in one fluid motion.

It roared, and the blood of dead men poured from its mouth.

The sight of it bearing a man to the ground shook me from my stupor. I drew my saber and yelled above the noise of battle. "To me! Form a line!"

My voice cut through the din. Men ran to me. I grabbed some stragglers and dragged them into the line, forming up near the south gate, twenty or so men, when the tiger in the courtyard took notice of us. It dropped the man it was shaking and roared again, baring its exposed ribs and rippling shoulder muscles.

It had no skin, no organs. It had been shot and skinned and left for dead. I had no time to wish the hunters had thought to take the teeth and claws.

It charged.

"Aim! Fire!" I yelled at the men, signaling with my saber.

A roar of musketry blasted the charging beast, tearing exposed muscle and shattering ribs. It checked the tiger's charge but a little, breaking its stride but failing to stop it.

"Receive charge!"

The men in the thin front rank dropped to one knee and drove the butts of their muskets into the ground. Their bayonets formed a glittering wall of steel.

The tiger crashed into them at a run, roaring, claws slashing. A dozen bayonets pierced it, releasing torrents of blood, both fresh and rotten. The animal howled as it seized a man and dragged him, screaming, into its waiting jaws.

I ran to the tiger's side and hacked its back with my saber. My arm shook from the impact as its spine shattered. Its back legs sank to the ground, but it continued savaging its victim, shredding flesh. I reared back and with a desperate yell, brought down my saber again and severed the spine completely. My third blow took it just behind its head.

The beast crumpled to the ground, the dead man hanging from its jaws.

The second beast fell with a thud beside us. Dead.

Sergeant Stuart called down from the parapet. "I put down your cat, Lieutenant. It were a bit bitey!"

I gaped at the sergeant – this man who had fought a tiger single-handed on the wall. His halberd was covered in gore, and the man looked like he'd been bathing in the leftovers of a butcher's shop.

"Sergeant Stuart! If you prefer to take care of the rest of our enemies, please feel so inclined!" I called back.

"*Sor*, arrangements could be made!"

The men laughed – it felt good to be alive.

Blasts of musketry sounded from the north wall, and then from the east and west. I ran up to the fire step and looked out. The wandering dead, previously aimless, now seemed purposeful, as if lead by an unknown force. They scrabbled at the walls, attempting to breach the fort. It was a grisly sight: rotten limbs coming apart on the raw timbers; bloat bursting under the pressure. And as they swarmed, they trampled one another under foot.

They were building a ladder of their dead.

I hurried along the wall; it was the same at each point: a slowly building ramp of dead; organs bursting and oozing in the moat. The night had been loud before: the roar of tigers; the shrieking of monkeys, now... near silence, bar the raspy scrambling of the dead.

A wind kicked up, and with it the stench of dead long-decayed. The men trembled on the walls. I walked among them, touching shoulders, whispering quietly, and did what I could to reassure them.

The morning would bring no relief, I feared. We could not send out runners now: we were fully surrounded. There was no way to make contact with the nearby town for reinforcements from their garrison. In fact, a steady trickle of the enemy was moving that way – their purposeful shuffle could be maintained all day.

I feared we were lost...

* * *

As dawn broke, so did Hell.

The first sliver of sun peeked over the horizon. And the first dead, finally mounting the ramparts, came over the walls.

"Fire!" I yelled.

A barrage of musket-fire tore down the first invaders, shattering bone and spraying guts. The men reloaded and fired, reloaded and fired, mechanical almost as the dead that mounted the summit and were torn down by the blasts.

It stretched on for hours. The fighting intensified as some demons breached the wall. The hand-to-hand fighting was gut-wrenching. Stabbing another man is hard enough, it's worse when he doesn't notice he should be dead and pulls the musket deeper, trying to reach you with rotten hands.

I filled breaches in the ranks, hacking at limbs and crushed bones with my saber. I wished for the heavier cavalry blade more than once.

A slight lull in the fighting brought Captain McKee to me.

"Nick!"

"Robert," I said.

"Seems we might hold after all. Your boys love a scrap!"

"So do we all, I hope. It seems long from over."

"Oh, aye, much killing to be done yet, but your boys have the stomach for it. Fighting for your life makes things more lively than in the drill yard, I reckon."

I had to laugh… until McKee's mirth faded as he looked over my shoulder to the dawn.

"What do ye make of that?" he asked.

I followed his pointed finger. A cloud of smoke was blooming on the horizon. I snapped out my own glass and peered through. My heart sank.

"Time to form up in the yard, I think." McKee nodded and hurried off as I yelled the order: "Off the walls! Form square in the yard! Form square! Now!"

Men leapt from the fire steps and hurried down the ladders, forming an orderly square in the yard. I was the last off our side of the wall, slashing and snarling at the demons snatching at me.

A thunderous crash rocked the fort.

"Roll up the artillery. Guns here, now! Hurry!" The gunners pushed the twelve-pounders into the formation and aimed them at the gates.

"Ready! Present arms!" The north face of the square drew up and leveled their muskets, the gunners waiting with leather-clad fingers and burning tapers.

Another crash and the men's muskets wavered.

"Steady men, steady!"

Another crash and the gate slammed down. A flood of demons poured through. My blood turned cold. A huge elephant pushed through the ruined gate and threw its head back, trumpeting so loud some men dropped their muskets to cover their ears. It had no tusks I could see, and it was covered in rot and putrid pus. It turned milky eyes towards us, but hatred of the living gave the dead orbs evil fire.

The demons poured around its legs and under its body, coming in a tide of rotten flesh that threatened to fill the fort.

The elephant trumpeted again and stumbled into a charge.

"Fire!" I bellowed.

The gunners put fire to touch-holes and the guns roared, thundered, and leapt back from the recoil. Two shots from the flank guns missed the elephant but left a long trail of shattered and ruptured bodies in their wake. The center gun hit dead on. The elephant's head burst like an over-ripe melon, and its guts blew out its sides. It wavered, stumbled, then fell.

The men sighed with relief and muttered prayers.

We opened fire on the remaining demons in the yard – fire, the crackling of muskets, and smoke surrounded us as those in the square battled for their lives.

Another trumpeting.

Thunderous on the air.

My heart fell.

"We killed the cow," said Sgt. Stuart, suddenly at my side. "Now we get the bull."

Another elephant appeared in the gates, straining at the small opening, cracking timbers and threatening to upset the whole wall. Demons popped beneath its feet like grapes. The stench made the gorge rise in my throat.

This monster had tusks – one broken halfway down.

Nothing we had could stop it.

"Load!" I shouted at the gunners, but they were well ahead of me, swabbing and ramming powder, their eyes wide and feverish as they prepared another volley. "Hold, men! The demons of India shall not linger!"

The guns fired, and this time they hit true.

The beast's sheer size made the cannons seem small. The flank guns tore at its guts, cracking monstrous ribs and shattering bone. Splinters flew in all directions – shrapnel that tore apart demons too close to the impact.

The center gun hit it in the chest, blowing its guts out the back and blasting rotten bits of dangling organs from the many oozing holes in its hide.

To our horror, our unthinkable, indescribable horror, it trumpeted again then lurched into a charge. The men rushed to reload before it could crash into the line – its speed was terrifying. "Fire! Load! Fire! Load!" Nothing else could save us but steady fire and discipline. The monstrous elephant bore down on us.

A trumpet call!

McKee and his dragoons burst from the smoke around the stables and charged the beast, yelling like insane banshees.

"For King and country!" McKee's voice roared over the din of battle.

The dragoons met the charging monster head on. They slashed at tendons, legs; muzzles flashed as they fired carbines and pistols into its head and sides – a ferocious and unrelenting sea of blades and bullets.

The elephant faltered; started to back up. It trumpeted in anger; slashed about with its tusks.

McKee's horse was gored and tossed through the air like a child's toy. I could only keep to my square, moving about the inside faces and checking on men, pulling some from the front ranks who were too tired to fight on, and helping haul back any dead.

The great elephant tried to rear on its back legs but the bones were too far gone and shattered under its remaining bulk. The dragoons dismounted and hacked into the beast's flanks, trying to quench the demonic fire that gave it life. I ordered the infantry to advance. I moved with the north face of the square to secure the fort walls.

We fought like demons ourselves, slashing and roaring bloody battle cries. The monsters fell beneath our steel; rancid blood burst and flowed, thick and stinking. Carnage.

Demons were ripped and gutted with twisting bayonets; heads burst by musket fire. I saw a man stomping on a little demon monster – a babe that had clawed its way out of its fighting mother's womb.

Such things no man was meant to see.

Finally, the demons were driven back and the north face of the fort secured.

We built a barricade of whatever we could find at the gate then climbed the walls again.

A ring of dead, twelve feet high, formed grisly ramps around our fort. We must have slain thousands.

And yet, and yet... the tide kept coming. But the demons now avoided our fort, as though some unknown force told them to bypass us. We'd saved our lives at some cost to the enemy. Whatever it was that drove them now knew we had teeth. The enemy could be seen for miles. We were a single tree standing against an avalanche. A single point of human sanity.

And the dead walked on.

They shambled past, oblivious to the now baking sun and the stench of rotten bodies.

I found McKee in the surgeon's tent, mending a broken arm.

"Have we stopped them, Nick?'

"For now, Robert, it seems so."

"Their disposition?"

"They avoid us, but walk on. South."

Roberts's eyes grew wide. "Towards New Birmingham."

I nodded.

"They have no walls. We must sally and harass the enemy. Someone must be sent to warn them!"

I nodded again. "The tide is coming in, Robert. We must be the sea walls."

He tried to stand but the surgeon held him back. "Sir, you're in no shape to be riding!"

McKee, covered in blood and gore, and his arm in a sling, grunted and lay back.

"We'll find a way to warn them. We must."

"We'll find a way." I walked out, worry stabbing at my bones. New Birmingham was a thriving colony town. They had only the protection of their garrison. Stout men, but with no walls.

I climbed our walls again and looked over that seething mass of dead. It was going to be worse, much worse at New Birmingham. But we would ride. We would battle the enemy, and make them fight for every shambling step.

God help us all, the demons marched on.

DEATH AT 900 METERS

Tyson Mauermann

The reticle tracked across the Iraqi landscape for what felt like the two-hundredth time this hour, searching for anything that would jeopardize the squad or their mission. So far, there'd been nothing to be concerned about, but in Fallujah, that could change in the blink of an eye. The marksman kept his M82A1 SASR rifle – his sasser – trained down range.

Sergeant Shane Hill was on his third deployment and looked forward to returning home. His long-time girlfriend, Lynn, had finally worn him down and made him commit to an engagement upon his return. In three short days, he and his platoon would rotate to the rear on their way back to Camp Lejeune, ending his tour of duty. He couldn't wait, but right now there was only the mission. One thing at a time.

The mission was simple: breach and secure the target location. The building wasn't much to look at, a strong front door with no windows on the first floor. The second floor had a few windows covered with dust, dirt, and grime. The door leading to the deck looked rotten and would likely fall apart with very little force. With luck, the unit would find a few Iraqis who the MCIA – Marine Corps Intelligence Activity – had deemed targets of opportunity. Capture if possible, kill if necessary, and get out without losing any friendlies.

The plan was to hit the target house right before sun up, only a short time away. It looked good to Shane. There was no activity in any of the surrounding buildings and the neighbor-

181

hood was quiet – perfect conditions for providing overwatch. Hill had chosen a large abandoned building to the east, knowing that as the sun rose into the sky it would be difficult for anyone to see the two-man *HOG* – Hunters Of Gunmen – team, the best of the best.

"Delta Whiskey Four to Overwatch, report," Platoon Leader Chavez called over the radio.

Hill knew Chavez was doing his best to take command of the unit. He'd just been transferred to the group, fresh from officer training. Hill guessed Chavez remained distant from the men because that's what the training manual recommended. Chavez rarely deviated from the manual.

"Delta Whiskey Seven, you're all clear," Sergeant Hill replied.

The mission was about to kick off. *Time to give the area another eyeball.* Hefting the heavy .50 caliber sniper rifle onto his shoulder and putting eyes on the target, he slowly worked his way to the left. Nothing piqued his interest; the streets as quiet as a tomb.

Hill glanced over at his partner, Lance Corporal Charles "Dog Pound" Turner, who looked through the scope on the smaller of their two rifles – an M40A5 chambered in .308. Turner surveyed the landscape with sharp eyes, looking for something to ten-ring.

Turner was a good guy to have watching your back, Shane thought, a bit of Navajo mixed with a little south of the border made for a compact man with rippling muscles and character. He was always at ease, regardless the situation. If Hill had to pick someone to be in a foxhole with, Turner was the easy choice.

Turner and Hill were on the roof of a three and a half-story dwelling disguised as a pile of shit and bricks. Five blocks from the target residence, they were roughly nine hundred meters from the target house – the tallest building in the immediate area.

If the two highly-trained and decorated snipers couldn't get the jump on the terrorists, no one could.

Hill returned to his scope and caught movement a few houses to the right of the target, on a second-story balcony. The area was dark and wouldn't see the light of day for a few hours, but something had drawn his attention.

"Overwatch to Delta Whiskey Four, you have a possible tango on your three o'clock. Watch your flank," Hill said into his comms.

"Roger that. Keep me posted if the tango advances."

Hill saw Turner move his scope to check it out.

"I don't see anything," Turner said. "You sure?"

Just then, a dark shape leapt the gap between the two adjoining balconies, little more than a blur in Hill's scope. Both snipers lifted their heads, and stared at one another.

"Overwatch to Delta Whiskey Four, tango is moving fast to your posit. Advise you secure your flank and hold."

"Delta Whiskey Seven. Repeat tango's last known position." Hill wasn't sure but it seemed as if Chavez' voice sounded a little shaky.

"Last sighting was three houses from target on your right, second floor. "

"Copy, Delta Whiskey Seven."

Through the scope, Hill could see his platoon leader snap instructions to the assault team, and he watched the men of the right flank reinforce their lines of fire preparing for the worst.

Hill moved his scope back to where the tango was last seen. He double-checked the dope, making sure that the range to target was correct. It was a waiting game; a game of which he was a master. Hill knew Turner was hot to get another kill, the fourth in the deployment. He was chasing Hill's kill record. If Turner could get one more they'd be tied. Hill knew the man was dying to get the record before heading home. Just as Hill was about to check back with the breaching team, he saw more shadows. A second tango crept along the terrace.

This time, however, Hill was able to see a few more details. The figure was big – not Turner big, but large enough to warrant caution. He was also deathly pale. Hill switched off his safety and slowed his breathing, preparing to take his first shot. He placed his crosshairs on the back of the tango's neck. If Hill's shot flew true, the bullet would sever the spinal cord from the body and put the guy down before he even knew he'd been shot. Hill visualized the shot, starting with the trigger pull and ending with the large tango crumpling to the ground. He did this before each shot. It was an attempt to see all the variables and make minute adjustments milliseconds before he actually fired.

The tango slowly turned, and then moved out of sight. Hill's practiced breathing froze. Red, glowing eyes had, for a second, made him doubt his normally perfect vision. He shook his head. Damn stupid time to be imagining things.

"Delta Whiskey Seven to Delta Whisky Four, you have a second tango – second floor, third house. We can't get a bead on them."

"Overwatch, we're sending a party to investigate while we commence the operation. We have to rock 'n' roll or we lose the element of surprise. If the tangos reappear, take 'em out if you see a weapon," Chavez responded with a little more iron in his voice.

"Roger that," Hill replied.

He watched as two marines moved toward the second house, the darkness and urban environment providing perfect cover. A quick look at the target house had the rest of the team stacking up in preparation to breach. They were moving a little early; daylight was still about half an hour away, but a few slivers of light were starting to creep over the rooftops. With luck they would secure the target house and exfiltrate to base before anyone on the block woke for the Morning Prayer.

"Oh, shit," Turner yelped. "Tango is right on top of them, and they're blind. I'm taking the shot."

"Belay that. Tango doesn't have a weapon" stated Hill.

"Dammit, Hill, you know as well as I do that they intend to kill our boys."

"That may be the case but 'no weapon, no shot' is the order from up top," said Hill

"Shit, the brass don't know what it's like out here. This is gonna go sideways fast."

Hill watched as Turner fumed. Just then, the two marines responsible for checking the team's flank could be heard going fully automatic. The radio burst to life as the firing stopped.

"Delta Whiskey Four to Delta Whiskey Six, report," came the call from Chavez.

"Delta Whiskey Six, we just capped two pale, motherfucking Johnnie Jihadis. They got the jump on us, but now the Hajis are down. We're all good here," PFC Staples replied.

Not long ago the platoon celebrated Staples' twentieth birthday in-country with some 'confiscated' beer. He was a good soldier who was shaping up to be a great marine. His melon-sized and balding head had earned him the unfortunate nickname of 'Pineapple'. It didn't make a whole lot of sense, but then again, nicknames given by the unit rarely did.

"Copy, we're breachin' now. Go, go, go!"

With the two tangos down, Hill quickly scoped over to watch as the three-man breaching team blew the door to the house then threw in a flash bang. The instant the grenade went off, the team moved in.

While waiting for the report to come in from Chavez, Hill switched back to scan the balconies for more bad guys. The way they'd moved and hid suggested there might be more waiting in the dark.

The comms system crackled as Chavez's voice came over the net. "House is secure. Seven dead. They're all torn up. Something out of a slasher film, arms and assholes are everywhere. We need to document it. The rest of the team is securing intel and photographing the scene. It smells like shit in here." Hill could hear Chavez's breathing over the comms. "Delta Whiskey Six, high step it to my location, you can help secure any intel."

It wouldn't take long before the team gathered what it could to take back to Forward Operating Base. The FOB was only a few clicks away.

"Delta Whiskey Four to Joker One Seven, requesting transport, we will mark location with strobe," stated Chavez.

Hill blew out the breath he was holding as Staples confirmed the order to help gather the intelligence and then entered the house. Joker One Seven, a Black Hawk helicopter, was their ride back to base. The mission was winding down and he was looking forward to a shower and some hot chow—

Gunfire erupted from the target house.

"Overwatch, the fuckers aren't dead—" Shots erupted over the headset as the team dealt with the new threat.

Both Turner and Hill set their sights on the front door. Flashes from the carbines cast light and shadow out the doorway.

"Delta Whiskey Four, report!" Hill said.

"The Tangos are not dead, I repeat, *not dead*. They're attacking with their fuckin' teeth. I have two wounded and two dead. Pineapple and I are going to the second story. Cover us. We are going to try and get some distance on them."

"Copy, Delta Whiskey Four." Hill looked to Turner. "This just got ugly. Wait for Staples and Chavez to come out and put down anyone that comes out after them."

"Fuck! Let's do it," Turner said, and Hill knew the other sniper was on mission now. He was out for blood, and it was blood he was going to get.

Hill watched as Chavez and Staples made their way onto the second-story balcony, fireman-carrying the wounded and hopping to the patio of the neighboring house. Their BDUs were covered in dark red splotches he knew was blood. Whatever happened in there must have been a nightmare. They would have to contend with the wounded as they fled. The dead could wait.

Hill watched as Chavez and Staples, with the wounded, made it to the second balcony. He saw them make it halfway to the next balcony when a small horde of tangos crashed through the nearest patio door.

Turner and Hill went to work.

Hill let Turner take the shot as the first tango came through the entryway. He knew Turner would have it lined up, and he wasn't disappointed as Turner's gentle pull of the trigger sent the bullet on its merry way. Hill watched through his scope as the shot entered the tango's head a little left of the bridge of the nose. The head snapped back with violent force as the legs went out from under him, like a puppet with its strings cut.

Hill lined up his own shot as he heard Turner chamber another round. A second tango crossed the threshold. Hill fired.

While the .308 was the perfect round for taking out a person, the .50 caliber was designed for tank warfare or long range targets. His SASR was loaded with Roufoss Mark 211 explosive rounds. The bullets were designed to blow through a wall or into an armored vehicle, where the zirconium trigger would ignite and smash a big exit and plenty of shrapnel, making it a very bad day for anyone hit. The person in Hill's scope was neither a wall nor armor, so the round ripped the head and the majority of the upper body off, exploding in a spray of red mist. The first two terrorists to stick their heads out had lost them, buying the team more time to reach safety.

Hill watched as Chavez and Staples made it to the third balcony seconds after the dead tangos hit the floor. They were working on a way to get to ground level and meet up with Hill and Turner. The snipers' shots echoed off every surface in the neighborhood. If people weren't awake when the operation began, they were now.

Hill watched through his scope, and saw that the ground rose up in front of the team enough to make the jump difficult but not impossible. The chance of breaking an ankle was still there, but not a definite like it would have been from the other two houses. Hill watched as Staples jumped first. He had the most *battle rattle* and the full pack would tell Chavez if he needed to be more cautious when he worked his way down. Staples had no trouble; he was fine and already covering as many angles as he could when Chavez lowered the two wounded down to him before finally joining what was left of his squad.

Hill's radio crackled to life as Chavez got on the horn, "Delta Whiskey Four to Delta Whiskey Seven, what's the clearest way out of here?"

"Delta Whiskey Four, continue two more houses to your right, and then come straight at us to the east. We're just shy of one click away. Turner will set up a strobe on the roof to alert our ride."

Hill peered over as Turner turned on the strobe light to mark the location. *It shouldn't be too hard to locate,* Hill thought; it was the tallest pile of bricks and mortar in the area. The helicopter wouldn't be able to land but it could hover while the unit made good their exfil.

Hill surveyed the area again. No one had exited the target house after he obliterated the second tango. The early morning grew quiet once more. To Hill, it didn't feel right, but he couldn't put his finger on what 'it' was. He moved the scope to check on Chavez, Staples, and the rest of the team. Then it hit him. The first two contacts Staples and his fire team had killed were no longer lying where they'd fallen. They were nowhere to be seen. Sweat dripped down Hill's spine, making him itch.

"Dog Pound, did you see anyone gather up the tangos Staples and his team shot up?" Hill asked.

"Negative, why?"

"They're fuckin' missing." Hill and Turner put eyes back to scopes and scanned the street.

A few seconds passed. "No fuckin' sign of them," Hill said.

"Well, that ain't good," Turner deadpanned. Hill knew Turner was a sarcastic son of a bitch in times of crisis, a stone cold killer with a dry sense of humor. It never surprised Hill what spilled out of the guy's mouth. Suddenly, Turner was all business. "Movement, second house, street level."

"Take the shot," Hill replied.

A single report rang out.

"Tango down," Turner said.

Hill looked down on the fire team as they made their way to the landing zone. *Halfway.* The going was slow for both Chavez and Staples under the weight of the wounded soldiers and having to cover every nook and cranny with their pistols while looking for more hostiles. As Hill moved the scope around the area to provide some cover for the retreating soldiers, he caught a dark silhouette creeping toward his friends. The hostile was making progress and, while Chavez and his team might not see them, Hill did. It was an easy shot from this distance.

He waited for the tango to line up inside his crosshairs, slowing his breathing as he prepared to pull the trigger. It gave Hill an opportunity to study his prey.

The man was dressed in a pair of dark black pants similar to Hill's and a ripped, dirty camo shirt. The man's skin was pale. Not what Hill expected to see in Iraq. He could be one of the Chechens who had entered the conflict to help their Muslim brothers. It wasn't common, but not unheard of. Whoever he was, he was seconds away from meeting his maker.

Two more steps, fucker, Hill thought. *Come on, keep moving.*

Without warning, the tango surged forward, ripping PFC Silao from Chavez's arms. The pale man dragged the wounded soldier away and bit into him, blood spurting all over the figure's face and Silao's BDUs. Hill lined up his shot. Wasting no time, he pulled the trigger.

The comedian, Gallagher, would have been proud. As the bullet entered the tango's head, it exploded like a watermelon. Blood gushed from his neck stump, a shower of red bathing Chavez, who'd moved to try and help Silao even as Hill had taken the shot. The .50 caliber left no doubt as to the fate of the attacker.

Hill now watched Chavez though the scope; he was dazed but not out.

"Delta Whiskey Four to Overwatch, thanks," Chavez croaked.

"No problem, Delta Whisky Four. Get moving before more of tangos hit you." Hill moved his sight to cover their six. Silao was down, but Hill saw Chavez gather the body and sling it over his shoulders. *No one gets left behind*, he thought.

"Got anything?" Hill asked Turner.

"Nada. Target house and the streets are clear," Turner answered, not taking his eye from the scope. "I had movement near the gas station on the corner, two houses down from target, but nothing now."

"Good, I'll radio the helo, see what's taking them so damn long." Hill changed comm frequencies. "Delta Whiskey Seven to Joker One Seven. Time to dustoff? We have wounded to casevac."

"This is Joker One Seven, time to extraction is five mikes, say again, five mikes."

"Roger, Joker One Seven. Sooner is better than later," Hill replied. He switched back to the unit channel. "Delta Whiskey Seven to all elements, extraction in five mikes, so haul ass, marines."

"Copy that, Delta Whisky Seven," came the terse reply from Chavez. He sounded tired and shaken. Having your commanding officer panic was not a good thing. Best to leave him off the radio or it could spread to the others.

"Did you hear that?" Turner asked.

Hill shook his head. "Hear what? I don't hear anything."

"Sounded as if someone was below us." Turner looked toward the edge of the building.

"Impossible. The claymores in the stairwell would have gone off. We put enough to bring the whole building down around them if they dared come up."

"Not from the stairs. Over the side of the building."

"Fuck, that's impossible," Hill said.

Hill watched as Turner moved to a tactical crouch, grabbing the M4 rifle he'd leaned against what was left of the hip-level wall. He made his way to the edge and peered over, then jumped back.

A pale, slender hand grabbed for the ledge. It was joined by a second hand, then a head.

Turner wasted no time opening the taps on his rifle. For a decorated sniper, Hill thought Turner's aim in this situation was severely impaired. The bullets hit just about everything except the intended target, only a few hitting the climber. The repetitive clicking of the rifle's hammer on the empty magazine was all that could be heard as the tango climbed over the lip of the building. The rounds hadn't slowed their attacker down one bit. The stare from glowing red eyes zeroed in on the two men

Turner grabbed a fresh mag from his pouch and slammed it into the lower receiver, but it was too late. The pale tango grabbed the sniper, dragged him forward, and bit him in the throat. Hill watched Turner die as the tango tore his throat open with his teeth, and tossed Turner's flailing body over the side as effortlessly as throwing a rag doll.

Hill didn't have time to mourn the loss of his friend as the hulking man turned to face him. Turner's M4 was too far away so Hill grabbed his Heckler and Koch Mk23 pistol.

Pfft, pfft. The silenced weapon spat, its load striking the man dead center of the forehead. The man stumbled back, falling to the ground.

Hill breathed a sigh of relief. That was too close for comfort. He took the time to look over the edge to locate the rest of his group. Turner's lifeless body lay at an odd angle in the sand. Staples would pick the body up and bring him home. The team would know where the charges were set and how to avoid them as they climbed the stairs to meet him.

Hill gave a silent prayer for his fallen friend, wishing him a safe trip to the other side. There would be time to mourn later; right now he had to stay frosty and make sure the rest of the team made it back alive.

Whoomp, Whoomp. The beautiful sound of the chopper's blades could be heard in the distance as their ride made its way toward them. In no time at all they would be returning to base. As Hill thought that, Chavez and Staples exited the stairwell, carrying their fallen comrades. They looked like warmed dog shit.

As the chopper made the minute adjustments in order to hover over what was a sorry excuse for a rooftop, Hill made his way over to the body of the man who climbed up the building. He was joined seconds later by Chavez and Staples.

The tango was very pale, his skin almost translucent. His jaw didn't look quite right. It was massive, and with weird muscle structure. He was hairless, and his clothes looked as if they'd been dug up and taken from a dead man, the style right out of the 1970s. Not unusual in this part of the world, but definitely not normal.

As Hill bent to take a closer look, the sun breached the horizon, bathing the rooftop in a golden hue. The body started to smoke and smolder, then burst into blue flames. Hill jumped away in surprise. Within seconds, there was little trace of the man, just a pile of ash blown into the air by the chopper's wash. Hill didn't know what to make of it, and wasn't sure how he was going to write it up in his report, if he even had the balls to put it in writing.

There wasn't time to talk about what they'd witnessed as the Black Hawk hovered over the roof, just low enough for the men to climb a board. The dead and wounded were loaded first, followed by Chavez, Staples, and finally Hill. No one spoke on the ride back to base.

Victory had come at a high price. Hill looked over at Turner's lifeless body. He wasn't sure, but thought Turner looked paler than he should. Almost luminous. A cold chill settled over Hill and he grabbed a spare magazine from his vest and reloaded his sidearm.

HOLDING THE LINE

Eric S Brown

The jeep sat sideways in the middle of the road, blocking it completely. Billy held the grips of the heavy machine gun mounted on its rear, nerves making his grip looser than he would like. He was new to the National Guard, and this was first time in the field. He'd joined to get the money he needed for school. There hadn't been a real terrorist attack on the United States in years and overall, it was a time of peace, so he'd figured it was a safe time to join. The more liberal party that had come to power in the last election was doing away with the 'War on Terror' and every other war or active police action they could. The news was filled with reports of troops being called home. Billy had figured it was safe to join up, thinking the worst things he could be doing would be sandbagging flooded areas and helping out disaster victims.

Jackson, who most folks just called Sarge, stood several feet from the jeep. The older man shook a cigarette from his nearly-empty pack and lit up. Billy watched him with a sense of awe. Sarge had seen real action, all over the world. How the heck the man had ended up back here in the middle of nowhere, North Carolina, was a thing that Billy couldn't even guess at. Sarge was one tough and cold mother: his off-duty bar fights were legendary, even to the new recruits

Pullman paced the road on the other side of the jeep from Sarge. At least he looked a touch nervous. That brought Billy some comfort, because he was scared and there was no denying it. His hands were slick with sweat where they clutched the jeep's weapon, and he could feel the pounding of his heart inside his chest.

They had waited here in silence for the better part of three hours. Billy couldn't take it anymore. He summoned up his courage and called out to Sarge. "Hey man, do you really think this crap they're telling us is real?"

Sarge finished a long drag of his smoke and turned to face him. Billy's cheeks grew heated as Sarge looked him up and down.

"This is your first time out ain't it kid?" Sarge asked.

Billy nodded.

"How come we always get stuck with the newbies?" Pullman asked, walking closer to the jeep, his M-16 held sideways in front of him.

"Stow it," Sarge grunted at Pullman, his eyes never leaving Billy. "Look kid, it ain't our place to believe or not, we just do our jobs. In this case, that means if something nine feet tall and hairy comes charging out of the trees, we fill it full of lead and leave its corpse rotting as a warning to any others that might come at us, and we do this until we get different orders."

Pullman smirked at Sarge's answer and added. "Ease up kid. None of this is real. It's all some kind of cover up or something. Has to be. There's no way on God's Earth that Bigfoot is real."

"So what they're saying about those creatures wiping out the town down the road is just a bunch of crap?" Billy asked, far from convinced.

"Seriously kid?" Pullman laughed. "A whole freaking tribe of Sasquatch just decides to come out of the woods and start killing people? That doesn't make any sense. Those things, if they do even exist, have spent all this time hiding – why would they just suddenly give that up and go feral? What could they hope to gain by taking out a town and revealing themselves to the world? It's more likely they're feeding the public that garbage to keep their attention away from whatever is really going on."

Sarge tossed the still-glowing butt of his cigarette to the

ground and crushed it out with a heel. "Pullman, you're as bad as the kid. Like I said, it ain't our job to think. Our job is to kill anything that tries to get past us here, whether it's some wild-eyed nut job in an ape suit or the real thing. We hold the line here, no matter who or what shows up."

The night was cold and the sweat that had bled from Billy's body into the cloth of his uniform wasn't making it any warmer. He shivered and wished this mess was over with already. Before they had left base, the last bits of news he had seen were calling this the 'Sasquatch Apocalypse'. Since whatever had hit the small town of Babble creek had gone down, there had been reports from all over the country of Bigfoot pouring in. Not the usual sort of sightings either, but stories of Bigfoot, or entire packs of the things, on the move and ripping apart everyone they came across. Billy didn't really know what to believe himself. He'd never bought into the tales of things like Sasquatch, the Loch Ness monster, or UFOs. His dad had been a hunter his entire life in these parts before cancer claimed him two years back, and had never once said anything about encountering one of the creatures. Still, Billy guessed that there had to be something going on or the three of them wouldn't be out here freezing their butts off. Sarge seemed to think the Guard, like the Army, was full of REMFs – rear echelon paper pushers – who enjoyed nothing more than finding new and cruel ways to make grunts like them suffer. Billy had to admit that the idea of the Sasquatch Apocalypse sure sounded crazy. There were plenty of wackos who believed the zombie apocalypse was just around the corner, but swarms of Bigfoot declaring war on mankind? That was just insane.

"Sarge?" Billy spoke up again. "If what they're saying is real, there can't be enough of those things to really matter can there?"

"How the Hell should I know kid? I'm a soldier, not a crypto-zoologist."

"How could there be?" Pullman laid his rifle against the jeep, propping it there as he fished a smoke of his own from his pocket. "There's no way the things could have stayed hidden this long if there were."

"We don't know anything about the creatures, Pullman," Sarge pointed out, surprising Billy. "We don't know where they live. We don't know what they do out there in the woods. Nothing. Who can guess at how many there are or what they're planning?"

Silence hung in the air like a tangible force around Billy until Pullman finally nodded and answered, "Nobody I guess."

He placed his cigarette between his lips, picking his weapon back up, and headed back to his spot on the road without another word.

Sarge looked Billy over. "You gonna be okay up there kid?"

Billy nodded from where he stood in the rear of the jeep.

"Good because—" Sarge started, but whatever else he was about to say was lost, drowned out by the half human, half animal shrieks that came from somewhere in the direction of Babble creek.

Sarge and Billy looked up from their conversation to see waves of monsters moving towards them. The things were all between nine and ten feet tall, covered in matted, brown hair. Where moments before, they'd been so quiet as to approach unnoticed, their footfalls on the road now sounded like thunder as they rushed forward. Their mouths were twisted in hungry snarls, and their red eyes burned with hatred and anger.

The chattering bark of Pullman's rifle as he raced to the jeep, firing over its hood at the advancing horde, snapped Billy and Sarge out their shock. Sarge spun around, jerking his own M-16 up. It spat burst after burst at the things. Billy swung the mounted fifty cal to face the beasts and opened up on them. Sarge and Pullman's rounds only seemed to be making the creatures madder as they came, without even slowing them, yet Billy's cut them down in rows. The heavier rounds of the mounted weapon sank deep through thick muscle, cutting down several of the monsters where they ran. Those creatures fell, feet entangled in their own intestines, to sprawl upon the road. Billy blew chunks of flesh away from the bodies of numerous others. One monster even lost an arm and stopped dead in its tracks to stare at the blood jetting from where the limb had once been attached. Resistance was useless though; there were just too many of the damn things.

As the creatures began to reach their position, Sarge screamed for them to fall back, but Billy had no idea how or to where. More of the beasts had emerged from the trees all around them. One of them picked Sarge up, as if he weighed nothing, and shook the big man in the air before it completely ripped him in two. With a roar, it flung the pieces in separate directions. Billy swung the machine gun to catch the thing dead in the chest with his stream of fire. The creature imploded under the sheer force and number of bullets tearing into it as a shower of blood covered the asphalt around it. Its twitching corpse collapsed unmoving on the road as the other creatures trampled it in their haste to get at him. Billy held his ground. He could hear Pullman screaming behind him but didn't dare turn to see what was happening to the man.

Billy kept his finger tight on the machine gun's trigger, swinging wildly back and forth in a wide arc, trying to take down as many of the beasts as he could. He felt a pair of massive hands close on his shoulders, then he was jerked from the back of the jeep and flung sideways onto the road. He struck the pavement hard. The pain jolting through him told him his right arm had snapped underneath his own weight. He struggled to yank his pistol from the holster on his hip as the beasts closed on him. Dozens of hairy hands reached out, digging into his flesh. He cried out, his eyes full of tears born of fear, and then pain as he was yanked apart. He saw one of the beasts raising his left leg to its yellow teeth and another scooping out long, red slicked strands from his stomach. He'd heard that a severed head lived on for a short time after being removed, and he soon found that it was true. The last thing he saw was a glimpse of the trees along the side of road as his head was tossed through the air and his world went black.

Thela Hun Gingeet

David Benton and W.D. Gagliani

The staccato throb of the Huey's rotors was practically deafening as the helicopter cut a path through the night sky between Command and Control Central in Kon Tum to the insertion point just south of Luang Prabang east of the Mekong in central Laos.

They were going *over the fence*. Flanking them on either side were their escort choppers, gunships loaded for bear.

Special Forces Sergeant Jake Carter, One-Zero of Recon Team Python, sat with the hundred-round drum magazine of the Russian RPD Light Machine Gun resting on his knee. He was staring out the Huey's open door, past the ride-along gunner. Below them an open field of elephant grass that the boys called the Golf Course stretched in all directions, illuminated by the glow of the nearly-full moon. In the distance he could see the flash of cluster bombs pounding the Ho Chi Minh trail. He sighed and turned away from the door, refocusing his attention on the team.

Sgt. Larry Kane leaned into Carter, yelling over the heavy *thrum* of the bird's engine and the rushing wind. "So what's the pucker factor gonna be on this drop?"

"Unknown, Kane," Carter yelled and shrugged broadly enough to be seen. "We should be in and out, two days. Not expecting anything out of the ordinary," he lied.

"So what you're saying is that we're screwed?"

Carter allowed a fragile smile to cross his face and leaned back into the seat. They knew the ropes. The truth was, he really didn't know what to expect. The mission briefing had been short and sweet. They were to observe whether there was 'enemy activity' at a godforsaken Taoist temple west of the Plain of Jars, far north of the panhandle. Though Carter had been team leader on a dozen MACV-SOG missions with Recon Team Python, none of them had crossed this deep into the interior. The main war zone was to the south and east, but they were flying a black op into the heart of Communist-controlled Laos and he had little idea as to why. Even if it were an NVA stronghold or training facility, it was too far from the front lines to be of major concern, especially considering that they were teetering on the cusp of the rainy season.

And, overall, it just didn't *feel* right.

There was something about this one – they'd been told ahead of time they were going in black. If caught, their existence would be denied. For all intents and purposes, they were dead unless they made the extraction point.

Carter, like all his men, had volunteered for dangerous assignments. No point grousing about it now.

The Huey jinked to avoid a barrage of anti-aircraft fire, glowing green tracers suddenly surrounding them and lighting up the night. Carter grabbed his seat to brace himself as the chopper swerved evasively. A handful of pounding heartbeats later, the assault was left behind as unexpectedly as it had found them.

The pilot turned, looking over his shoulder with a grin.

"Laugh a minute," he shouted.

The teams never found the pilot's sense of humor contagious, but you did what you had to do to get clear of the fear.

RT Python was comprised of seven men; three grunts and four Yards. Outside of Carter, Sgt. Kane was One-One, and the newer guy, Sgt. McBride, was One-Two. The three of them were Special Forces – Green Berets – and what they'd all volunteered for was duty in the Studies and Observations Group, so they had to be either crazy or gung-ho. Their Montagnard companions were all from the Bahnar tribe: Mock, Jek, Phut One, and Phut

Two. The whole team were designated Bushmasters, specially trained for jungle combat. And this wasn't their first rodeo.

Something nagged at him about that, but it was gossamer in a delicate night's breeze.

Carter pulled a square out of his pocket, lit it with his Chinese Zippo copy, and took a deep drag. The *mission* was nagging, of that he was sure. Yeah, a few nerves were normal. The adrenaline rush of getting dropped into the boonies – into the unknown – was something he lived for. But this was different. It was as if that voice inside his head was warning him. Whatever they ran into, they were on their own. There wouldn't be any Hatchet Forces or Air Cav sweeping in the clean up if they ended up in deep shit... they were already too far out, and blacked out on top of it. Why, he didn't know. He wasn't supposed to know. Even if they did call for an extraction, it would take hours for a slick to arrive. This was gonna be a clean fight, RT Python against whatever they found out there. But that wasn't what was bothering Carter.

No, maybe it was that slimebag spook, Pearson of the DOD. He'd been at the briefing, quietly lurking like the snake that he was. Sure, Pearson wore Hawaiian shirts like banners and was friendly enough to your face, but it was that fake friendly of someone who was gaining your trust so you wouldn't expect the knife when it slipped into your back. Carter didn't like him, or any of his cronies. They were chickenshit in Carter's opinion, but when you were deployed in Uncle Sam's clandestine army you had to deal with the devil. It came with the package. You didn't have to like it.

The choppers headed north along the hazy border between Laos and Thailand trying to steer clear of Charlie's known nests. The flight seemed to take forever. Carter thought that it was probably similar to what a man would feel like on his last day on death row... waiting. The roar of the Huey's rotors made conversation difficult – impossible if you didn't want to blow your voice out. They didn't want to talk anyway. They knew what needed to be done. They just wanted to get in and out alive and get back to base with the intel. And then maybe do it all over again.

He saw them all gripping their weapons, an assortment of French MAT submachine guns, Russian RPDs, and Chinese AK47s for the Yards. If they were caught or killed, none of their gear was US-made.

And *that* had made him nervous, sure enough.

Turning east, they flew into the mountainous region south of Luang Prabang. These weren't the mountains Carter was familiar with from his youth, growing up in Colorado. The mountains he'd explored as a kid were mostly outcroppings of solid rock, with evergreens sprouting in the foothills. Those trees' acidic needles kept the undergrowth to a minimum in the thin soil. No, these mountains were covered with lush growth from base to summit. They always reminded Carter of some kind of prehistoric jungle lost in the folds of time. If he'd seen a pterodactyl wheeling across the sky he wouldn't have been surprised. There were all sorts of creatures down there – though not dinosaurs – and they were plentiful. Just about every manner of creeping crawling thing was well represented down below the upper canopy, some of them extremely dangerous.

For some reason, Carter wasn't worried about the fauna. He tried to shake away the nagging internal voice, the sound of...

"About five minutes to insertion," the pilot yelled back over the seats, displaying the five fingers on his hand to make sure he was understood above the noise.

Carter nodded and took a quick inventory of his equipment, for the hundredth time. He sighed and crosschecked Kane, making sure his gear was secured as well.

The Huey and its escorts came in low. They weaved between the looming mountains, cutting their path above the valleys like a river carves its own channel through living rock. The full moon was above, but there was no light from below. No sign of a nearby village, or hootch, or any people at all. And nothing to give any indication that they were near anything like an NVA military base, if that's what they were looking for. All of which was relatively good.

"Here you are," the pilot called out like a New York cab driver, giving Carter and the others a thumbs up. He held the Huey hovering above the wavering treetops.

Carter grasped the steel bar and leaned out the open door, staring down into the sea of blackened greenery. It was dark as midnight down beneath the triple canopy, but below that their newfangled night-vision gear would help them avoid breaking their legs when they reached the ground.

He deployed the clumsy and heavy Soviet PNV-57 night vision goggles that had been slung around his neck. He wished they could be using US-made SU49 NVGs, but they were incognito and all tell-tale gear had been nixed. He hated wearing these damned Soviet albatrosses. They felt like strapping a brick to his face and another to the back of his head, but they mostly did the trick in extremely low light – working on the same principle as a green eye. Down there where there were only the faintest traces of moonlight, there was enough light filtering down to make the goggles useful. Under a full moon like tonight's, however, the goggles were next to useless. Above the canopy they'd be blind. Once below it, the goggles would give them what they needed. The Yards would be going in without the night gear – their eyes were accustomed to the jungle's blackness.

Carter signaled to Jek, and the Yard fast-roped from the slick into the jungle below. Next was Phut Two, followed by Mock, then McBride, Kane, Phut One, and finally Carter himself took to the wire and dribbled downward like a spider weaving a web.

When he reached the jungle floor, the rest of the team had already set up a small perimeter around the insertion point. The three choppers wheeled away, heading back to CCC, as soon as he touched ground. The thunderous din of their spinning blades faded slowly and soon the raucous nocturnal jungle fauna had once again taken over.

The mosquitos were on him immediately, and Carter slapped one that was tickling the hairs on his neck. He could feel its not-so-tiny crushed body curled beneath his fingers.

Goddamn insects. They made life in the bush miserable. And then there was the rainy season.

"Glad to get out of the egg-beater," Kane muttered. "I can barely feel my legs."

Carter shushed him. He wanted to move the team away from the insertion point in case any dings had seen or heard the choppers.

They headed east by northeast, sticking to the lowlands. Jek took point, followed by the slack man, Phut Two, then Mock, McBride, Kane, and Carter, with Phut One walking sweep.

With difficulty they cut their way through the thick under-growth with machetes that would dull much too soon. And the 'magic' goggles just weren't good enough to help them keep moving rapidly through the forest depths out here in the boon-docks. After a while they were all wearing the gear slung around their necks again. When they were about a couple hundred yards from insertion, Carter stopped them. They were already dragging due to the night's heat.

"We'll stay here 'til morning," he announced. "Jek, Mock, keep an eye out for watchers." The Montagnards melted away like ghosts. The others hit the ground, grateful for the respite.

Carter threw his rucksack down and settled himself on the ground next to it. He opened the ruck, pulled out his canteen, and took a deep tug of metallic water. Finally he took off the damned goggles, tucked them and their power pack into the bag, leaned back, and closed his eyes. The machine gun lay across his legs, his finger resting on the trigger guard. He wouldn't sleep. It wasn't fear of the enemy that would keep him awake – it was responsibility for the team. So he listened to every sound while resting his eyes. His mind raced, not for the first time.

The sounds of night insects and tree frogs lulled Carter, calming his hardened nerves until he heard something else whispering between the endless night chirping. He bent his ear to try and capture the sound. At first he thought was that it was an enemy patrol, their gear clinking.

He listened carefully.

No, it was laughter... a child's laughter.

He opened his eyes and turned to survey the perimeter.

There, barely visible through the fronds and vines stood a slender Asian girl in a *chang-ao*, a traditional Chinese garment. The girl stared at Carter and held her finger up to her smiling lips. Then she beckoned him with a wave of her tiny hand.

He rose slowly from his position on the ground, checking the shapes of his sleeping teammates. No one had stirred. No one had heard the laughter. No one was awake.

He hesitated, not sure what he was doing. Or why.

He thought he might be asleep, dreaming. He pinched himself and felt it.

She was still there, half-hidden in the dense undergrowth, waving at him, beckoning him toward her.

He shrugged. Then he began to follow her.

Jesus, what am I doing?

His eyes had become remarkably well-adjusted to the dark and he followed her at an unintentional distance, unable to keep pace with the girl who was now running with one hand gathering the material of her robes. He hadn't initially realized that he had left his machine gun behind, and when he did, he was far from the others. Too far to go back.

He was abandoning his post, but he felt compelled.

You never leave your weapon! his internal voice screamed at him.

But he had, and he couldn't go back. He would lose the girl.

His back itched, as if someone watched from afar.

Barely in control, he pressed on through the darkness.

In time he couldn't quite measure, Carter came to a clearing in the jungle. It was no natural clearing – the area had been burned to ash, maybe in a rogue napalm strike and Carter could still smell the characteristic petrol residue hanging in the air. It had burned the vegetation and anything else that had stood here into oblivion, leaving behind a hellish scorched landscape.

But this was too far from the war. *What had happened here?*

The girl was still there, a moving shadow in a sea of gray. And her rippling laughter sent chills of recognition through Carter. Yet now he set off through the ash field. With his first step he heard a *clink*, like he'd kicked a tin can with his foot. He looked down. There, half-wrapped on the toe of his combat boot was a set of dog tags. He reached down and picked them up, trying to study them in the dark. He flicked his fake Zippo and held them close together until he could read the letters.

It was a name he recognized: Sgt. Samuel Lund.

The memory struck Carter like a physical force. Lund had been on Carter's first two missions with Recon Team Python. Until a booby trap left by Charlie had eviscerated him. Carter had called for a dustoff, but it was too late. Lund died while Carter tried to hold in his guts, his hands squishy with thick blood.

Carter shoved the tags into his pocket and took another cautious step. Again he heard a metallic sound, and the ground just didn't feel right beneath his weight. Glancing down, he dreaded what he would find. He almost thought: *mine!* But it was as if he knew it couldn't be a mine, that it was something stranger and more dangerous.

Beneath his feet more tags crunched. Dog tags hidden under the ash. *There were tags everywhere, hundreds, maybe thousands of them.*

How was this possible? This wasn't even a war zone.

Carter jerked awake.

Shit.

He *had* been dreaming.

His hand was trembling. He had drifted into sleep. It wasn't like him, not at all, yet he had. He was still at the campsite.

Dog tags were all the more peculiar to dream about, because none of them wore theirs for this op in order to remain essentially orphaned in terms of nationality. If caught, they could be tortured and shot.

He took a ragged breath and surveyed the area around them again. The faintest traces of weak daylight were beginning to filter down through the jungle. Nothing had happened. He wiped the sweat from his brow and got to his feet. He heard the echo of a child's laughter in the back of his mind, but the dream had already begun to fade.

He kicked McBride's booted foot, leaning in and whispering. "Get up. Get the others up."

When everyone had assembled in a group around him, Carter spoke to them in measured tones. "Our objective is approximately nine clicks to the north, but a ways up in elevation. We'll stick down here in the valley, sweep around this mole hill on its eastern flank then approach our target from the southeast. Until further notice, no communication other than hand signals unless absolutely necessary. Standard marching order with a five-yard spread. Stay sharp, everybody." Carter checked his Soviet watch and wrist compass. "All right, let's head out."

The team wove their way through the thick foliage, Jek leading the way at point. Though the filtered sunlight was beginning to brighten the jungle in angular patterns, night's shadows still fought for dominance beneath the canopies, and gray phantoms seemed to lurk wherever Carter trained his eyes. Despite the lingering darkness, RT Python efficiently cut their way through the valley and headed east-northeast around the base of the towering green mountain. They were pros. They got it done.

The rain that started spitting at them before morning had come fully into flower. It swept in so rapidly that Carter felt the first fat drops falling through the leaves before the storm clouds swallowed the sun. The lush growth offered little resistance to the downpour. Rain catching on leaves high above coalesced and then gushed down in heavy streams, quickly turning the rich black soil into slippery mud, covered with even more treacherous wet discarded leaves. Water dripped from the brim of Carter's boonie hat, obscuring his vision. His dyed black fatigues – lacking any trace of insignia – were soaked through to the skin in minutes.

Apparently they had passed the cusp and the rainy season had begun. Just like that.

The team pressed on, muttering.

Goddamn rain.

As suddenly as the torrent had started, it disappeared. But instead of granting relief, the rain was followed by an oppressive heat that threatened to choke them with its cloying humidity. The jungle seemed to exhale, giving its moisture back to the air. The atmosphere grew heavy and thick. Within a half hour the rainwater that had permeated Carter's clothes was replaced with sweat. For him there was no difference – he remained wet.

Occasionally he thought he heard a sound out of place in the tapestry of jungle noises, but when he turned it was gone. If they were being followed, the followers were good. The sense of being watched was unnerving, and he never took his finger off the trigger.

They trudged on through the heat of the day. The under-growth was thinner here and they gave their machete arms a rest. Rounding the eastern slope, they found a narrow slow-running stream and followed along its western bank. The water was brown and murky, stirred by rainwater runoff. Judging from the steep banks, Carter guessed that the stream ran more like a river during the height of the rainy season. They forded the river where it bent its course to the west. Jek entered first and the lower half of his body disappeared in the creeping, putrid water. He trudged through the slow current across to the far bank, holding his AK47 above his head, the rest of the team following close behind.

"Ain't seen hide nor hair of Charlie," Kane said to Carter with disdain. "Exactly what the hell are we doing here?"

"Keep your voice down, damn it."

Carter threw down his rucksack again after pulling out his canteen. He sipped the lukewarm water then wiped off the few drops that rolled down his chin with his sleeve. "Jek, Phut One – take a look around," he ordered.

The two tribesmen quickly and silently vanished into the jungle, and in seconds it appeared they'd never been there at all. Thin and whipcord tough, the mountain tribesmen became ruthless fighters when trained. They matched, man for man, just about every Green Beret Carter had ever known – but they were temperamental and their loyalties were sometimes difficult to pin down.

"Come on, One-Zero," Kane persisted, the others looking on. "What the hell's going on? What kind of recon is this really?"

"You know exactly what I know, Kane. We get to the top of this shit pile and have a look around. We relay what we find. We haul ass. That's what we're doing here."

"Well I don't like it," said Kane. "We ain't anywhere near the war." He pulled a filterless cigarette from his shirt pocket. Carter tossed him his knock-off Zippo. "Thanks." Kane lit the smoke.

"Do you *ever* like it?" McBride said, half-smiling. He was sitting on a bamboo log with his boot off, checking to make sure there weren't any bloated black leeches on his leg. If there were, the bites could become infected fast, and that meant trouble.

"Mock," Carter called out quietly. "Give me those funny books." The indigenous soldier came at a run, grinning.

The Yard reached into his ruck and produced a handful of curled maps, handing them to his One-Zero. Carter unfolded them and took a look, mostly to placate Kane.

"Look here," Carter said to Kane. "This is where we are. Right by the blue line," he pointed at the map, "and this is where we're heading. We should be there by sundown."

McBride had joined them and was standing beside Carter. He pointed upslope. "Up there?" he asked. Carter nodded.

Kane said something, but Carter found himself suddenly transfixed by the praying mantis that was moving in slow motion over Kane's shoulder. He heard the sound of pieces of tin clinking together. Carter slipped his hand into his pocket and ran his fingertips along the metal edges of the dog tags that rested there. A wave of dizziness swept through him, and he was suddenly afraid to pull the dog tags out, afraid of what he would find, afraid of the name he would find press-punched into the metal.

Lund, Samuel.

Or Carter, Jacob?

"Are you all right, Carter?" Kane was grabbing his shoulder.

Carter looked up and saw the mantis flit away. He shook his head, trying to clear it.

"Yeah," he said. "Yeah, I'm fine."

"Well, check it out, you looked like there was nobody home for a minute there, know what I mean?" Kane's brilliant blue eyes were set in a piercing stare.

Carter pushed Kane's hand away. "I said I'm fine. Where the hell are Jek and Phut One? We need to get this show on the road. I want us to be up there while there's still light." He took another tug from the canteen, his hand trembling.

As if on cue, the two Yards burst through the vegetation. Phut's arm was draped over Jek's shoulder, his eyes wide and staring. All the color seemed to have drained from him. Jek was holding his kinsman upright.

"What the hell happened?" Carter demanded.

Before Jek could answer, Phut stammered and spit out something in his dialect.

Carter shook his head; he didn't speak the indigenous lingo. It all sounded like gibberish to him. The Yards spoke halting English, enough to be understood by their American allies, so he had no idea why this one was trying his patience. Carter's nerves already frayed, he felt ready to explode. The men sensed his anger and eyed each other silently.

Jek spoke, keeping Carter from losing his shit. "He say that he see his mother... out there, in the jungle."

Carter shook his head, confused. He couldn't even form a sentence through his frustration. His hands and feet tingled.

"How the fuck is that even possible?" Kane asked.

"It is not," said Jek with his thick accent. "His mother is dead, many year."

Jek helped settle his countryman on the ground. Phut practically collapsed into a shaking heap, curling into himself in a semi-fetal position. He cried helplessly.

"Did you see *someone*?" Carter asked, "Anyone? Something?"

Jek shook his head, his face sober.

"Kane, take Mock and have a look around. Mac, hang with me."

Kane sighed, but followed the orders.

Carter reached into his pocket. His heart stopped beating for a painful moment.

The tags he had held there a minute before were now gone.

He shook his head to dispel the mounting haze.

What the hell is going on?

Pearson. That son of a bitch spooky cocksucker had done something to them. Had to have fucked with them somehow.

Maybe he'd slipped something funny into their Dapsone... maybe some kind of hallucinogen? Or maybe they'd sprayed it in the air before inserting the team? Maybe there was another team out here, watching them, seeing what happened, judging how they reacted?

Typical DOD voodoo shit.

Who knew what the bastards were up to here in these dense jungle locations.

Carter rubbed his temples. He asked Jek, "Is he gonna be all right?" He jerked his head at Phut One.

"Yah, he will be ho-kay," Jek answered, nodding too rapidly. Then the Yard knelt by his shaken compatriot, talking quietly in their Bahnar language.

A chill raced through Carter; he had a bad feeling about this op. He took one more swig from his canteen before stowing it back in his rucksack as he waited for Kane and Mock to return from their sweep. Around him the jungle was teeming. Life was so thick here you couldn't move without it touching you, breathing on you, leaning on you. Carter had learned to ignore most of it because the inability to tell the difference between a bead of sweat running down the back of your neck and a poisonous spider crawling down the collar of your shirt could drive a guy nuts. But today he couldn't seem to blot it out. He was having trouble sorting out the important information from the trivial. His nerves seemed on edge while his senses felt dulled.

Today it all seemed new, and Carter was overloading.

He sensed it, but couldn't stop it.

Something rustled in the undergrowth. Carter crouched and trained his machine gun on the movement. He relaxed his finger off the trigger. It was Kane and Mock, breaking quietly through the thick growth.

"Nothin' out there, Sarge," Kane said, disgusted. "And I mean nothing. No trace of Charlie whatsoever. No footpaths, no huts, no sign of anyone even somewhat civilized," and with a sideways glance at Phut One and Jek, "...or their mothers."

"All right then, let's move out," said Carter.

"Move out to where?"

"We're going to the top of this mountain."

"There's nothing out here, man. We're literally in the middle of nowhere."

"Then it'll be like a vacation, right?"

They left the riverbank and resumed their ascent. The higher they moved the more hostile the growth became, broad leaves became saw blades, stems seemed encrusted with nasty barbed thorns, and tangled vines grew into impenetrable walls of vegetation. Biting and stinging insects seemed to grow in both size and number. It was as if the land itself were trying to dissuade the team; keep them from completing their mission.

Ahead, Kane signaled Carter: *get down.* Carter turned to wave down Mock, who was now taking up the rear in lieu of Phut One, but he could see no trace of him. He scrutinized the underbrush, but nothing moved. Leaves and branches hung motionless. Carter was about to retrace his steps when a small stone bounced off his shoulder. He jerked, swiveling the RPD's muzzle around, his finger brushing the trigger.

Kane, trying to get his attention down the path they'd made.

Jesus.

Kane and McBride were conferring. They beckoned Carter.

"What's going on?" Carter whispered, approaching cautiously at a crouch.

"I don't know," McBride said, "I – I lost the rest of the team."

"*What?*"

"I don't know where they went, Sarge. I was right behind Phut. He was right there..." McBride motioned with his hand, "and then he was just *gone.*"

Carter rose up from his crouch, and stood looking over his shoulder where Mock should have been. The other two special ops soldiers followed suit.

"It was like... like the jungle just *swallowed* them," McBride mumbled, almost in a daze. Trying to convince himself.

"What are we gonna do, Carter?" Kane grabbed him by the elbow. "Are you all right?"

"Yeah, I'm fine," said Carter. "We're gonna finish the mission."

He wasn't fine though, was he?

"No really, check it – it's like you're out of it today."

"I'm *fine*, Kane! Let's get to the top of the fuckin' mountain and get the hell out of here. Sound like a plan to you?"

He realized he'd turned the RPD to face them, then turned it away again.

"What about the Yards?" McBride was jittery, his eyes searching, never still.

"We'll have to report them missing, but first we need to accomplish what we were sent out here to accomplish."

"Which is?"

"Look," said Kane, "something's seriously fucked here."

"I know, I agree. But the top of this mountain is gonna be our best extraction point if we can't make the scheduled rendez-vous anyway. Can't go back down. We might as well hightail it up there. I don't like it either. As for the Yards... I don't have an answer. I... I have some theories. Nothin' I'd say out loud in sane company. Not that you guys are sane."

McBride and Kane looked each other up and down and nodded. Reluctantly.

"We all right, then?" Carter asked. "Let's head out. Mac, take point."

Nervous and twitchy, fingers on triggers, the three remaining members of RT Python continued their climb, McBride in the lead.

In time, after struggling against the heat, the voracious insects, and the nearly impenetrable vegetation, they made the summit just as the hazy setting sun bathed it in a red firelight glow. They stood just inside the jungle's crown, catching their breath, attempting to calm their racing hearts.

The flat mountaintop was oddly devoid of vegetation, with one exception. Near the center of what looked like an open field, a single huge tree stood like a lonely sentinel. Unlike its brethren in the jungle below the summit line, here the tree was not required to stretch upward for life-giving sunlight, but instead could expand outward – and it had. This tree had branched out low on the trunk, and often, creating the appearance of a gigantic bush.

As Team Python cautiously entered the courtyard, the reason there was no plant life clogging the peak became clear. Sometime in the temple's long history, the priests had meticulously paved the area with large flat stones, leaving only the cracks between each slab to foster the sparse plant life, which turned out to be mostly stunted weeds. At the far end of this manmade clearing at the mountain's summit squatted the temple itself, its columns and crumbling walls bound with twisting vines. The stone walls themselves were stained green with moss.

Carter's nerves didn't keep him from wondering how in goddamn hell those flat stone slabs, each of them the size and thickness of a king-size bed, had been transported up the mountain. It hadn't been helicopters, as the paving was clearly hundreds of years old.

Kane kicked at a weed poking up from between the massive stones. "Looks like an NVA stronghold to me," he said sarcastically.

"Stay frosty," Carter ordered. "We've already lost four men on this mission."

"They probably realized we were out of our minds and ditched us."

"That's enough, Kane." Carter motioned his remaining team members into flanking positions. Even though the temple seemed abandoned, he wasn't taking any chances.

After the others had repositioned themselves, Carter moved

forward in a crouch and took a sheltered position behind that strange single tree. McBride and Kane stayed near the jungle cover on either side of the courtyard.

Carter poked his head around the tree's bulk and stared into the shadows inside the abandoned temple. It certainly didn't look occupied. At least not for the last hundred years. He motioned his men forward until they had flanked the building's entrance. Then Carter moved forward, his gun muzzle trained on the darkened doorway. The three soldiers came together and, with his RPD still aimed at the shadows, Carter made a motion and Kane stepped up through wall-rubble and entered the temple. The darkness swallowed him as if he had never been there at all. McBride followed him and duly disappeared, fading into the darkness. Carter brought up the rear.

Carter's eyes took a few moments to adjust to the low light. He cursed himself for forgetting to try the night vision gear, but he figured it wouldn't have worked. Slowly details became clear. The temple was destroyed. Half the roof had caved in and a matting of vines had thatched the hole like a chaotic spider's web. Shade-craving plants had grown between the indoor stones as tenaciously as their sun-loving kin in the courtyard. It was obvious that no one had called this place home in an impossibly long time. Not home or temple or even shelter.

The mission was a bust. Carter had to wonder for the hundredth time about the intel on this one. Or had Pearson, the DOD's favorite spook, been playing them all along for some twisted voodoo experiment?

He lowered his rucksack to the stone floor.

"All right, fuck this, I'm calling in an extraction," he said.

Carter's voice echoed in the empty shrine.

"Hey, Kane. Mac? Hey, where the hell are you guys?"

He whirled, his gun trembling in his hands. Suddenly it was so heavy he wanted to drop it. He lowered the muzzle and shuffled around the floor, on which the moist remnants of dead leaves clung, forming a mucky slurry.

Hell, there aren't even any footprints outside of mine.

How could it be?

"Kane! McBride!"

He stumbled back out into the gloaming. Night was settling in quickly, and the crimson sky had turned a deep purple, like a bruise on the universe.

And he was alone.

"Kane! Mac!"

Carter walked the perimeter of the courtyard in jagged steps, calling out to his missing men. An increasingly loud chorus of insects, nocturnal birds, and animals answered him from the edge of the flat mountain, where the jungle resumed its dominance, but there was no other answer.

The shock of his complete isolation shot a sudden chill through him, and he shivered like a man with the ague. He turned in a staggering circle, aiming his RPD at the phantoms. The machine gun was heavy again, and the muzzle drooped as his muscles could no longer hold it upright. He dropped the gun with a clatter that echoed loudly and drove birds from their perches and caused something else to rustle in the thick vegetation.

If this was the enemy, he was now unarmed.

"Mac?" he whispered, his voice cracking. "Kane?"

The jungle fell abnormally silent, as if it were also listening for a response. Paranoia washed over him in a sudden wave. Carter felt the eyes on him, watching. But it didn't feel like a person hiding behind the tree line observing him, but more like the jungle itself was just a reflection and behind the mirrored glass something scrutinized his every move.

He stumbled back from the jungle's edge and into the temple proper, dug the radio from his sack, and called for a Huey slick. When his trembling finger released the chunky push-to-talk button, static was the only reply.

Static and *something...* something he couldn't define.

A sudden gentle breeze stirred the clearing and behind him Carter heard a tinkling sound, like muffled windchimes and light creaking in the one tree's branches, and something else...

It was a child, laughing.

He spun around.

It took a long moment to register, but the bush-like tree in the courtyard had changed. All of its leaves had fallen to the stones below, where the breeze stirred them in tiny circles. They had been replaced on the bare branches by dog tags, thousands or maybe millions of them, jingling in the wind.

Carter blinked rapidly. Suspended from two of the thicker branches were Kane and Mac, hanging by their necks, vines wrapped around them. Their eyes were bloody holes.

Stumbling forward in a trance, he tripped over his abandoned RPD, landed on his knees and barely felt the pain.

He looked up, blinking again. Now he could see the bodies of the Montagnards suspended in the same way.

He cried out, a single strangled scream that died before it had completely escaped his throat.

Beneath the tree, he saw a girl dressed in a *chang-ao* sitting on the back of a huge black tortoise. She was giggling, one hand almost concealing her childish smile. Carter was transfixed by her as the tortoise slowly ambled forward, scraping over the stones. The girl's eyes seemed to glow with white light.

Though he didn't initially notice, the tortoise somehow transformed into a crane and flew into the night sky with the child still on its back.

Carter watched them soar upward, the white feathers of the bird becoming brighter and brighter until he had to shield his eyes from the light. And he felt its wings beat down with hurricane force winds that blew through the tree and made the tags jingle.

Then the crane was gone, replaced by a bigger bird, a Huey gunship – its cold spotlight glaring down on Carter like a single cyclopean eye. It took him into its body.

* * *

Pearson, known as *the spook* behind his back at Da Nang Air Force base, stalked into the darkened room fresh from the helipad, a stack of tan files clutched in his hand. "Has he said anything?" he asked.

Colonel Denning glanced over his shoulder at Pearson and shook his head. "Still not a word."

"So we still have no real idea what's happening to him?"

"Nope."

Pearson stared into the bright interrogation room through the one-way mirror. Sergeant Jake Carter was seated at a non-descript government-issue table facing them, a blank expression pasted on his face. Another soldier was in the room with him, on the other side of the table questioning him – a captain. There seemed to be no response from Carter, no matter what the captain said or asked.

"Has he been like this the whole time? Two months?"

"Yeah, more or less." Denning waved a hand. The time no longer mattered, as far as he was concerned.

"Why are we here today?"

"Well, today he made a face."

"A *face*? You got me here from Saigon because Carter *made a face*?"

"It's considered quite the event among the medical staff," the colonel said, frowning. "As if you cared." Carter was one of his boys. *He* cared.

Pearson ignored the snideness. "What's the deal with him again? Remind me."

The colonel sighed. "The docs say it's traumatic psychosis – dissociation disorder. He's semi-catatonic. But there is something going on in there, in his brain. Something continuously traumatic. "

Pearson looked in at the sergeant, who seemed to be staring at him through the glass. It made the agent uncomfortable, so he stalked to the other side of the room.

"I've lost four teams," Pearson said. "His was the first, he's the only one who came back, and we don't know shit about why. Or what they saw up there."

"With all due respect," Denning said, displaying very little of it, "*we* lost the teams. *You* have lost control of your fucking mission. Maybe you and your spook buddies should just give up and move on to some other sampan on the river."

Pearson ignored the tone; he was used to it. "That's a good reason to send in another team, right? We need to find those missing soldiers and Yards."

Carter's stare from the other side of the mirror once again focused on Pearson. The agent nonchalantly moved around the room to avoid the sergeant's burrowing eyes. They made him unaccountably nervous.

"What exactly are we dealing with, Agent Pearson?" Anger rose in the colonel's voice. "What the hell have your people been up to, on that mountain? I don't think you care about the missing teams, not at all."

Pearson looked away from the colonel and the glass partition, both. "We don't know what it is, but the natives are scared shitless by it." He combed his rough hair with a tanned hand. "We don't need something like that falling into the enemy's hands."

"You're assuming they saw a *weapon*?" Denning was incredulous. "That's *it*?"

Pearson ignored him. He'd gotten good at doing the Company's bidding, wielding rank and power, and ultimately dismissing the Army's objections to every little thing.

"I'd say that's quite enough, Colonel. We don't need any new offensive tools used against us, and Charlie's using his influence in Laos to aid the enemy. We damned well *do* assume it's a weapon. It seems to be working on you."

The colonel muttered a curse and turned away. He knew who swung the bigger balls, unfortunately. Anywhere else...

Meanwhile Pearson had noticed that in the other room, the sergeant's eyes seemed to glow, surreal light shining from behind his staring irises. The spook kept pacing, trying to get out from under Carter's zombie gaze.

He made up his mind. "Just send in another team, Colonel. That'll come across your desk as an order within the hour."

"Goddamn you, isn't it enough..."

The colonel's voice faded in and out as Pearson was suddenly entranced by Carter's eyes, which grew brighter and brighter until he had to squint to avoid the painful glow.

Pearson felt a breeze blowing, and when he opened his eyes he was staring at a golden sunset as the wind fluttered the weeds on a flat mountaintop. Behind him there was a light ringing sound, like muffled windchimes clanking in the tree branches and, he would later swear, a child's mocking laughter.

* * *

The staccato throb of the Huey's rotors was deafening as the helicopter cut its path through the night sky. The insertion point was just ahead, south of Luang Prabang and east of the Mekong in central Laos.

They were going *over the fence.* Their escort, two gunships loaded for bear, flanked them.

Special Forces Sergeant Jake Carter, One-Zero of Recon Team Python, sat with the hundred round drum magazine of the Russian RPD Light Machine Gun resting on his knee.

He was staring out the Huey's open door, past the ride-along gunner.

Below them an open field of elephant grass that the boys called the Golf Course stretched in all directions, illuminated by the glow of the nearly full moon.

He sighed and turned away from the door, refocusing his attention on the team. Kane and Mac and others.

In his memory, some windchimes and a child's laughter seemed to play over and over, like an out of tune recording. It was a tape loop, and it was always out of tune.

A familiar flat mountaintop temple awaited him for the hundredth time, and he tried to remember his team members' names.

Maybe this time it'll be different.

He wasn't sure what the voice in his head intended to say, all he knew was that he hoped so.

"Five minutes to insertion..."

Carter got ready to face it all again.

THE SHRINE

David W. Amendola

A ll right, Schultz, stop here."

The Mark III ground to a halt on the hill crest, engine growling in idle. Dust powdered the tank's steel armor, subduing its dark gray paint and the black-and-white German cross on the side. The turret bore the white number 525. On the front hull was a yellow Y with two ticks – the emblem of the 9th Panzer Division.

Stretching to the horizon was bleak, empty steppe, tall grass rippling in the moaning breeze like an endless, brown ocean. The relentless afternoon sun blazed orange in a cloudless sky. About three hundred meters away, stark and alone at the bottom of a flat, shallow valley, stood a little church of white stone, its black onion dome topped by the three-barred cross of the Russian Orthodox Church.

Sergeant Langer, the tank commander, stood in the cupola and pushed up his dirty goggles. He wiped his tanned, sweaty face and scanned the church with binoculars.

"Looks deserted," he said into the throat microphone of the intercom.

The voice of Private Schultz, the driver, came over his headphones. "So what do we do?"

"Secure the area and wait, those are the orders. A special detachment is supposed to rendezvous with us."

"I hope so, Herr Sergeant," said Private Koch, the radioman, who sat below in the front hull next to the driver. "We're way out of radio range now."

"They needed someone here in a hurry and we were the only ones available," said Langer. "Everyone else is pushing to link up with Guderian and cut off Kiev."

"Lucky us," said Private Hoppe, the loader, raising his voice so he could be heard above the engine noise. The tank was open for ventilation and he sat halfway out of the left turret hatch. "If Ivan decides to show up we'll have problems." Ivan was slang for the Russians.

That prompted a grunt of agreement from Corporal Meyer, the gunner, sitting in the right turret hatch. A grunt was his usual contribution to any conversation.

"Well, hopefully Ivan is more worried about Kiev right now," said Langer.

"Hopefully," said Hoppe.

"War's almost over anyway," said Koch. "In a month Stalin will be finished, we'll march in a victory parade in Moscow, and then we can go home to Vienna."

The crew was Austrian, like everyone else in 9th Panzer. After their country had been annexed by Hitler in 1938 it was renamed Ostmark, they were declared citizens of the Reich, and their military was absorbed by the German Army.

By now – early September 1941 – they were veterans of Hitler's wars. All of them had earned the Panzer Combat Badge for having been in at least three tank battles. They had fought together in the Netherlands and France the previous year, then in Greece and Yugoslavia last spring before the division was shipped east for the invasion of the Soviet Union.

Langer and his men did not question the rationale for it all. The Führer commanded; they obeyed. Such was the way of things. And thus far they had seen only victories. Germany seemed destined to rule all of Europe.

"Headquarters sent us all the way out here to capture an old church?" asked Schultz. "What's so special about it, Herr Sergeant?"

"The lieutenant didn't say. Strange place for one though. According to the map there isn't a village within a hundred kilometers." Langer twisted around and raised his binoculars. "Looks like our colleagues have arrived."

A gray column of vehicles rumbled up a dirt road behind them, brown-red dust rising in a choking cloud in its wake. In the lead was a sidecar motorcycle. It was followed by a heavy eight-wheeled 231 armored car, a Volkswagen field car, half a dozen three-ton Opel Blitz transport trucks, a communications truck, and an anti-aircraft gun mounted on a halftrack. A light 222 armored car brought up the rear. One truck had a Nazi flag spread over its top for air recognition.

Langer noted the double lightning-bolt runes emblazoned on the registration plates.

"SS," he said. "Can't tell which unit."

"A sun wheel swastika is the Viking Division and a key on a shield is the Hitler Bodyguard Regiment," said Koch. "Those are the two Waffen-SS units in the Ukraine right now."

"I don't see any insignia at all. Not even a tactical symbol. Odd."

They watched the convoy pull up behind the hill. Their platoon commander, Lieutenant Krugmann, climbed out of his tank and walked down to the Volkswagen. He exchanged salutes with two officers riding in the back. They conferred briefly and Krugmann returned to his tank.

His crisp voice came over the FuG 5 radio. "Provide over-watch while the building's cleared."

The platoon's five tanks stood ready on the hill as an infantry squad jumped down from the trucks. Each soldier was clad in the field-gray uniform of the German Army but with the collar runes, cuff title, and sleeve eagle of the Waffen-SS. The cuff title would indicate their unit, but at this distance Langer could not read it.

The church had one entrance, a heavy, iron-bound wood door. There were no windows. The squad circled around the hill to approach it obliquely, an SS-Sergeant in the lead followed by a machine-gun team and several riflemen. Upon reaching it they edged along the front wall to the door. The sergeant kicked it in and charged inside, followed by the others.

Half a minute later he emerged and held up his weapon to signal all-clear, followed by shrill blasts on his whistle. In response the SS vehicles rolled up to the church and parked.

"Form a hedgehog," said Krugmann. The tanks fanned out into a defensive ring around the valley, facing outwards. "We'll be escorting the convoy back once they're finished here. Everyone can relax in the meantime, but stay alert."

Engines switched off. The silence was deafening as Meyers, Hoppe, Koch, and Schultz emerged, grateful to get out of the hot, stinking tank. Because of the heat they had stripped off their black wool jackets and just wore the gray shirts, sleeves rolled up.

The other tank crews were taking advantage of the lull to get fresh air, stretch cramped legs, and relieve themselves. Shadows lengthened as dusk neared.

Meyer munched on sausage. Despite being as skinny as a rail he seemed to have a bottomless pit for a stomach and never passed up a chance to eat. Schultz hopped on the rear deck and popped open a maintenance hatch. Grit was always getting into the engine and he fretted and fussed over his "Liebling." Langer stayed in the cupola, observing the activity at the church through his binoculars.

"Who's the fat one?" asked Koch. "He looks like he's on parade."

Langer focused on the Volkswagen. The two officers had stepped out. One was tall and lean and wore the collar tab of an SS Captain. The other was an SS Colonel, a rotund, spectacled man dressed in the prewar black SS uniform complete with shiny jackboots and red swastika armband. His bulging uniform looked crisp and new and boasted no decorations at all. He hardly seemed to fit the idealized SS image with its emphasis on physical fitness.

"Must be an SS part-timer who still has the old uniform," said Langer. "His rank's probably honorary. Civilians have to wear uniforms in occupied territory so this may be the first time he's actually had to put it on."

Hoppe snorted with contempt. Digging out a crumpled pack of cigarettes, he lit one and passed the rest around.

They watched as the SS officers gazed up at the church, the captain pointing out various details while the colonel bobbed his head in agreement. Once the latter was satisfied, the former barked out orders. Moving at double-time, a second squad dismounted and hauled out equipment and crates, carrying them inside. One truck towed a generator trailer; a power cable was unreeled and run into the church.

"What's in there?" asked Koch, swatting a fly on his neck. "Supplies?"

"No idea," said Langer. "Seems too small to store much though."

"Maybe loot," said Schultz, closing the maintenance hatch. "Icons and so forth."

"Souvenirs for Herr Göring's art collection," said Hoppe, a sour look on his face.

Hermann Göring, commander-in-chief of the German Air Force, was notorious for his extravagant lifestyle and took full advantage of Hitler's conquests to appropriate whatever valuables he could from the occupied territories.

The sun sank into its pyre in the west and a gibbous moon glowered down like a gleaming skull. The night was quiet except for the rattling drone of the generator, the church door outlined by a strong light inside.

The generator sputtered and stopped; the light blinked off.

A horrific bedlam of screams rang out.

The crews scrambled into their tanks, banging hatches shut. Engines roared into fierce life, spouting exhaust; turrets swiveled to aim at the church.

The screaming ceased.

A long, tense silence. Then the radio crackled. "I've lost contact," snapped Krugmann. "Five-two-five, investigate and report!"

Langer repeated and acknowledged the order and dropped down into the turret. Schultz swung the Mark III around, keeping the headlights off. Langer looked through the cupola's visor as they rumbled down the slope, wheels and tracks squeaking and clanking. Hoppe opened an ammunition locker, ready to load armor-piercing or high explosive shells as Meyer peered through the 50-millimeter cannon's telescopic sight. Koch double-checked the ammunition belt of his MG34 machine-gun in the bow.

The tank stopped just short of the parked SS vehicles, silhouettes in the pale moonlight. All was still – still as a tomb. The only sound was the tank's engine.

Langer opened the cupola. "Herr Colonel?" he called out. "Herr Captain? Anyone?"

No answer.

"Dammit, we're going to have to get out and check," he said. "Meyer, Hoppe, Koch – come with me. Schultz, stay here. Keep the tank buttoned up and the motor running."

The four crewmen climbed out and buckled on flap holsters holding Walther pistols. Hoppe, Koch and Meyer exchanged looks and drew theirs; Langer unfolded the stock of an MP40 submachine gun and snapped in a long magazine. Led by him, they ventured forward.

They approached the 222 armored car, kneeling beside it. Langer rapped on the hull, but there was no response. Peering inside through the open driver's visor, he flicked on a flashlight.

Slumped in their seats were all three crewmen – motionless, mouths gaping, eyes fixed in the glassy stare of death. He could not see what killed them, but there was no blood. Langer turned to the others and made a slicing motion across his throat. They hissed profanity.

At Langer's gesture they moved on. Circling the building, they checked the other vehicles and found the same thing. Dead drivers or crews. After scavenging three more MP40s to better arm themselves, the crew crept up to the church.

The heavy wooden door stood ajar, the generator cable snaking in through the crack. They snapped back submachine gun bolts. Motioning for the others to wait, Langer stepped inside, crouching, finger on the trigger. His eyes darted around, probing the pitch blackness for lurking enemies.

Nothing.

He switched on his flashlight and swept its beam around. Then he lowered his weapon and beckoned for the others to enter. Hardened to the horrors of war, their only outward reaction was to raise eyebrows at the sight their flashlights revealed.

The SS soldiers were sprawled dead across the floor.

Hoppe glanced over the nearest corpses. "Don't see a mark on them."

"We didn't hear any explosions," said Koch.

"No shots either, and no casings on the floor."

"So what killed them?"

"I don't know," said Langer.

They looked around. The interior did not resemble the layout of an Orthodox church. Normally it would be divided into vestibule, nave, and sanctuary, but there was only a single, domed chamber, empty except for the dead, and the stone walls were completely bare. No altar, no chairs, no icons.

"There's nothing in here," said Koch, puzzled.

As Langer stepped among the dead men he scrutinized their uniforms. Sewn on their lower left sleeves was a black diamond bearing a white branched rune, a specialist patch he did not recognize. Below it was a black cuff band with the abbreviation RFSS stitched in silver.

"Reichsführer-SS," he said. "This is the cuff title for Heinrich Himmler's personal staff."

Langer stopped beside the corpse of the colonel and searched the man's pockets, finding civilian and SS identification cards. They stated he was Doctor Ernst Ziegler, a professor of astronomy. What was an astronomer doing in a war zone?

Deepening the mystery was a special pass declaring that Ziegler, 'by order of the Reichsführer-SS, carries out research of a special and urgent nature about which the details may not be divulged.' Cooperation was requested of all civilian, police, and military authorities.

Langer checked the captain next and found a Waffen-SS paybook. It contained a summary of the officer's military record: personal data, training, promotions, awards, and so forth. Flipping through he learned the man's current assignment was SS-Sonderkommando Ziegler – SS Special Command Ziegler – which meant nothing to him. The SS routinely created a multitude of temporary task forces for a variety of duties and each was usually named after its commanding officer, in this case the unfortunate colonel.

The captain also carried a leather map case. Glancing inside, Langer saw the security classification and special handling caveat marked on a document cover for something code-named Aktion Kosmisch (Operation Cosmic) and read no further.

He returned to the tank and radioed his findings to the lieutenant.

"Must have been poison gas," said Krugmann. "A booby trap."

"We didn't smell anything unusual," said Langer, "and the bodies don't show any of the signs. No burns or blisters, no pale skin. No vomit or diarrhea. It's like they just dropped dead."

"What else could have killed them? You say there aren't any wounds."

"True, Herr Lieutenant, but if it was gas, why weren't we affected?"

"It could have dissipated before you got there. Maybe the Russians have developed a new non-persistent agent no one's heard of before, one that leaves no external symptoms. Put your masks on. And put on gloves before touching anything. I'm coming down there."

Langer dug out the crew's M38 gas masks, decontamination tablets, gas capes, and gloves. Telling Schultz to don his mask, he slipped on his own before carrying the rest in to the others. As he passed on the lieutenant's instructions, Meyer beckoned to him.

He pointed at the floor. It was paved with heavy flagstones and he shone his flashlight down on a large one set in the center. It had an old, faded Cyrillic inscription with what appeared to be a year: 1801.

"Fresh pry marks along the edges," said Langer, kneeling to examine it more closely. He glanced over at the equipment the SS soldiers had brought in. Much of it was excavating tools: pry bars, hammers, mattocks, shovels, and a block-and-tackle hoist on a tripod had been erected. "They were trying to raise this."

Hoppe raised an eyebrow. "Grave robbing?"

"Maybe. Can anyone read Russian?" The others shook their heads.

A floodlight had been set up, but when Langer tried to switch it on it did not work. The bulb looked fine, so he went out and checked the generator. Despite having plenty of fuel it would not start. Upon closer inspection the wiring appeared to have melted somehow. The building itself had no electric lighting, only empty wall sconces for candles.

"Get these bodies out of here," said Langer, arms akimbo. "Tell Schultz to come help."

Meyer fetched Schultz and the four crewmen began snapping off identification disks and collecting paybooks from the corpses before carrying them outside.

Krugmann strode in with four other tank crewmen, all wearing gas masks and gloves. The others snapped to attention, but he motioned for them to stand at ease. His crew joined Langer's men in their gruesome task.

Langer handed Krugmann the map case, the identity cards of the two SS officers, and Ziegler's special pass. The lieutenant switched on his flashlight and inspected them.

"Did you read any of this?" he asked Langer at length, giving him a sharp look.

"Only the identity papers, Herr Lieutenant."

"Well, this was a unit of SS Special Command Ziegler, a detachment that doesn't fall under any of the main departments of the SS. It's part of Himmler's personal staff."

"What was it organized for?"

"Seems SKZ was created just before the war for the purpose of 'retrieving artifacts of special scientific importance from frontline areas.' They had orders to capture this shrine."

"What for, Herr Lieutenant?"

"I'm still trying to piece that together. These other documents reference an SS file classified Secret State Material, which for obvious reasons would never be taken out into the field. So this is a redacted summary. One thing's clear though: the Russians thought the shrine was important too. According to this intelligence report, it's the only religious building in the area the Communists didn't demolish. NKVD security troops defended this sector until yesterday when they were pulled back to help defend Kiev. That gave SKZ the chance they needed. Our division was closest so Himmler requested we assist."

"Why would Stalin's security police be guarding a religious shrine?"

"Good question. I'll send a preliminary report to headquarters. I'll have to use the long-range radio in the communications truck since our tanks' radios won't reach."

Krugmann returned shortly, irritated. "Radio doesn't work. See if your men can fix it. And get one of the trucks ready. We don't have room in our tanks to carry anything."

"Koch, Schultz, take care of it," said Langer. The pair hurried off.

Krugmann resumed reading. "On April 15, 1801 a meteorite landed here. The czarist authorities investigated, but the findings were kept secret and have never been released. The Holy Synod was so alarmed it ordered everything at the site buried and had this shrine built over it."

"Why would SKZ be interested in a meteorite?"

"Because when Doctor Ziegler analyzed old news reports he concluded it wasn't a meteor. He calculated it was traveling too slow and the impact crater was too small. Eyewitnesses claimed it zigzagged across the sky before it hit. Ziegler thought what actually crashed was some kind of craft. But no one's ever excavated the site to see what's buried here. The Orthodox Church forbade any digging, a prohibition that's continued under the Bolsheviks."

Langer frowned. "There weren't any aircraft in 1801."

"No there weren't."

"God, what a crazy story."

"Exactly what our Air Ministry's technical office and the Army Ordnance research office said. They consider it nonsense from superstitious peasants. After all, when a meteorite blew up over Siberia about thirty years ago the locals thought the destruction was caused by some pagan god. Since the military wasn't interested Himmler ordered SKZ to get involved. If what's buried here really was from another planet there might be useful parts left. Recovering advanced technology would be an incredible coup if it could be reverse-engineered into something of military use. And the Reichsführer is always looking for ways to increase his power and influence."

Koch and Schultz returned. "Herr Lieutenant," said Koch, "none of the radios in the truck can be repaired. The wires and tubes are burned out and we have no spares."

"None of the trucks will start either," said Schultz. "Nor will any of the other SS vehicles. All their electrical systems are shorted-out."

"I found the same thing when I tried to restart the generator," added Langer.

Krugmann let out an exasperated sigh. "Then siphon off as much gas as you can for the tanks. No sense leaving it for Ivan." Krugmann turned back to Langer, "We can assume headquarters would have ordered us to take over Operation Cosmic."

"What happened to their vehicles?"

"I don't know." He pondered this for a few moments. "Never heard of poison gas causing an electrical overload. It can't have been that after all." He pulled off his mask. "Go ahead and take them off," he told the others.

"Why weren't our tanks affected? Or us?"

"It must have a limited radius."

"And if we disturb it we're liable to trigger it again."

"We'll have risk it. We're digging it up, whatever it is."

"Yes, Herr Lieutenant." He tried to keep misgivings out of his voice. Orders were orders.

At Krugmann's direction Langer's tank was moved back to the hill. Another crew stood watch on the crest, scanning the moonlit steppe for signs of the enemy. The ominous clatter of diesel engines had been heard way off in the distance.

Inside the shrine the flagstone was pried up and ropes were slipped over it. These were hooked to the hoist, moved into position to raise it. The heavy slab rose in slow jerks as the platoon's strongest men, stripped to the waist, pulled in unison, the pulleys creaking. The atmosphere was tense.

But nothing happened. Under the flagstone was a pit. The slab was swung to one side and lowered onto the floor. Everyone crowded around the edge and shined flashlights down.

A couple meters deep, it was lined with stone like a burial vault. At the bottom were two hollow hemispheres about a meter in diameter, made of a shiny, aluminum-like metal. The outer surfaces were studded with crystalline protuberances resembling the contact detonators of a naval mine. Krugmann jumped down, put on his gloves, and picked one up.

"Well, that's definitely not a meteorite," said Hoppe.

"Looks like the halves of a big, hollow ball," said Koch.

Krugmann set down the hemisphere and shone his flashlight around. He spotted fragments and picked one up. It was a jagged, curved shard of an unknown substance, pale blue and smooth as glass. Clambering back out, he continued his examination, turning the shard over in his gloved hands. He tested its strength. It snapped easily in two.

"Any ideas, Herr Lieutenant?" asked Langer.

Krugmann rubbed his chin. "They probably lifted the slab just enough to see if anything was under there, poked around, and triggered whatever killed them; some anti-tampering device. Then the slab fell back in place."

"What was in the sphere?"

"No idea. All I found were these pieces." He turned to the others. "Four of you get down there and start digging. See if anything is buried."

A ladder was lowered and four men descended with spades

and buckets. Handling them carefully, the hemispheres and blue fragments were brought up and laid out on the floor. The men found a hole in one corner, just big enough to admit an adult. The smallest of the men, a lean, wiry fellow, crawled in to take look.

"What's in there, Hans?" asked a colleague.

"A tunnel of some sort. Has a funny smell."

Up above, Krugmann stared at the inscription on the flagstone. "I studied Russian at university before the war, so I should be able to translate this," he said. Frowning, he brought out the SS documents again, looking for a particular reference. When he found it he compared it with the inscription. His scowl deepened.

A slight tremor shuddered through the shrine. Everyone stopped and looked around.

"Earthquake?" an anxious crewman asked.

A second, stronger tremor shook them. The men in the pit scrambled out.

Krugmann's eyes widened with sudden realization. "Get out of here! Now!"

The crews rushed outside and dashed for their vehicles. Even as they ran the ground heaved beneath their feet again and this time it did not stop. Two men stumbled and fell. Krugmann dragged them to their feet and exhorted them on.

The platoon jumped into the Mark IIIs, relieved the engines were still warm so they could use the electric self-starters instead of standing outside and hand-cranking them. The noise of them firing up was drowned out by a deep rumbling.

"Herr Lieutenant, what's happening?" asked Langer over the radio. He strained to hear the officer's reply over the din.

"Fools!" said Krugmann. "Ziegler should have read the inscription. The translation was wrong. It's a warning from the Holy Synod."

"What was in the sphere?"

"An egg! Opening the sphere let it hatch!"

Langer twisted around in the cupola to look. Even as he

watched a great fissure opened beneath the crumbling shrine and swallowed it up, the SS vehicles tumbling into the yawning abyss after it. The crashes were drowned out by the tremendous roar. A cloud of dust was thrown up, and through it huge slimy tentacles thrust from smoking cracks in the earth. Leprous and gray in the moonlight, ever more limbs sprouted as they grew at an impossible, unearthly rate. A great, reeking stench wafted out.

Then a huge mechanical beast rumbled into view. Langer's blood froze. It was a Russian heavy tank.

Most of the Soviet tanks they had fought thus far had been obsolete prewar machines. Combined with poor tactics, they proved no match for the panzers. But this was one of the new models, a KV-1, a 47-ton monster with armor so thick the only German weapons currently capable of penetrating it were the big guns of the artillery. And the powerful 76.2-millimeter cannon on the behemoth's massive turret could easily punch through a Mark III.

Tentacles lunged for the KV-1, coiling around its hull like serpents. Vapor rose as their rows of suckers, apparently secreting some sort of acidic enzyme, started melting through, trying to get at the helpless crew trapped inside.

With blinding speed the thing also turned on the Germans, engulfing four of the Mark IIIs in a storm of flailing tentacles. Langer's tank, farther back, was ignored for the moment.

"Open fire!" he ordered. "Machine guns only!"

The bow and coaxial machine-guns erupted with buzzing roars as Koch and Meyer slashed at the tentacles entwining the other vehicles. Lines of green tracers streaked across, 7.92-millimeter bullets shredding pale rubbery flesh and splattering sticky blood, ringing and ricocheting off the smoldering steel. The desperate voices of the other tank commanders flooded the radio. The thing, whatever it was, grew new limbs as fast as they were blown off. The voices disintegrated into screams.

Langer's crew cursed helplessly as the other four German tanks were reduced to corroded, entangled hulks. Hatches were thrown open on a couple, but no one emerged. The radio fell silent. The KV-1 still fought the creature, but tentacles were inexorably dissolving through even its thick armor. The running gear on one side had already melted and collapsed, immobilizing it.

The thing turned its attention to Langer's tank next. He dropped into the turret and slammed the hatch closed as the Mark III was seized.

"Schultz, get us out of here!"

Schultz shifted into reverse and floored the accelerator pedal. The 300-horsepower Maybach engine bellowed like a bull, but the straining Mark III could not move. He wrenched the steering levers back and forth, desperately trying to wrestle the tank free.

"I can't break loose!" he said.

The metal around them began to bubble and hiss. More tanks rattled out of the gloom. Through the visor Langer recognized the silhouettes of the T-26, a light Russian tank considered easy meat for German anti-tank gunners. They had destroyed untold numbers of them in battle. Three raced up in what looked to Langer to be a suicide charge, a brave but futile attempt to divert the thing's attention.

Their gun barrels were shorter than normal. A moment later he realized why when their stubby muzzles aimed upwards and long yellow-white streams of fire jetted out. These were KhT-133 tanks, a flamethrower variant of the T-26 designed for assaulting fortifications.

The slimy tentacles ignited instantly, recoiling as fire flashed along their length and wreathed them in orange flames. Langer's tank and the KV-1 were released. The blazing, writhing limbs shrank back into the crevasse and disappeared from view. Oily black smoke rose; Langer gagged on an even more horrible stench.

"Burn, you bastard, burn!" said Koch.

Russian infantry, engineers judging from their equipment, jumped down from the tanks and hurried forward to the edge. Langer guessed they would set demolition charges to turn the lair into a tomb, burying the horror forever.

The KV-1's turret began rotating back towards him.

Langer jerked a cable repeatedly. In rapid succession smoke canisters mounted on a rack at the rear of the Mark III dropped to the ground.

"Back us up!" he said.

Schultz reversed into the thick cloud billowing up. The tank's front armor was the thickest so he kept that towards the enemy, but he also tried to face it at an angle, giving them a chance that an incoming round might ricochet instead of penetrating.

The KV-1's cannon boomed and a loud clang deafened the crew. Meyer and Hoppe cried out; hot pain stabbed Langer's leg. The shell had glanced off, but the impact sprayed spall across the compartment like shrapnel. Moments later a second screeched past, missing entirely, the Russian gunner's aim spoiled by the smoke screen.

Schultz kept going backwards until they were behind the cover of the hill, then slammed the levers to spin the tank around, the tracks ripping up the dirt. He shifted into forward gear, stomped down the accelerator, and roared off at full speed into the night.

Gritting his teeth against the pain of his wound, Langer watched for signs of pursuit, but saw none. The KV-1 was disabled and the flamethrower tanks were still finishing off the creature. The Germans drove on in silence, shaken by the vision of the nameless thing they had stirred up, thinking of the comrades they had lost – and for what?

As Hoppe opened a first aid kit, Langer sourly reflected that Heinrich Himmler would have to concoct a new scheme to impress the Führer.

PTEARING ALL BEFORE US

Steve Ruthenbeck

Five men on horseback rode through a sea of grass.
And then there were four…

A sun so hot it might have been the devil's eye fried Grant's face. Sweat turned his blue uniform black, and the yellow gloves tucked into his belt flopped with each step of his horse. Grant couldn't tell which smelled worse, him or his mount.

Grant tried to take his mind off his discomfort by reading a newspaper. Headlines included: *Alexander Graham Bell receives a patent for an invention called a telephone; Dakota farmer discovers a dinosaur skeleton in wheat field; Morgan Bulkeley elected President of the National League of Professional Baseball Clubs…*

Success stories everywhere, so why couldn't it happen to him?

Envy raised Grant's temperature further. He removed his hat to mop perspiration from his brow, swallowed the last gulp of tepid water from his canteen and turned back to see how the rest of the party was doing.

Breckenridge slept in his saddle. Stubble covered his cheeks, and dust turned his sunburned skin to the ashen tone of a corpse.

Webster rode behind Breckenridge. Webster had been overweight when he joined the Third Cavalry, but two years of living mainly on beans and hardtack so tough it could double for bricks, if a mason was desperate enough, had turned him into a wisp.

Paulson scanned the horizon for threats. He didn't bother with surveying the immediate area. If Indians were within killing range, a person wouldn't see them until the bullets started flying.

Bringing up the rear, a roan stallion plodded along with something like supplication in its manner. It saddle was empty.

"Whoa," Grant stopped his horse. He tucked the newspaper under his saddle and waved a swarm of buffalo gnats away from his face before their bites could swell his eyelids.

"What is it?" Breckenridge jerked awake. "What's wrong?"

"Where's Jack?" Grant asked.

Jack was short for Jackrabbit Otter, an Indian scout who helped the white men due to a longstanding feud with the Cheyenne. Grant once saw the man divine the nature of an Indian party from the position of the urine puddles left by their horses (war parties seldom used mares). Such skills were unnecessary in this campaign, however. The Indian trails they had come across were over half a mile wide. The ground looked like a plowed field from all the lodge poles dragged across it. Area wildlife was also stirred up by the multitudes passing through. Grant and his party had come across a mountain lion even though the Bighorn Mountains were fifty miles away. These sights compelled Jackrabbit Otter to sing *Amazing Grace*, which he had adapted as his new death song.

"He was here a minute ago," Paulson answered Grant.

Guns came up and eyes scanned tall grass – a high-stakes Indian Button Game. In the Button Game, one team watched another team pass, or pretend to pass, a button back and forth. If they guessed the man who held the button when the passing was finished, they won. Now the button was potential targets and guessing was guns.

Grant calculated. If they were in the middle of an ambush, Jack was as good as dead, and they were next in line. However, if Jack had succumbed to heat exhaustion and fell off his horse, he'd disappear in the tall grass, and they'd have to backtrack to find him.

Breckenridge revealed he was thinking the same thing. "Jack wouldn't have gotten sunstroke. He was Sioux."

"What's on his doggy?" Webster slid his hand along the shoulder of Jack's horse as it sidled past him. His palm came away red with blood.

"Ride!" Grant shouted.

Grant spurred his horse before the order fully escaped his lips. The wind of passage dried the sweat of his brow. Hooves beating against the soft soil of the Montana plain sounded like fists pummeling a man to death. Grant knew he didn't dare push the animal long. It'd burn out in this heat – all their horses would – and they'd be overtaken. He figured they were midway between the Tongue and Powder Rivers, which would intersect with the Yellowstone thirty miles ahead. That's where they hoped to rendezvous with old 'Hard Ass' himself. In the meantime, the terrain left little options: nothing but grass to the north, too many Indians to the west and what looked like a rock formation to the east.

"Come on, Cerberus!" Grant urged his horse toward the rock formation, swatting its rump with the flat side of his saber for that extra motivation. Grant turned back to make sure the others followed. They did, riding low in their saddles. Blisters burst on Grant's thighs as he faced front once more. They had been pushing hard since coming out of Fort Fetterman and harder still since the Indians turned back the rest of the Third at Rosebud Creek. Grant volunteered for leading the detail to warn the Seventh Cavalry. The Seventh had to know that General Crook would no longer be coming up from the south to support them.

Cerberus began to flag. Grant cherished the horse, once punching a man in the jaw for trying to ride him without permission, but he gave the animal no quarter in this race. Cerberus was a fine mount, and the Indians would surely keep him if they killed his master. Hence, Cerberus could rest once they reached their destination.

The rock formation was approximately twenty-five yards in circumference. Its western side was taller than the rest, with sheer walls nearly fifteen feet high. If the four of them could get to the top, they could hold off a large number of Indians. All they'd have to worry about was running out of ammunition, which shouldn't be a problem. Indians typically didn't lay siege, and each man carried a Spencer rifle with one hundred and forty rounds and a Colt revolver with thirty.

Grant pulled back on the reins as Cerberus reached the rocks. He flipped his leg over the stallion's neck, grabbed his rifle and supplies (which were rolled up in a blanket) and clambered up onto the formation. He found cover in a shallow crevasse and aimed his Spencer back along the way he had come. Paulson, Breckenridge and Webster weren't far behind. They jumped off the horses, gave them slaps on the hindquarters to get them out of the line of fire and joined Grant on the rocks.

"Webster, cover north side!" Grant ordered. "Paulson, east! I'll watch south! Breckenridge, get up top!"

Grant surveyed the southern expanse through gun sights. No Indians pursued. The grass swayed with the wind, and clouds moved across the sky. A thin haze of alkaline dust made the horizon appear indistinct. The only thing that moved was Grant's newspaper, which had fallen from his saddle and drifted on a breeze to nowhere.

Maybe they were in the clear, but Grant didn't believe it. His sweat-soaked clothes felt clammy despite the day's heat. The feeling in his gut was something he had never experienced before, even though uneasiness was the state of being for a cavalryman. Forty miles a day on beans and hay, wishing one would never come across an Indian, yet half-hoping one would, have it done with and go home.

"Oh hell!" Breckenridge cried from atop the rock formation. His bass voice sounded on the verge of cracking into a tenor.

"What is it?" Grant pressed.

"It's Jack!"

Grant squinted to the limits of his southern view, trying to make out a distant rider. "Where? Is he being chased?"

"Not out there! Up here! *Jack's up here!*"

Confusion replaced Grant's unease. Jack couldn't be on top of the rock formation. Wherever Jack was, he was without a horse, and he couldn't have outraced the four of them at the pace they had set. Grant didn't doubt Breckenridge saw someone on top of the rock formation, however. Maybe it was a trick; maybe Jack turned turncoat; or maybe another Indian was up there in disguise, playing possum, waiting for Breckenridge to get closer so he could pop up, screaming and swinging his tomahawk…

"Watch my side!" Grant ordered Webster and scrambled up a cleft to the top of the rocks. Grant pulled himself onto the formation's summit, which was flat as a plate and as wide as two chuck wagons. When he saw what was up there, what felt like a shot of whiskey came up from his stomach, and he forced it back down. Grant had seen bad sights before: men bristling with so many arrows they looked like pin cushions and men mutilated because the Indians believed they'd enter the afterlife maimed. But this was the worst case of such brutality yet. This victim wasn't just missing eyes or organs. He didn't have his tendons cut or muscles split. His body was *strewn*.

"It's Jack," Breckenridge said helplessly.

"How can you tell?" Grant asked.

Breckenridge kicked a head out from behind a rock.

"Holy—" Grant averted his gaze upward. He saw a low-flying bird – a heron, perhaps – with puffy clouds high above it. Then the bird disappeared, and Grant closed his eyes, thinking he was close to passing out if he was hallucinating birds like a punch-drunk boxer.

"What's going on up there?" Paulson called.

Grant bit down on his composure. This excursion was his chance to shine, after all. If successful, an officer's commission was sure to follow. "You and Webster get up here!" Grant managed.

While looking away from the mess, something else caught Grant's eye – petroglyphs carved into the rock formation. Indians must have used the site as a camp during their hunting trips, or while passing through on their annual migrations. Many of the tribes were nomadic, only stopping in semi-permanent camps during the winter. This was a huge disadvantage in their fight against the white men because they had no industrial base to support a war. In effect, the Indians retreated even when they won because their supplies were exhausted. Furthermore, the military forces rooting them out knew this and ruthlessly attacked the Indians' winter encampments, destroying whatever surplus they managed to squirrel away and leaving the Indians weaker with each passing year.

A buffalo, deer, fish, thunderbird, rabbit and wolf – Grant ticked off the animal drawings that made up the petroglyphs. He considered the Indians savages, but he respected their ability to live off the land and hunt the animals that shared the territory with them. The Indians used wildlife for everything from food, shelter and clothing, to boats, tools and, in the case of buffalo chips, fuel for their fires. Grant admired the practicality of it, to get rich off what one could pluck from the earth. Too bad it wasn't that easy in white-man world. Money and reality were all that counted there. That's how Grant knew the Indians were doomed. They still believed in birds so large their wings could create thunder. But how could that compete against people who believed in the bottom line?

"Holy Jesus!" Webster exclaimed when he got to the top.

Paulson followed and went white, despite his leather-like tan.

Webster considered the parts of Jack that remained recognizable as human. "But how? The Indians would have had to grab Jack, throw him on a horse and ride over here… all without us seeing."

"Then that's what happened." Grant saw little point in questioning the horsemanship of the Indians. Ever since the Spanish introduced the animals to North America, the Indians had taken advantage of their benefits, which changed their whole culture. Horses enabled Indians to trade with tribes hundreds of miles away, uproot entire camps and hunt with greater efficiency. Grant had seen cavalrymen ride their own horses to death trying to keep up with Indians who didn't want to be kept up with. "We don't need to worry about how they did it," Grant said. "We need to worry about whether or not they're still out there. We'll stay here for the night. If any Indians are still around, they'll have a hard time getting to us."

"We should keep moving," Breckenridge disagreed. "We're just four men, and the Indians got bigger fish to fry with more blue coats coming in from the east and west. The ones that hit us are probably happy they got Jack and already hightailed it out of here."

"You sure about that?" Grant asked. "What if they get a bee in their bonnet about us? We aren't going to outride any Indians the shape we're in."

"If we stay, more might come," Breckenridge argued.

"I'm with Breckenridge," Webster chimed in. "You've seen the trails, Grant. Too many redskins around for my taste. We need to link up with the Seventh as soon as we can."

"Who's in charge here?" Grant reminded them.

"Jesus wept," Webster shook his head. "What do you think, Paulson?"

Paulson stood with his back to the group, staring off into the distance. "I think you should stop taking the Lord's name in vain."

"And what'll you do if I don't?" Webster challenged.

Paulson turned. "Ask you again."

Webster grinned despite the tension.

Grant watched their easy camaraderie with irritation. He could never find his niche among his fellow soldiers, even though they were an eclectic bunch: book keepers, farm boys, dentists, blacksmiths, salesmen ruined by drink, ivory carvers, Bowery toughs, some out to escape women and some in the army to learn to read and write. Grant knew there had to be others like him, who joined up to get famous, but he never came across them in his travels. Grant had visions of single-handedly defeating a superior force, coming across a mother lode of gold while chasing Indians through mountain passes or rescuing the grateful daughters of homesteaders snatched by raiding parties. Something. Anything. Then he would ride the results to fortune and fame. Instead, all he got was riding here and riding there under the summer sun and winter sky. Plenty of Indians died, to be sure, but what was that worth? Even the market for scalps had dried up. Sadly, promotion had become the best option. Grant figured if he could achieve a high enough rank, maybe he could acquire the status to join a stage show as a trick shooter. Entertainment was the ticket these days.

"You want to know what I think," Paulson said. "I think we're worn out, and I think the horses are worn out. We're in enemy territory, but we're in a defensible position in enemy territory with the bulk of the Indians to the east and heading north by all signs. We have two days to link up with the Seventh at a location that's a day's ride away. I think we should take an hour or two to collect ourselves. Then we can reevaluate riding on at dusk." He turned to Grant, his face inscrutable. "What do you think?"

Grant knew Paulson was finding a middle ground to keep the peace. Still, it wouldn't do to weaken one's authority by acknowledging it.

"We need to round up the horses," Grant ordered. The animals had wandered a short distance away to graze on wild alfalfa. Grant knew if he sent Breckenridge and Webster to wrangle their mounts, they'd talk about him behind his back. "Paulson and Breckenridge, you got the duty. Webster and I will take care of Jack and keep a lookout."

"Fair enough." Paulson led Breckenridge down the rocks.

Grant set about tossing pieces of Jack over the side. The summit wouldn't be so bad if they could get rid of the larger chunks. The blood would quickly dry up in the heat. Grant knew Webster watched him and measured him, so he showed no ill effects even as his stomach churned. He tried to think of the parts as nothing more than firewood. That helped a little. He pointed out a leg.

"You want to get that, Webster?"

"I ain't touching it."

"Afraid you'll get kicked?"

The lines of Webster's face grew taut as the indignation of having his manhood insulted outweighed his disgust. He picked up Jack's leg and threw it over the side. He wiped his hands on the seat of his pants while he watched flies pursue the discarded limb.

"It looks like the back of a hospital tent up here," Webster spat.

Grant found the comparison apt. Doctors loved their amputations. Amputations for frost-bite; amputations for gunshot wounds; amputations for fractures; and amputations for dislocations. Grant remembered one man getting shot in the hip during a skirmish. The company had to transport him one hundred miles back to civilization. In agony, the man begged to be killed the whole way, only to end up getting his wish when the surgeon, unsurprisingly, treated him with an amputation.

Webster's next observation came out toneless and sudden. *"Breckenridge is gone."*

Grant straightened up. "What are you talking about?"

Webster pointed at the grass below. There, Paulson – and nobody but Paulson – led the horses to the base of the stones.

"Where's Breckenridge?" Grant yelled.

"Behind—" Paulson turned and stopped when he saw that he was alone. He drew his pistol and tried to look everywhere at once.

Grant's bad feeling returned. "Get those horses squared away!" Without their mounts, their position would become even more precarious. Grant rushed down from the summit. The east end of the rock formation ended in a pincher shape. There, Grant waited for Paulson to lead the horses into this natural corral and secure their reins to outcroppings.

Webster joined them. "Breckenridge!" he called.

"Quiet!" Grant snapped. "Can't you see the man's gone?"

"If we wouldn't have stopped, he wouldn't be gone!" Webster glared, the line of his shoulders bull-like.

"Get down, both of you!" Paulson growled. "I'm going to fire into the grass. If anything pops up, you guys hit it. Ready?"

Grant and Webster gave grudging assent.

Paulson's gunshots blasted across the prairie. The horses perked up at the noise but were too used to gunfire to panic. No Indians revealed themselves. The grass continued to sway. Cloud shadows chased each other across distant hills, and sweat dripped from the brows of the three men, the only precipitation the rocks had seen in sometime. The silence became as stifling as a muddy sheet. The Indians wouldn't have to speak, Grant knew. Despite the many different tribes of the plains, all of them shared a common sign language. Plus, Grant heard tales of how much Indians valued silence anyway. If Cheyenne babies cried once their needs were met, the mothers would hang them on a bush, alone, until they cried themselves out. The babies quickly learned that excess noise accomplished nothing.

Webster shouted, "What are you waiting for, you chicken shits?" His eyes roved over the grass like drops of water across a hot skillet.

Paulson pulled fresh cartridges from a pouch and pushed them into his rifle. "They're waiting for us to crack, which you're doing."

Webster's tongue stopped flapping, but his cheeks started twitching.

"They can't get to us without crossing open ground," Paulson reminded him. "If there were enough to take us in a stand-up fight, they would have charged already. Understand?"

Webster nodded, controlling his nerves with a shaky breath.

"I want you up top," Paulson said. "*Gary Owen*, right?"

A rueful smirk crossed Webster's features at the mention of the cavalry's anthem. *"We are the boys who take delight, in smashing limerick lamps at night, and through the streets like sportsters fight, tearing all before us,"* Webster recited a verse. He rose to his feet and headed for the summit in a crouch. "Just don't leave without me…"

Grant admired Paulson's tact even as he resented Paulson for usurping his command. Now was not the time to seek retribution, however. To everything there was a season, and Grant could practice tact, as well. "Why haven't the Indians shot at us? You think they don't have guns?"

"They all have guns," Paulson said. His jaw muscles tightened and released. "We take their hunting grounds, and the Indian Bureau gives them guns so they can better hunt the land they got left. Then we take that land, too, and they kill us with the guns we gave them."

"You sound like a sympathizer."

Paulson shook his head. "The Indians get cheated on what they're promised, and traders and political hacks make profits. Accepting the fact they fight back isn't sympathy. It's recognizing human nature."

"Some say Indians aren't human."

"Hell," Paulson scoffed. "A man's a man."

Above, Webster continued to sing *Gary Owen* to himself.

"Instead of spa, we'll drink brown ale, and pay the reckoning on the nail, no man for debt shall go to jail—"

The song broke off into a scream.

"Webster!" Paulson scrambled for the rock formation's summit.

Grant didn't want to expose himself, but if the Indians were up top, he was as good as dead. Fighting offered the best chance to survive whether he liked it or not. He followed Paulson. Webster's screams, meanwhile, took on an odd dwindling quality. Grant started up the cleft, pebbles from Paulson's assent bouncing off his hat. He kept his finger off his rifle's trigger so he didn't accidentally shoot himself. That wouldn't improve his odds any. Grant reached the summit at Paulson's heels.

The top of the rock formation stood deserted.

Webster may as well have disappeared into thin air.

"Where the hell is he?" Incredulous, Grant rushed to the edge of the rock formation and peeked over the side. He had the sudden impression of an Indian lurking below with an arrow notched and pointed straight up, ready to perforate his skull from chin to crown.

"Anything?" Paulson asked.

"Nothing," Grant replied. The imagined Indian was gone, a mirage born of anxiety. Only bits of Jack lay below, now black with flies. Grant turned to Paulson. "How could they have gotten up these walls? They're sheer. And how'd they get Webster down so fast?"

Paulson's face creased in thought, drawing his mouth into a grimace. "I don't know, but it'll be dark soon. We stay up here, back-to-back."

* * *

The sun set; the stain of night spread across the sky, and a quarter moon rose to hold sway over all. The prairie took on an eldritch cast. It might have been a sea and the rock formation an island. Stars glittered indifferently overhead. Despite the heat of the day, the night took on a surprising chill that pushed comfort just beyond reach. The men knew cold. On some winter campaigns, they'd awake frozen to the ground. That didn't make this night any more bearable, however. Cold always had teeth.

Grant and Paulson sat cross-legged, wrapped in Grant's blanket. They held their rifles across their knees and their pistols in their hands. Grant wondered if the Indians would start lobbing arrows at them, but such a thing did not occur. They saw nothing moving in the dim moonlight, and the only sound was the wind.

Grant thought about Jack's remains. Had Breckenridge and Webster been reduced to the same? One minute men, the next minute parts…

Grant grew thirstier and regretted finishing his canteen earlier that day. Remembering the sensation of gulping it empty increased his craving. One wasn't supposed to gulp water, of course. A cavalry health pamphlet recommended swishing and spitting only. Apparently, one could die from drinking too much on the trail. Grant didn't believe it, however. He had seen men follow that advice, taking along only a little water to stave off temptation, and ending up opening veins in their own arms to wet parched lips. Grant wasn't to that point yet, but the desire to go down to the horses and grab a canteen was maddening. Such a thing would be foolhardy, yet he couldn't stop thinking about that itch in the back of his throat. He tried to concentrate on something else, but the only other thing that filled his thoughts was finding Jack.

"If the afterlife's real," Grant asked, trying to keep his tone light. "You think Jack went into it cut up?"

"People have perfect bodies in heaven," Paulson said. "But even if people did go to heaven maimed, that's still better than hell."

Granted shrugged. "I don't believe in heaven or hell. I believe this is all there is, so you better get while you can."

"There's a Bible verse for that outlook. 'What does it profit a man if he gains the world and loses his soul?'"

Grant waved a dismissive hand.

"You can be wrong a long time, and God will give you chances to wise up," Paulson said. "It's not smart to let those chances run out."

"Neither is believing in things that aren't real—"

"Quiet!" Paulson cut Grant off. "You hear that?"

Before Grant could respond, Paulson crawled to the edge of the rock formation. Suddenly sweating, Grant followed with his heart thudding in his ears. If he believed in anything, he might have prayed to keep hearing it thud. He crept up beside Paulson and looked out into the murk. Now, stealthy sound reached his ears as a shape moved through the taller grass thirty yards away. Neither Grant nor Paulson could make out details, but the shape appeared to be of human height.

Paulson counted to three, and flames flashed from their Spencers. The shape collapsed as gun blasts dwindled to echoes.

"We got him!" Grant exclaimed.

An ungodly cry split the night, and the noise raised the hair on the back of Grant's neck. He recognized the sound but couldn't immediately place it. Surely, it was too inhuman to come from a man, and then Grant realized what the cry was and why it was familiar. Back at Fort Fetterman, two soldiers decided to have a horse race the month before. They took off outside the camp in a burst of hoof beats. A short distance later, one of the horses stepped in a gopher hole and broke its leg...

"It's Jack's horse!" Paulson beat Grant to the realization. The animal must have continued to plod along after the rest of them took off for the rock formation. It took all day to cover the distance, perhaps stopping to graze, but now it had finally caught up to them.

The horse continued to scream.

"Damn it!" Grant cursed. He put his rifle back to his shoulder and could just make out the patch of thrashing grass in the moonlight. He emptied the rest of his rounds into the area, and the horse fell silent.

* * *

Both men dozed off sometime after the incident with Jack's mount.

Grant dreamed of the Button Game. He played by himself within a cloud. Every time he opened his hand it contained a wooden button with a petroglyph animal carved into it: a buffalo, a deer, a fish, a thunderbird, a rabbit, and a wolf. Grant placed them into groups, but he kept rearranging them because the groups didn't fit together. The buffalo, deer, rabbit, and wolf seemed to match because they all had four legs, but that left the fish and the thunderbird by themselves. The fish lived in the sea. The thunderbird wasn't real. Grant tried again. He put the deer, fish and rabbit together because they weren't a danger to man, but that left the buffalo and wolf together and the thunderbird alone once more. Grant found himself growing frustrated with the strange logic of dreams. The carvings *had* to fit together. Next, he put the buffalo, deer, fish, rabbit and wolf together. That *felt* right at least. Shrugging, Grant put the thunderbird with them, which felt *exactly* right. It wasn't a satisfying feeling, however. It frightened him.

When Grant awoke, the sun was an hour into the sky. He rubbed his face and grimaced at the gummy slime that had collected at the corners of his mouth. Thirst burned in his throat and turning around to check on Paulson awoke a deep ache in his back.

Paulson was gone.

Grant wobbled to his feet, his pistol drawn and his hand on his saber.

"Relax. I'm over here."

Grant spun on newborn-colt legs. Paulson sat with his feet dangling into the cleft that descended from the rock formation's summit.

"I was waiting for you to wake up," Paulson said. "I'm going down to get food and water. You all right to cover me?"

Grant tried to speak, but his throat was too dry. He nodded instead.

"Back in a minute." Paulson lowered himself out of sight.

Grant holstered his pistol. His mouth started to water at the thought of food, which loosened his shriveled tongue. He willed Paulson to be quick. The idea of gulping from a canteen was joy, peace and celestial choirs. He scanned the surrounding area and saw no signs of danger. The sun's morning light was tranquil rather than torture. The horses still stood in their makeshift corral, waiting. The whole world stood there, waiting.

It's going to be all right, Grant told himself.

They could reach the Yellowstone by dusk, and if they made it through the night, they could make it through the day. Below, Paulson reached the horses. He moved with quick, furtive movements, grabbed his canteen and food pouch and heading back the way he had come.

Grant kept his eyes peeled for the enemy, and movement arrested his attention. It took him a moment to realize what he saw – thirty yards away, black feathers flitted above the surface of the grass.

Feathers! Headdresses! Indians!

Grant raised his rifle and stopped himself from pulling the trigger.

It wasn't Indians. Rather, buzzards fed on Jack's horse. Faint sounds of tearing flesh reached Grant's ears. A familiar dizziness spiraled up from the base of Grant's skull, like when they discovered Jack, and he looked up into the sky and saw a bird disappear...

A buzzard hopped out of the tallest grass. Its legs, bald head and beady eyes appeared more reptilian than avian. It ruffled its feathers and shook a piece of dangling meat from its beak. It cocked its head, as if hearing something. A moment later it exploded into the air with a squawk that sounded afraid. Five of its mates followed.

Just like that, *gone.*

Jack *gone*…Breckenridge *gone*…Webster *gone*…

Torn meat on a beak…

Jack was *torn* apart…

Compelled by instinct, a subconscious urge and the fear of the buzzards, Grant looked up and realized why the thunder-bird button of his dream belonged with the "real" animals. The bird he had seen flying through the air when they discovered Jack was no hallucination. It only *appeared* to fly low due to its huge size. The bird was actually high enough to fly *behind* the clouds, making it *look* like it disappeared.

Now the thunderbird dove for Grant, a creature with a wingspan of at least twenty-five feet – white, leathery and with a tail. A horn grew out of the back of the creature's skull. The wind whistled over its wings as they pivoted at muscular shoulder joints, and an overpowering smell of carrion and snake brought tears to Grant's eyes.

"Paulson—!"

The thunderbird snatched Grant's arm in a reptilian talon, lifting him airborne. The sun shone through its wings, revealing bony structures. A broken-off arrow stuck out of the creature's ribs, showing it had been a man eater for some time. The bird cocked its head and measured Grant with a slit-pupil gaze. Its beak clicked open and shut hungrily.

"No!" Grant shrieked, imagining that beak picking him apart the way it had Jack, Breckenridge and Webster.

Gunshots crashed from below, and Grant felt the thunder-bird shudder as bullets slammed into its flesh.

Earth and sky switched places.

Grant's stomach flip-flopped.

Sight became a spinning blur.

Crashing impact.

Bouncing off rubbery flesh.

Bitter mouthful of grass.

Crawling.

Paulson ran toward Grant and drew his revolver.

Wounded and grounded, the thunderbird still continued the hunt. It folded its wings and scurried after Grant. Six-inch talons perforated the soil. A cross between a roar and a squawk emitted from its throat, and its beak went before it like a knight's lance.

"Look out!" Paulson cried and fired his Colt.

Blood burst from the thunderbird's breast, and a third nostril appeared in its beak.

Grant tried to run, but his feet entangled. He screamed as the thunderbird lunged toward him like an egret going after a fish.

Paulson grabbed Grant by his collar and yanked.

The thunderbird stabbed the ground between Grant's legs. Its beak clacked like a pair of two-by-fours slammed together.

Gun empty, Paulson drew the saber from Grant's belt.

Giant chicken feet stomped on either side of Grant's face. His vision was blocked as the bird clambered over him, and vile skin rubbed against his face. Amid the madness and the muffling, the creature screeched and went limp. Grant became soaked as the creature's bowels let go.

Shrieking, Grant wrestled out from underneath the acrid wet and stink. Free, he snatched up handfuls of grass and rubbed his eyes and nose clear. He peeled off his jacket and flung it far from him.

The thunderbird was dead, Grant saw, and Paulson would soon be joining it. Paulson had managed to stab the saber through the creature's throat, but it had put its beak through his chest. It stuck out of Paulson's back, red with blood. Paulson's eyes were half-lidded with the pain.

Grant saw there was nothing he could do for the man, so his gaze slid to the thunderbird. Part of him refused to accept it, but seeing was believing. He did one better than the farmer in the newspaper, and if he was a college professor, he'd be wiping egg from his face. To think, what academics called extinct, Indians called by name.

And then it fell into place for Grant. His opportunity for fame and fortune had finally, literally, dropped out of the sky.

What would a university pay for such a specimen? Better yet, what would regular people pay to see such a thing?

A vision of a signboard swam into Grant's skull.

See Jonathon Grant's Terrifying Thunderbird! $1!

Even the best stageshow couldn't compete with that...

"You'll never be able to carry it whole," Paulson whispered. "Slow you down too much. Not good in this territory."

Grant was taken aback at how Paulson had divined his thoughts.

"I'll take my chances," Grant said.

Paulson coughed, and blood wet his lips. "No, I don't think you will..." Then he slumped forward, silent.

Grant grabbed Paulson's canteen. The man would not need it anymore. He drank until his thirst was slacked. Then Grant grabbed the saber sticking out of the Thunderbird.

He had a lot of work to do...

* * *

Grant rode all day with the carcass of the thunderbird split among the horses of Paulson, Webster and Breckenridge. He pushed the animals as hard as he could, sometimes seeing ominous dust clouds on the horizon and crossing too many fresh Indian trails. It wouldn't do to get killed now, not when he was on his way into the history books. Buttons cascaded through Grant's mind. No petroglyph animals this time, just dollar signs.

Paulson's words came back to Grant.

What does it profit a man if he gains the world and loses his soul?

Grant rubbed his arm where the Thunderbird had snatched him. The flesh had turned an ugly purple. If one looked into the bruise long enough, it almost looked like it contained an answer to that question. Grant looked away before he could make it out.

Maybe such questions would be relevant in the future, but not for a long, long time.

Eventually, Grant topped a hill and spotted sanctuary. The column of horse soldiers was long and formidable. Plus, such troopers were an eclectic bunch. Surely, a taxidermist was among their number…

Smiling, Grant sang a verse of his own from *Gary Owen*.

"In the fighting Seventh's the place for me; it's the cream of the cavalry; no other regiment can ever claim; its pride, honor, glory and undying fame…"

Finishing the song, Grant kicked his spurs, and Cerberus carried him into the midst of the Seventh Cavalry – as General George Armstrong Custer led them all toward Little Bighorn…

A Time of Blood

Kirsten Cross

A huge, sickly-yellow moon hung over Salisbury Plain. This was no glorious, golden 'Hunter's Moon', resplendent in the heavens and, thanks to an optical illusion of cosmic proportions, apparently thousands of miles closer than it would be normally. This wasn't a moon worthy of salutation by a bunch of druids pratting around in white sheets. This was a greasy yellow orb, producing a phosphorescent glow that made healthy plants look diseased and wasted, and trees on the skyline take on the appearance of twisted, deformed skeletons.

The Stones loomed on the horizon like silent sentinels – guardians of a landscape saturated in legend, death, war, and blood. At night, shadows clustered around the mighty Sarsen obelisks like the spectral fingers of long-dead ancestors who had raised them up thousands of years before, caressing the pits and ruts on the weathered surface. Stonehenge was a monument to man's ingenuity, a testament to his ability to create something astonishing, and a demonstration of his fear of what terrible reprisals the Gods might rain down upon the land and tribe if homage wasn't forthcoming, usually in the form of blood sacrifices.

Many theories had been bandied about concerning the Stones.

They were a temple.

A meeting place.

A shrine for the dead.

A celebration of the solstices.

The truth? Nobody really knew. So the new age brigade and the 'Druids' laid claim to the place, sanitising it and diluting its majesty with drumming, chanting and a shit-load of hugging and love-ins. They conveniently airbrushed out the bloodier facet of the Stones' past in this hippy-trippy interpretation. A brutal, savage past. Just like the unforgiving landscape, these Stones didn't care if you sang to them, drummed at their feet or laid out the entrails and still-beating heart of a human sacrifice on the ground to please the Gods. They were stone. They were immortal – reminders of a time of blood.

Sergeant Mick Jones of Her Majesty's own arse-kicking bastards, 2Para, stared at them and sniffed, singularly unimpressed. Lumps of rock. Admittedly, bloody *big* lumps of rock, but nevertheless, just lumps of rock. But there was something odd about them, even from this distance. He frowned and muttered to himself quietly. "Ya know? I swear them buggers look bigger in the dark."

"Yeah. That's what he says about his cock." Snorts of laughter in the darkness were followed by a sharp rebut.

Mick rounded on the nearest crouched figure and snarled. "Cox, shut your damn mouth and keep your eyes open!"

"Oh, lighten up, for Christ's sake! It's an exercise, Sarge! Seriously, how the holy hell did you actually manage to get through the obstacle course during basic with that stick jammed up your arse?"

"Daft bastard wants to be a Rupert, don't ya, sweetheart? Trouble is, he couldn't make the cut at Sandhurst."

"Fuck off, Jonno."

"That true then, Sarge?"

"Bollocks."

"So that's a yes, then?"

"Go fuck yourself!"

Gary Cox giggled. "Is that an order, *sir*? Because I know for a fact there's a steaming hot little redhead in the pub we passed about half an hour ago. Just want to make sure I keep my pecker up for Queen and country, sah!" Cox ripped off a salute and the rest of the unit chuckled.

Mick Jones glowered at the gloomy hump he presumed was Private Gary Cox. "You know who's playing the enemy, Cox? Those mad fuckers from Hereford. They'd probably take great delight in relieving you of your pecker and presenting it to Brenda as a trophy! I promise you son, they don't know the meaning of the words down time."

"Nor do you, you uptight twat." The muttered comment came out of the darkness.

"Go fuck yourself with a cactus or something, Armstrong!"

Jones could practically hear Phil Armstrong's eyes rolling in the dark, and wasn't in the least surprised when the college-educated twat started getting all pedantic. "Cacti, you ignoramus. And cacti are not indigenous to Wiltshire. I could try go fucking myself with a stick of rhubarb or summat, if that would make you feel better about life in general?"

"Actually, you know Phil, as much as it pains me to say, he was correct. Cactus is the singular of cacti. Theoretically, you'd only need one cactus to go fuck yourself, not several."

"How much rhubarb would you need?"

"Wait, *what?* What is *wrong* with you people?" Jones now had to get a particularly unpleasant mental image involving rhubarb out of his mind's eye.

"A whole fucking crumble's worth, mate. Goes limp quickly, see?" Jonno giggled like a schoolgirl.

"Just like Jonesy." Cox's reply was predictably caustic.

"Fuck off, Cox. And seriously? You're weird, Jonno."

"I'm not the one comparing rhubarb and cacti as sex toys. Now that's weird."

Jones lost his shit. "For the love of *fuck* will you lot *belt up!* Eyes open, mouths shut!"

An uneasy silence descended over the Unit. In the privacy of the darkness, Mick Jones glowered at the crouched figures, waiting for one of the smart-mouthed bastards to start up again. They were a bloody disgrace to the uniform. This wasn't his first time out on the Plain leading a unit of wet-behind-the-ears rookies, but it was crystal that these little bastards had bugger-all respect for him or for the situation they were in. These weren't serious soldiers. These were fuck-abouts. Why the hell they hadn't joined the Territorials instead of the regulars, he'd never know.

Salisbury Plain could be a weird old place. You could get mazed out here. Turned around. The official term was 'royally fucked up'.

The huge open sky could feel like it was pressing down on you, crushing the life out of your body and the air out of your lungs. The way the wind howled around the Stones sounded like children crying. The massive slabs seemed to tower three times higher at night, and there were rumours that the closer you got to the Stones, the more likely it was that your equipment would start going haywire. You needed to stay sharp. Alert. Focused.

Mick felt alienated.

Alone.

Angry.

So *bloody angry*.

This wasn't how things were supposed to have been. He had wanted to follow his dad into the Paras ever since he was a nipper. Now he was here, and determined to do the memory of his dad proud. His old man had copped a bullet in Belfast just two days before the withdrawal. Dumb luck shot for the IRA bastard pulling the trigger. Shit out of luck for his dad. That had brought it home to him. This wasn't a fuck-about job for numbnuts. People died. This was a job for professionals. And this bunch of pillocks were making a mockery of everything he believed in.

The anger frothed in his brain, setting his heart pounding and his teeth on edge. Just at the limit of his senses, he could almost hear his dad's voice whispering: "They're laughing at you, son. At me. At the *Regiment*…"

Anger. So much anger. Choking, vomit-inducing anger.

A boiling, churning rage that turned his guts into knots and made his throat tighten. An anger so utterly consuming it made him want to let loose a primal scream, tear his clothes from his body and bludgeon every one of those pathetic dick-cheeses who had the bloody nerve to call themselves his 'oppos' to death with his bare hands.

It was the same kind of anger he'd felt when he'd walked into a pock-marked mud-brick building in Helmund and found it littered with the bodies of dead children. All girls. The local schoolteacher had had the audacity to teach little girls to read. The Taliban had disagreed with that policy. They didn't make particularly good school governors. And they'd disagreed by using AK47s on the helpless children and their teachers. They'd spared the boys.

Jones had felt his heart break as he listened to the tortured wailing of children, terrified and alone. Vomit on the floor, shit and piss everywhere. They'd got the all clear to go in after an ATO had dealt with an IED strapped to the doorframe. Finally, they'd managed to get the little boys out, but it was too late for the eleven girls. A pile of bodies lay in a lake of blood. But then, a tiny, filthy finger had twitched, causing three fully-grown and battle-hardened men to jump out of their skins. They'd scrabbled to dig the child out from underneath the bodies of the dead, but as Jones had scooped her up in his arms, she'd gasped a final death rattle and fallen limp in his arms. That rasping, final breath had echoed in Jones' mind for months afterwards.

That was an understandable trigger for that eyeball-aching rage that descended. But why was the flippancy of a few newbies causing him to feel the same way? Was it because they were belittling the seriousness of what was out there? Or had he brought some of the war back home with him?

Now it seemed the little girl's death rattle was surrounding him on Salisbury Plain, as if the ghost of that child had followed him thousands of miles from that sad little grave in Helmund Province.

He looked up again at the Stones. They seemed to shimmer, resonating that gasping, rasping noise of a dying child's last breath back at him, but intensifying and amplifying it a thousand-fold.

Briefly he tried to get back control. For a split second he knew that he was having the mother of all flashbacks. *No. Not now. Not fucking now*! He was on night manoeuvres with those nutjobs from Hereford after them, babysitting a bunch of newbies who didn't know their arses from their elbows. *Not fucking now, for Christ's sake! Not now!* He needed to focus. Jones shook his head, trying to clear the fog of the flashback; getting the images of dead children out of his mind. These little shits might be newbies, but the last thing they needed was their UC going fruitloops on them in the middle of a night exercise.

But every time he looked at the Stones, the rage seemed to intensify. He stared at them, mesmerised. They filled his world with a white-hot fury that flooded his brain with adrenaline. He could hear the blood pounding in his ears. The confusion of images started to thin out and his focus turned to Gary Cox.

His smirking face.

His smart-arse one liners.

His total disrespect for the chain of command.

Mick's consciousness started to shift. He couldn't focus on the mission. All he could think about was what he'd like to do to that son of a bitch.

A resonant hum seemed to be punching and pulsating through his skull, making his brain vibrate, and sending savage images cascading through his mind. Images that were so real, so foul, so *gloriously violent*…

A pile of bodies, contorted and soaked in blood. That strange pulsating movement underneath the surface of the skin as the maggots started to do their work. His detached consciousness walked through the carnage, seeing through unfamiliar eyes. A sense of hunger filled him – a five thousand-year-old hunger that demanded to be sated…

He would stand up. He'd walk over to Cox, as silent and as unfeeling as the Sarsen Stones that stood silently on the skyline. He'd stand over him, examining his victim, savouring the rising smell of fear and uncertainty that tainted the air like acrid smoke. He'd reach down, slicing the cloth of Cox's jacket aside with his knife. Clawing his fingers, he'd force them through the soft, yielding skin, sinking through flesh, pushing aside the other organs – they could be spread at the feet of the stones later for the ravens to dine upon.

He'd ignore the screaming, the frantic and futile grabs by his victim at his wrist as his hand sunk deeper into the man's chest. He'd feel the pulsating, throbbing heart, pumping furiously, as if it knew it was about to be torn from the warm safety of the body.

His fingers would close around the pump and slowly, agonisingly slowly, he would tear out Cox's beating heart and hold it up, blood dripping between his fingers, paying no attention to the pathetic bastard's pleas for mercy and blood-frothed gurgles as he died.

He'd lick the still warm heart, letting the blood and fluid coat his tongue, savouring its deliciousness, He'd take a bite and swallow, letting the hot lump of tissue slide down his throat, the coppery flavour filling his mouth, giving him strength, vigour, *power*.

Then he would crush what was left of the organ between his fingers, amused by the sheer fragility of the soft muscle tissue as he turned what was the most precious of all organs into a useless mush of bloody pulp.

The images were so real.

Was he actually doing it?

Or was it some kind of horrific, waking nightmare?

No. Not horrific.

Sensual.

Powerful.

God, the rush of power he would feel would be unlike anything he'd ever experienced! He was getting a feeling of sexual arousal as the images in his mind became more and more vile. He could feel a pressure building behind his eyeballs and screwed his lids tight shut, fearful that they'd pop out like a couple of ping-pong balls shot out of a Thai whore's fanny…

"Movement! On the left!" Jonno let out a hoarse whisper.

Mick's eyes snapped open and he swivelled around. Cox was still very much alive, his beating heart still firmly ensconced in his chest. Mick battled as hard as he could not to puke like a drunken teenager, swallowing back the mouthful of vomit that threatened to spew out.

What the *fuck* just happened?

He fought back against his body's gag reflex and tried desperately to snap himself back into the here and now. Sweat poured down the back of his neck, even though the wind was icy cold and the temperature was nudging the 'brass monkey' zone.

Barrack-room banter was instantly forgotten. Any second now a couple of flash-bangs followed by a beating of epic proportions would descend on their heads like a huge, painful pile of SAS-shaped crap. The Hereford crew had a tendency to forget they were on 'exercise' and go in hard and fast. Not surprising, really. It's what they were trained to do. Trouble was, sometimes they forgot that the ordinary squaddies from 2Para were on the same damn side as they were.

Jones and his team took the exercise seriously, but in all honesty, with deployment to the Falklands just a few weeks away now, how relevant was a night exercise on Salisbury Plain to their training? Sure, the Plain had the same kind of unfeeling, unkind and windswept remoteness that the islands of the South Atlantic had, but was there one single penguin within a thirty-mile radius to their present position? Was there fuck.

And why ask Hereford to play the enemy anyway? Bit of a sledgehammer/nut scenario, really. For all the good it would do, you might as well get the bloody Catering Corps to play the bad guys and come at them with spatulas, egg whisks and their notoriously liberal attitude to 'Best Before' dates.

Mick scanned the horizon, then cursed himself for being such a FNG. The 22nd wouldn't stand on the skyline like extras from a dodgy cowboy film. They'd stay low. Hidden. Unlike Bravo Unit, they wouldn't be wearing MTP cammo. They'd be in their usual ninja black.

"Boo!"

Mick spun around, swinging the SA80 up – and straight into the line of fire of a C8. His gaze travelled away from that snuffling snout, up the barrel and towards a pair of steel-hard eyes peering from behind the slot in a black balaclava. "Oh, *bollocks! C'mon!*"

"Bang, bang. You're dead, fella. Shit, that was too fucking easy." The owner of the eyes gave a little chuckle, and lowered his gun. "Seriously. We're what, two hours in? Did you stop off for a Maccy D's or summat? They *did* tell you we were coming for ya, right?" The eyes squinted in a frown. "Jesus, fella, you look like absolute hell. You need a medic?"

"Perhaps you literally frightened the crap out of the little gobshite." A harsh Scottish accent came out of the dark, presumably from one of the other 22nd members.

He looked around to see each member of his Unit in exactly the same position as him, and to a man they were all staring at the business end of a bunch of C8s. When you were playing with these guys, you really, *really* hoped they'd remembered to put blanks in. The 22nd had done it again. He looked back to his captor, anger boiling up once again – that insatiable, unstoppable anger. He could feel his cheeks burning like someone had chucked napalm in his face. "You were supposed to give us a two hour head start!"

"Oh, boo-fucking-hoo, Shirley Temple! You think the enemy'll go 'One, two, miss a few, ninety-nine, a hundred! Coming! Ready or not!', do you? What are you, five?" The black-clad soldier grabbed Mick by the neck and hauled him to his feet. "Tell you what, princess. Lucky for you, I got sucked off last night by a blonde with the biggest tits you've ever seen in your life, so I'm in a relatively jovial mood. Know what I'm gonna do? I'm gonna cut you some slack, fella. But so help me God, you tell anyone and I'll personally bend you over the heel stone in yonder monument and buttfuck you 'til you scream, got it? You have exactly five minutes to bugger off." He looked at Mick and leaned in. "Are... you... *still fucking here?*"

"Move out!" Mick didn't need telling twice; nor did the other lads in Bravo Unit. They grabbed their kit and yomped out of there like the devil himself was after them. They needed cover, and they needed to be as far away from the mocking laughter of the 22nd as they could.

"Oh, and watch out for the grunt crushers! They're trundling around due north of here! You can't miss 'em, mate, they're those fuck-off great green things with tracks and a bloody great gun sticking out the front!"

The words and the laugher were finally lost on the wind. Now all Jones could hear was the sound of his team's ragged breathing as they stumbled over the uneven ground, eyes forward, trying to avoid the plough ruts that would snap a misplaced ankle like a twig. "Keep to the left of the Stones! And stay tight!" He threw the words back over his shoulder, not knowing or even caring if his Unit heard him. He kept running, trying to put as much distance between him and those Hereford nutters as he could. He knew this unexpected second chance would be their only one. After this, there would be no quarter given. But Bravo Unit were Parachute Regiment Pathfinders. It was their job to work as scout units, evade enemy patrols, get as far behind enemy lines as they could, recon, and then – and this was the tough bit – get back again with intel and a way in. Satellite imagery might have made some of their job redundant, but there was nothing that could compare to 'eyes on the ground', gut instinct, and an up close and personal approach.

What Jones and the rest of his unit didn't want right now was another up close and personal interaction with the black-clothed bastards behind them. They didn't have five minutes. He knew the 22nd would be on their heels within seconds.

The sound of laboured breathing made him glance sideways. Keeping pace but struggling under the weight of a 30lb kit bag and an extra few kilos of SA80 was Cox. The newbie glanced back, meeting Jones' eyes. The cocky, self-assured personality of before had evaporated. Yeah. Staring down the barrel of a C8 will do that to a man.

The two men stumbled forward over the uneven ground, making painfully slow progress towards the Stones. It felt like running through treacle. Jones suddenly wished that some of his civilian mates could do this. *Try running over a ploughed, muddy field carrying a shit-load of kit in the pitch black with a bunch of insane SF bastards baying for your blood sometime, and then fucking tell me that life in the modern army is piss easy,* he thought viciously to himself.

"Sarge, where're we headed?" Cox's words came in between gasps. The going was, in horseracing terms, soft to shitty.

"There're some old bunkers close to the Stones. We can hold a position there.

"You serious? There's only one way in! We'd be cornered!

"We'd have a defensive position, you prick! And they'd be walking straight into a shitstorm of *our* making for a change! Now pick up the fucking pace!" Jones shoved Cox in the small of the back, sending him stumbling forward.

"I'm just sayin'…"

"Fuck me, are you *seriously* questioning my order when we've got the 22nd climbing up our arses? *Move!*" The shove this time was a damn sight harder and Cox measured his length into what looked like a soft pile of mud, but had a distinctively musky odour that suggested to Jones that it wasn't.

"Cunt!"

"On your *feet*, soldier!" Jones ignored the insubordination, grabbed the webbing strap on Cox's backpack and hauled him to his feet again. "*Run!*" Another shove and Cox jogged forward, muttering darkly and spitting out globules of 'mud'.

Jones stumbled forward another dozen steps. It was rough going that sucked the energy out of your legs in seconds, making them feel like they were turning into lead. Every step became harder. *Jesus, I'm getting too old for this shit!* Without warning the ground gave way beneath his feet. He tumbled head-first into a void, closely followed by the yodelling Cox. "*Bollocks!*"

He tumbled and spun, crashing painfully into unyielding walls and finally landing in a grunting heap on a hard, uneven and slimy floor. For a few seconds he lay motionless, trying to get his bearings and to quell the sense of panic that falling any great height without a packet of silk and a ripcord attached to your back generates in a member of Airborne.

Finally, Cox let out a string of expletives. "What the actual *fuck*…"

"Bunker, Cox. We've dropped into a bunker, that's all. Stay calm." Jones shoved the prone newbie off him and stood, switching his head-torch on.

The two men looked around the chamber. "Bunker, huh? So they used stone slabs to line their bunkers during the Cold War then, did they?" Cox pressed a hand into the small of his back and arched his body. "Shit, Sarge. I thought dropping on you I'd have a bit of a cushion. But you're knobblier than a sackful of rocks!" He flexed again. "I think I've cracked a rib!"

"Jesus H Christ, will you *please* give your damn mouth a rest for two seconds!" Jones stared at the walls, puzzled. This was no Cold War concrete bunker. For starters, it was circular. And huge. And as Cox had so ably pointed out, it was also lined with stone.

Jones stood and dusted himself off. As his eyes adjusted to a different kind of darkness, he could see that the chamber they had so unceremoniously landed in was huge. And it stank. Dear God, it stank! A vile odour you could practically chew. It made the air feel thick and suffocating, like being smothered by a rancid blanket. The curved ceiling of the chamber was lost in an ocean of thick, black shadows that made it feel oppressive and much lower than it actually was. In the middle of the inky blackness was a slightly lighter patch – the break in the ground they'd tumbled through. The gap was framed by whiskers of silhouetted grass stems, and Jones could make out a few distant stars twinkling above. Gronking to itself, a raven flapped lazily across the night sky, its guttural calls echoing around the landscape.

Not a bunker, then. Something older. A tomb, perhaps? One of the barrows that littered the landscape? There were plenty of them, most of which had been excavated by archaeologists over the years. Was this one of the hundreds that had already been documented across the south of England, dating back to a darker, more savage and bloody era? Or was it a previously undiscovered one, secreted away for thousands of years?

Jones sniffed, and immediately wished he hadn't. The smell in here was truly god-awful, like someone had left a whole box full of dead rats out in the sun. "Right then. We're stuck in a shitty old tomb that smells worse than your mother's fanny. If we were archaeologists, I guess we'd just about be pissing our pants with excitement right about now. But seeing as we're serving soldiers in Her Mage's army, it's now our duty to get out of here in one piece and report this as a hazard. This fucker's big enough to swallow a grunt crusher whole, and that roof couldn't support our weight, let alone sixty-two tons of Challenger Two." Jones looked up to the gap in the roof. "Bollocks. Even standing on my shoulders, you're not gonna reach that."

"Sarge, the entire US basketball team standing on each other's shoulders couldn't reach that!" Cox's voice sounded strained. "Try radioing for help."

Jones pulled his comms out of its holder and depressed the squawk button. Nothing.

Jones tried the radio three more times, battling to suppress a rising sense of panic. He didn't like this dark, enclosed space, even if it was the size of a cathedral. He balled his hands into fists, trying to disguise the tremor that shook his normally steady fingers.

Jones pulled out his mobile phone. "No bars." Shit. Shit, shit, *shit*! He jammed the phone back into his pocket. So they had no comms, no way up to the surface, and nobody knew where they were. And... seriously, what the *hell* was that smell? "Cox, have you shat yourself or something?" Jones switched to breathing through his mouth.

"Fuck off!" Cox's voice was sounding more panicked by the second.

Jones sniffed again and almost threw up. The smell was getting stronger... and now he recognised it for what it was.

It was the same stench that had hit him like a wall when he'd walked into that Taliban slaughterhouse in Helmund. It was the smell of decomposing flesh, body fluids and putrefaction. "Jesus!" He gagged and put a hand over his mouth. It was coming in waves now, and it was worse every time they moved. "Stand still, Cox."

"Why?"

"Just stand still!" Jones aimed his headtorch at the floor and nearly vomited on the spot. In the bright, white spotlight he could see the entire floor was slick and covered in slime. It had a marbled appearance, with swirls of darker patches in a larger expanse of paler fluids. He crouched and touched a gloved finger to the floor. As he brought his hand back up, a strand of jelly-like goo stuck to his glove, the viscosity the same as baby snot. He stood and flicked the disgusting stuff off his glove. He knew exactly what the slime was. And it wasn't baby snot, that was for damn sure.

"Sarge..."

"Easy, Cox. Easy." Jones could now hear genuine fear in Cox's voice. *Not so cocky now, are you, you smart-mouthed little shit?* he thought viciously. But the newbie was under his protection, despite his earlier and deeply disturbing mental image of ripping the son of a bitch's heart out of his chest. His job now was to get them out of here, and quickly.

Jones stood in the middle of the chamber, directly underneath the hole that led to the outside world – a world where the floor wasn't coated with the rotting remains of decaying bodies. A world where the darkness didn't press in on you like a vice. A world where horrific thoughts of disembowelling your fellow man could be dismissed as a sick by-product of PTSD, and talked through with a shrink over a nice cuppa and a biscuit. In here, in the womb of the earth and so close to the ritualistic carnage that had saturated this landscape in blood for centuries, the familiar form of an SA80 didn't seem to be such a comfort.

Jones tried to quell the panic he felt was about to hit him like a tsunami. He scanned the chamber, and the spotlight of his torch revealed a stone-lined wall so well made you wouldn't be able to get a blade between the unevenly shaped slabs, let alone your fingertips. As he did a three-sixty rotation, the torch beam landed on a much larger lump of stone and he stopped in his tracks. Carefully, in case the slime caused him to lose his footing, he made his way over to the massive stone.

"Sarge, for fuck's sake, talk to me!" Cox's panic was now clearly audible.

"Stop panicking, fella. We're not dead yet. So calm down and breathe slowly. Preferably through your mouth. If you're gonna throw up, do it in a corner. Somewhere I'm not going to step in it." He ignored the sounds of Cox dashing to the side of the void and throwing his guts up, focusing only on the massive megalith in front of him. "We must be right next to the Henge. This looks like the arse-end of one of the Sarsen Stones."

"How's that possible?" Cox spat the last remnants of bile from his mouth and straightened, feeling slightly better for voiding ration pack number sixteen out of his twisted guts.

"What, you think the bloody things levitate, you daft sod? They're buried into the ground, how do you think they stay up? There are legends about underground chambers beneath the Stones, but shit, I thought it was just a bunch of new age bollocks…"

Jones slowly reached out his hand and brushed his fingertips over the surface of the stone.

The jolt threw him backwards clear across the chamber.

He landed and slid through the slime on his arse, trying to stop himself from slamming into the opposite wall. His head-torch went spinning across the floor, the light dancing and contorting like a ballerina on acid. It smashed into the side of the chamber, then blinked out. Jones finally came to rest a few inches from the wall, feeling like he'd just been hit with the mother of all tasers. He gasped, unable to get a lungful of the putrid air. Jones felt Cox cradling his head and heard the panicked man's voice at the edge of hearing, but couldn't respond. His mouth felt like it had been stuffed full of cotton wool and a million ants were crawling all over his body. He shook violently, his muscles convulsing and twitching as he tried to focus on bringing his breathing under control.

"Sarge! Jesus Christ! Sarge!"

The shock sent Jones' brain into shutdown mode. His oppo's words became muffled and distant, as if Cox was shouting at him from the opposite side of a parade ground. He wanted to tell Cox that he was okay, but that was a bloody lie. He quite clearly wasn't. And Cox's obvious inability to function under extreme stress was starting to send the younger man spinning towards full-on hysteria. *Well, tough titties, kiddo. Your sergeant's down. It's up to you, now. It's called 'teamwork', fella...* Jones started to embrace the unconsciousness that kept threatening to over-whelm him...

* * *

Cox cradled Jones' head, instinctively pressing two fingers to his neck to check his pulse. He felt about a hair's breadth away from total pissing your pants and crying for your mummy meltdown. He held Jones in his arms, trying to comprehend what had just happened and to shut out the crushing fear that was filling him. He was not normally that bothered by the dark or enclosed spaces – he'd always believed that they were phobias only pussies got. But right now those pussy phobias seemed to contain other, more threatening horrors. Where were the bodies that had produced the copious amount of corpse fluids that turned the floor into a slime-covered, foetid skating rink? Why had his sergeant just been thrown across the chamber after touching the foot of the Sarsen Stone?

And was his terrified imagination playing twisted tricks on him, or did a part of the blackness have a distinctly bipedal form?

He turned his headtorch towards the spot, expecting the beam to light up a human form; please God, perhaps one of the 22nd who'd yomped down the hole and was going to pull them to safety.

There was nothing there. The shadow form had slid sideways to just beyond the edge of the beam, away from the light. Still cradling the drooling, semi-conscious Jones in his arms, Cox swivelled his head, sending the torchlight scampering across the stones. No matter where he looked, that bipedal form was always just out of the path of the beam.

His headtorch flickered and dimmed. "Oh, no, no, *No*! Shit! C'mon, do *not* do this!" He batted the side of the torch, willing the beam to power up again, but the torch suddenly winked out. The chamber was plunged into darkness. But at last a shred of his training kicked in as Cox remembered his NVGs perched on his helmet. He flicked them down and suddenly looked out into an eerie, vivid green chamber.

Glancing down, he could see the prone body of Jones, still shaking and convulsing. "S'alright, Sarge, you're gonna be fine. Take it easy." Cox took a deep breath and tried to stop his own hands from shaking so violently, afraid he'd drop Jones' head and shoulders back down into the slime that covered the floor. Cox shifted his weight and positioned his thigh underneath Jones' shoulders, keeping the man's head and neck clear of the ooze. "Easy, Sarge. Easy. I'm gonna get you out of here, okay?" Cox frantically scanned the chamber. It was huge – far bigger than the limited glow of the headtorches had revealed. The night vision goggles allowed him to see details, but still there was something just at the edge of his peripheral vision – something that seemed to be taunting him in a sick game of Marco Polo. Wherever he looked in the chamber he could sense it…

He looked down again at Jones. "Sarge, c'mon, stay with me!" He slapped Jones' face gently, garnering a moan in response. "Sarge, hey, Sarge…" Cox looked up – straight into the wild, staring eyes of a massive figure. "Jesus Christ!"

He scuttled backwards, ignoring the crack as Jones' head hit the hard stone floor and propelled himself away from the figure. *Gun! Gun! Grab your gun!* He swung the SA80 up, and then realised that it would probably be more effective as a club. This was not a live ammo exercise. It was a 'shit and thunder' romp across the Wiltshire countryside, with plenty of flash-bangs, noise and piss and not much else. The SA80's magazine was full of blanks, which made it about as much use as chucking confetti at a seven-foot tall… what?

What the actual *fuck* was it?

Human? Hell no, he'd never seen anyone that big. And even though it was showing up in his goggles, it seemed to have an almost ethereal quality, as if it was trying to exist in two alternative dimensions at once. Here, and as long as you were looking directly at it, the figure appeared solid. But glance at it out of the corner of your eye and it flitted in and out of phase. He also felt wave after wave of hatred coming from the thing, slamming into him like the Atlantic on spin cycle. This fucker was majorly pissed off, and it seemed majorly pissed off at Jones in particular. It loomed over the prone man, a snarl contorting what would otherwise pass as a face. Broken and rotting teeth dripped pus and drool, and the massive muscles on its arms and shoulders flexed.

Moving faster than anything that size had a right to, its right arm shot down towards Jones and taloned fingers slashed at the front of his MTP camouflage jacket, shredding it into ribbons. Jones screamed as the claws sliced into his flesh.

Cox's scream matched Jones', only his was one of fury at what this *thing* was doing to his sergeant. "*No!*" Cox scrabbled to his feet and fumbled for his bayonet, willing his shaking fingers to do what they were told. The bayonet clicked and locked into place. He picked up every ounce of courage he had left and charged at the creature.

He got three steps, tops.

The thing looked up, flicked a hand and Cox was sent spinning across the chamber by an invisible force and slammed into the wall. The creature's hand stayed outstretched towards Cox, and he slowly raised it, as if it were conducting some demonic orchestra to a crescendo. As he did, Cox slid painfully up the wall, pinned to the rough stone and unable to break free. The stone slabs jarred against his vertebrae and no matter how hard he struggled, he could only watch, helpless, as the creature turned its attention back to the whimpering form of Jones…

* * *

Jones stared up into the eyes of a creature that had no fucking right to exist. Not here. Not anywhere. The thing snorted then pressed its palm against Jones' forehead. Instantly, Jones was engulfed in a wave of flashing images bursting through his brain. The stinking piles of corpses he'd seen in that slaughterhouse; the dead child, expiring in his arms, her fingers grasping at his hand in a vain attempt to hang on to life; his mate Chris, when that IED had taken his legs off at the knees and blown the shreds of the poor bastard's skin and muscle tissue into Jones' face. Foul, tainted images of combat in a distant land, etched into his soul and twisting like rotting fibres in his mind. He wept, crying for everything he'd suffered.

Then new images came. More savage, more horrific than he'd imagined possible. This place, filled with the screams of the dying as a circle of hazy figures chanted incessantly, calling to the darkest god of the Stones – Aeron, the Celtic god of slaughter. Images of a war waged by the real druids against the Roman Legions filled Jones' mind. He saw them hunting Aeron in the Welsh Preseli Hills, capturing the God using trickery and guile, bringing him back here and entombing him in the bluestones that were erected at the entrance of this portal to the Underworld. Here, on the open Plains, Legionnaires were lured to their doom, tumbling into the cavern as its roof gave way and they were deposited at the feet of a starving, angry god. A god who revelled in slaughter. A god who could sense the mind of a soldier and lure him to this place, calling him with images of unimaginable savagery and a lust for power.

And now, Aeron had a soldier crawling and pissing himself in terror at his feet, and another crying and raging against his helplessness, pinned to the chamber wall like a butterfly collector's prize possession. He felt the pulsating power throbbing through his loins and into his blackened soul. Time to feast once more.

It had been too long. Far too long...

* * *

275

Aeron stood over Jones, examining his victim, savouring the rising smell of fear. He reached down and, clawing his fingers, forced them through the soft, yielding skin, sinking through flesh, pushing aside the other organs. They could be spread at the feet of the stones later for the ravens to dine upon.

He ignored the screaming, the frantic and futile grabs by his victim at his wrist as his hand sunk deeper into the man's chest. He could feel the pulsating, throbbing heart, pumping furiously, as if it knew it was about to be torn from the warm safety of the body. The screams grew weaker, interspersed by choking gurgles as blood filled the man's throat.

His fingers closed around the pump and slowly, agonisingly slowly, he tore out Jones' beating heart and held it up, blood dripping between his fingers, paying no attention to the pathetic, blood-frothed gurgles as his victim died in agony, twitching and convulsing.

He licked the still warm heart slowly, letting the blood and fluid coat his tongue, savouring its deliciousness. It had been so very, very long since he had tasted such fear – the fear of a warrior in the throws of his agonising, prolonged death. He took a bite and swallowed, letting the hot lump of tissue slide down his throat, the coppery taste filling his mouth, giving him strength, vigour, *power*.

Then he crushed what was left of the organ between his fingers, amused by the sheer fragility of the soft muscle tissue as he turned what was the most precious of all organs into useless mush.

Jones died badly, a victim of his own horrific fantasy. Aeron feasted on his flesh, tearing at his throat and moaning with pleasure as the still-warm tissue slid down his throat.

Aeron stopped mid-gorge and turned his eyes towards the terrified form of Cox and smiled lazily, blood and flesh dripping from his teeth. He stood, and strolled across the chamber towards Cox, relishing the sensation of Jones' warm blood swirling around his feet and mingling with the juices of decay that coated the floor. He stretched out a taloned hand towards Cox's chest, hungering for the pounding heart caged behind the man's ribs. It called to him. It *sang* to him. And the screams of the doomed man made the song so much sweeter...

BLANK WHITE PAGE

(Songs in the Key of White)

James A. Moore

Lucas Slate sat astride his dark horse and stared into the sprawling affair with little or no expression on his gaunt face. He looked upon the collection of hastily assembled buildings and well-used tents with eyes half-lidded. An unwary sort of soul might have thought he wasn't paying attention, but he was.

"It occurs to me, Mister Crowley, that this place looks too much like other areas we've both seen in the past."

The air had a hard bite to it. The wind was dry and cold and cutting. Winter was well and properly on its way and the people in the small town knew it. They were shilling their goods with a sort of cheerful desperation that said at least a few of them could think of better places to be. He wondered if any of them would succeed in finding those better places before the winter came properly.

Jonathan Crowley, who was riding his own horse and sitting only a few feet from Slate, allowed himself a small smile and shook his head. "And, what, exactly, is it that you think we're going to find here, Mister Slate?"

Slate did not bother turning to the sound of Crowley's voice. He knew what he would see. The same lean, plain features and brown hair, brown eyes. Same offensive smirk on the man's longish face, though at the moment it was hidden behind almost a month's worth of beard growth. They'd ridden across half the

Arizona territory, riding past patrols of Cavalry and Indians alike, because something inside of Lucas Slate told him he had to be here, but he had no idea what that something was.

He just knew it chewed at him.

Only a short time ago he'd been quite a different man. His hair white, and his skin was as pale as snow, same as always. He was an albino, after all. But beyond that there was remarkably little that was the same.

When he'd lived in Carson's Point, Colorado he'd stood at least eight inches shorter and he'd been told more than once that he had the face of a woman. True, a few of the folks who'd made that claim had been drunk and desperately lonely, but he knew that his face had been different, as surely as his body had changed.

Slate stood over six and a half feet now, and while he still sported the same hat he'd taken to wearing as the local under-taker – a fine old hat that served him well and looked somber enough for funerals – he could no longer fit in his old suits and had been forced to buy new shirts and new pants as well; rawhide in this case because the damnable cold would have sunk through anything less.

He had always been thin. Now he was gaunt, and his muscles were cords of leather under skin that had long since stopped being supple and soft. No one would ever mistake him for a woman these days. Instead they'd contemplate whether or not someone sharing his old profession should have buried him. He was not dead. He just looked the part.

He had always been soft spoken, but these days his voice was lower and seldom seemed to want to come out as much more than a whisper. The only thing that had not changed was the cultured southern drawl that moved through his words. "I'm intending to find answers, Mister Crowley."

Crowley nudged his horse closer. Slate looked toward the man and considered the beard he was growing. Jonathan Crowley did not look like a man who should have a beard to him. It didn't seem to fit his long face. "I am very fond of answers, Mister Slate.

But I have to ask, what, exactly, is the question?"

He looked at Crowley. The man was dressed in fine clothes. A cotton shirt, a charcoal, pinstriped suit with a vest, and over that a great duster that kept the cold and wind from touching anything under it. He sported a gambler's hat on the top of his head, and a heavy wool scarf of a dark, somber red hue.

Slate offered a thin-lipped smile of his own. "I believe the question is the very one you've been contemplating since we started riding together. What, exactly, am I becoming?"

Crowley nodded. "That is a question worth answering."

"Indeed it is, sir."

* * *

You could hardly call it a town, really. More a collection of shops and brothels all shoved together and becoming a town already called Silver Springs, Arizona. The place was an assortment of thieves and whores and criminals, as could be expected in a boomtown. The rumors of silver had driven herds of people into the area and the fortunate few who had struck solid claims guaranteed they'd stay. There were white folk, red folk and black folk, all of them in the same area. Crowley imagined if he looked around he'd even see a few Chinese as well. That seldom happened in places that were properly called civilized. There were too many who considered the other races as enemies for that. Here, where money was more important than opinions, there was less need of being selective.

Crowley rather liked that part of the situation. He'd never much cared for the need to believe one people were better than another. One on one, most of them seemed all right. It was only when you gathered any of them in groups they tended to be stupid.

The ground was as dry as the air, which is to say most of the folks in the area would be getting their water from wells, or from the barrels a few enterprising people were bringing with them. It was a commodity. The Verde River was a few hours ride from the area, and he had already seen a group of men at the edge of town working on figuring the best way to get the water from there to here. What they lacked in equipment they seemed to make up for with enthusiasm.

He could see that Lucas Slate was tense. Slate, who seldom seemed bothered by much of anything since he'd begun changing. Slate, who calmly and methodically followed through with some very grisly work, was currently as taut as a bowstring.

"We have traveled through Indian territories and been shot at several times, Mister Slate. Who do you think is most likely to be of assistance to us in this situation?"

The two of them were still at the edge of the crowded area. Someone, somewhere, had claimed they found silver in the area. A week later the first building seemed old. Now? Now the crowds kept coming and the buildings kept popping up like mushrooms after a rainstorm.

Slate looked slowly over the area and then finally shook his head. "I'm sure I have no idea."

Crowley smiled. "Look around us, Mister Slate, and tell me what's different about the people here?"

"Nothing that I can see." He spoke even as he once more scanned the crowds. "Ah. I see it now."

"What do you see, Mister Slate?"

"The Indians. They're more afraid of *me* than they are of *you*."

Crowley chuckled. "Well now, don't you think that deserves a bit of investigation?"

Slate took off his hat for a moment and ran long, pallid fingers through his long, thin, white hair. "Indeed I do, Mister Crowley. Indeed I do."

They rode forward at a leisurely pace, two men who scared most people without even trying.

* * *

Silver Springs wasn't old enough to be on any maps. The town had been hastily assembled and that tended to make navigating the structures challenging. There were no rules, really, except the ones people managed to force on each other. Most of the folks who saw the strangers eyed them warily, rather like one might contemplate a substantial rattlesnake that was minding its own affairs but was looking at you with one ophidian eye.

To be fair they struck quite a few notes that qualified them as unusual. The gaunt man rode on a pale grey horse that didn't seem to breathe. It did not snort, nor did it whinny. The beast seemed oblivious to most of the other animals in the area, though the same was not true in reverse. A good number of dogs made it a point to be elsewhere when the horse got too close, and they made certain to bark their dissatisfaction just as soon as they were far enough away to assure the great horse could not easily get to them.

The man riding with him seemed of particularly good humor, with an eager smile that did not sit well. More than a few of the faithful crossed themselves when they saw his broad, even teeth. When Crowley was not smiling he was hardly remarkable, but there was something inherently wrong with his grin. There was something about the way he moved, the way he looked at folks, that left them a mite worried that he could just possibly take note of them. His horse was only remarkable in that it did not run from the larger grey beast the gaunt man rode.

Both men sported weapons, but that was hardly unusual in this area. The gaunt man had a long rifle draped across his saddle, held in place by the weight of his hands. A shotgun rested near his leg, and a careful eye would make out the two Colt Navy revolvers tucked into saddle holsters. There was a knife hilt at the top of each boot and at least one large blade strapped to his hip. He carried enough weapons to promise mayhem, even if his deathlike face and grim pallor hadn't already advertised a penchant for destruction.

Crowley slipped off his horse with an unsettling grace. He didn't bother stretching or adjusting his posture as so many did. Instead, he seemed perfectly relaxed and comfortable. Lucas Slate dropped down with substantially more difficulty and looked around the area with hooded eyes.

"You're not feeling well, Mister Slate?"

"Something's wrong. I don't quite know what, or why, but I'm feeling decidedly ill at ease."

Jonathan Crowley adjusted his wide brimmed gambler's hat and looked around carefully. "In the time I've known you I've run across remarkably little that put you under the weather."

"Indeed, sir. It is a rarity." Slate's soft southern drawl was more pronounced. "And one I daresay I do not enjoy."

"Close your eyes, Mister Slate."

The man did as Crowley suggested.

"Now, tell me what you feel both in your body and outside it."

To most, the conversation would have seemed foolishness, but Lucas Slate knew better. He was changing and his changes included some very devilish alterations to his senses. He could often see past the lies that presented themselves to most people, and he could occasionally feel much more than he should have been able to consider.

"Well now…"

Crowley said nothing, but he watched the man very carefully.

Slate turned his head slowly to the left and tilted his ear higher, as if trying to catch a sound. "Well now," he repeated. "That's something, isn't it?"

"What might that be, Mister Slate?"

"I can hear something. Sounds almost like music, but nothing that makes sense."

Crowley nodded slowly. All around them people were going on about their business and giving a wide berth to the two of them. "Then I might suggest you investigate. Shall I come with you?" He made the offer already knowing the answer.

"Not at this time, Mister Crowley. Though perhaps I could count on you to remain within shouting distance."

Crowley nodded again. "I expect I can make myself available to you, should the need arise."

Crowley turned his horse away and started on a parallel course. The smile dropped from his face as he merged with the people moving about the bustling area.

* * *

Crowley knew that if you sit long enough, people tell the most amazing stories. It wasn't hard to find a place that was selling food, but finding one where the food wasn't dubious was more of a task. Still, Crowley managed well enough.

There was a tent not far from the first stable that had slices of roast beef, a thin gravy, and potatoes for a few pennies. A single penny bought a plate of beans from a pot that looked diseased. The establishment also had a bar, and that almost always guaranteed conversation. Crowley bought his food and settled in to listen.

Most of the people were talking of only two noteworthy things. The first was the silver in the area – amazing how many wanted it and how desperately they were willing to search for instant wealth. The other major topic of conversation was the ongoing Indian wars.

War might have seemed too harsh a word for some, but Crowley didn't think so. There were soldiers moving through the area, and they were there for the main purpose of pushing any red men they saw onto the reservations they had set aside.

Crowley had no idea why. Until a little over a year earlier he'd made a very strong point to stay well away from human beings in general, and while he was once again obligated to deal with people, he had no desire to get involved in their politics. One thing hadn't changed in his time on the planet: people got together and made messy political situations and then other people came along and tried to fix them. In the process there was normally a great deal of bloodshed. He didn't worry about politics. He worried about the things that tried to break into the world and take it for themselves.

A man standing a few feet away from him was speaking. The man was short, stout, and stank. He needed a bath far more than he needed a whiskey, but the drink was what he was after and what he was enjoying.

"Big as a bear," Stinky said, "and white as snow, and looking around like he's waiting to kill something."

Crowley could guess whom the man was speaking about.

The man pouring whiskey was taller, leaner and looked about as friendly as an executioner. Still, he nodded and poured and listened.

"Thing is, all the Indians is looking at him like he's gonna kill 'em and cook them up for dinner." The thickset man smacked his lips noisily and slurped down his whiskey like it was water. His mustache, desperately in need of a trimming, trembled as he spoke. "Far as I can see that would be an improvement."

Crowley kept his tongue. Ultimately, he didn't much see a need to involve himself in the discussion. Still, it was interesting to hear.

When the bartender finally spoke it was softly, but with an edge. "Don't much care for the Indians, but I'm just fine keeping the army out of here, too."

"Oh to be sure," Stinky said. He had a sloppy smile on his face and he nodded his head so hard Crowley wondered how it managed to stay attached. "Any ways you look at this situation, I prefer to avoid having a hundred soldiers coming along and shooting the hell out of everything again. I already had that problem in Maryland, Virginia, and in Alabama. I'm done with men in uniform."

Crowley snorted at that, not even trying to suppress the noise.

Stinky looked his way. His brow knitted. "You think soldiers are a good idea, mister?"

"No. I just don't think men in uniform will ever go away."

"How you figure?"

Crowley cut a piece of beef and chewed on it for a moment before answering. "You have silver mines here. People are staking claims and digging and some of them are making money. Those people are going to want to protect what is theirs, so they'll either hire men in uniforms to protect it, or they'll demand men in uniforms to protect it. Either way, you're going to get men in uniforms. Then you have your Indians, who maybe don't care about the silver and maybe do, but either way probably don't like getting pushed from place to place. They're going to get upset sooner or later and they're going to push back, and sure enough, more men in uniforms will come along to stop that from happening. I believe that's why you currently have men in uniforms heading in this direction."

Stinky looked at him for a long moment and then a smile broke on his face. He had a good smile. It made his face round and cheery. "Mister I like you. Let me buy you a drink."

"By all means," Crowley said. "But I'd ask you to do me the kindness of standing downwind. I'm still eating and you have a ripe odor on you."

Might be that some people would have taken offense to that, but stinky did not. Instead he laughed. "It's been a long few days riding to get here. Haven't found the baths yet."

The bartender pointed. "That way. Three doors down."

Crowley finished his meal and Stinky, who had forgotten all about the offer of a drink, went to get himself cleaned up. Really, that was better for everyone involved.

* * *

Captain Henry Folsom looked around the settlement and glowered from under the brim of his Hardee hat. The men with him were tired and hungry and they needed supplies. He wasn't overly fond of the way the place looked, but they would simply have to work with what they had available.

There were Indians moving among the people in the camp and he didn't much care for that. His job was to make sure the Apache stayed where they belonged and that was a task he took very seriously.

"Sergeant Barnes." Folsom spoke clearly, with a hard, barking note in his voice that perfectly matched his disposition. "Find stables and a spot upwind from this filth."

"Upwind, sir?" Barnes asked.

Barnes was one of those people Folsom always found offensive: they'd all been on the road just as long, but Barnes was neat and clean and not a hair was out of place.

"I have no desire to smell the people here if they reek as badly as the area looks."

Barnes snapped off a hard salute and broke away from the men.

When Folsom slid from his horse's saddle and landed, it was with remarkable agility. "Sergeant Fowler?"

"Yes, sir?"

"Take your squad and ride a circuit around this cesspool. I want to know how many Indians are here and why they are here."

"Yes, sir!"

A moment later the commander of the Seventh Battalion strutted toward one of the only solid structures he could find in the town. It was two stories of wood rot and sagging boards, but it was an actual building and that had to stand for something. The man who walked beside him was not Indian, yet he was not a proper white man, either. He said he was from China. All Folsom knew for certain was that Chi Chul Song was a better tracker than anyone else he'd met and that the fellow worked hard for a small wage. He did not speak to Song and the Chinaman returned the favor, but Folsom was happier with the man beside him than he was without. Song stood next to him with his muscular arms crossed over his broad chest and continued to say nothing while Folsom commandeered the Silver Springs Hotel for himself and his soldiers.

* * *

Lucas Slate felt the tugging at his body and soul like iron shavings might feel the pull from a magnet just exactly too far away to make them move. He could have resisted, but part of him did not want to. Part of him wanted this, needed to know what was behind the silent summons. What bothered him was he couldn't decide if that part was what he liked to think of as himself, or as the thing that was changing him. There had been a time when he could tell the difference with ease, but familiarity was not being kind to him.

What had once been a distant voice inside his soul was now a part of him, much as he hated the notion. The endless whispering influence that had already changed his body was now better positioned for chipping away at his mind. He still knew who he was, but recent events argued that he might not stay that way too much longer.

One nameless town, one odd beastie – odd enough that Crowley had never heard of it before – and the thing inside him had taken over, nearly drowning him in the dark waters of his mind. The change had happened so quickly that he couldn't fight it off. One moment he was himself and the next something else had controlled his actions. It had worked out to the benefit of Slate and Crowley alike, but it had put a strain on their relationship, and though Crowley did his best to act as if nothing was different, Slate's mother hadn't raised any fools.

His horse clomped along as calmly as ever. The dogs in the area, and there were a goodly number of strays, barked and raged and backed away. The horse didn't care. It wasn't really a horse anymore, of course. It had been snakebit a while back, when he and Crowley were in the middle of the badlands. The horse had reared up and run a hundred yards and then fallen on its side. By the time he'd reached the thing, it was dying. The muscles in its body were shuddering and the beast was soaked in sweat, surely as good as dead. Crowley had come along, moving at a leisurely pace. He'd stopped long enough to shoot the snake dead and then followed, but the look on his lean face said he knew what Slate knew: the horse was a goner.

And for only an instant, that dark whispering voice that seldom spoke loudly enough to be noticed on a conscious level had reached out and taken control. Slate had leaned down and grabbed the dying horse's head, wrenching it roughly around until the animal's open mouth was aimed at his face. He'd leaned down and exhaled a powerful breath into the horse's mouth and then held it closed with his hand.

He stayed that way until the animal shuddered and then shook him off. A minute, perhaps two, and the horse was up and fine and Crowley was looking at him with a calm that was even worse than the man's damnable smile.

Something needed to be done about what was happening inside Slate's body and his soul. He had no idea what that something might be, but he believed with every fiber of his being that the answers were somewhere near him, somewhere in this place. Just then he saw the palest man he had ever seen. Deathly white, actually. An Indian, that was obvious, but there was nothing natural about his hue or his demeanor. The man walked past him in the middle of a crowd, hunched over to the point where he looked easily a foot shorter than he should have. He had a shawl drawn over his head and if Slate hadn't felt that something was wrong, he'd likely have dismissed the shape as an old squaw.

The face that peered from under that shawl was drawn and ancient, thin and angular. The eyes were hidden in shadow, but he could feel them scrutinizing him just the same. The man stood up quickly and let the old cloth fall from his head and his shoulders, dropping it to the ground. Around them, most of the people paid no mind, but every Indian backed away as surely as if they'd been hit with boiling water. A few of them screamed, to boot.

When he smiled, it was worse than Crowley's. He spoke words that were not English. Slate should not have been able to understand them, but he did.

The old man said, "I know you."

Slate shook his head. He spoke in English but knew the man understood every word. "I have never met you before. I'd remember you."

"You will know me better soon."

It was at that moment the Cavalry riders broke through the crowd. Slate had been so busy looking at the pale man that he'd lost track of everything else. The soldiers came on horses trained to bull their way through crowds. One of them had an old Indian woman by the wrist and was dragging her along beside him. Another had rope around the wrists of three younger women, also Indians, who were crying and trying to keep up with the rider and his horse.

Slate felt that other presence slither through his mind, but did not take the time to pay it any attention. He had other concerns. He was not fond of men who mishandled women. As a half-breed himself, he didn't much care what race they were.

He rode his horse four paces toward the first of the riders and allowed himself a very small grin of satisfaction when the horse reared up and threw the rider. The horse didn't like Slate's mount. Most animals didn't. As he rode forward a little more the rest of the horses grew skittish and backed up, despite their riders' urgings. The first of the soldiers looked up from where he'd landed on his tail end and glowered at Slate. Slate looked back down and kept his face deliberately expressionless.

"Watch where you're going, you damn fool," the soldier said. The old woman backed into the crowd as the soldier stood. Slate supposed he should have known the man's rank in the Cavalry, but he did not. He had never much cared for the soldiers he'd met and the feeling had always been mutual.

"I did nothing, sir, but continue on my way."

The man had risen to his feet and was still scowling, at least until he saw Slate's face a little better. As he shaved himself when he needed and looked at the changes in his features with a sick fascination, he knew what the man saw and that it was not particularly pretty.

"Well you've interfered in a military operation!"

"Wrangling squaws is a soldier's business these days?" Slate kept his voice as calm and soft as ever. Oh, he'd been riding with Crowley far too long. "I'd have thought you might actually try to find a few braves to fight instead of simply stealing their women."

"Get off of that horse, you bastard. You'll be coming with us."

Slate looked at him for a long moment and rested his hand on the grip of his rifle. "As I am neither a squaw nor a brave, I believe I will stay exactly where I am."

In the distance the other cavalrymen had managed to calm their horses – while successfully moving several feet back – and were carefully watching what happened. Apparently the man who dragged old women around was in charge.

"That's a direct order!" He was furious, the soldier, but he was not very wise. He came toward Slate with one hand holding to the butt of his service revolver.

Slate spoke softly, his expression remained calm. "I am not

now, nor have I in the past, been a part of your army, sir. I do not answer to you."

"Are you a Confederate, boy? Is that the problem here?"

The man was likely a few years younger than he was. Not that it much mattered.

"In fact, sir, I was on the side of the North in the conflict, though I was not a soldier. I agreed with the notion that all men are created equal. I should think that would include red men, would it not?"

"What?" The soldier scowled and came closer still. Slate suspected he intended to sneak up and attack. He lacked in subtlety.

Slate sighed. "I am not a Confederate. The war is over, by the by. I am a gentleman. You might have run across a few in your journeys, though I fear it is just as likely you've never run across anything but gutter trash."

That seemed to be enough for the soldier. He stepped forward with every intention of pulling Slate off of his horse. His gloved hands grabbed at the reins of the horse and tried to lead it roughly away.

The horse did not move.

"You'd do well to leave my mount be, sir. He doesn't much like you."

"Piss on your goddamned horse!"

Slate sighed and climbed down from the saddle. The great grey beast looked at him with only the mildest interest. Rather than bother with the horse Slate took hold of the cavalryman's ear and pulled savagely. The man screamed as cartilage snapped. While he was howling in pain, Slate punched him across the jaw and broke bones.

The next of the soldiers was already drawing his firearm.

Slate looked at the man and did the same. "Don't. It won't go well for you."

The man did.

It did not go well.

* * *

Stinky came back a while later. His actual name was Owen Napier, and he was a man without much purpose in his own estimation. "I come from a family of lawyers. They make a good living and I am fortunate enough to share in that, but I don't much like the law. Thought I might come this way and find something more interesting to do with my time."

"So you decided to try mining?" Crowley considered shaking his head at the notion because Owen-the-less-stinky didn't strike him as a very physical man.

"Lord, no!" Napier shook his head hard enough to rock his jowly face. "I figure if anything I might report on what happens here. Send articles back to a friend of mine in New York."

"Not a lot of money in that, is there?"

"I have a family. They'll keep me fed." He patted his belly. "As you can see that's not much of a consideration for me. Besides, they're glad to have me out here. I can't get in the way and I might have useful information for them, too." For a man who was carefully not admitting to being sent away from the family as an embarrassment, Napier seemed cheerful enough. When he patted his belly it also showed the bulge in his vest where he was smart enough to hide a small two-shot Wesson. It only took one bullet to kill a man if you were fast enough.

"So where are you from, Mister Crowley? I can't quite place your accent."

Crowley looked at his new acquaintance and smiled. "Here and there." Before Napier could ask any more questions, Crowley turned the tables. "What is it you have against Indians?"

"Hmm? Oh, nothing at all. But I keep hearing about raiding parties burning peoples' homes down and taking their women. That's a godless thing to do."

"Are you a scholarly man, Mister Napier?"

"I like to think so." He nodded. "Yes, I am."

"Look into your history a bit better and you'll find that raiding parties, houses being burned down, and women being taken from their families are not at all new notions. I don't believe there's a part of the world where it hasn't happened for as long as there have been people."

"Well, certainly not among civilized folks."

Crowley smiled again and Napier got a nervous look on his face. "Whatever makes you think a few buildings brings about a civilized human being?"

Before Napier could answer, Lucas Slate walked into the room, looming over everyone in the place. Most of the conversations died in an instant. Slate's voice remained as soft and cold and low as ever. Napier looked toward him and blanched. "Mister Crowley," said Slate, "I believe I'm going to need your assistance."

From outside the tent a slowly growing sound caught Crowley's attention. It was a noise he'd known for many, many years and one he never had much affection for: the sound of many men on horseback. Like as not, they were men in uniforms and their intentions would not be much to his liking.

"What have you gotten yourself into, Mister Slate?" Crowley did his level best not to smile, but it wasn't easy for him.

"There were a few men in uniform decided they had to take some ladies from this area without their agreeing to be taken. I intervened."

Outside there were the noises of commands being barked and repeated, horses coming to a halt and whinnying their displeasure, and a few dozen men working quickly to become organized in a chaotic situation. In other words, soldiers in action.

Crowley sighed and placed his hat on his head. "And did your intervention result in injury or worse to the men?"

"Indeed it did, sir."

"Well now, this should be something."

The man pouring whiskey looked uninterested. Napier seemed eager to hear more. He also studied Slate with wide eyes. He stopped when Slate turned quickly and stared back just as hard. Might be things would have gone wrong from there, but a collection of Cavalrymen came into the tent before things could get worse.

Of course, them coming in rather took care of worsening matters all by itself.

* * *

Folsom looked around. They were an unpleasant lot to be sure. The tent was filled with people, and most of them were unwashed and underfed. Folsom looked at the crowd and found the man his soldiers had reported with amazing ease. The gaunt albino was as tall as he was thin and looked like death. He was dressed like a savage in rawhide, sported a coat made of some sort of animal fur, and carried two large pistols on his hips. Despite his uniform and the men behind him, Folsom hesitated for a moment. Then the Chinaman, Song, moved a bit to the side and a few more soldiers stepped into the tent beside them both.

Having an audience never failed to make Folsom feel the need to be brave. "You!" He stabbed a finger at the albino. "What in the name of God did you do to my men?"

The gaunt man looked at him. Next to him a smaller man with a feral smile looked in his direction with nearly feverish eyes. Most of the people were looking toward him, but what made those two different was simply that they were not afraid of him. Not in the least, and that was a worrisome thing.

The albino said, "I did nothing to your men that they did not provoke, sir." He had a southern accent. Little existed that was more contemptible in Folsom's eyes.

"I have four dead soldiers and a handful of men who swear you killed them. Attacking a soldier is a hanging offense." Folsom stepped forward and Song moved with him, a graceful, silent man with the eyes of a cat. Song always looked like he was ready to pounce, to kill, though Folsom had never once seen the man strike first.

"And I repeat, Mister Crowley, I do believe I'll need your help." The albino murmured to the smiling man next to him, seemingly unable to speak louder than a whisper.

The man with him slipped forward and stood between Folsom and his prize.

"Don't make this concern you, mister."

The stranger's smile grew broader and ice rimmed the inside of Folsom's stomach. He had no idea why, but the man scared the hell out of him. Still, there were the troops to consider and justice to be handled.

"I know you. Henry Folsom. How's your mother? Ruth, I believe?" The man did not speak. He purred. Folsom felt that cold in his guts spread. His mother had passed when he was only ten. How the man could possibly know her was a mystery. Still, he seemed familiar,

"I do not believe we've met before."

"I know you. I know your father, Alexander. Your mother, Ruth. I knew your sister as well, Loretta." The lean man looked away for a moment, his eyes staring past Folsom toward something only he could see. Folsom barely remembered his older sister. She'd been involved with a man in Boston. There had been a scandal, of course, though his father did his best to hide it. Loretta died and died badly. The thought was enough to twist his heart into a knot.

"And your name?"

The stranger smiled. "I'm Jonathan Crowley."

Folsom backed up, his eyes growing wide. That was impossible, of course. He remembered Crowley. The man had seemed a giant to him when he was a child. He'd been tall and lean and he'd had the most terrifying smile.

"Good Lord." Folsom's lips barely moved. "How is that possible?"

Crowley's smiled dropped as fast as it had shown itself. He ignored the question and countered with, "I expect your men might have told you one version of the tale. Why not hear the other version before you decide how to handle the situation, Captain?"

The request was reasonable enough, but Folsom did not like the tone of voice any more than he liked that damnable smile. He didn't like the fear that seeing the man caused in him, either. "Your friend will have a chance to tell his side of the story when he stands trial." He wanted to dismiss the man, planned to, in fact, but the man stayed where he was and damned if that smile didn't come back and grow broader still.

Crowley's brown eyes regarded him for a moment and then he shrugged. "He won't be standing trial. He has things to do and so do I." That was the end of the argument as far as Crowley was concerned. His tone said as much. Folsom looked closely at the man for the first time and shook his head. "Sir, you should take yourself away from this situation before it grows any worse. I have witnesses that say a man with skin as white as snow killed four of my men. I see exactly one man with skin as white as snow in this area, sir. In fact I'd hazard there are no more albinos for a hundred miles in any direction."

"Would you indeed, sir?" The albino's face crept into a strange smile as he spoke. His eyes glittered under lids at half-mast.

"Have you seen yourself?" Folsom asked. "Your skin is as white as milk."

"Indeed it is. Has been my entire life. I did, however, have a conversation with another man not long before I saw your men, and he was just as pale as me."

The smiling man laughed; it sent shivers down Folsom's spine. "Well now, I would hazard a guess you might be mistaken, Captain." His tone was dry and mocking and Folsom found him distasteful in the extreme. That damnable laugh, however, echoed in the back of his mind, brought back thoughts of his sister, and how he'd felt when he found her body.

No. The past was just that, and he'd not let the grinning fool confuse him with what had to be half-truths or blatant lies. How he knew about Folsom's family was irrelevant.

He had every intention of brushing the nonsensical claim aside, but before he could the man he'd observed pouring shots of whiskey spoke up. "Saw him myself. He's a little shorter, a lot thinner, and looks like he's an Indian, but his skin is just as pale."

"Nonsense." Folsom shook his head. "Corporal Bridges, kindly put that man in irons." He pointed toward the gaunt man.

Bridges nodded and took a step forward. The corporal was a burly man, large and heavyset and capable with his hands. He'd knocked several men larger than him down a few sizes in his time and he would likely do so again.

The smiling man shook his head and blocked Bridges. "Let's not make a mistake here, gentlemen. My friend and I are perfectly willing to leave town right now and end this without any additional troubles."

"Are you deaf, sir?" Folsom's voice was as harsh as a whip crack when he spoke. "I have dead soldiers on my hands!"

"Your soldiers died trying to shoot me down." The gaunt man's voice remained as calm as ever, but the expression on his face belied his tone. "They were a mite bit offended, seeing as I stopped them from taking a few squaws to have their way with."

Folsom nearly balked at that. Was that guilt in his chest? He tried to tell himself that it was not, but he also remembered his sister and the scandals she'd been involved in and that feeling bloomed inside him. With an effort he crushed the emotion down. "It is our duty to curtail the growing Indian problems in this area. And in addition to confessing to killing my men, you've just confessed to interfering with that duty." He looked away from the gaunt man and barked at the corporal, "Bridges! Lock that man in irons!"

Bridges nodded and started forward. Before he could take two steps, the smiling man moved forward and struck him a solid blow that dropped the larger man to the ground.

"That's enough of this!" Folsom grabbed at the pistol strapped to his hip.

By the time he'd drawn, several of the soldiers with him were doing the same, and the two men he was facing had both managed to draw as well.

The smiling man had two Peacemakers. One of the large-bore barrels was aimed at Folsom. The other was pointed at Song, who was crouching slightly and looked like he might well enjoy taking a bite out of the gunslinger.

The albino aimed a heavy shotgun at the whole lot of them. He'd swept the damned thing from under his coat with ease, and was looking hard at Folsom.

"Anyone pulling a trigger might well wish they'd reconsidered, gentlemen." A round-bellied man walked forward. His voice shook, but he had a pleasant enough smile on his round face. "Might I suggest we put weapons down and come to an understanding before anyone else is killed?"

Folsom didn't like him. He spoke like a lawyer. Still, he offered a chance to the captain not to get his head blown off by two different men. Outside of the tent several of his men let out bellows of anger and shock. The ground trembled lightly and while he feared taking his eyes off the two men aiming at him, he risked a look around to the entrance of the tent.

"Would someone kindly tell me what the hell is going on out there?"

Private Bronson called out loud and clear from the other side of the tent flap, "Captain! We got injuns coming our way! A lot of injuns!"

The smiling man laughed again. It was a humorless, bitter sound.

* * *

There was a point where no more could be tolerated. That point had come a long time ago as far as Alchesay was concerned. His parents had been murdered and scalped when he was a boy. His wife had been taken only a few years ago. His family had been attacked and slaughtered again and again over the years, first by Mexicans and now by the round eyes. Enough.

Several of the tribal elders wanted peace, but that time was past. They came into the area and looked for silver, and when they found it, they started digging. Most of the *Dilze'he* were already stuck in this desert land, forced here by the white man, and now they were being told to move again.

And maybe they would have. Maybe even Alchesay would have accepted this – though he was not truly sure if he would or not – but now these fools had come and dragged several women from the town. They thought the women did not understand their words, but they were wrong. His sister was among them and she'd heard what the men intended to do.

And according to her, a Skinwalker had saved them.

Whatever the case, it had only taken the word of his sister to send him toward the town, and because many of the men were just as tired of being pushed and pushed, they came with him.

There would be no more of their women raped or scalped by the white men.

The men in blue uniforms were gathered in one area when Alchesay charged into town with his men. In numbers they looked to be stronger, but they were all busy looking at one tent and before they were aware, Alchesay and his men were in range.

The first rifle shots cracked through the air before the soldiers did much more than look around with open mouths. All around the area people of all colors were running, wisely clearing away from the charging horsemen. Four of the bluecoats fell before any of them considered attacking in return. Two of their horses fell too, shot by who knew. Men and horses alike screamed.

And then the soldiers turned and grabbed for their weapons.

Alchesay had planned for this. Instead of staying at a long range, he and his men charged their horses into the enemy. Flesh fell before the hooves of his mount. Men screamed and fell, and the horse stumbled but kept its footing. He was too close to shoot, so he swung his rifle and hit whatever he could with the butt of the weapon. Someone fired from nearby and a bullet cut past his head. He had no time to consider that. Instead he hit another bluecoat and felt bone break.

There were screams, of course. And then there were battle cries. He called out for his men and they called out as well. The cavalry recoiled as if hit by boiling water.

He charged forward.

The tent was closer now. And the time was finally here. He would kill them all, every last one of the soldiers. They would all pay for what they had done, what they had planned to do. There would be no mercy.

Unfortunately, the men in the tent felt the same away.

There were more of the soldiers than he'd expected. They came from inside the large tent and started shooting and they were far enough away that they could still aim and shoot and kill.

Beside him Mangas stopped his battle cry when a bullet tore his skull away. He fell from his horse and into the tide of men being crushed, and that was the last Alchesay saw of his lifelong friend.

The bluecoats kept coming, and Alchesay jammed his heels into the horse's flanks and charged forward into the crush of soldiers.

And men screamed.

And men died.

And Alchesay roared his challenge for all of them. His skin felt hot. His bones were blades of ice. His heart thundered in his chest and his eyes shook in his skull.

And then the change came, and Alchesay roared his challenge a second time as his teeth grew and his body twisted into a new form.

* * *

Halfway across the camp he'd crouched in the dirt and made markings with one pale finger. His other hand had poured colored sand into the markings and filled them in.

The Navajo called his kind Skinwalkers. It was as good a name as any, but he knew better. There was more to them than just changing shapes. Most of his kind were gone now. They tended to kill each other off. It was not something they could, or wanted to, control. Like the weather or the stars, it was simply what was supposed to be. They felt a dislike for each other that could seldom be set aside for long. The one he'd seen earlier was a child, barely born into the world and likely knew nothing of himself.

He probably wanted to know more about what he was. And why he existed. The old one could have told him, but that was not what he planned this day.

What he planned was violence and carnage and blood and suffering, the things he fed on best.

And so he'd finished his simple spell and looked at the characters he had drawn in the dirt and then at the Apache charging into town. They had plans, too, and those plans were of blood and violence.

So the old one helped them along.

His hands had scooped up the colored sand and dirt and held the mixture out and blew it at the Apache as they rode past.

He did not hit all of them, but he'd hit enough.

He waited until they were engaged with their enemies and the bloodshed had begun before he said that words that made the spell awaken. And just that easily, the anger within the warriors was given a face and a form.

The old one settled down and watched and waited.

Soon enough he would feed.

* * *

Crowley shook his head as the cavalrymen turned away from him and from Slate alike. Slate stared at them with an expression that was either shock, outrage or both. Whatever the case, it made Crowley chuckle.

"You find this situation amusing, Mister Crowley?" Slate looked his way with an expression of disappointment.

"Not at all, Mister Slate. I find you amusing."

"And why would that be?" Damned if Slate didn't sound offended.

"Because you look so very annoyed that the men who want to hang you are no longer bothering with you."

Slate blinked and a quick, embarrassed grin flashed on his face. "Yes, well, when you say it like that."

"We should leave."

"I agree." Slate pointed at the men flowing out of the tent. "But there are men in our way."

"This is a tent, Mister Slate. We can climb out from under it if we must."

The bartender looked at them and shook his head. "Could just go out the flap at the other side, too."

Crowley smiled and tossed the man a coin.

And as they were walking away from the soldiers, ignoring the screams and the gunshots, a deep roar shook through the air and the tone of the screams changed from anger and pain to deep, abiding terror.

And he knew before it happened of course. It was inevitable, really.

Someone out in the front of the tent let out a shriek and someone else called out, "Help me! Oh, Lord, help me!"

Crowley shook his head.

"You don't have to, you know." Slate's voice, as soft as a whisper.

"Oh, but I do." He shook his head again. "Can't you feel it? Whatever is out there, it's not natural." He spoke as if he regretted what was going to come next, but still the smile pulled at the edges of his lips and his heart beat faster in his chest.

"Well then, shall we do this?"

Crowley spun hard and nearly ran for the men at the opposite end of the tent. Many of the soldiers were coming back in, their eyes wide and frightened. He could understand that. There were a lot of things out in the world to be afraid of.

* * *

Folsom had planned to come out with guns blazing and eliminate the threat before it could become something larger. He'd half expected to run across a few of the savages in town, but when he heard the horses, and the sound of Apache battle cries, he felt a cold knot of dread in his stomach.

Had he, perhaps, turned a blind eye to his men having their way with the squaws? Yes. Why? Because happy soldiers performed better. What he had not truly considered was what might occur when the red skinned brutes found out about what was happening with their women. That was the very first concern when he heard the sounds of his men screaming. It shouldn't have been, but truth be told the guilt had been gnawing at him for a while.

The guilt went away the second he saw the monsters.

He'd pushed through the crowd of his men to assess the situation and was looking directly at the Indians when they changed. Not all of them, only a few, but it was enough. The man at the front of the charge was a stocky brute in leathers. He wore a canvas coat that had seen its best days a few years earlier and was coming apart at the seams, and his rage was a brutal thing to behold.

The coat tore itself apart, shredded right before the captain's eyes, and the clothes beneath it did the same, peeling away even as the man continued charging forward on his horse. One pace and the fabric was splitting. Another step forward and the horse was knocking two soldiers aside. A third step and one of the soldiers fell to the ground while the other kept his balance. A fourth step and Folsom was drawing his weapon, intent on killing the fool horseman. A fifth step and everything changed all at once. The horse let out a shriek and lost its balance, falling forward and crashing to the ground. He was a horseman himself and knew instantly the beast had broken its neck. The rider fell forward and blurred as he caught himself on his palms. That was the only way he could think of it. The fabric on his body was torn apart and so was the flesh beneath it. Folsom looked and his eyes refused to see properly. Great flakes of flesh and hair split away from the shape of the man and when he moved forward, standing instead of sliding across the ground, which seemed an impossibility by itself, he was not a man anymore but something entirely different.

The thing still had two legs and two arms, yet beyond that he would have been hard pressed to say what might seem humanoid about it. The body was wrong. Too broad, and covered in wiry fur. The head seemed to grow directly from the torso, and while he knew the thing must surely see, the only features that made any sense were the teeth that filled a mouth far too large for the rest of the hellish shape.

The thing roared again and Folsom aimed and fired, and then fired twice more. His aim was true, and a hole blossomed in the center of the demon's chest. It stepped back and then fell back and landed in the dirt, rolling and thrashing, slamming into the shuddering, dying horse, which once again let out a scream of panic and pain.

His men did their best to get away from both shapes, but even as they tried to escape, the other horsemen were coming and they, too, changed. While Folsom was busy trying to kill the first nightmare, a pack of equally-unsettling things dropped from their horses, snarling, bleating, screaming, and attacking the members of the Cavalry.

They were none of them the same. Each was a different form of nightmare; some thickset and low to the ground, others long-limbed and far too tall for a human. The horses fled, kicking and screaming up a hellish noise, crushing everything that got in their way as they made as much distance as they could from the hellish things.

The only thing they had in common was that each and every one of the nightmares was, indeed, as white as snow. They were ghostly, horrid things that scared him to the point he thought he'd piss himself.

The thing he'd shot got back up. It wasn't completely white anymore. There was a lot of blood spilling from the wounds he'd put in it, but that didn't seem to be enough to stop it. There was no face, just that damnable mouth full of fangs as it screeched and leapt at him.

And then the pale white man he'd been ready to lock in irons pushed past him and fired a shotgun blast into the open mouth of the thing. The barrel was just past Folsom's face and he felt the detonation as much as he heard it. After that he wasn't hearing much of anything. His ears seemed too stuffed with cotton to make sense of the words spoken.

Just the same, he understood the gesture when the albino swept him aside and fired the second barrel of his weapon. The thing he shot did not get up again. They were tough, but they were not indestructible.

Crowley was next, moving past him with no sign of a weapon in his hands and that mad grin of his spreading across his face.

His hearing was coming back enough that he heard the words from the smiling man's mouth. "What are they, Mister Slate?"

The gaunt man shook his head. "No idea, Mister Crowley, but I believe they are connected to whatever is drawing me here."

One of the things, too thin and too tall and reaching for a private who was screaming and staring down at the stump where his hand had been, turned its attention to the man named Slate and let out a sound like a cat hissing, if that cat was the size of a bear.

Crowley stepped around the gaunt one and blocked the oversized hand that reached for the albino. He struck hard enough that the nearly-skeletal thing reared back in shock. It was almost twice as tall as a man and had a face that was stretched and thin and filled with teeth the size of knives.

"No. I don't think you want to do that." Crowley kept smiling.

Folsom shook off his confusion and decided to handle the matter. The revolver kicked when he pulled the trigger and he watched the left half of the thing's neck explode in a gout of crimson that splashed both of the men.

Slate flinched as the thing screamed and clutched at the wound. That made Folsom feel a little better about his own fear.

Crowley stepped in closer and kicked the spindly leg of the thing with the heel of his boot. Bones snapped and the ghostly white demon fell as surely as if struck by an axe.

Folsom felt something touch his leg, and almost shrieked. He looked down and aimed his Colt at the source of whatever was touching him. It was Song. Half of the Chinaman's face had been carved into bloody red trenches and his eye was missing. He clutched at Folsom's pant leg and let out a sound. And then he died.

Folsom shook his head, angrier at the loss of the heathen than he would have ever expected. "That's enough of this madness!" he roared, and all around him the soldiers stopped their panic, or at least calmed it down. They were soldiers and they were used to combat. What they needed, what they always needed, was someone to lead them. "Kill these damned things!"

To make his point he aimed at the next of the things close enough for him to hit, and fired. The shot went astray and only clipped one overly large ear on the beast. When it looked at him,

305

really looked at him, Folsom knew he'd made a horrible mistake. He'd have apologized if he could have found the words, but it was on him far too quickly. Folsom let out a yelp as clawed fingers ripped into his coat and the beast lifted him into the air, baring impossible teeth and roaring directly into his face.

Folsom aimed his weapon and fired, and nothing at all happened.

He tried again.

Nothing.

"Well, damn." It was all he could think to say.

* * *

The captain was staring at his death, and Crowley was tempted to let it take him. As a boy he'd been a scared, confused little thing. As a man he smacked of too much cocky attitude and too little common sense. Worse, he was actually making himself useful. It was easier to ignore men who were useless and cocky about it.

Still, at the moment there were other considerations, like the damned things chewing their way through a dozen soldiers. They were monsters, yes, but nothing he'd ever seen before. They did not reek of the demons he was used to, and they were not spirits in any sense he was familiar with.

When he'd come to the New World he'd done so to study these exact sorts of creatures. There had been a definite excitement in finding new and interesting beings in a land he had never been to before.

That excitement had not changed. Adding to it was the sheer variety of shapes that these creatures took. They were, he had no doubt, of similar ilk. They had to be.

Even things that ran in packs seldom liked to mingle with different creatures.

That was the part that made him smile.

Crowley saw Lucas Slate grab the thing holding the captain and haul it backward by the scruff of its bullish neck. It let out a yowlp of surprise and so did the Cavalryman. The good news for the captain was that it let go of him. That was also the bad news for Slate. The thing he was holding onto moved like a sack of cats held over a roaring fire. It twisted and whipped its arms in wide arcs and screeched as it turned on Crowley's companion, and both of them stumbled back and fell.

Before Crowley could get to them, they were lost in the crush of people.

A soldier aimed for the area where they'd fallen and Crowley knocked him aside, throwing off his aim as he waded into the crush of flesh. People moved and thrashed and pushed in and out of his view. Crowley ignored them all, save to push them aside. Somewhere ahead of him, not but a few feet to be sure, but in the press of struggling bodies it might well have been miles, his companion was down on the ground and fighting.

When the bullish thing flew through the air, it was as limp as a sack of horse dung. The thing trailed blood, and as it rose into the air, Lucas Slate stood, covered in the same crimson stains and looking truly enraged.

His shirt had been torn apart and deep cuts ran along the left side of his muscular chest. Those cuts bled, a reminder that he was still at least partially human despite his appearance.

Slate looked around and stooped long enough to grab his fool hat from the ground. That hat had seen better days and likely would have been thrown away by most people, but the battered old thing with its dusty band and the broken feathers sticking from the same went back on Slate's head before he looked around and the rage faded from his expression.

It was a calmer expression he wore as he reached for his Navy revolvers and started aiming.

Crowley had the good sense to stay well away from the man as he pulled the triggers. The first bullet blew a hole through a white, scaly thing with too many eyes, and also took the hand from one of the Cavalry. The creature flopped to the ground and twitched. The soldier fell to his knees and screamed. By the time those two things had occurred, Slate had turned his attention to the next target and fired with that same dead expression on his face. *Boom!* The creature fell. Slate's mouth twisted into a feral snarl and he fired again. The bullets from his weapon were a reminder that death could be sudden and violent. Another explosive noise and the Indians and the soldiers alike were quickly backing away from Slate. He stood taller than any of them and he looked like the Grim Reaper ready for the harvest. The only things that didn't run were the white nightmares around them. They should have fled but it seemed beyond them to reason that well. Instead they charged toward Slate and he fired again and again until the last of them fell at his feet.

Through it all, Jonathan Crowley watched with his eyes narrowed to slits and a grin frozen in place.

When the final beast had fallen, Lucas Slate looked at Captain Folsom and shook his head. "I do not currently feel inclined to go with you for trial." Both of the weapons were still in his hands and the barrels of the Navy six-shooters were smoking in the cold air.

Folsom stared at the spectre before him for ten heartbeats without responding and then finally he said, "Currently, I do not feel much inclined to argue the matter, sir. We have all of us had a day already."

"Indeed."

Folsom called for his men to gather the dead and the wounded. His voice was weaker than before and his hands shook. That did not make him a coward in Crowley's eyes. It merely made him human.

He rather envied the soldier that.

* * *

Folsom sat in his newly-appropriated office in town. He thought about the day's events. All told, if you counted the Chinaman – and he did – he had lost seven men, and the number of wounded was higher still.

Somehow he had avoided getting injured himself. The men looked up to him and none of them had missed that he was in the heart of the combat. They knew he hadn't stood behind the lines and watched them take the damage. No, he had come out to the assistance of all when the damned Indians had attacked.

Being as he was in the middle of town when the attack took place he should have expected some sort of coalition of towns-folk, but he was caught flatfooted. The men who came before him were dressed, as gentlemen should dress, in proper suits with vests and with matching shoes. That was an accomplishment at least half the time; at least it had been since he crossed into areas across the Mississippi from home. That said, they needed a good wash and not a one of them seemed familiar with the idea of shaving. The facial hairs were long and the facial expressions were dour.

They'd been droning on for a while now, long enough for him to get the gist. They wanted the soldiers gone. Or they wanted assurances, or they wanted the Indians dead. Something of that sort.

When he'd heard enough he raised one hand and the con-versations stopped. "What exactly do you gentlemen want? Pick one thing. I haven't the time to listen to every complaint you have. I need to report the deaths of my soldiers and I need to prepare your town for any more possible Indian attacks."

A black haired man sporting the most impressive mustache Folsom had ever seen, spoke. As his lips moved, his mustache jittered and jumped. It was nearly mesmerizing. "There wouldn't be any Indian attacks if you'd left well enough alone." The man leaned forward and planted his hands on the long oak table the captain had commandeered to act as his desk. "We had us an understanding. We didn't piss on them and they didn't come along and try to kill us. You notice how they only went for soldiers? There was a reason for that."

Folsom stood and gave the man his best hard look. It was a good one because the fellow took two paces back, shaking his head. "Do you know who I am, sir? Do you even begin to know why I am here? I'm here because I was called here by one of your own. A telegram was sent to Washington, D.C. and that in turn was considered and then acted upon. I am the result of that telegram."

"And who the hell sent it?" The mustache trembled with righteous indignation. Folsom knew the man he was speaking to had eyes, but he had not yet been able to focus on them enough to consider the character they might reveal.

"Allucius Sheppard." Folsom reached into his jacket pocket and fumbled out the original paper. "Says here he's the mayor of this town."

The mustache tightened for a moment and then trembled even more. "Al? Al Sheppard not only isn't the mayor of anything, he's dead!" Several voices murmured their agreement. "The damned fool drank himself to death. Passed out and choked on his own regurgitation. And besides, he was never in charge of a damned thing around these parts."

Folsom felt a flush run into his cheeks. "Be that as it may, I have my orders to get rid of the red man in this area and I intend to follow those orders." He leaned onto the table and heard it creak threateningly under his weight. "I've spent time listening to your concerns, gentlemen. Until I hear otherwise, my duty is to remove the Indians from this area and keep your town safe. Good day."

"We were already safe!" Mustache shook his fist and looked like he might even consider using it against Folsom but decided at the last moment not to get himself shot. "Leave us to our own devices, sir! We have to live here when you're done with your damned orders."

The man turned his back and stomped away before Folsom could respond, and after a brief hesitation the rest of the sorry lot followed suit.

Folsom settled back behind his desk and started composing his explanation of the day's events. Colonel Hartshorn would want to know what had happened and he'd need to offer a proper defense. The loss of so many and that on top of being caught unawares, was not going to sit well. Folsom dreaded the shit storm that would surely be coming his way.

He had no idea.

* * *

Lucas Slate squinted at his reflection in the dusty mirror. The clothes were nice, a gift from Crowley, and they fitted properly.

The tailor had a suit that was supposed to be picked up and never was – the man had died, apparently – and while it took a bit of waiting while the adjustments were made, the final result was worth the patience.

Crowley eyed him critically enough to make him wonder if the man had ever spent time as a tailor himself. Finally he nodded his satisfaction and counted out coins for the man who'd sold the suit.

"There is a haberdashery at the edge of the saloon over that way," the tailor said as he pointed vaguely, which, as the town had no proper streets, was the best that could be managed, "should you like a new hat as well."

Slate stared at the man for a moment and then simply shook his head.

Crowley walked for the door of the shop after thanking the tailor.

Slate watched Crowley break into one of his smiles. "What?" Slate was slipping his hat in place and almost managing a scowl.

"I have seen men less devoted to their wives than you are to your hat, Mister Slate."

"And had I a wife, perhaps I'd care less about my hat, sir."

"I should rather not consider the ramifications of that statement."

Slate reared back as if slapped and then chuckled. "You've a vile mind, Mister Crowley."

"Now, tell me about the pale thing you saw before everything went mad."

"He was tall and thin and pale. Looked to me as if he might be an Indian, but as washed of color as me." Slate looked away. "He spoke to me in some language I have never heard, but I understood him. He said we would meet again."

"You were pale when we met. You are an albino, after all, but you are a different sort of pale now."

"How do you mean?"

Your skin lacked pigment before. Now it has more color to it, but that color is white. That's really the best way I can put it."

Slate nodded and pursed his thin lips. "He was too thin."

"What do you mean?" Crowley looked puzzled.

"I mean I am thin, but I am still a possibility. He was taller than me and thinner than me. He looked impossible. His body is too thin and his arms and legs so very long and his head shape was thinner even than mine."

Crowley stared at him for a long moment and finally nodded. "That thing we dealt with in Carson's Point was a bit like that. But only a bit."

"I never truly saw the thing but towards the end, and frankly I was a bit too unsettled by what was happening to me to much care at that point."

"You touched a stone. The stone went into you. We've discussed that before, of course. We know that the stones were put into the – whatever the hell it might be's – chosen victims and they changed, but it wasn't the same as these things. These were sudden and the bodies didn't stay changed."

Slate looked at him. "Did they not?"

"No." Crowley looked back just as hard, his face impossible to read past that damnable grin of his. "They became what they once were when they died. They were Indians, but we knew that."

"Why do you suppose they attacked?"

Crowley shrugged. "I neither know nor care. Humans do stupid things to humans all the time, Mister Slate. I don't allow myself the luxury of paying much attention."

That was a lie and Slate knew it. They discussed many things on their travels and inevitably what they talked about most was the state of the world around them as gleaned from various newspapers. Crowley bought them and read them insatiably. Still, he did not call the man on his lie.

"And the soldiers? How do you feel about them being here, Mister Crowley?"

"I've never much taken to soldiers. Been one before, fought in my share of wars and followed orders, but I've never liked it. Soldiers are expected to follow orders, no matter how foolish those orders might be."

Crowley paused a moment and then asked, "And you? Do you side with the Indians?"

"No sir, I do not. I side with the people on the streets who are getting caught up in this conflict. I knew what those men intended when it came to the squaws." He shook his head. "I do not believe that women should be misused."

Crowley nodded.

"And you, Mister Crowley? Do you side with either group?"

"The Indians were minding their own business. The army was sent by someone. They do not, as a rule come without orders. They are summoned. So one is doing what they have always done and the other is following orders from elsewhere. I can't say as I much care either way."

"You keep saying that sort of thing, and yet, here you are, grinning and wading into conflicts."

Crowley's voice dripped with sarcasm. "My pale companion has gotten himself into trouble and asked for my help. What is a man to do?" His plain face looked around the shop for a moment and then back to Slate. "How does the suit feel?"

"Like proper clothing, and I thank you for it, Mister Crowley." Slate ducked his head briefly for a moment, feeling an unaccustomed flash of shame. "I fear I cannot possibly pay you back any time soon."

Crowley waved it aside. "I have the money to spare and you have lost all you owned before we met. As we are traveling together for the present time, I can hardly expect you to settle into life as an undertaker again, though I imagine you could have made fair compensation this particular day."

"Just the same."

"Should I decide you owe me, Mister Slate, you may rest assured you'll be informed of such debts. Until then, merely accept that under our current circumstances I do not mind investing in your clothes." He snorted. "Besides which, you were beginning to look too much like an Indian and I need to not confuse you for any other white-skinned Indians we might encounter."

"Do you suppose that's a strong likelihood?"

"You've run across one already and I am fairly certain you are looking forward to a second encounter."

"What makes you say that, Mister Crowley?"

"Because you have a need to understand your place in the universe, Mister Slate."

"And you don't?"

"I have known my place in the universe for a very long time, Mister Slate. And we are still looking into your position."

Neither spoke of what might happen when that position was known.

* * *

Finding rooms proved challenging, but not impossible. Apparently having a giant albino looming over your shoulder made people more willing to find space for a man in a negotiating mood. The rooms were comfortable enough, and as an added bonus seemed bug free.

In the morning, Crowley looked at the growth on his face, and trimmed the hairs down to manageable levels rather than shaving them away completely. He knew it wouldn't last but for the next few days at least he had a neatly-trimmed beard and mustache to fight off the cold.

When he came downstairs, Slate was already waiting for him, and the small gathering of tables were all filled except for the one where the albino waited. His hat had been mended and looked mostly like it had in the past. Crowley chose not to feed into his obsession and ignored the thing completely. Within twenty minutes they'd eaten and after ten minutes more they were on their way.

"Where are we going, exactly?" Crowley asked, though he already knew the answer.

"I'm off to find the other one like me. You are along to keep me out of trouble."

Crowley nodded. "I seem to remember something about that."

"As it was your idea, I should hope so, sir."

Despite the violence of the day, before the crowds were moving about, many of them looking to buy wares and others looking to sell. It was distinctly possible that there were even more wretches moving into the town.

There were soldiers everywhere they looked, though for the moment none of them seemed to be causing too much trouble. Crowley had no doubt that would change soon enough.

Folsom had made clear his intention to clean the Indians from the area for the safety of all involved, regardless of how the people felt about that. As it had been Indians starting the shooting the day before – excluding what Slate had accomplished all by himself – it seemed perfectly reasonable to expect the captain and his men to be as prepared as possible.

A pickpocket tried to steal from Crowley. He stopped the attempt without causing a scene. It was a bad time to be a thief and a worse time to be a child. He decided to let someone else deal with handling the young boy with the grabby hands. The things they'd been bothered by the day before were far more worrisome. Besides which, Crowley kept most of his money hidden where it would never be found. A moment later he changed his mind, and contemplated going after the kid and teaching him a lesson, but it was too late. The would-be thief was long gone.

* * *

He watched the other Skinwalker from a distance, and noted the man who walked with him. They were both powerful, as was expected of any Skinwalker, but the one with him, the smiling man, he was a different sort of powerful. He carried himself with confidence and he smiled at almost everything. Not a pleasant smile but a baring of teeth, a warning that the man was deadly beyond most people's reckoning. Where they walked, people scattered away from them, perhaps without even being aware of it.

The Skinwalker was aware, of course. That was why he was following them. They were dangerous and they could well be dangerous enough to cause him harm. He would find out soon enough.

The wind blew and whispered its secrets and he listened as he had learned to long ago. The stories of the wind were all about the Indians coming toward the town. There had been a great deal of blood spilled and the Apache in the area wanted to settle the matter. They did not wish to talk any longer. There is a point where anyone can lose hope of a simple resolution and that time had come and passed.

All around him people moved and milled and sought desperately for what would make their lives complete. An urchin moved toward him, furtive and worried. He bumped into a man in front of the Skinwalker and plucked a few coins from his victim's pocket. A moment later he was bumping into a young woman and apologizing even as he lifted a small item from her bag. And then he bumped into the Skinwalker, mumbled an apology and continued on with a small silver nugget the Skinwalker had been carrying for the last three days.

The silver meant nothing to him. He had taken it from a dead man he found on his way to the town. The corpse had been torn open by what at first glance appeared to be wolves, but the Skinwalker knew better. He could smell shapechangers and found the notion amusing.

The fact that the boy took it merely meant that he had managed to catch the old sorcerer's attention. That was enough.

A whispered word as he crouched and grabbed at the soil. The arid earth crumbled in his hand and he spat into it, rubbed it between his fingers and his palm until it became a doughy mass. He stood just long enough to throw that simple lump at the thief, striking him on the back of his neck. The boy reached reflexively for what hit him and the old man smiled and continued on his way. Only a few seconds later the screams started as the boy fell to the ground, swelling and choking and trying to breathe. It was not the first time he'd spread a sickness and it would not be the last. This was a minor one and would only kill a few, but it would leave them all afraid.

Somewhere behind him a woman screamed as the boy's flesh rotted away and spilled his bodily fluids into the street.

Up ahead, far enough along that they did not seem to notice, the other Skinwalker and the strange creature walked on.

* * *

Crowley noticed Slate cock his head to the left. "What is it?" he asked.

"That damn song again," Slate replied. "Every time I hear it something goes wrong."

"You are hearing a summoning spell. Whatever this thing we're looking for is, it summons energies and what I can only call demons, even if they don't feel like the ones I'm used to."

"Then how do you know?"

"I've been testing your limits, Mister Slate. Seeing what it is you might be capable of, but I have my own abilities."

"You've never much discussed what they are."

Crowley cast a sideways look in Slate's direction. "We don't much talk about what happens if I decide you are a threat. We both know the answer already, yes?"

"Of course." Slate nodded, but his voice remained soft and dry. "I might be a threat and you might need to eliminate that threat. We've already seen a little of what something like me can do. If I don't maintain control, I understand what you'll have to do and I condone it."

"Do you?"

Slate looked at him and his mouth trembled for a moment. "I've no desire to become the sort of monster I was raised around."

"You were raised around monsters?"

"I was raised an albino and a mulatto in an area where many considered that a sign of the Devil, sir. Had my family not had a certain level of influence I'd have been killed. As it was, I remained locked inside my house most times to avoid a beating. There are all sorts of monsters, Mister Crowley. Not all of them cast spells or have fangs."

Crowley nodded. "Agreed. Very well, Mister Slate. A few facts for you. I can see the dead. I can communicate with them. Mostly I choose not to."

"Why is that?"

"Because the dead are not of interest to me. They are dead, and often they make demands when they know they can be heard. I am not interested in their demands and I have no desire to be plagued by them any more than I have been in the past." Crowley's face grew troubled for a moment.

"Are the dead around here?"

"Some. Not as many. Not too many have died here yet, though I imagine that's to change soon."

"Are there any dead around us now?"

"Oh, yes." He looked past Slate's shoulder at the faint ghostly image of Molly Finnegan and nodded slowly. She looked at him, implored him, would have begged if there was enough of her left, but there was not. Something had stolen most of her away in Carson's Point, not too long ago, and left just enough to ensure he was haunted by her. He had not yet resolved to destroying that remnant or sending it on to whatever lay beyond this realm. If he didn't think about it, he could tell himself she wasn't suffering. Sometimes, most times, really, he didn't much like himself. He promised himself that he would release her soon. Very soon. Just not yet.

"What else do you see that you do not speak of, Mister Crowley?"

"I see a lot. I hear just as much. I heard the spell that was cast. I'm still trying to understand it. I know that it came from behind us, but so do you."

Slate nodded in agreement. "I do indeed. I've been trying to decide how to handle it."

"Well, perhaps you should confront your enemy and be done with it."

"Is he my enemy?" Slate's voice carried an uncertain note.

Crowley stopped walking and stared hard at him. "I should imagine he is. He's killed several people with his actions, and a few moments ago he killed a young boy who was seeking enough to stay alive in this hellhole."

"Did he?" Slate shook his head. "How do you know that?"

"Because currently the dead boy is standing over his rotten remains and screaming his rage into the skies. You cannot hear the dead, Mister Slate, but I can and I do."

Slate closed his eyes and nodded. "Then I suspect he is, indeed, my enemy."

Crowley heard the sound of gunfire and screaming from the far side of the small town, same as they had the day before. The screams were not pain or suffering. They were war cries. "Well, things are likely to get confusing right about now." Crowley spat the words, but again his smile crept out.

"I suspect you are right, Mister Crowley. And should I confront my enemy or wait?"

"It might be that the fighting won't reach us."

Slate nodded again and spun hard on his heel, moving back the way they'd come.

Crowley watched him, watched the crowd that had turned toward the sounds of dying part before Slate as easily as calm waters part before a ship's prow, and watched also as the small shape he approached unfolded itself from a stooped position.

Lucas Slate was taller now than most of the men around him. He was taller than Crowley by a few inches, though they had only recently stood almost the same height. Crowley had once stolen a suit of the man's because it fit well enough to allow it. As tall as Slate was, the thing that stood before him was taller by almost a foot. How it had hidden itself in so small a form was a mystery that Crowley would try to solve later.

The thing was the same color as Slate, a white that seemed too vibrant for the cadaverous shape. It had long white hair tied back in a braid, and wore clothes that looked like rawhide but that Crowley knew immediately were human flesh.

It had a very long body and a long face, eyes as dark and black as pitch and as shiny as polished glass. When the nightmare smiled his gums were gray and his teeth an unpleasant shade of yellow.

Slate and the thing spoke to each other, and Crowley listened and understood not a word of it. In the distance a dead boy kept screaming his outrage at being murdered and further away still, the gunfire continued in sporadic bursts.

* * *

The Indians came in hard and fast, and this time there were more of them and they were better organized.

Folsom's men were doing their duty, guarding the town, and none of them took their task lightly. The day before had been reminder enough that their work was dangerous.

So when the red men came, the alarm was quickly called. Folsom stepped outside and prepared himself for the battle. The men were ready and so was he, and by God, he'd see the savages pay for their bloody assault.

The men rallied quickly and he called for them to assume the various posts he'd laid out the night before. They were ready and they were more than willing after seeing their companions taken down. One or two might well have been worried about whatever sort of monsters the Apache had brought with them the day before, but they rallied just the same and he was proud of them.

Captain Folsom walked away from the hotel and headed for the sounds of combat, his heart pounding with the thrill of combat. He was not afraid. The Lord had blessed him with a brave heart and a noble purpose. He would see the day through and take no prisoners. The savages had earned a quick death for their troubles.

Up ahead of him, Sergeant Barnes had taken a position on top of a two-storey mercantile, firing as quickly as he could into the crowd below. The man was hell with a rifle, and with each shot, an Indian dropped, but damned if it didn't seem there were endless numbers of them this time around.

He had dealt with the Lakota before but never with the Apache until the previous day. They did not seem cut from the same cloth. They seemed more determined to stand their ground and take whatever it was they wanted.

"Fowler! Where is Sergeant Fowler?"

"Sergeant Fowler is on the other side of town, standing his

ground and waiting, sir!" The man that spoke to him was just out of his sight, but he recognized the voice of Private Herbst. The voice was as distinct as the man himself, a red haired brute nearly as strong as an ox. He turned to bark an order at Herbst and saw the private's body jerk twice, saw the blast of meat and bone that came off his left shoulder and then saw the man hit the ground, screaming.

Damned foolish of him to look away from the conflict. He looked back toward the crush of Indians charging into town and the chaos of people getting away from them. The civilians ran, as well they should. The soldiers stood their ground.

Folsom drew his revolver and took aim at the closest savage, a lean old man on a black horse. The old man saw him and charged, riding hard to reach him. The bullet Folsom fired caught the old man in his thigh and blew through the leg and the horse under it with ease. The old man screamed, the horse screamed, and both collapsed in a sliding heap. Neither was dead, but he intended to remedy that. One step closer, and the bullet from the next Indian caught Folsom in the chest, tearing through the rib above his heart and then through the organ itself. He tried to aim his weapon but his traitorous fingers dropped it. The pain, when it showed up, was as large as a mountain and crushed his chest in its grip. Folsom tried to scream, tried to do anything at all, and managed only to fall backward and land hard on the ground. The horse and rider stomped over his body as they continued into the town, followed by several other natives.

* * *

Crowley watched on from a distance, his face calm and almost expressionless, his eyes intensely focused. Slate did his best to ignore the man, which, considering the nightmare in front of him, was not that difficult.

"You have questions," the thing said. It was a statement rather than a question. Again it was spoken in a language other than English, one completely unknown to Slate, but he understood just the same.

"What are you? What am I?"

Those vile teeth flashed and the impossibly thin, tall man chuckled. "You were given a seed. It was planted in your body. I do not see it." It stared for a moment and then pointed to the small bump almost perfectly centered in its own forehead. When he touched it the skin parted like an eye blinking and for just an instant a greenish-gray stone showed before the skin sealed itself again. "It would be similar to this, but not exactly the same."

Slate remembered touching the stone, feeling it; remembered that pebble, too, had a song to sing. He nodded but did not speak.

"That seed is what you are. What you are becoming. We are not many, there have never been many, but we are powerful."

"What do I do about it?" Slate asked.

"Embrace the changes. I fought mine and in the end it caused me nothing but pain."

"What is the song I hear?"

"That is magic trying to tell you how to grow and become strong."

"Do you hear that same song?"

The thin man looked at him with a cold, sly expression. "I am the song."

"I don't understand."

"We are a part of the world. This world and others. We can listen to the song and we can sing notes from the song and create wonders. But we must feed if we listen to the song."

He wasn't sure if the thing was being deliberately vague or simply lacked the ability to explain itself. Either way, he was starting to dislike the thin man.

"What do we have to feed on?"

"Mostly pain, and others like ourselves." That smile grew larger.

Then the thin man reached for him and placed a hand on his chest and something inside of him pulled and twisted and shook through his body like a tree's roots being ripped from the ground. Lucas Slate tried to step back, tried to break free, but the thin man's hand on his chest burned at him and left him unable to move a single muscle. He stared at the yellowed teeth in darkened gums surrounded by white, smiling lips, and felt hatred rip into his heart.

In a lifetime full of predatory people who thought he was easy prey Lucas Slate had proven more than his share of people mistaken. He could not make his body move. He could not make his anger known by any of his previous methods. He could not, by God, even call out to Jonathan Crowley a dozen strides away. Instead he listened to the song that called to him and tried to understand the things it was saying.

The pain fought for his attention. The song had been trying to get his notice for longer.

He let the song win.

* * *

Crowley stared hard at the two pale men, waiting as they stood face to face and spoke. He could not understand a single word they were speaking and that, too, was something he was unaccustomed to. He did not understand because the words were new to him, but they were also not words, not exactly. Damned if it didn't sound like to two of them were harmonizing.

As a counterpoint to their song, the battle raged close by and drew closer. The Cavalry was fighting against the invading Apache and by the sounds of screams, cries, and gunshots the conflict was in a full fury.

Crowley stared toward the sound of battle and saw the soldiers retreating, heading at a slow crawl toward where he stood and watched another war taking place.

Sometimes the conflicts seemed impossible to escape.

The gaunt man facing off against Lucas Slate slapped Crowley's companion in the chest and Slate started jittering where he was, standing still and twitching, seizing again and again. The usually calm face pulled down, drawing into a pained expression and Slate's eyes raged silently.

Crowley'd planned on doing nothing at all about this. He made it a habit not to get involved in several different sorts of situations, not the least of which were cases when one monster fought another.

323

Did he think Slate was a monster? That was the question.

Not far away the dead boy kept screaming his anger to the skies. He refused to be placated by whatever it was the afterlife was supposed to offer him. From the corner of Crowley's eye he could see the vaporous spectre of Molly Finnegan, dead since the previous winter, buried by none other than Lucas Slate, and whose body once pushed itself out of the ground at the behest of whatever sort of creature Slate was becoming.

Behind Molly a Cavalryman's head snapped back violently and he flopped to the ground without making a sound that could be heard from the distance. Molly looked at the body expectantly. Crowley looked away.

Helping Slate would be a hideous mistake. The events of the last summer had proved that beyond a doubt. The man had muttered words and shattered the ground at his feet. He was no longer human.

And yet, as Slate asked for help in the tent earlier, Crowley was still allowed to respond now. He was freed from his usual constraints when asked for assistance by a human being.

And he was freed when asked by Lucas Slate.

"Damn me," he muttered.

The gun was in his hand in a second. He cocked the hammer, aimed and fired. Aimed, fired. Aimed, fired, and then again.

All four bullets slammed into the thin man. The first shot surprised him. He had apparently forgotten Crowley was there. The bullet tore his right arm apart, dragging it from Slate's chest. Slate staggered backward, gasping. The second bullet took the thin man in the left shoulder blade and spun him where he stood so that he was looking toward Crowley's feet. The third round punched into the thin man's chest and blew a hole through his left lung. The fourth round hit him in the stomach and doubled him over as sure as if he'd been kicked by a horse.

The thin man gasped and grunted and then fell to his knees, trying to balance himself on his hands. He bled from each wound, streams of blood flowing to the ground. Crowley took three strides forward and looked down at where Slate lay on the frozen soil. Slate looked at him then sat up, wincing. Where the thin man had touched him, his shirt was torn and the skin underneath was already bruising, showing an amount of red that would have been alarming on most people, but for all Crowley knew, the color was perfectly normal in an albino who got himself bruised properly.

"I wasn't sure if you were going to help me or not." Slate's voice was more raspy than usual.

Crowley did not answer. To his left he saw the thin man getting to his feet.

"Mister Crowley!" Slate's eyes grew wide.

The thin man was looking hard at him and he was scowling. His face, already long and thin, grew longer still as he opened his mouth to speak. What he said meant nothing at all to Crowley. It was just gibberish. Just the same he felt his body hurled backward and did his best to prepare himself for impact.

The good news was that he landed on a canvas surface. The bad news was that a cast iron stove was under that canvas. He felt his ribs break on impact, and his right arm snapped in three places. He did not black out. He was not that fortunate.

* * *

The Skinwalker looked at his prey and smiled again. The wounds hurt, but he would heal. He would take from the younger, weaker Skinwalker and he would feed on the essence as had been done for as long as there had been Skinwalkers. Each was born, each created their seeds, each offered the seeds to worthy humans and then left. Later, after the seeds had a chance to grow, they came back and harvested their children. This one was not one of his, but that did not matter. He would feed and he would feed well. If the one who created this one took offense, he would feed on the progenitor as well.

The young Skinwalker stood, shivered. His chest was an angry red mass. The bruising was no doubt painful. The seed was deep inside this one's chest, near his heart. That was why he'd grabbed him there. Most Skinwalker's chose to place the seeds in the forehead. It made it easier for their children to see with their new senses and it also made harvesting them easier.

"I will kill you now. If you stay still I will try to make your death simple." It was a mercy he was willing to offer.

The young one nodded and said, "Fuck yourself." The shotgun rose and both barrels of the weapons fired.

The Skinwalker had been alive for a very long time and he was familiar with European weapons. Familiarity, however, did not prepare him for the pain. A hundred tiny pellets rammed through his flesh and burned into muscles, into bone. One of the tiny shots tore open his right eye and the agony was greater than he had felt in lifetimes.

He yowled and fell back, clutching at his face. He had planned to be merciful. That plan was finished.

He looked through his good eye in time to see the young one breach the shotgun and pull out the hot shells. As he watched two more were inserted and the gaunt man came closer, scowling down at him.

He raised one arm and sang. His right arm was ruined and hadn't had time to mend, but his left worked well enough. His fingers clenched the air and he pulled with his song, with his mind, willing the seed deep in the other to come to him, to tear free of its moorings and come to him.

* * *

Lucas Slate dropped the shotgun and clutched at his chest. Was this a heart attack? He had no idea, had never felt one before. The pain grew larger and he fell to his knees, crying out.

Had any pain ever been this large? His hands held tight to the front of his chest, and under the palm that touched his pallid skin he felt something moving, twisting. He remembered the day he'd swallowed the oddly carved pebble he'd been given as a gift. It was a memory he'd done his best to forget, a fevered dream he never wanted to recall.

Much like the pain tearing him in half.

Lucas Slate screamed, something he hadn't done since his transformation had started. The sound was not remotely human.

* * *

For three seconds Crowley had a fantasy about Molly. Her body was next to his and she whispered in his ear, a warm breath that tickled pleasantly. Then the pain kicked in and took him from his reverie.

There was magic about and while he often hated that notion, Jonathan Crowley was healed by the presence of the supernatural. His skin ached and his bones shrieked a symphony of pain, then the agony faded into a deep fiery itch as they pulled themselves to where they belonged and healed within him.

Crowley opened his eyes and stared at Slate and the thin man. Both of them were on their knees, straining and bleeding and locked in some sort of silent struggle. Slate did not seem to be winning. He would rather Molly whispering in his ear, but she was dead and the past offered him little solace.

"All right then," he moaned. It took only a moment for him to stand.

The sounds of gunfire grew closer, drowning out the cries of the dead pickpocket and the unsettling scream coming from Slate.

Crowley started walking, heading for the two of them.

The first of the Indians came into view and almost immediately reined in their horses. They stared at the thin man and Lucas Slate with expressions of dread that were nearly comical, and grew almost as pale as the two of them.

He had no idea why the Apache were so afraid of the pale men and he did not care. What mattered at that moment was that the whole marauding lot of them watched for all of five seconds, and then their leader let out a command that had them turning tail and leaving the area at high speed.

As Crowley had witnessed, the Indians in the town had been scared of Lucas Slate. Apparently two of his kind in the area was a bit too much for them to stand. Crowley smiled at the notion, even as he looked back to Slate and the thin man.

Slate screamed again and blood spilled from between the fingers clamped over his chest. His eyes were wide and his mouth moved like a trout out of water seeking a gasp of proper breath.

"Move your hands, Mister Slate!" Crowley bellowed the words and the thin man ignored him.

Slate looked at him and managed a puzzled expression. "I am... I can't. What do you need?"

"I need to see what he's reaching for inside of you."

Slate stared at him for a moment and slowly, carefully let his hands fall away. The lump that was revealed was the size of an apple. That Slate's chest had not exploded was something of a miracle in Crowley's opinion. Heavy lines of red stained a great deal of his body and in addition to the heavy lump trying to tear free of him, there were other lines, other things moving under his skin. All of them seemed connected and all seemed determined to come out.

Crowley looked away from Slate for only a moment to assess the thin man. He'd been beat down a good bit. Four holes from the bullets Crowley himself fired and more still from a shotgun blast or two. Only one eye remained and it stared only at Slate.

The bastard was smiling.

Crowley hated when other people had a reason to smile. Well, at least when they were enemies of his. He walked closer, scrutinizing the thin man's face.

One eye was gone. One remained. Centered above them was a small opening in his head, and that at least was something Crowley was familiar with.

He had seen similar stones in Carson's Point. They had caused him no end of troubles.

Two fast steps had him picking up his pistol. Three more strides and the barrel was one inch from the center of the thin man's forehead.

As he cocked the hammer back, the bastard finally noticed him and his one remaining eye opened wide. Crowley pulled the trigger and ripped the top of the thin man's head away with one shot.

The thin man launched backward and slammed his ruined head into the frozen ground. Deep within his skull a collection of grey things wriggled. They all seemed to be seeking something that was no longer there.

Crowley looked at the body for a moment and then checked

the remaining portion of the skull. The bullet had managed to destroy that damned stone, whatever it might be, and though he couldn't be sure, he suspected that was a mighty fine thing, indeed.

Slate fell forward and caught himself on his hands again, whimpering.

The sounds of combat were gone. The noise of people screaming had died as well, though in the distance a dead boy wept with less fervor, perhaps one step closer to accepting his fate.

Crowley put his weapon away and helped Lucas Slate to his feet.

"Are you well, Mister Slate?"

"I am not, sir. But I am alive and I thank you for that." His voice was fainter than usual.

"You'll have to be well enough." Crowley squinted as he looked around. "You take the Indians and I'll handle the soldiers."

"What do you mean?"

"I intend to stop this damned fighting before one or both of us is killed."

Lucas Slate nodded, hefted his shotgun and looked toward the direction the Indians had gone, the direction of most of the fighting.

As he walked, he murmured under his breath, words to a song that no one else in the vicinity could hear or understand. The furious red marks on his torso rapidly faded, first to pink and then to the same color as the rest of his flesh.

He was learning. The song had many, many notes and Slate suspected he would not know them all for years, but for now he learned how to heal himself with the song and it was a start.

* * *

Crowley found Sergeant Fowler and his men gathered near the far side of town, following orders. They were there to make sure the Indians didn't storm in from the other side of the area, and likely to clear a path should it become necessary to flee Silver Springs.

Crowley walked directly up to the sergeant while the man watched warily.

"Sergeant?"

The man nodded and came toward him with caution. There was no telling where a man might stand on the Indians. Most agreed they should be sent away, but wise soldiers didn't take that for granted.

The spell was simple, and one of the very first he'd learned ages ago. Crowley didn't like using sorcery on human beings, but if he had to, he made exceptions.

"Sergeant, I'm sorry to inform you that your captain and most of the rest of your soldiers are dead. They were killed by the Indians, who are fleeing even as we speak. You've won the battle, but the cost was high."

There was truth to his words, but only as much as he needed. He could have told the man that it was the heart of summer and he'd have agreed. That was how sorcery worked.

"I'm sure they fought bravely." The sergeant's voice was slightly slurred.

"Of course they did. They fought valiantly and they won. But wouldn't it be best if you returned to your base camp and reported in? If more Indians should come back they might see your presence as a challenge and you can't do your duty if you're all dead."

The sergeant looked around uncertainly. There were seven men with him. The rest were elsewhere or dead.

"Yes, of course. We'll head for home."

"An excellent idea, Sergeant. You have to make sure your men are safe, after all."

He finished the incantation. The sergeant would forget having seen his face. The men around him would remember only that the sergeant had been informed of their pyrrhic victory and nothing else.

A short walk had him reuniting with Slate and with the man who stood near him. Stinky Napier was clean and sober, his eyes haunted by the sights that Crowley didn't need to see to understand. There were dead men up ahead and likely a lot of them if the sounds from earlier were anything to be judged by.

Crowley smiled broadly for him. Napier flinched a bit but stood his ground.

"And is the town still alive, Mister Napier? Or are we the only survivors?"

"Oh, there are more, Mister Crowley. The Indians only wanted the soldiers. They were good about not shooting anyone else." He frowned a moment. "Can't say the same for all the soldiers. Some of those boys shot anything that moved."

"Still think the red men are all heathens?"

"Absolutely. Doesn't mean I have to hate them. I just know they do not properly worship Jesus Christ."

Crowley shook his head and said nothing. That was a story he was wise enough not to touch on.

"Your friend is very persuasive." Napier's voice caught him off guard.

"How so?"

Slate chuckled to himself. He was looking remarkably healthy for a man whose chest had been nearly broken open twenty minutes earlier.

Napier eyed him dubiously but continued on. "Walked right up to the Indians where they were getting ready to have a bit of fun with the soldiers and put a stop to it."

Crowley's grin was quick and savage. "And what did you say to them, Mister Slate?"

Slate looked directly at him. "Leave." He shrugged. "They left."

"So the Indians are gone and the soldiers are leaving." Crowley nodded, a satisfied expression crossing his features and feeling decidedly alien there.

"Can't be that many soldiers left." Napier's frown deepened and he looked around. "I don't reckon that's a bad thing just now."

Slate spoke up, his voice still pained. "Might we be on our way, Mister Crowley? I'm feeling a bit faint."

Mister Napier opened his mouth to say something else, but one look from Slate silenced him.

* * *

When the morning came the two men claimed their horses from the stables. A surprising number of the Cavalry's horses were gone, despite the lack of riders, but no one was foolish enough to try for theirs.

Outside, the remaining soldiers were gathering together, preparing to head northeast, toward Camp Woodbine, if Crowley was remembering properly.

"Where are we headed today, Mister Crowley?"

Crowley looked at his companion and shrugged. The weather was hideous, but that was hardly unusual. "I took the time to listen to a few men chatting last night, after you had gone to sleep. The men were French and talking about *Loup Garou*."

Slate frowned. "Werewolves?"

"You speak French, Mister Slate?"

"Not as well as I speak English, but I can manage. Spent a bit of time in Louisiana and dealt with my fair share of Cajuns."

Crowley nodded. "We're heading west, Mister Slate. We shall discuss what happened here when you feel more inclined to discussing the matters, but we are heading west to see if there are, in fact, werewolves hiding somewhere in the region."

"You don't suppose it's merely wolves?"

"No. In my experience, wolves very rarely attack wagon trains."

Slate nodded. "Well then, I imagine this will be an interesting journey." The man seemed distracted and Crowley simply nodded. Let him have his time to think.

* * *

As they rode, Lucas Slate listened to the song that always played for him and, in listening, began to comprehend.

Thanks for supporting Cohesion through all the changes over the last couple of years, and thanks for purchasing SNAFU. We hope you enjoyed it.

Small presses thrive on reviews, so if you could drop one at Amazon, that would be great.

Also, watch Tim Miller's Love, Death + Robots on Netflix if you want to see some stories from our SNAFU series br

Geoff Brown/Amanda J Spedding
July 2018

Printed in Great Britain
by Amazon